when you call my name

when you call my name

Tucker Shaw

HENRY HOLT AND COMPANY
NEW YORK

Henry Holt and Company, *Publishers since 1866*
Henry Holt® is a registered trademark of Macmillan Publishing Group, LLC
120 Broadway, New York, NY 10271 • fiercereads.com

Our books may be purchased in bulk for promotional, educational, or business
use. Please contact your local bookseller or the Macmillan Corporate and
Premium Sales Department at (800) 221–7945 ext. 5442 or by email at
MacmillanSpecialMarkets@macmillan.com.

Library of Congress Cataloging-in-Publication Data is available.

First edition, 2022
Book design by Trisha Previte
New York skyline image © by atlantic-kid/Getty Images
Printed in the United States of America

ISBN 978-1-250-62486-4 (hardcover)
10 9 8 7 6 5 4 3 2 1

For Steven
I've never missed you more.

We can never go back again, that much is certain. The past is still too close to us.

—Daphne du Maurier, *Rebecca*

One

JANUARY 1990

So welcome to the world, yeah.

—The Beloved, "Hello"

ADAM

Soon, Adam will know every part of the boy. Every plane, every crease, every shadow, every ridge. He'll tally and retally the freckles that swirl across his skin like constellations, over his chest and around his shoulders and into the shallow dimples at the base of his back. He'll know the vibrations of his voice and the lines of his palms and the steady rhythm of his sleep.

Soon, but not today. Today Adam only knows what he can see: a boy, or maybe a man, standing in the January sunshine with his collar turned up against the cold, waiting for an answer.

"Will you come?" he asks again. He is not impatient. He smiles.

Look at him. Look at how tall he is, a head higher than Adam. Look at his eyes, at how they are set asymmetrically, the left higher than the right. Or is that just the way he's tilting his head? Look at the rebellious curls at the edge of his watch cap. Look at his beautiful nose. Just look at him.

An icy gust swipes Adam's face, blowing his hair into his eyes. He squints through the strands. He shivers. Why can't he ever remember his hat?

Adam twists one foot inward, making pigeon toes. He presses down to feel the sidewalk beneath his sneaker. Gravity. He studies the boy's eyes, first the left, then the right, then back again. Clear eyes. Placid. Hopeful.

Will you come? It's a simple question. Adam knows how this works. He's seen it in a thousand movies, rehearsed it a million times in his mind. A stranger stands before you. He says his line. He asks his question. Now it's your turn. Answer, and your story will begin. Adam bites his lower lip, conjuring courage.

A taxi scrapes around the corner, dragging its damaged muffler across the asphalt as it rolls toward Christopher Street. The clatter sends up sparks and Adam can feel its vibration in his teeth. It's one of the old cabs, a Checker, and when you see one of those you get to make a wish. Adam makes his wish. The taxi lurches through the intersection and away.

His eyes drift to a gathering of freckles at the side of the stranger's face, just there, just at the temple. Look carefully. See? A pulse, his pulse, steady and expectant and alive.

Will you come?

Adam will say yes. Adam is seventeen.

BEN

The lenses of Ben's eyeglasses are smudged with pomade and the bus windows are fogged up with everyone breathing, so he can't see much as the Greyhound lumbers through Midtown. It rolls with excruciating sluggishness, taking a half hour just to cover the final few blocks into Port Authority.

Its slow pace fits the day. The ride down from Gideon should take an hour and change but today it took a lifetime. You can't ever tell with traffic. Ben's already read, cover to cover, the copies of *Vogue*, *Interview*, and *i-D* that he bought at the station on the way out, and he's listened to the Beloved's *Happiness* CD all the way through three times. He'd listen to it again if his Discman's batteries hadn't died. He should have taken the train.

4

Ben pulls his hand into the sleeve of his sweatshirt and swipes it across the window to create a little peephole in the foggy glass. He knows it's a clear day, but you can barely tell here in the shadows of Midtown. The sun is up there somewhere, but a hundred buildings obscure it.

Streams of people in winter coats of gray and brown and olive and black course along the sidewalk, gathering into antsy pools at the intersections to wait for the walk signal. They hold their scarves to their throats and turn away from the wind to shield their faces.

When the signal comes, some dart across, leaning into the cold. Others trudge slowly, each step a groaning labor. No one looks happy. It's all so beautiful. Ben loves New York.

Suddenly, a man in a shockingly bright orange bomber jacket breaks from the drab stream of pedestrians and steps off the curb, scanning the traffic as if to jaywalk. He looks familiar. Could it be? Ben swabs at the window again. Yes. It is him. Marco. Right there on Ninth Avenue. Ben would know him anywhere.

Two years ago, when Ben was a sophomore, a junior named Marco got jumped at the end of the school day. They pushed him into a maintenance closet outside the music room and broke off the doorknob, trapping him inside. They spray-painted *QUEERS GET AIDS* across the door and vanished. No one found Marco until the next morning, when a custodian dismantled the door and found him huddled against the wall, vomit covering his shoes. The administration called in a hazardous waste specialist to disinfect the closet—the door said *AIDS* after all—but they never called the police. Soon everyone was saying that Marco brought it on himself. You can't just walk around with earrings in both ears and a Culture Club T-shirt without consequences, they said. It was conspicuous. Marco got what was coming to him.

Marco stands tall, a confident posture. Just then, a swirl of

5

steam from a manhole envelops him, the white cloud amplifying the electric orange of his jacket. It looks like a fashion photograph in one of Ben's favorite magazines. If he were the stylist, though, Ben would swap out the orange jacket for something less obvious. Oxblood maybe, or emerald. Something just as arresting, but a little less garish.

Ben blinks, and Marco vanishes, swallowed back into the city. The bus pulls into its berth at Port Authority, and everyone jumps up and into the aisle, pushing and sighing and clicking their tongues. Ben waits until the whole bus empties out, then takes down his duffel bag and goes in search of a pay phone. He needs to call his brother. He needs to call Gil.

ADAM

"Will you come?"

It's not such a big deal. The boy—or man? no, let's go with boy for now—is only asking Adam to see *Tremors*, the new Kevin Bacon horror movie that's supposed to be more funny than scary. It's just that no one's asked Adam to the movies before. Not like this. Not a customer.

Sonia's Village Video had been thronged all morning with harried customers stocking up on movies before the snowstorm Sam Champion promised on *Eyewitness News*. Sonia loves storm warnings, because nothing is better for the video rental business in New York. But busy days deplete inventory, and Adam spent most of his shift disappointing customers from behind the counter. *No, you can't rent more than three tapes at a time; no, we don't have* Drugstore Cowboy *on Beta; no, we don't carry* that *kind of movie here, but check over at the Pleasure Chest on Seventh Avenue.*

Soon it was one o'clock, the end of Adam's shift. The rush had slowed to a trickle. Adam peeled off his stiff retail smile and took his pale blue parka down from the hook. "I'm clocking out," he said, shrugging the jacket over his shoulders.

"Gimme two more minutes?" Sonia asked. "I have to pee." She darted through the green-and-purple beaded curtain she'd hung over the entrance to the back office. It rippled and clacked in her wake.

There was a customer standing at the register. A very tall customer. A very tall, very cute customer with messy, uneven curls matted slightly on one side. Bed head or hat head, one or the other. Adam considered both.

"Can I help you?" he asked.

"I think I have a tape on hold. The name is Keane."

Adam let go of his parka zipper, still unsecured. "Key?"

"Keane," the customer said. "Callum Keane."

"Callum Keane." Adam enunciated the sounds. Two hard guttural clicks with a hum in between and a fade-out finish. *Callum Keane.* He didn't know yet that he would remember this name forever.

Adam crouched down behind the counter, where two shelves held the reserved videos, each labeled with a pink Post-it note. He scanned the names: *Ramón, Barillas, Inkpen, Zakris, Keane.*

"Here it is." He placed the tape on the counter. "Bach Violin Concertos."

"Ah," Callum Keane said. His shoulders slumped in disappointment. Adam's stomach sank. "I was hoping for the Carlos Kleiber rehearsal. This is the Seiji Ozawa. I've already seen this one."

Callum pushed it back across the counter, his denim coat riding up on his arm to reveal a flannel lining against a lean wrist cuffed with ruddy freckles. Adam's eyes lingered, studying their shapes.

"Sorry," Adam said.

"Oh well." The customer stuck his tongue between his teeth when he smiled. "It's hard to find."

Just then, Sonia swept back through the beaded curtain in a cloud of jasmine body spray, fastening a hoop into her earlobe. "Adam? What are you still doing here?"

"You asked me to stay."

"Adam was helping me." Adam was startled to hear Callum Keane say his name.

"He had a tape on hold," Adam explained. "But it turns out it wasn't the tape he needed, so—"

"Okay, this story is already too long." Sonia tapped her watch and pointed at the front door. "Goodbye. Where is your hat? It's January. Crazy cold."

"I forgot it."

"You're worse than my kids. Zip your parka."

Adam bowed his head and walked stiffly to the door and away from this awkward moment, avoiding eye contact with Callum Keane and hoping he wouldn't trip. If he walked fast, he could make it to Astor Place in fifteen minutes for the haircut he desperately needs. But he only made it to the end of the block, because behind him, Callum Keane was calling his name, because he knew it now.

"Adam!"

And now here they are on the corner.

Will you come?

What would Lily tell him to do? Just a few weeks ago, on New Year's Eve, she'd insisted on a shared resolution. *It's a new decade, Best. The eighties may have made us, but we make the nineties. It's time to start living. Time to start taking risks. This is our time. This is the Decade of Yes. Say it with me: YES.* They toasted it with cheap, sugary sparkling wine pilfered from her mother's liquor cabinet.

Adam takes a deep breath and straightens his spine.

Callum's smile grows wider.

Adam smiles, too.

"Yes," he says, finally. "I will come with you."

Callum pumps his fist in victory. "Yes! But we better hurry. It starts at one thirty at the theater over on Sixth. You know, the one by the basketball courts? Now, which way should we—"

"This way," Adam says, pointing toward Christopher Street.

"Really?" Callum is looking the other way, down Bedford.

"Trust me," Adam says. "I've lived in this neighborhood my whole life."

BEN

Gil doesn't answer, so Ben hangs up to save the quarter. He'll try again in a little while. He tells himself not to worry. Gil will say yes. He always does. When he first moved here after accepting his position as a resident physician at St. Hugh's Hospital, Gil told Ben he could come whenever he wanted a weekend away. *Just call first,* he'd said. *I need forty-eight hours warning.* Ben always honored the forty-eight-hour request. He would have honored it this time, too, if he'd known two days ago that he was coming down to the city. But he hadn't known, not until early this morning.

It started a little after sunrise with a gentle poke on his shoulder. It was his mother who delivered it, using the finger she'd broken yesterday by slamming it in the car door after they'd had another fight. One minute she was saying he'd be sorry if he didn't start being nicer to her, the next she was wailing loud enough to bring the neighbors in the next unit to their door. Ben helped her into the passenger seat and drove her to the emergency room. It was a clean break, the doctor said. Just a simple splint and plenty of aspirin and ice. "No codeine this time," he'd said, and then to Ben, "Make sure she sleeps with her hand resting on a pillow, to help reduce the swelling."

Maybe she had a point. Maybe he wasn't very nice to her yesterday. She'd asked him to cheer her up after work—a perennial, unspecific request—but he'd said no, he wanted to be alone. He'd had a difficult day. Cue the *you'll be sorry* speech, one he's heard a hundred times before. His mistake was tuning her out. The car door slam was designed to get his attention. Her finger got in the way. Or maybe she put it there on purpose. He'll wonder about this for a long time.

"Ben," she said this morning when she poked him. "Benjamin."

For a moment he wondered if she'd picked the lock to his room, then he remembered that he'd been up twice in the night to check the position of her hand as she slept. He probably forgot to lock it.

He sat up and felt for his glasses on the nightstand. She was wearing a pair of tapered jeans underneath her purple flannel bathrobe. She was barefoot, her toes tangled in the threadbare shag carpet, worn to wisps from years of brutal treatment by their ancient vacuum cleaner. She held her injured hand up to the side of her face, as if to remind him of her pain.

"Are you all right?" he asked.

"No."

"Is it your hand?"

"I'm not equipped to deal with this," she said. Her voice was grim, cold, desolate.

Ben tugged at the neckband of the Depeche Mode T-shirt he'd fallen asleep in. He pulled harder than he should have, snapping its threads and leaving it cowled around his collarbone. Great. Another one of his favorite T-shirts trashed. "Deal with what?" he asked.

She pointed at a shoebox on his dresser. "With this."

Inside the shoebox, Ben knows, is a stack of glossy magazines he'd found in the men's room at the train station a year ago—*Honcho, Inches, Mandate*—and brought home in his backpack. He kept them hidden in the crawl space downstairs because she was always snooping around his room. They stayed hidden down there, except when he needed them. He'd needed them last night. He must have left the box out.

"Do you have a death wish or something?"

"What are you talking about?"

With her good hand, she took a tissue from the box on his bedside table. She dabbed her eyes and wiped her nose, then crumpled it up and placed it on the copy of British *Vogue* he'd been reading before he fell asleep, the new one with Linda, Naomi, Tatjana, Christy, and Cindy on the cover. The import that cost him nine bucks. She hated how much he loved his magazines. She held his eyes while she took another tissue, wiped her nose again, and set it next to the first. A point made.

"If you die, what will I do?"

"If I die, then I'll be dead. So I guess you'll have to figure it out by yourself."

"Is that what you want to happen? You want to die?"

He didn't answer.

She wiped her nose again. Another tissue on his magazine. "It belongs in the trash."

"Then put it in the trash," he said. "I don't care."

She locked her eyes on him. "It all belongs in the trash," she said. "All of this."

He got it then. She wasn't talking about the magazines. She was talking about him.

It numbed him, and then it nudged him. He knew what to do

next. He pulled back the covers and got out of bed. He pulled his duffel bag out from under the bed and began to pack. He moved calmly, not rushing. Some T-shirts from the stack in his closet. Two sweatshirts. One more. Three pairs of jeans. He filled his dopp kit with hair stuff and deodorant and two eyeliner pencils from the top drawer of his dresser. He made sure she saw those go in. He gathered socks, underwear, and his toothbrush from the bathroom. She didn't speak. She just stood to the side and watched.

He took his time choosing CDs from the case—New Order, Erasure, Cocteau Twins, Book of Love. Only a dozen or so. He untacked the magazine pictures that he'd put up on the back of his closet door—Iman in Halston, Marpessa in Dolce & Gabbana, Gia in Armani, Grace Jones in Alaïa. He folded them together and slipped them into his backpack.

Gil had given him an envelope with five twenty-dollar bills a few weeks ago, and Ben cashed his seventy-eight-dollar paycheck from his job at the Poughkeepsie Galleria yesterday, so he consolidated the money and tucked it into his backpack. He packed backup eyeglasses. Chapsticks. A fake Swatch.

He got dressed. Black jeans, leather cuff, charcoal sweatshirt, black Chuck Taylors with the black toe caps. He zipped himself into his black parka and secured his black baseball cap tightly over his head. He didn't bother with his hair. Not today.

She pointed at the shoebox again.

"You can keep those," he said. "They seem to matter more to you than to me." He hoisted his duffel bag, accidentally knocking the box off the dresser and scattering the floor with glossy naked bodies. She covered her face with her broken hand.

At the front door, he turned to look at the mirror by the coatrack as he always did. He adjusted his baseball cap, tucked in the errant hairs, wiped the smudged eyeliner from his lower lid. He should remember to take that stuff off before he goes to sleep. He squared his jaw. He squinted at himself. Why can't he be beautiful? Everything would be easier if he was beautiful.

In that moment, before he opened the door to leave, all she had to stay was *stop*, and he would have stopped. *Wait*, and he would have waited. *Come back here*, and he would have turned around, apologized, and tried again.

But she didn't say anything. Not *stop*, not *wait*, not *come back here*, not even *happy birthday* on this, his eighteenth. He didn't say anything, either. She knew he was leaving. He knew he was leaving. Everything would be different now, for both of them.

Ben wonders how many other people here at Port Authority aren't sure where they're going to spend the night. He grabs the handset from the pay phone and tries Gil again. Still no answer. He's relieved, a little. More time to rehearse. The favor he needs isn't a small one.

ADAM

Adam leads Callum through Sheridan Square and across West Fourth Street, adjusting the route as they walk to make sure they're on the sunny side, a futile bid for a ray of warmth. But it's too windy to matter. They walk fast. When they turn the corner onto Sixth Avenue, the sharp wind stings his eyes. He runs the last half-block to the ticket window. They each slide five dollars under the Plexiglas, and the attendant waves them in with fingerless gloves.

"Hey, what's wrong?" Callum asks in the lobby. "You're crying."

"No," Adam says, rubbing tears from his face. He laughs nervously. "It's the wind. It makes my eyes water."

"Oh, look at your ears. They're bright red. Come here." Callum rubs his palms together several times, then presses them against Adam's ears.

Adam's eyes snap left, then right. Is anyone watching? This is the Village, the gayest neighborhood in the city, but still. You think about these things.

"Don't worry," Callum says confidently, as if he's reading Adam's thoughts. "Warm now?"

Adam nods and twists out of his grip. "Thanks," he says.

Just then a gleeful grin takes over Callum's face. "No way!" He points at the photo booth in the corner of the lobby. "Come on."

"Really?" Adam hasn't used the photo booth here since *Gremlins* came out.

Callum's already at the booth, holding back the curtain and gesturing for Adam to enter. "It's a first-date requirement. Go ahead, and I'll squish in next to you."

First date. Adam's stomach jumps when he hears those words. "Okay."

Adam sits on the bench inside, and Callum piles in after him, twisting and folding his long body into the space and draping his legs over Adam's. "Am I crushing you?"

"Nope," Adam says. It's a lie. He's being crushed, but he doesn't want Callum to move.

"Okay, here goes." Callum feeds a quarter into the slot. "Smile!" Adam smiles. The flash fires.

"Now make a funny face!" Callum shouts. Adam crosses his eyes. Another flash.

"Smile again!" Flash.

"Stick out your tongue!" Flash.

Callum tumbles back out into the lobby, laughing. Adam follows, looking around. Is anyone watching? No.

After a minute, the machine spits out a little strip of four black-and-white photos. In each picture, Callum is in the foreground, beaming, laughing, bright. Behind him, Adam is stiffer, awkward. *Smile, funny face, smile, tongue.*

"So cute." Callum rips the strip in half and hands the top two pictures to Adam. "A memento."

"I'll treasure it forever," Adam says, trying to flirt, not sure if it's working.

Callum smiles again, his tongue between his teeth. "Okay. Let's go see these monsters."

After they sink into their seats and the lights dim, Callum leans over. "Are you scared?" he asks quietly, his warm breath on Adam's skin.

"A little," Adam says.

"Don't worry," Callum whispers. He presses his knee against Adam's. "I've got you."

Tell me when you knew for /ure.

It was pretty early. I was up at my grandmother's house in the mountains, staying with her while my parents were away. We were watching the gymnastic competition at the summer Olympics in Montreal, so what was that, 1976? I guess I was four and a half. I kept calling it the 'Lympics.

She was going on and on about how amazing Nadia Comăneci was on the uneven bars.

"Isn't she beautiful?" she kept saying during Nadia's famous perfect-ten routine. "Beautiful. Just beautiful."

I sat on the floor beside her easy chair, looking at a special section of the newspaper devoted to the Olympics. There were photographs of many of the famous gymnasts—Nadia, Olga Korbut, Nellie Kim, all the favorites. But I was focused on a picture of Kurt Thomas high on a pommel horse. His legs were extended wide and his muscles were straining against his USA tank top and white gymnast pants. I ran my finger across his feathered Shaun Cassidy hair and said, "Beautiful. Just beautiful," the same way she did. I looked up at my grandmother for affirmation.

But the look on her face was strange. She tilted her head to one side and took in a sharp gasp that sounded like she'd just seen an unwelcome visitor at the door, or a wild animal in the yard. I remember feeling strange. Like I was different. Maybe it was embarrassment or shame, I'm not sure. I didn't know those ideas yet. I didn't want her to be upset with me so I went outside to play in the yard by myself.

Later, when she was on the phone with my mother, I heard her say, "He's such a sensitive boy." She really emphasized that word, sensitive. My ears still prick up when I hear that word. It's like the way people say, he's so colorful or isn't he creative or he prefers individual sports. They all mean the same thing, like it's some kind of code.

BEN

The wind out on Eighth Avenue steals Ben's breath, reminding him that it's winter. But the city doesn't care about the cold. It's always kinetic. Vibrating. He turns toward the subway.

To walk in New York is to enter a sprawling civic choreography with a cast of millions, and Ben falls effortlessly into its rhythms of haste, purpose, possibility. He knows the steps because he listens to the city call them out. He sees where the woman approaching him is going just by the position of her hips and the curve of her neck, and when she comes directly at him with no hint of slowing, New York tells him to count a beat and twist his shoulders just as she does the same. They pass cleanly, like two models on a runway swooshing elegantly past each other without missing a step. She moves on, and so does he, and soon he's dancing with another stranger.

Ben belongs here in the city, not in Gideon. Up there, he's constantly reminded how much of a misfit he is. *Weirdo*, they call him, or *freak*. But down here, in the city, an odd boy with a dull expression and black eyeliner fits in just as well as anyone. He's nothing special. Inconspicuous. He belongs. That's why he comes down so often. The difference this time is he's not going back.

At a newsstand on the corner, he stops to look at the cover of *Women's Wear Daily*. It features a photograph of a model he doesn't recognize in a windowpane newsboy cap and matching jacket. Is it by Kenzo? Moschino? He looks for the caption. *How breakout designer Anna Sui is turning downtown upside down, page 5.*

Anna Sui? Ben hasn't heard of her. But he likes the look of this outfit so he buys a copy for seventy-five cents and stashes it into his backpack for later. He also buys fresh batteries for his Discman.

He sees a phone booth and tries Gil once more. Still no answer. He feels inside his backpack for the envelope of cash. He has enough for a hotel for a night, or maybe two, but that's it.

He descends the stairs into the subway and slips a token into the slot. He'll take the C train or the A train, whichever comes first. It doesn't matter. They're both going his way.

ADAM

If you want sweets to take home on a snowstorm day, you'd better get to Rocco's early because by afternoon, the usual abundance of sweets in the giant glass case—pasticciotti, cheesecake, and cannoli—is depressingly thin. But luck shines on Adam today. He spies a few slices of chocolate espresso cake on a shelf behind the counter as soon as they step inside.

"Follow me," he says, tugging Callum over the tile floor toward a small café table near the back. He drapes his parka over a chair and points Callum to the other. "Save my place."

"Yes, sir," Callum says, taking the seat.

Adam returns to the counter and tugs a number from the ticket dispenser, hoping the three customers before him don't steal away the cake.

The indecisive man at the front of the line ties up the staff with unanswerable questions—*Do I like lemon cream better than pistachio? Will the tiramisu give me an upset stomach?*—while behind him, a woman in a calf-length quilted parka and pom-pom hat glares impatiently. A toddler wriggles free from her arms and lunges at the glass case, slapping her open palms against it and squealing "*coook-kiiieee!*" at the last few lemon meringues. Adam smiles at her. He was that toddler once, smudging his own fingerprints on this same glass case while Pop picked up his weekly pound of pignoli cookies.

When Adam's number appears on the NOW SERVING display behind the register, he waves his ticket over his head. The woman behind the counter smiles wearily at him. "Adam, right? What'll it be?"

He points at the chocolate espresso cake. "Two please. For here." He points to Callum.

"We'll bring it over, hon."

Adam slips into the restroom to wash his hands, then fills two small glasses of water at the self-service fountain. By the time he returns to their little table, Callum's already halfway through his slice of cake. He looks up, grinning as he chews. "I couldn't wait," he says.

"It's my favorite thing here," Adam says, relieved. He takes a seat and takes a bite, pressing it against the roof of his mouth with his tongue, mashing the cake together with the coffee buttercream. "I'm just glad there was some left. The case is usually overflowing."

"Lucky us," Callum says. His foot bumps Adam's under the table. Adam slides away, but Callum follows, keeping contact. Adam's stomach spins. Anxious, but in a good way.

He clears his throat. "So, what's the video you were looking for this morning? I forget. Something about classical music."

"Carlos Kleiber. The greatest conductor ever. I'm studying to be a conductor. Well, I'm planning to study to be a conductor. Need to save up first."

Adam imagines *Amadeus*, the movie about Mozart that won all those Oscars a few years ago. He pictures Callum in a powdered wig and brocade jacket, triumphantly waving his arms at an orchestra. "A conductor," he says. "The one down in front. With the wand."

"It's called a *baton*, monsieur," Callum says.

"Ah, *oui*," Adam says. "*Pardonnez-moi.*"

Callum's foot presses closer. Adam nearly loses his breath.

"You'll have plenty of time to learn all the important vocabulary when you accompany me on my first world tour," Callum says. "Paris, Vienna, Tokyo, the Sydney Opera House. It'll probably be in about twenty or thirty years from now, give or take. You in?"

"I don't even really know what a conductor does."

"It's simple, but also not simple."

Callum pulls a folded-up piece of paper from his back pocket and smooths it flat on the table. It's sheet music, horizontal lines across the page with musical notes and italicized words woven through.

"Here. This is music, right? It's like a set of instructions. I can read this and know what notes to play. It spells out the melody, sets the timing, and gives me a few clues about whether it should be loud or quiet, fortissimo or mezzo piano, and whether the notes should be quick, staccato, or slow, legato. See? This tells me what the music should sound like. But the instructions don't say much about how the music should make me feel. You know?"

Adam watches Callum's eyes as he speaks, the way they dart and dance, like hummingbirds.

"Now. Everyone interprets the instructions a little differently. When you have forty or sixty or ninety musicians all following the same set of instructions but interpreting them differently, you need someone to make sure they're all in the same zone. That's the conductor. You tap your baton, raise your hands, make sure every-one is ready to go, and then you move, and the musicians begin to play, and the room fills with music. It's like you're extracting the music from the musicians, drawing it into the air for the audience. Everyone watches you, and if you're good, everyone believes you. You create a moment. You create a mood. You share it. That's who I want to be."

"That's really cool," Adam says, meaning it.

"What about you? What do you want to do?"

"With my life? I don't know. Maybe something with movies."

"Like a director?"

"I don't know. I just like movies. That's why I work at Sonia's. I get unlimited free rentals." His own ambitions seem so murky against Callum's. His dreams are nowhere near as clear.

"What's your favorite?" Callum asks.

"My favorite movie?"

"Yeah. Ever."

Oh, this dangerous question. Adam doesn't want to get this wrong. Your favorite movie says something about you. When he was seven it was *The Wiz*. When he was eleven it was *Fame*. When he was fourteen it was *Desperately Seeking Susan*. But now?

Titles race through his brain. *Vision Quest, 9 to 5, Harvey, Purple Rain, The Last Unicorn, Moonstruck, After Hours, Local Hero, Clue, Harold and Maude, Educating Rita, Evil Under the Sun, Smithereens.* All are movies that he loves, none is his favorite.

"Well?"

"*Amadeus*," Adam blurts out, surprising himself. Why would he say that? He's only seen it once.

Callum's eyes widen. "Are you serious?"

A pit drops in Adam's stomach. Has he made a mistake? Does Callum hate *Amadeus* the way serious boxing fans hate the *Rocky* sequels? Does he think *Amadeus* sucks?

"I can't believe you said that. I love that movie so much. I saw it seven times when it came out."

Uh-oh, Adam thinks. What if Callum wants to talk about *Amadeus* now? Adam can't remember any details except the clothes and the wigs and Tom Hulce's deranged laugh. He resolves to rent it again to bone up. But right now, he'll change the subject.

"How does a person become a conductor anyway?"

Callum sighs. "School. A lot of expensive school. I've been saving up for it for the last couple of years, working as an usher at Lincoln Center. The pay isn't great but I get to see most of the concerts for free from the standing-room-only section. That's about all I do. Work, go to concerts, save money, study music at home with Clara."

"Clara?"

"My piano. I got her for seventy-five bucks at the flea market in Chelsea. Cost almost twice that much to have her delivered to the apartment." His eyes glaze over, changing focus, as if they're searching for a memory. Adam wonders where he's gone.

After a moment, Callum's eyes return. His expression softens into the easy smile that Adam already knows.

"Can we get another piece?" Callum asks. "I don't want this cake to end."

BEN

When the train comes and the door opens, Ben sees an open seat underneath a poster for an AIDS hotline. DON'T DIE OF EMBARRASSMENT, it reads. NEW YORK STATE HEALTH DEPARTMENT. He settles into it, next to a woman with beaded braids and faded jeans, and across from a young man reading a picture book to a child who's much more interested in the couple making out at the far end of the car. He rests his duffel bag on his lap and slips his hand inside to feel for his Discman. By touch, he changes the batteries and presses play. He positions his headphones on his ears, tipping the thin metal headband behind his neck because it won't quite fit over his baseball cap.

At the Thirty-Fourth Street stop, a crush of passengers floods the train. A group of middle school boys in Knicks jerseys and high-tops. A woman in a belted houndstooth overcoat and yellow pashmina. Three thin, sullen-looking girls about his age clutching leather portfolios that read ELITE MODEL MANAGEMENT.

The train lurches forward again. Ben notices the sullen girls looking at him and whispering. His throat seizes. Does he look weird? Is there something on him? He looks at his knees, hoping the bill of his baseball cap will obscure their view of him.

At Twenty-Third Street, two men step onto the train. One looks like he's about Gil's age, early in his thirties, with dark skin and soft eyes. He's wearing a track jacket under a down vest. The other, shuffling behind on a rubber-tipped cane, appears much older, with patchy, thinning hair and a crooked hunch. He wears a heavy sweater that buttons up the front, with worn leather patches on the elbows. He waves his cane at Ben. "May I?"

Ben stands up quickly, hoisting his duffel with him. He gestures at the seat.

The man lowers himself onto the bench. He winces as he lands, then smiles with relief. Ben sees now that this man isn't any older than his companion. He's ill. Ben feels an elemental impulse to move away, to increase the space between himself and evident illness. But he quells it. The man says thank you to Ben, and Ben nods back.

The train continues its jerky journey downtown, blasé New Yorkers bouncing like bobbleheads as it goes. Ben bobs, too, in time with his music.

ADAM

The late-afternoon sun is low and lazy in that kind of midwinter way that sends long, alien shadows across the streets, distorted spidery shapes. They walk slowly, unrushed, happy that the wind has settled for now. At the corner, Callum holds up his hand to cast a rabbit-eared shadow puppet on the side of a bus. "Do you think I'm cute?" the bouncing bunny asks.

Adam makes a shadow crocodile. "I think you are delicious," it says, before opening its mouth and devouring the bunny. They laugh like children.

The sidewalk is crowded with people in chunky scarves cradling paper bags of groceries on their hips and smoking cigarettes. Adam recognizes faces as they pass. There's the guy with the thick neck who runs the hat shop on Christopher. He nods, Adam nods back. There's the manager of the diner on Greenwich whose fake eyelashes always seem lopsided. She smiles, Adam smiles back. There's the delivery guy from Grand Sichuan with the ten-speed bike. He waves, Adam waves back.

"It's like you know everyone in this neighborhood," Callum says.

"Yes," Adam says. "So you better behave." He's flirting freely now. Lily would be proud.

Adam nudges them on deliberate detours through the Village, extending the afternoon. Callum doesn't object. They pass the coffee wholesaler, the Afghan import shop, a handful of gay bars—Ty's, Boots & Saddle, the Stonewall. Adam speeds up when the sex shop comes into view; the array of color-code bandannas and glossy posters of scowling porn stars make him nervous.

At the corner of Perry Street, Callum stops abruptly outside a brick rowhouse. He points up to a window on the second floor. It's been left open—a common practice in these old buildings even on cold winter days because so few people can control their radiators. "Hear that?" he says. "Music."

Adam looks up at the window. He can just barely hear soft notes from a piano, *tink-tink-tink*.

"Chopin," Callum says as the quiet key strikes get louder, faster, coalescing into a melody. "This is one of his études, number ten, I think." He holds his hands up like a mime, playing an invisible keyboard in perfect time with the increasingly rapid notes from upstairs. He gets every note right, every pause, every emphasis. It's like a perfect lip sync, only with his fingers. He sways dramatically as the tune comes to a crescendo, and ends.

Adam claps. Callum bows. The window above slams shut, breaking the spell.

"I love New York," Callum says, ebullient. He shouts up to the window. "Music everywhere!"

Adam smiles. He is smitten now. Smitten with this tall, playful, mysterious creature.

Suddenly, a familiar voice from behind him. "Adam?"

Adam spins around to see Lily in an oversized faux-fur coat that reminds him of Tippy Walker's outfit in *The World of Henry Orient*. She waves her single braid at him, thick and deep brown and dyed garnet at the tip. "Yoo-hoo!" she coos.

Adam takes an instinctive step away from Callum. "Hey, Lily," he says.

She lowers her Ray-Bans and looks up at Callum, her expression a mix of curiosity and suspicion. She holds out her hand like a duchess greeting a courtier. "I'm Lily. Adam's best friend."

Callum takes her hand and deposits a graceful kiss on her knuckle. "What a pleasure."

"You say that to all the girls," she flirts. "Now, who are you?"

"Callum Keane, at your service. Adam and I have just been to see *Tremors*."

"Have you now?"

"Yes. He generously escorted me. I'm too much of a wimp to see horror movies alone."

"Well, isn't he a prince," she says, slyly shifting her eyes to Adam. It's a signal: *You are busted*. Adam was supposed to see it with her. She's obsessed with Kevin Bacon.

"You have new hair," Adam says.

She wiggles her braid. "Manic Panic Vampire Blood. It's dramatic, no? You know how I love a little, ahem, *drama*."

"I love it," Adam says. "Anyway, I'll call you later, okay?"

"You can try, but honestly, I'm not sure I'll be available tonight. I have so much to do. But you may leave a message on my machine if you wish." Adam knows she's lying. She has no plans.

"I hope we meet again very soon," Callum says. He holds out his hand to shake, but she swats it away and pulls his head down for a double kiss, one on each cheek.

When she leans in to kiss Adam, too, she whispers, "I hate you, but he's gorgeous."

"Bye, Lily."

"*We're all connected, New York Telephone*," she sings. Another signal. Call her later, or else.

"She seems sweet," Callum says, watching her go.

"Usually," Adam says.

Soon they're at the little park on Bank Street and Hudson.

Adam points at the boxy redbrick apartment building across the intersection, the one that looks like it's slowly sinking into itself. "That's me," Adam says. "The lopsided one on the corner."

"You say it's lopsided," Callum says. "I say it has character."

Adam squints up at him. "How tall are you anyway?" he asks.

"I'm not sure," Callum says. "Too tall?"

"Just right."

"Whew."

Now what? Do they hug? Shake hands? Kiss once on each cheek? Adam looks at the ground.

Callum takes Adam's shoulders, one in each hand, and squeezes. It's not quite a hug, and definitely not a kiss. But it feels like it means . . . something?

"Can I call you?" Callum asks.

"I don't have a pencil," Adam says.

"That's okay. I have a good memory. Try me."

Adam recites the seven digits of his telephone number, and Callum repeats them back perfectly.

"Do you have far to go?" Adam asks.

Callum points uptown. "Horatio Street."

"That's close."

"Four blocks."

Callum reaches over and tucks Adam's hair behind his ear. His hand grazes Adam's cheek. "Your hair is the color of maple syrup," he says. "My favorite flavor."

Adam leans into the warmth of Callum's palm, and in that moment, he feels something fall into place, something essential, structural, a missing part finally found.

Kiss me, Adam thinks. *Kiss me like George kisses Lucy in* A Room with a View. *Kiss me, and this corner will transform into a field of barley overlooking Florence, and the music will rise around us, and I'll go limp in your arms and we'll both be changed forever. Kiss me and everything will be perfect. Kiss me.*

But Callum doesn't kiss Adam. He just lets go and returns his hand to his pocket. "You better get inside," he says. "You'll freeze to death out here. And then who will answer when I call?"

Adam says goodbye, reluctantly, and crosses the street. At his doorway, he turns back to see Callum, still standing there, watching. "I had to be sure you made it!" he yells before turning uptown and walking away.

Adam slips his key into the lock, and starts waiting for Callum's call. It won't be long.

BEN

Ben exits the train at Fourteenth Street, about halfway down to Tribeca. He'll kill some time at Dome Magazines before trying Gil again. It's just a few blocks down from the subway.

He catches his reflection in a storefront window. All in black. He looks like a poseur, he thinks, but what else can he do? He can't afford great clothes. The next best thing is to wear all black. It's the closest you can get to looking good without spending all of your money on designer jeans and coats. The only trick is to get your blacks to match, and his jeans have started to fade. They don't match his shoes anymore. Ben hates that. He'll save up for a new pair.

He feels a rush as soon as he steps into Dome. This is his favorite place in New York. Thousands of magazines from around the world, stacks and stacks of them, on shelves and tables and display racks, even piled on the checkout counter and under the candy rack. Glossy, gorgeous faces smiling from every direction. Fashion magazines, design magazines, music magazines, art magazines, all filled with beautiful people wearing beautiful clothes doing beautiful things in beautiful worlds. Bad things don't happen in those worlds. Ben wants in.

"Hi, Ali," Ben says, nodding at the shop manager behind the raised counter. Ben takes a tissue from the box and wipes his glasses. "Can I leave my bag here by the counter?"

Ali looks up from a copy of the *Economist* and smooths his shirt. He nods. "Of course. New British *Vogue* in today, by the way," he says. "February."

"Already?"

"Right on time, for once."

"Do you have any Januarys left?"

Ali points to a cardboard box at the back of the room. "In there. I was about to toss them." He turns up the radio, tapping his hands on the counter to Paula Abdul.

Ben peeks into the cardboard box. There it is, the cover of British *Vogue*, shot by Peter Lindbergh. Naomi Campbell, Linda Evangelista, Christy Turlington, Tatjana Patitz, and Cindy Crawford. The holy trinity plus two, in soft black-and-white with bright pink letters that read: *THE 1990s. WHAT'S NEXT?* A good, clean copy to replace the one his mother dropped her Kleenex on this morning.

He studies their faces, as familiar to him as anyone in the world. Naomi is the best on the runway. Linda is the best poser. Christy is the most glamorous. Tatjana has the best smolder. Cindy is the most famous. Right now, Linda is his favorite. Last week it was Naomi. Before that, Christy. Sometimes he favors Veronica Webb, Helena Christensen, Nadège, Carla Bruni. He's fond of both Claudias, Mason and Schiffer, and he loves Gail Elliott and Gurmit Kaur.

He opens up a copy of *L'Officiel*. Look, there's Yasmeen Ghauri wearing Claude Montana for Lanvin. Maybe she's his new favorite. And what about Stephanie Seymour in Versace? She's so Versace. Gianni must love her.

"She's very nice," Ali says, nodding at the photograph of Stephanie. "Very nice."

Ben's eye catches a photograph of Madonna on the cover of a gossip magazine. It's a paparazzi picture of her with Warren Beatty coming out of a restaurant in Los Angeles. Her hair is bleach blonde again, and her smile is wide and aggressive. Warren is scowling. "You can do better than him," Ben says aloud. "You're the most famous person in the world. He's a has-been."

"Did you say something?" Ali asks.

"Oh, nothing," Ben says. "Just talking to myself."

He picks up a copy of *Harper's Bazaar*, with Karen Alexander on the cover. She should be a bigger star, he thinks, but *Bazaar* needs a redesign. He keeps browsing. The other fashion magazines: *Elle, Mademoiselle, W.* The music magazines: *Q, Spin, NME.* The imports: *Match, So-En, Tatler, Grazia.* He would buy them all if he could. He would live inside a magazine if he could.

He should get going. He sets the January issue of British *Vogue* on the counter.

"Just this?" Ali asks. He's reading *Sassy* now.

"Trying to save money," Ben says.

"I hear ya," Ali says. "Well, this one's on me. It was out the door anyway. Oh, and there's a new *GXE* if you want it." He points to the freebie table by the door.

Ben always takes an issue of *GXE*, the glossy free biweekly that covers New York's gay nightlife and news, although half of it is personal ads. The new cover is a close-up of an orange Speedo stretched tightly across a butt that barely fits inside, with the words *DIVE IN!* overlaid in bright blue neon letters.

"Thanks, Ali," he says. "I'll see you soon."

"Be careful," Ali says, like he always says. He turns back to *Sassy*.

Out on Eighth Avenue, the wind has died down. Maybe he'll just walk to Gil's from here. His bag isn't too heavy. Tribeca's not so far. Straight down Eighth Avenue, then east on Canal, right on West Broadway, and then a few more blocks. He'll be there in a half hour. If Gil's still not home by then, Ben knows a diner nearby where he can wait.

Tell me what you thought life would be.

I was in second grade when we first got a color TV, and that whole school year I kept coming up with ways to fake being sick so that I could stay home and watch it all day. My mother never stayed home with me because she had to work. But it was better that way. I could watch all the game shows I wanted. The Joker's Wild, Press Your Luck, The Price Is Right. But especially Name That Tune.

Do you remember that one? The host, Tom Kennedy, would jog onto the sparkly set and introduce the contestants, and then the band, all wearing matching tuxedos, would play a few notes of a song. The contestants would have to guess the title just from those few notes. It was always some old people's song, like "I Left My Heart in San Francisco" or "Born Free." Sometimes Kathie Lee Johnson would come on and sing a lyric. You know her? She's on that morning show now with Regis. Anyway, I knew every single tune.

I was convinced that when I grew up, I would fly out to Hollywood, California—the music capital of the world according to the announcer—and compete. I'd win every round. I'd get a La-Z-Boy recliner and Radarange microwave oven and a four-night trip to Hawaii, and then I'd make it to the $25,000 Mystery Tune round. I'd name it in two notes, jump up and down for a couple of minutes, and walk out with a giant check. If I

33

could just win that round, I would never have to worry about anything again. I could buy a big apartment in New York City and live all by myself and do whatever I wanted and no one would bother me anymore. I really thought that would happen. I thought game show winners were rich forever.

What?! I was only eight years old! I didn't know.

ADAM

Adam's family's apartment isn't accessed through the main building entrance; instead, the door to their flat is a few feet away, behind a little gate and down a few stairs. Pop would correct Adam if he called their place a basement apartment, because according to Pop, it's *garden level.* He says it sounds less cheap that way, even though it probably is the cheapest three-bedroom in the neighborhood.

No one else is home. Good. Adam doesn't feel like fielding the *how was your afternoon* questions or the *what have you been up to* questions. He wants to chew on the day by himself for a little while longer. He hangs his parka on the hook and kicks his shabby Sambas onto the shabby rubber mat underneath. It reads *Home Sweet Hom* in swirly gray letters. Clarence, the family cat, ate the *e.* Typical. Clarence does what he wants. Clarence doesn't care what you think of him. Clarence knows you'll love him no matter what. Clarence is pure confidence. Adam wonders what that feels like. He admires that cat.

It's just the four of them here in this choppy, cluttered little apartment with linoleum floors: Mom, Pop, Clarence, and Adam. Mom and Pop moved in here in 1970, before Adam was born, back when Mom was a flower child and Pop was trying to break into musical theater. The rent was on the steep side, three hundred fifty a month, but it was just the right size for a pair of hippies who might want to start a family.

Pop gave up on auditions a long time ago. Now he works as a tour guide on one of those double-decker buses you see in Midtown. You know the ones: hop-on hop-off. Pop likes it. The work is steady and he always gets a round of applause. Mom, meanwhile, runs a bookkeeping business from home. Her clients are all artists and writers and musicians in the neighborhood whose language she speaks. The kitchen table is always a mess, piled high with ledgers and folders and staplers and pencils and curly ribbons of paper from her calculator. She keeps a giant office calendar tacked onto the back of the broom closet door, covered in notes detailing client meetings, filing deadlines, dentist appointments, birthdays. She calls it the Brain. Nothing happens here that isn't noted on the Brain.

He grabs a chipped coffee mug from the cabinet, an old one with a *WKRP in Cincinnati* logo and a faded photo of the cast. He fills it with water from the tap and grabs a handful of M&M's from the ashtray he made in fourth grade. Plain M&M's, not peanut, because she thinks peanuts are health food. *If I want trail mix, I'll buy trail mix.*

Adam slides across the linoleum and into his bedroom. He locks the door behind him. His window opens onto the Hudson Street sidewalk, right at shoe level. When he's bored, he watches the shoes walk past and makes up stories about who's wearing them. A stockbroker on the way to make a million dollars. A detective closing in on a suspect. A lover hurrying to a date. Sometimes he sees a pair of shoes at the deli that he recognizes from the window, but the owner almost never matches what he'd pictured. Old ladies love skateboarder shoes.

Bookshelves dominate the room, and they are packed full.

The rest of the shelves are packed with books. Too many books. Some he still reads, like the collection of movie reviews by Pauline

Kael and the world atlas that he looks at when he can't fall asleep. Some he hasn't opened in forever, like *Tuck Everlasting* and *Tiger Eyes* and the Lord of the Rings trilogy, which he tried many times to get into. No luck. He fared better with *Postcards from the Edge* by Carrie Fisher and *Lulu in Hollywood* by Louise Brooks and a copy of the *Double Indemnity* screenplay. He has a couple of Edward Gorey collections, and several Stephen King paperbacks. His newest book is a gift from his godfathers Jack and Victor: *The Celluloid Closet* by Vito Russo. Jack said he hoped to have a chance to introduce Adam to Vito one day.

At least two shelves are occupied with movies Sonia let him keep because no one rents them anymore: *Brewster McCloud*, *Eyes of Laura Mars*, *Watership Down*, *Lust in the Dust*, *The Big Blue*. The one marked *WarGames* actually contains a copy of *The Beastmaster*, which Adam only watches when his parents are out.

The tiny closet next to the bookshelves bulges with nearly eighteen years' worth of clothes and shoes and toys that Adam has long outgrown. Rubik's Cubes and incomplete Lego sets and a *Pong* console that no one's plugged in since 1981. It's a mess. Every now and then, Adam's mother declares that *today's the day* but as soon as she opens the door she just says *holy shit* and slams it shut.

He stands in front of the mirror behind his door. He stacks one foot on top of the other, pushes his hair back on his head. Maple syrup? He takes off his shirt, strips to his underwear. He crosses his arms across his concave chest, turns to the side, cranes his head to look at his nonexistent butt. He sucks in his stomach, searching for abs. No luck. He inspects his nipples. Why is one bigger than the other? He wonders what Callum looks like in his underwear.

Adam checks again to make sure the door is locked, then gets in bed to think about it.

BEN

Tribeca is the opposite of Midtown. There's almost no one on the sidewalk down here. No shops open, hardly any restaurants, no interior lights spilling out onto the street. It's bleak, and now that the wind has picked up again, even bleaker. Ben walks past building after building covered in scaffolding, temporary plywood walls obscuring construction zones inside. Row after row of temporary wheat-paste posters cover the plywood, advertising upcoming concerts or record releases. MC Lyte. Fine Young Cannibals. Henry Rollins. Eric B. & Rakim.

At the entrance to Gil's loft on Church Street, Ben presses the buzzer. No answer. He presses again. No answer. He wishes he'd picked up a couple of those cheap hotel brochures at the bus station.

He buzzes again. This time, an answer.

"Yeah?"

"Gil? It's me. Ben. I tried to ca—"

The buzzer cuts him off, unlatching the door. Ben enters, then hikes up to the third floor, into a rough hallway with peeling paint and a huge pile of two-by-fours stacked neatly at one end. Ben takes his backpack out of his duffel and slips it on his shoulders, then stashes the bigger bag behind the lumber. He'll get it later, either to bring it inside when Gil says he can stay, or to carry back out on his way to somewhere else.

Ben takes a breath, then opens Gil's door. The loft is cavernous, a giant unfinished room with double-height ceilings and soaring windows covered in massive sheets of plastic. The walls are bare Sheetrock with wires poking out of holes where electrical outlets should be. A shop vacuum that looks like R2-D2 sits next to a makeshift workbench with a band saw. The place is a mess. Gil says he's nearing the end of the renovation, but it doesn't look like it. Ben wonders how he can even afford this huge place, let alone the construction, but doctors make a lot of money. This is a long way from Gideon.

Gil appears in a doorframe next to the sleek kitchen, the first room he finished. He's an inch taller than Ben and much broader, with thick black hair sticking out in a million directions. He's in a wrinkled set of pale blue scrubs. His sleeping scrubs, he calls them.

"Hi," Ben says. "Were you sleeping? It's only seven."

Gil rubs his eyes. "You don't know much about doctors, do you? I had an eighteen-hour shift."

"Sorry," Ben says.

Gil raises an eyebrow. "Everything okay?"

Ben answers swiftly. "Yes. I just wanted to come down to the city for a couple of days or so. Okay if I crash on the couch in the study?"

"What do you mean by *or so*?"

Ben shrugs.

Gil scratches his stomach. "Whatever. Just keep it down."

"Are you hungry?"

"I'm sleeping."

"But will you be hungry? I can make us something to eat."

"There's no food here. Just wine and fortune cookies."

"I'll shop. I have money. I'll make the spaghetti that you liked last time."

"Suit yourself."

"I promise I won't be in the way," Ben says.

Gil tilts his head in recognition. He knows these words. Growing up, the biggest sin in their family was to be in the way. It encompassed almost any offense: taking up too much room, being too inquisitive, needing help. You're watching *The Electric Company* too loud, you're in the way. You need a hand with a homework problem, you're in the way. You lost your milk money and need a quarter, you're in the way. You're in the back of the car and you really have to pee, *for chrissakes, stop whining and hold it. You're always in the goddamn way.*

"There's some money in the drawer next to the fridge," Gil says.

"Okay," Ben says.

Gil turns back down the hallway. "Happy birthday!" he yells before disappearing into his bedroom.

ADAM

It's just after seven when Adam emerges. His mother is back at the kitchen table, filling out a tax form and singing along to Gloria Estefan on the clock radio.

She locks eyes with him, shimmies, then leans her head back in triumph for the final beat. "*Gonna get you . . . tonight!*" she shouts. "Whew. Rhythm got me. Hello, sweet pea."

He notices she has two pairs of reading glasses on top of her head, in addition to the pair on her nose. "Um, Mom? You have, like, three pairs of glasses on—"

She holds up a hand to stop him. "One pair to read, one pair to hold my hair back, and— I know what you're thinking, but there is absolutely no truth to the idea that I forgot that the other pair was up there. I absolutely did not spend a half hour digging through every corner of this kitchen looking for them. No way that happened. Nope. Not a chance. Not here."

"You know there are at least two pencils in your hair, too."

"You call it my hair," she says. "I call it my office supply closet. I may or may not have a stapler up there, too, along with a bottle of Wite-Out and several IRS forms, in triplicate."

"I'm impressed." Adam reaches for the bathroom door.

"Your father's in there." She holds her Muppets coffee mug out to him. "Zap this for me, will you? Twenty seconds. I hate cold tea."

Adam places it in the boxy microwave on the counter.

"Don't forget, it's Bus Stop night. We're meeting Jack and Victor at eight. They're excited to see you."

Normally, Adam would be excited, too. He loves the Bus Stop diner and he loves his godparents Jack and Victor. But Adam is still spinning after his day with Callum. He can hide it from his parents, but Jack and Victor would see it immediately, and they'd know that it's a boy, and it would turn into a whole thing. Adam's not up for all that. He wants to keep Callum to himself for now.

"I'm going to skip," he says.

She peers over her glasses. "Everything all right? You feeling okay?"

"Yeah. I just feel like staying in."

"Jack and Victor will be bummed."

"I'll see them next time."

"Weren't you going to get a haircut today?" She taps today's date on the office calendar. "Yes, right here. *Adam/Astor Place.* Clear as mud."

"I forgot. I'll do it tomorrow or something."

"All right. I'll update." She licks the tip of her pencil. "I noticed you forgot your hat today."

"Mom. I'm almost eighteen."

"And I'm forty-four. What's your point?"

"Are you going to be on my case about my hat when I'm at NYU next year?"

"Oh, sweetie, yes. I can't wait to barge into your dorm room

41

swinging your hat from my finger. I'll wear my Pink Panther socks with Birkenstocks and flirt with your roommates. You'll be so popular."

"Your specificity is terrifying."

"It's a gift. Oh, I almost forgot. Lily wants you to call her."

Pop bellows from the bathroom. "Do I hear my boy?" The door handle jiggles and he bursts into the kitchen, still wearing his HOP-ON HOP-OFF sweatshirt. He grabs Adam's ears and kisses him on the forehead. "You ready for a big night on the town? The Bus Stop is hotter than Studio 54, you know."

"He's not coming, hon. And Studio 54 closed ten years ago."

"What?" Pop pokes Adam's shoulder. "Are you sure this is my son? He's never said no to a grilled cheese in his life."

"I'm just gonna watch a movie or something," Adam says.

Pop turns to Mom, aghast. "You're not ditching me, too, are you, Frankie?"

She gets up and hugs Pop. "You got two chances of me ditching you, Popsicle."

"Fat and slim?"

"Jackpot."

Pop dips her like a tango dancer. "Kiss me, Frankie. I'm coconuts about you."

"I hate to interrupt this touching moment," Adam says. "But I need to call Lily." He takes the phone and walks it back toward his room. Clarence pounces at the cord, but misses.

"Sure you won't come eat?"

For a moment, Adam reconsiders. Maybe he should go. He could tell Pop and Mom and Jack and Victor all about the tall stranger who asked him to the movies, about the pictures they took, about the cake they ate, about their long walk home. But then he imagines their reactions, their clumsy expressions struggling not to start giggling with one another about young love and teenage crushes and what it was like back in *their* day.

"No thanks," he says. "But say hi to them for me."

Pop musses Adam's hair. "We'll bring you back a grilled cheese, okay?" He takes a step closer and knits his brow. "Are you taller than me?"

Adam's a good two inches taller, but he plays along. "Never."

"Good boy." Pop winks. "Tomato soup on the side. Extra croutons."

"Thanks, Pop."

"You bet, kid."

BEN

The awning above Angelino's Fruit & Flowers spells out the details: BEER. PRODUCE. CIGARETTES. LOTTO. In other words, a typical neighborhood grocery. Ben wonders how it survives down here. Maybe it's by selling sandwiches to the construction crews during the day. And cigarettes.

Ben smiles at the woman behind the cluttered counter, but she doesn't smile back. She simply tips her graying head to one side and blinks lazily, a vague acknowledgment of his presence. She's engrossed in a word search. The chain connected to her glasses is tangled in the top button of her blouse. Behind her, displays of cigarettes, cough medicines, eyeglass repair kits, and condoms surround a tiny black-and-white television playing *Wheel of Fortune* with the sound off.

The shop has three short aisles, filled floor to ceiling with breakfast cereal and dog biscuits and four-packs of Yoo-hoo and individual rolls of paper towels and boxes of light bulbs and cans of soup and boxes of fancy crackers. No square inch of shelf or wall space lies empty. Ben starts gathering ingredients. A box of dried spaghetti, one pound. It's enough for four people, but Ben's hungry. A big can of crushed tomatoes. A green can of powdered cheese, because there's no real cheese in the refrigerator case. A pound of butter, way more than he needs. A large onion and a head of garlic, chosen from a basket by the refrigerator. While he's inspecting the onion, a chubby cat appears from underneath the basket, looks up at Ben, sneezes, and retreats back out of view.

He carries his ingredients over and lines them up in front of her, then takes a stack of four chocolate cookies wrapped in plastic from a basket on the counter. They look homemade and delicious.

"Do you have any red pepper flakes?" he asks.

She reaches under the counter and brings up two small packets, the kind you'd find in a takeout pizza box. "Five cents each."

"Okay." Ben holds up the butter. "I only need one stick. Can I buy just one stick?"

"Two," she says.

"Okay. Two."

She opens the box and removes two sticks for his pile, then hands the other two sticks to Ben. "Put these back," she says. He complies.

When he returns to the counter, she is carefully punching the buttons on her register. She searches for each key, then checks the display to make sure she's hit the right number. After each entry, she places the item in a paper bag.

"New machine," she says, adjusting her glasses when she finishes. "Twenty-one twenty-two."

Ben looks at his twenty. He always forgets how much more expensive everything is here in the city. "I guess I better not take the cookies," he says.

The woman sighs, voids the sale, and starts over. After she taps in the prices again, she says, "Nineteen forty-seven." He hands her the twenty-dollar bill. "She doesn't like anyone, but she likes you."

"Me?" Ben says. "She who?"

"Madonna." The woman points to the floor, where the cat is now sitting just inches from Ben's foot, looking up at him.

"Your cat's name is Madonna?"

"It's not my cat. She just lives here. She takes care of the mice, so I feed her. The only other person she ever liked was my son Dominic. She sat in his lap when he was sick. She never sits in mine." She hands him his change. "Fifty-three back."

Ben takes the bag in his arm. "Thank you," he says, but she's already looking away, toward the back of the store, her mind on something else now.

Back up at the loft, Ben closes the door quietly so he doesn't wake Gil. But just as he sets the bag down on the counter, the phone rings. Before he can reach it, the answering machine picks up.

"Gil. It's your mother. Pick up. Benjamin is missing."

Her voice is slow, sleepy, and sad. Ben finds the volume dial and turns it almost all the way down, leaning over to the speaker to listen.

"Gil? Pick up."

He should answer. He should do the right thing and let her know that he's safe, make sure she's all right, remind her that there are leftover meatballs in the fridge that she can heat up for dinner. But he knows it wouldn't be that simple, so he doesn't.

"Gil," she says, one more time, and the phone cuts off.

Ben waits a moment, then presses the ERASE button. He hears the little cassette inside the machine spin and whir, wiping itself clean. Gil will never hear it now.

He begins unpacking the groceries. Inside, he finds the chocolate cookies wrapped in plastic, the ones he didn't have enough money to pay for. New York is the best place.

ADAM

Lily answers in a very high pitch. "*Kiss!*"

Adam can hear Prince playing in the background. "Kiss" has been Lily's favorite song since ninth grade.

"It's me," he says.

"No kidding," she says. "We have Caller ID now, you know."

"Fancy. What are you up to?"

"I'm working on my beauty mark."

"I didn't know you had a beauty mark."

"I do now, thanks to liquid eyeliner. It's a little too Cindy Crawford at the moment, though. I want something a little more Lisa Stansfield. You know what I mean?"

"There's a difference?"

"Oh, Best. Have you learned nothing from my fashion and beauty moments over the years? My Irene Cara moment with the legwarmers, my Chrissie Hynde moment with the caterpillar eyelashes, my Lisa Bonet moment with the bowler hat, my Bananarama moment, my Sade moment, my three distinct Debbie Harry moments, my Martika moment, my 'Papa Don't Preach' mo—"

Adam interrupts. "Your *Preppy Handbook* moment with the Bermuda bag."

She gasps. "How dare you. We don't speak of those dark days."

"Sorry. You were spinning out of control. I had to stop you."

"Oh, my complex eighties fashion story," she says with dramatic wistfulness. "Everything was so different then. We were so young, so naive. Innocents."

"The eighties ended like five minutes ago."

"Ancient history. Yesteryear. I can barely remember it."

"You're listening to a song from 1986."

"That's different. 'Kiss' is the best song of all time. So far."

"So there are loopholes for music."

"Yes. And for fashion. But they are very strict loopholes and subject to change at any time, at my discretion. But why are we even talking about this? You went to see a Kevin Bacon movie without me."

"I thought you'd be proud," he says.

"Stop appealing to my maternal side."

"Aren't you the one who said it was the Decade of Yes?"

"Very good. You're forgiven. Now, spit. Who is he, where did you meet him, why haven't you mentioned him before, and how far did you go? I require details."

Adam is happy to provide them. He starts at the beginning. He tells her everything, from the tall customer at the back of the store, to the wrong tape on hold, to the question on the corner, to the photo booth, to the movie, to the chocolate espresso cake, to the music up in the window, to seeing Lily on the sidewalk. The only part he leaves out is when Callum tucked his hair behind his ear and touched his hand to Adam's cheek. He wants to keep that part to himself.

"Okay, hold on. Are you saying you *didn't* kiss him?"

"That's correct."

"At all?"

"No."

"You mean I got more action when I double-cheeked him good-bye than you got all day?"

"I just met him!"

"I don't follow," she says.

"Oh, Lily. It must be so hard for you to put up with me."

"What can I say? I'm a giver. And besides, we belong together. We're like that Pet Shop Boys song. You know, me with the brains, you with the looks, us making lots of money."

"Brains, looks, money," he repeats. "Got it."

"Ugh, Best. It's not fair. I never get to go on dates."

"You had a date last weekend. Rob, was it? Or wait, he has a nickname."

"You refer to Throb?"

"Why do I think that he came up with that nickname all by himself?"

"Not only that, he wears rugby shirts like it's 1983. Straight people are so slow."

"Wait, aren't you straight?"

"Don't get technical. I'm trying to make a point, which is, I want to date someone like Calvin."

"Callum."

"Like I said. Callum. I love that tall, skinny rock-star thing he's got. Like Mick Jagger, only twenty years younger and six inches taller. What do you think he looks like naked?"

Adam sighs. He does not want to speculate on Callum's naked body with Lily. He can do that by himself. Time for a subject change.

"He's going to be a conductor," he says. "Symphony, not train."

"*Oooh, rock me Amadeus,*" she sings, aping Falco's Austrian accent from the old pop hit. "Sexy. And how old is he?"

"I didn't ask," he says. "Older than we are. Definitely not in high school."

"Good," she says. "Seriously. You're almost eighteen. That makes you an adult. Personally, I'd go up to twenty-two or twenty-three. Older guys are better at everything, you know what I mean?"

"I'll make a note of that."

"Besides, look at Diana and Charles, the world's foremost ambassadors of true love and marital bliss. She was nineteen when they got engaged."

"Nineteen? How old was Charles?"

"Thirty-two."

"Okay, well, Callum is not thirty-two."

"Where does the love machine live, anyway?"

"Horatio Street."

"Really? That's weird. Why haven't we seen him around the neighborhood before? Pretty hard to miss a six-foot-four hunk of junk like that."

"I gave him my number," Adam says.

He expects a happy squeal, but instead she pauses for a moment. The song in the background ends. She asks quietly, "So do you think you're going to be boyfriends now?"

"I just met him."

"Do you want to be?"

"I don't know," he says, but he's lying. Yes, he wants to be. He doesn't know what it means, *to be boyfriends*, not really. But he's always wanted it. Maybe too much. "I don't even know if he'll call."

"He'll call," she says, her tone a mix of confidence and resignation. She sounds almost sad.

Adam wishes they were sitting together in person. He'd like to touch her hand. "I'll go see *Tremors* again with you if you want."

"Oh, I don't care about that," she says, her voice bouncy again. "I'm sick of Kevin Bacon."

"What? I thought you loved him!"

"Not anymore. I just decided."

"I love you, Lily."

Tell me how you got away.

I think it was fourth or fifth grade. I was at the arcade where I went to play Frogger and Centipede, but I saw that they had a new game, Ms. Pac-Man. I wanted to play it because I was good at regular Pac-Man. But this group of older guys that were always at the arcade were standing around making fun of it because it had a sexy Pac-Man with eyelashes and makeup instead of the normal, boring Pac-Man. So I stayed away from it. You can't play a game that everyone else is making fun of.

Finally those boys left and I went over to the Ms. Pac-Man machine. I got through a bunch of levels with my first quarter. I played two more quarters before I ran out of money. When I turned around, I saw that the same boys had come back in. They were standing in the doorway and snickering.

"That's a girl's game," one of them said. "It's for girls."

"And homos," another one said. "Are you a homo?"

I pretended not to hear them. I could see the arcade attendant in his booth at the back shaking his head at me. I zipped up my coat really slowly, trying to think if there was another way out of the arcade, like a back door. But I couldn't think of one. The only way out was straight through them, so I walked over to the doorway. "Excuse me," I said.

They stepped aside to let me through, but then one of the guys pushed me from behind. When I jerked forward my teeth clacked together and pinched the inside of my cheek, but I didn't fall. I just kept walking as fast as I could toward the bus stop, trying not to switch my hips back and forth because I knew that switching your hips back and forth was for girls and homos also.

Those boys didn't chase me down that day. Not that time. That didn't happen until later.

BEN

The sauce for the spaghetti is easy to make. Ben melts butter in a pot and waits for it to foam before adding the onion, which he's cut into four equal pieces. As it sizzles, he smashes four garlic cloves with a knife and drops them in, too. Seconds later, they release their aroma. Ben inhales. Garlic is his favorite smell. He adds a fifth clove, and then a sixth. The garlic will burn if he doesn't move quickly now, so he opens the can of tomatoes and pours it in. When it begins to bubble, he turns the heat down to a lazy simmer and covers the pot. It will transform over the next little while into something much deeper and more complex than the simple ingredients would suggest. He fills another pot with water and adds a hefty dose of salt, then sets it on the burner to boil. Ben likes cooking in this kitchen. It's so much nicer than the one back in Gideon. All the burners work, all the equipment is shiny. For someone who doesn't know how to cook, Gil put a lot of thought into it. Or someone did.

Gil shuffles into the kitchen, freshly showered. "It smells good in here," he says. He draws a glass of water, then sits on one of the barstools by the kitchen island to watch Ben cook.

Ben empties the box of pasta into the boiling water and gently stirs it to make sure the noodles don't stick together. He fishes the onion out of the tomato sauce and sets it aside. It's done its work. He squishes the tomatoes with the back of his spoon, just enough to break up the biggest pieces. He tastes it. Not bad. He adds a few red pepper flakes for heat. He stirs the noodles again. *They should swim like eels in the sea*, he thinks. He wonders where he heard that. Probably on television. *Great Chefs*, maybe, or one of the other cooking shows he watches.

The pasta is cooked through now, just the way Ben likes it. Chewy and not mushy. He uses Gil's creaky tongs to extract the noodles from the water and drop them into the pot with the sauce. He takes a couple of bowls out of the cupboard and ladles a bit of pasta water into them to warm up the bowls. Hot pasta should go into hot bowls, so it stays hot. He saw this trick on television, too.

"Do you want a glass of wine?" Gil asks. "I have a bottle of red here."

"No thanks," Ben says. He empties the bowls of water, then fills each with a big portion of spaghetti. He sets the cylinder of powdered cheese on the counter, then sits down across from Gil.

Gil uncorks the wine and pours himself a glass. He sinks a fork into his bowl and spins it clockwise, gathering noodles in the tines. He closes his eyes as he chews.

"This is good," he says.

"It's easy," Ben says, happy that Gil's happy.

"Did I hear the phone earlier?" Gil asks. "Was there a message on the machine?"

Ben swallows. "I tried to turn down the volume so it wouldn't wake you, but I got confused with the buttons. I think I erased it."

Gil narrows his eyes. "Those buttons are pretty well marked."

"Sorry," Ben says, his face hot. "I'm a klutz."

"It might have been important."

"Hopefully they'll call back," Ben says. *Hopefully not.*

Gil takes another bite. "God, this is good. Did you put extra garlic in or something?"

"A little."

"Do me a favor, all right? Don't mess with the answering machine again." Gil pours himself another glass of wine. "Now, why did Mom kick you out?"

"Not technically," Ben says. "But I had to go."

"Did she do something to set you off?"

"Nothing new," he says evasively. "I'm just sick of failing."

"Failing?"

"To make her happy."

"It's not your job to make her happy."

"Tell her that. She acts like it's my main purpose in life."

"Running away is a pretty shitty thing to do."

"I didn't run. She stood there and watched me pack. She wanted me to take more stuff."

"But now she's up there alone."

Ben doesn't answer.

Gil takes another sip of wine. "She's not a monster, you know. She hasn't had it easy."

She called me trash, Ben thinks. He gets up to clear the plates.

"You don't have to do the dishes. You cooked. I can clean."

"It's okay. I don't mind." Ben runs hot water into the sink. He needs something to do with his hands right now. Something to do besides sitting at the table and listening to Gil.

"Why don't you use my dishwasher? I'm very proud of it. No one else in this town has one."

"They get cleaner by hand," Ben says, squirting a few drops of dish soap into the water. He watches it foam up into shiny little bubbles, each one a rainbow.

"Some birthday," Gil says in a sarcastic tone. He balls up his napkin. "Okay, listen. I don't understand what you did, and I'm not sure I'd like it if I did understand. But you can stay. A few days, a couple of weeks, a month, whatever. But you will go to school. Every day. You will be on the train to Gideon every single morning at God knows what hour. I will buy you a Metro-North pass."

"But the commute will take forev—"

"No negotiation. People commute all the time. If you miss a day of school, you're out. Capisce?"

Ben nods.

"Oh, and if Rebecca comes over and I need the place to myself, you go for a long walk."

"Who's Rebecca?"

"Someone I know. You'll meet her. Or maybe you won't. It doesn't matter. The rule is, if I need privacy, you're gone. And I'll talk to our mother. Otherwise, she'll just keep calling."

"She called?"

"Give me a break, Ben."

Ben didn't anticipate feeling so small tonight. When he left Gideon this morning, he felt brave. Now, he's once again at the mercy of someone else. He's traded his mother in Gideon for his brother in Tribeca. The transaction comes with a price. He's got to make himself wanted here. Useful at best, unbothersome at least.

"I'll cook for us," Ben says.

"You bet your ass you will. That was the best meal I've had in a month." Gil swallows the rest of his wine. "Jesus, are you really eighteen?"

ADAM

It's freezing out here. Everything feels colder in the dark. The wind is blowing again. Adam holds his breath and dives into it. It's only a few blocks.

At Horatio Street, a man in an overcoat and fur trapper hat

crosses the sidewalk in front of Adam and trots up a shallow set of stairs. He presses a buzzer in a doorway between two arched windows, then leans against the wall to wait for an answer.

Horatio is a short street, only four blocks long, or four and a half when you count the short stretch between Eighth and Greenwich Avenues. It's also a quiet street, especially at night. No restaurants, no shops, mostly residential buildings and a couple of industrial warehouses down at the end by the river. A timeworn playground on the north side of the street, with its crumbling basketball courts and anemic trees, attracts outdoor drinkers on summer nights, but not in January. Besides the man in the overcoat, who is inside now, no one else is out tonight. The bald trees cast brittle, sinister midwinter shadows. Their spiky branches shiver in the wind.

He walks the length of the street in both directions, first toward the water, then back toward the city, looking up at the warm lights in the windows overhead. He imagines the men and women and children who live upstairs, some alone in their apartments, others crowded together. Somewhere up there, in one of these buildings, is Callum.

You could shoot a period movie on Horatio Street very easily. There's no fancy new architecture or anything. It would be a cinch to make it look like the 1880s or 1920s. All you'd have to do is get rid of the contemporary cars and take down the anti-Bush signs. The New York City Sanitation truck would have to go. But Adam will leave it in place for his movie.

He starts to write it in his mind. It will be a long movie, a big epic, scene after scene sprawling against decades and continents. Drama and comedy and struggle and victory and sorrow and joy and romance. A tall, handsome hero. A cast of wise-cracking sidekicks and doomed villains and sage counselors. Million-dollar sets, faraway locations, and languorous, syrupy golden-hour love scenes soaked in sentiment. And music. Oh, the music will win awards.

The opening scene is easy. Exterior: Greenwich Village. The beginning of a new decade. A gust of wind, a lucky taxi, a question. *Will you come?* And then the rest will unfold in mysterious and surprising ways. But there will be no happy ending, because there will be no ending at all. The movie will last forever.

He feels for the photographs in his parka pocket, the ones they took in the photo booth. He's memorized them by now, engraved the images onto a panel in his mind. Callum's curls. Callum's smile, with his tongue stuck between his teeth. Callum's shoulders. Callum's freckles, tossed like magic dust across his crooked nose.

The wind stings his cheeks. The snow is not far now. But Adam will walk for a few hours anyway. He's remembered his hat.

Two

APRIL 1990

I couldn't ask for another.

—Deee-Lite, "Groove Is in the Heart"

ADAM

There's a spot on the inside of Adam's cheek that he chews on when he's anxious. It doesn't hurt, not really. He doesn't bite hard enough to draw blood. Just enough to sting, to take his mind off everything else. It soothes him while he waits for Saturdays. Saturdays are Callum days. They've had two months of Saturdays together. Two months and counting. Except for that one week.

Sometimes they talk on the phone during the week but only for a few minutes, because Callum is so busy. He works every afternoon and evening except Tuesday and Saturday, and on Tuesdays he practices music with some friends from work. Once, Adam tested this boundary by asking Callum to play hooky from music practice to see a movie, but Callum only laughed. *I'll never get to Carnegie Hall without practice, practice, practice*, he'd said.

Every Saturday Adam worries that Callum won't come, but every Saturday Callum shows up at Sonia's at one o'clock, smiling with his tongue between his teeth. He'll hand Adam a subway token or a roll of quarters, and Adam will ask where they're going, and Callum will press his finger across his lips to shush him. *It's a surprise*, he'll say. *Follow me.*

Maybe they'll go down to the Battery and ride the Staten Island Ferry back and forth across the harbor. Maybe they'll go to the Chinatown Fair arcade and play *Galaga*. Maybe they'll take the subway out to Coney Island to ride the Cyclone over and over.

They'll go to slurp noodles at Grand Sichuan and make up songs about dumplings. They'll go for haircuts and sing "Father Figure" to each other while waiting in the vinyl chairs for their turn. They'll stand outside a little storefront electronics shop on Fourteenth Street trying to memorize all the words to the Queen Latifah rap that's cascading out of the boom box in front. They'll buy shawarma from a cart that's playing ragtime jazz. *Just like I told you*, Callum will say every time they hear a song. *Music everywhere.*

There was one week when Callum didn't come. He just didn't show up. Adam called, but Callum didn't call back until Sunday. He said he wasn't feeling well. Just a cold, just a little flu or something. *I'll bring you chicken soup from Second Avenue Deli*, Adam said. But Callum said no. Don't worry. He had plenty of cold medicine. He'd just sleep it off. He'd be better by next Saturday.

And he was better by the next Saturday. They went to Theatre 80 that afternoon, where they sat in the back row holding hands all the way through a Technicolor noir double feature, first *Leave Her to Heaven*, one of Adam's all-time favorites, and then *Niagara*, which he'd never seen before. Afterward, they snuck into the little garden behind the Jefferson Market Library. A surprise springtime snow squall surrounded them there, covering the hyacinths in wet flakes. Callum picked one for Adam. *Happy birthday*, he said. *Eighteen. You're catching up.*

Maybe one of these Saturdays Callum will invite Adam up to his apartment. It hasn't happened yet, but maybe that's how it's supposed to be. Maybe it just takes time. How would Adam know?

BEN

Ben's not sure how long it took before Gil figured out that he wasn't going back home to Gideon in a few days, or a few weeks, or ever.

He stays out of the way as much as he can, and, as promised, he cooks dinner almost every night. If they're both at home, they'll eat together in front of the television. If Gil's at work, Ben will leave leftovers in the fridge—macaroni and cheese, chili, meatballs for sandwiches. He does all the grocery shopping, even for wine. They never ask for his ID at the Corker over on Broadway. They never ask for ID anywhere.

He's followed Gil's rules. He's been at Grand Central every single morning for the 7:12 train to Gideon. He struck a deal with his history teacher, Mrs. Clovis, to do an independent study instead of going to her afternoon class. He chose his topic—the history of the garment industry in France after World War II—primarily because he's become obsessed with Christian Dior and Cristóbal Balenciaga. And because Mrs. Clovis loves fashion, too. There are no useful resources at Ben's school, so she connected him with a friend of hers who is a professor at the Fashion Institute of Technology. He boards the 1:05 train back to New York every day, does his homework for biology, calculus, and English on the train, then spends an hour or two at the FIT library working on his Dior/Balenciaga project. After a quick stop at Angelino's Fruits & Flowers, he's back at Gil's in time to make dinner.

Ben's year-end report card won't be perfect like Gil's was, but it will be the best he's ever had. Gil will have to be happy. Ben's not sure what he'll do with his good grades. It's too late to apply for college in the fall, but maybe he can enroll in the spring. He'll ask the registrar at FIT if that's possible. He'd love to go there.

There are two men that Ben sees all the time on the afternoon train. Handsome, about Gil's age. They always sit together, always on the same side of the train, the side by the river. The shorter man always sits by the window. The taller one drinks Perrier. They wear suits sometimes, and sometimes jeans and sweaters, and they talk softly to each other. Sometimes the tall one falls asleep.

Two weeks ago, Ben watched them argue. He couldn't hear what they were saying, but it was tense and sharp and it made him worry. When they arrived at Grand Central, the shorter one got up and stepped over the tall one to get out, not saying goodbye. The tall man was crying. Ben hasn't seen them since.

ADAM

"Meeting in the ladies' room," Lily says, and hangs up. Adam grabs a sweatshirt and, following the protocol the two friends set back when the Klymaxx song was a hit, heads to their usual rendezvous spot outside the Banana Express supermarket, halfway between their apartments. She's chewing gum so vigorously he can see her mouth moving from across the street.

"Everything okay?" he asks.

"Yes. No. I don't know. I dumped Brent." She blows a big, perfect bubble.

"What?"

"He told me he wanted a hand job in the chemistry lab and I told him it was stupid idea because there are plenty of better places in the world for a hand job. He got mad and called me a bitch."

"Seriously? He went straight to bitch?" They start walking toward Carmine Street. Meetings in the ladies' room usually involve walking around this block three or four times.

"I told him to go to hell. I really wish there was a word to call a guy that hits as hard as *bitch* hits a girl, especially in a situation like that. We need a straight-guy-specific insult and it has to hurt. It's like the only option is *asshole* but that doesn't pack much heat, you know?"

"I'll work on that with you. A project. Linguistics."

"Sounds dirty."

"Everything sounds dirty to you."

"By the way, I was right. It's a fact. The chemistry lab really *is* a stupid place for a hand job. What kind of weird Thomas Dolby fetish is that?"

"Not to mention the various mystery burns a person could end up with in that situation. On god knows what part of the body."

"Now you're making me wish I'd done it. *What's in this beaker? Oops, sorry about that!*"

"Diabolical," he says, smiling.

"It's so frustrating, Best. I thought I liked him. I thought he liked me. He was being so sweet right out of the gate. But then two weeks in, and he's already acting like it's my job to get him off?"

"He's an idiot."

"Yes. But there was something about the way he flipped out so quickly. Like, he assumed I was going to say yes. Like he expected it. Is that what guys think of me? Is that my reputation?"

"Screw reputations," Adam says. "And screw him. You're a goddess. He's a squirrel."

"I just want high school to be over. I'll change my entire identity when I get to college. No one in the wilds of the Yukon will know me. I'll be as pure as the driven snow again. Do you think the snow ever melts up there? Or is the whole place just encased in ice?"

"Lily, Hunter College is on Sixty-Eighth Street. That's barely even uptown."

"Don't remind me. I'm going to freeze. What do people even wear above Fourteenth Street? Frostbite is a serious concern, you know. I could lose my toes. And then how will I wear flip-flops on my eventual honeymoon?"

"Your toes will be fine," he says. "You'll be Julie Christie in *Doctor Zhivago*. And I'll bring you hot toddies on my dogsled."

"All the way from NYU?"

"All the way from NYU. Remind me to get some dogs."

"Oh, Adam. You're the best Best a girl could ever have," she says. "Now, let's talk about more important things. Have you and Too-Tall Jones done it yet?"

"Done what?"

"Sex!"

"Define sex," he says, then quickly retracts the bait. "No, wait, don't—"

But he's too late. "Sex," she is saying, "is when you take your thingy and you stick it—"

"Stop," he says. "I don't know what kinds of things you're picturing in your overactive imagination, but no. We haven't done any of those things. We haven't even kissed. Not really."

"You haven't even *kissed*? Are you kidding? Oh, Adam. I feel like a bad mother. You two need to get a bottle of wine and take your shirts off and see what happens."

"That could go so wrong. Don't you remember when I made you watch that old movie *The Blue Gardenia*? The one where Anne Baxter drank too many Pearl Diver cocktails and forgot who she was making out with? She ended up whacking Raymond Burr with a fire poker."

"Totally understandable. I, too, have become confused mid-kiss."

"I think the lesson is, no booze on the first kiss."

"So unadventurous," she says. "But fine, skip the wine. Just take your shirts off and make out. Something's gotta happen here. I mean, are you guys in love or what?"

Adam doesn't know how to answer. He *wants* to be in love. He thinks about it all the time. His mind is on Callum every minute of the day, and sometimes in his dreams. Is that love?

"I just wish I knew what he was thinking," he says.

"Oh, Best," she laments. "What am I going to do with you?"

"Now you really sound like someone's mother."

"Luke, I am your mother," she says in a *Star Wars* voice.

"Yes, Lily Vader."

They round the corner back to Banana Express. The meeting in the ladies' room is almost over.

"Don't you *want* to do it with Callum?" she asks.

"Yes," he says. "I do. I really do."

BEN

Ben's starting to feel like a permanent resident in Gil's loft now. A few weeks ago, when the contractor finished construction in the living room, Ben helped Gil move the sofa out of Ben's room—they call it that now, *Ben's room*—and into the living room, where it was always supposed to go in the first place. Gil got a new television set for the living room, and the contractor built an alcove for it so that when they slipped it in, the screen was flush with the wall, almost like the screen was flat, with no tube behind it. Ben imagines hanging a television on the wall, like a painting or a calendar. Wouldn't that be cool? He doubts it will ever happen.

But think about it. When CDs first came out, no one could believe those either. And now, no one even thinks twice about them. Same with cordless phones and one-hour photo labs. Soon there will be flying cars, pocket computers, video phones, gay weddings, vacations to the moon, invisibility cloaks. All seem equally likely, or equally unlikely. Ben wants the vacations to the moon the most. Although an invisibility cloak sounds great, too.

Gil had an older, smaller couch in storage, so they brought that up for Ben to sleep on. He would love a dresser, but he won't ask for it. He's got his stuff piled neatly along the wall. His stack of magazines grows every week.

The brothers don't talk much, even when they're both at home. At first, Ben thought it was because Gil was annoyed with him. He has plenty of reasons to be. Ben's been there for months now. But maybe this is just how grown-up brothers coexist. Not a lot of talking. It's fine with Ben. He just keeps his head down and stays out of the way.

"You're going to have to call our mother sometime, you know," Gil said the other day. "You owe her that much."

Ben said that he already tried to call. It was true. He'd called her twice, because he wanted to make sure she wasn't home. He wanted to sneak in and grab some more clothes. But both times she answered, so he hung up. He felt bad about it, but only for a few minutes.

ADAM

Adam's mother is standing in front of the fridge wearing a Howard the Duck sweatshirt with the hood cut off. "I swear I left half a pastrami sandwich in here," she says, scratching Clarence with her toe. "Did you take it?"

"I hate pastrami," Adam says.

"Oh, right. So does your father. Men are so weird." She grabs a handful of M&M's and sits down at the table. "These will have to do. Good morning, sweetie. Nice T-shirt. We should go there sometime."

Adam looks down to remind himself what he's wearing. It's his Mount Rushmore T-shirt.

She smooths out the morning newspaper. On the front page there's a story about independence talks in Lithuania, and another one about job discrimination against immigrants. There's an item about the ongoing investigation into the plane crash in Lockerbie, Scotland, and a headline that says: BUSH, IN FIRST ADDRESS ON AIDS, BACKS A BILL TO PROTECT ITS VICTIMS. She flicks her finger at the photograph of the president, like she's flicking an ant off a picnic table.

"His first address on AIDS," she hisses. "A year and a half into his term and he can finally bring himself to do something about it. He's just as bad as his old boss Reagan. I can't believe we have two more years of this bargain-basement dipstick."

"Or six," Adam says, crouching down to tie his Sambas.

"Take that back," she says. "By the way, have you registered to vote? You're old enough now."

"I will. Right now I'm late for work."

"Wait, there's a message here for you someplace." She rustles through some papers on the table and hands him a Post-it with Callum's name. "He seems very polite."

He knows they know about Callum, even though they haven't talked about him. He should probably stop being so weird about it. But he knows that once he breaks the dam and acknowledges that he's dating someone, they'll never shut up again. *How's Callum? When can we meet him? Why doesn't he come for dinner? Are you guys familiar with safe sex?*

"What time will you be home?" she asks.

"I'm not sure. Probably late."

"Same here. So many errands to run. Bigelow's Pharmacy, Western Beef, oh, and Li-Lac Chocolates. I need a gift for Bryan. He loves chocolate-covered cherries. Should I get milk, or dark?"

"Assorted. I have to go. I'm going to get fired."

"All right. Be careful out there. I don't want you to get hit by a truck, or—" She taps her pencil on the photograph of George Bush. "Just be careful."

Be careful. She has no idea how much those words weigh.

A bike messenger in a jeep cap is trying to fix a flat at the top of their steps, blocking Adam's way out. Adam says excuse me, but the guy just looks at him blankly, showing no signs of moving. Adam scowls at him, then climbs over the gate to jump just past the bike. He lands right in front of an old man pushing a baby stroller full of grocery bags.

"Hello, Mr. Carson," Adam says.

The old man nods, but he doesn't seem to recognize Adam. That's normal. He will next time, maybe. Mr. Carson has lived in Adam's building since World War II. Every few weeks, Pop sends Adam up to knock on his door and ask if he needs any tasks done around the apartment, or any errands run. Mr. Carson always says no, but sometimes he asks Adam to sit and listen to his stories about the 1950s and 1960s, when no one in the neighborhood had any money but everyone had fun. *Homosexuals everywhere*, he'd say, *and I was their Mama Rose. Oh, they adored me. They brought me orchids at Christmastime and strawberries in June. But now my babies are gone. They all got sick and now they're gone.* The first time Mr. Carson told this story, Adam wasn't sure what he meant. Now he does.

It's warmer than Adam thought it would be today, no clouds or wind. Summer is on its way. Freedom. Nothing but time to spend with Callum.

He steps off the sidewalk and into the street, walking through that strip of space between the curb and oncoming traffic, avoiding cars and pedestrians at the same time. He jaywalks across Hudson, cutting the angle just right so he clears the street and a short block at the same time. No time to wait for the light. No time to follow the rules.

Be careful.

Adam makes it to work five minutes late but Sonia doesn't notice. The store is pretty quiet all morning, and Adam busies himself reshelving returns and updating the log of rentals and returns. He's behind the counter when Lily approaches the register in a long-sleeve *Rhythm Nation 1814* T-shirt. He hadn't seen her come in.

"One rental please," she says. She pushes a tape across the counter.

"You have new hair," he says. "It looks nice."

She blows her bangs off her forehead. "Nice? Don't hate me because I'm beautiful, Best."

"Sorry. I meant gorgeous. Gorgeous and stunning and enchanting and devastating. I don't know how you even made it here today without every man in New York throwing himself at your feet."

"It's a burden." She sighs. "But I manage."

He opens the log and writes down the title of Lily's selection. *The Rachel Papers.* "Haven't you already rented this, like, twice?"

"I like Ione Skye, all right? Anyway, I have news about the prom."

"Are we going to the prom?" Adam asks skeptically. It's never occurred to him to even consider the prom.

"Of course not. But that's not the news. The news is you and I will be celebrating our release from the tyranny of adolescence at the Mirror Ball."

"The what?"

"The Mirror Ball! Don't you watch *Behind the Velvet Ropes* on public access? It's the party of the year. A fundraiser for something, but I forget what. Something gay. Last year it was at Roseland

and everyone was there. Dianne Brill, Joey Arias, Quentin Crisp. Lahoma Van Zandt and RuPaul came. Even Sylvia Miles showed up. Although they say she shows up for anything. Anyway, Larry Tee DJed and they had naked contortionists suspended from the ceiling. Zero high school students. Heaven."

"Sounds great," he says, suspicious. She's always coming up with plans that don't pan out.

"Your enthusiasm is overwhelming," she says. "But I got the tickets. You owe me a hundred bucks."

"What? A hundred dollars? Are you kidding? Lily, you know I don't have—"

"Did you not hear me say 'party of the year'? It's going to be amazing. We could meet Rupert Everett. He could ask you out! Or me, whichever he prefers!"

"Yes. That will definitely happen."

"Look at me," she says with a serious tone. "I'm serving notice right now. Me and you, the Mirror Ball, house music all night long. Promise right now."

"When is it?"

"Last weekend of April, right before I leave for Greece. I'll be gone for May and June visiting the cousins, remember?"

"You're skipping graduation?"

"I'm sorry, have we met? My name is Lily, and I don't do caps and gowns."

"Right. My mistake."

"Anyway, Mirror Ball. Promise."

"I promise."

"Good. Now. You're going to need to get an outfit together. I'll help. I'll be wearing a little leather-and-lace number from Trash and Vaudeville. It's slit all the way upstairs, with metallic rickrack around the neckline. I still don't know what to do with my hair.

Maybe I'll go Elvira. You know, kind of witchy. Or maybe something kooky, like the B-52's. What do you think? I could do an Annie Lennox."

"You'd never go that short."

"Dare me."

"No, because if I dare you, you'll do it, and you'll blame me and probably kill me, and you'll spend the rest of your life in a women's prison upstate eating crappy food and resenting my memory."

She shudders. "Upstate. Yech."

"Look, Lily, why don't you rent something new? Have you seen *Night of the Comet*?"

"A hundred times."

"*Sammy and Rosie Get Laid*?"

"You're killing me."

"*American Werewolf*?"

"I swear to god, if you say *Heathers* or *Mystic Pizza* I will throw something at your head."

"Suit yourself." He taps the register. "Two-thirteen."

"Two-thirteen what?"

"Two dollars and thirteen cents." Adam nods at the customer behind Lily to signal, *I'll be right with you*, then leans closer to Lily and whispers, "I've used up all my free guest rentals this month."

Her eyes narrow. "I see." She sets her giant purse on the counter.

"You're the one who told me to get a boyfriend. Nice purse."

"Oh, are we using the word *boyfriend* now? I can't keep up. And thanks. Canal Street."

She starts digging though her bag. She pulls out a Walkman, a cylindrical hairbrush, a subway map, a dog-eared copy of Tallulah Bankhead's autobiography, a laminated photograph of Maria Callas, a package of Hubba Bubba, a container of dental floss. "Where is my stupid wallet?"

"Forget it," he says. "I'll get this." He hands her the tape.

"Thanks. What time are you off? I'm hungry."

"I'm off at one. But I already—"

"Of course. My mistake. It's Saturday, isn't it?" She slips the tape into her bag and drops her sunglasses over her eyes. "Don't forget the Mirror Ball. You promised."

"I know. Call you tomorrow?"

"If you want, but don't go out of your way." She mimes a double air-kiss, then turns to the line behind her. "Next customer!"

BEN

"I need you to do me a favor," Gil says as he slings his messenger bag over his shoulder. "I'm supposed to meet Rebecca at Time Café in thirty minutes but I just got paged to work. I can't reach her. I need you to run up there and let her know that I had to go into surgery."

"Right now?" Ben asks.

"Yeah. It's up on Lafayette, up there by Bond Street or Great Jones or something. You know where I mean. There's a sign."

"I can find it. But I have no idea what she looks like."

"Red lipstick and an attitude," he says. "You'll know her when you see her." And then he's gone.

Thirty minutes. Ben grabs his backpack and baseball cap and goes, bolting the door behind him. He's heard about Time Café, of course. He's seen it in that downtown magazine *Details* and in the *Village Voice*. It's supposed to be a notorious model hangout. Which, Ben knows, probably means that no real models ever actually go there, at least not the famous ones. As soon as a place like Time Café is mentioned in the paper as a place where models gather, only wannabes show up.

He walks fast, and soon he's on Lafayette Street, right in front of Time Café. He's five minutes early. He should be able to catch her on her way in.

He sees his reflection in the window and lingers on it. He should have spent two more minutes at the loft picking out a different shirt. This black one doesn't match the black of his jeans. He hates that. He runs a finger under his eye to clean up a smudge of leftover eyeliner.

He turns back to the street, and suddenly, there she is. Gil was right. He knows her instantly. She's standing on the edge of the curb, stamping out a cigarette. She's in faded jeans and leather boots and her black hair is pulled back tight into a ponytail at the nape. She's wearing a charcoal, silver, and black jacket that looks familiar. Is it a knockoff of the Patrick Kelly motorcycle jacket he saw on *House of Style*? It can't be the real thing. You'd only see a real Patrick Kelly jacket in Paris, or on a photo shoot.

"Rebecca?" he asks, his voice tentative, almost too quiet to hear.

She lowers her sunglasses. "Who's asking?"

"I'm Ben. Gil's brother."

"Ben," she says, and her sharp face dissolves into a smile. Her eyes are clear and gray and still, fixed on him. She has a bit of leftover liner on her bottom lid, just like he did. Her lipstick is, as promised, deep red. She holds out her hand. The black polish on her nails is chipped. "I've heard a lot about you."

Ben is already spellbound. "Nice to meet you," he sputters.

"Where's Gil? I've been trying to call him to cancel lunch. I got a last-minute job."

"He sent me up here to tell you he can't make it, either. He got called into surgery."

"Are you kidding?"

Ben shakes his head.

"Perfect," she says. "Mutually canceled plans are the best plans."

He looks down at her boots. They're covered in dust, with scuff marks on the insteps, but—wait. Are they the Chanel motorcycle boots he read about in *Vogue*? He didn't think they were out yet.

"Like my boots?"

"Are they, uh—"

"Yeah, they are," she says. "I shot some pictures for Chanel a few months ago."

Ben's eyes widen.

"Not a campaign," she says. "Just some one-offs. Between you and me, I don't know why they hired me. I guess they're trying to dirty up their image. But they said I could have the boots. Not bad, right?"

Ben's eyes dart from her boots to her jacket. If she's wearing real Chanel boots, doesn't that mean she could be wearing a real Patrick Kelly jacket? "That jacket," he says.

"What?"

"Patrick Kelly?"

She nods. "Gil was right. You really know your stuff."

"I read a lot of magazines," Ben says, trying to keep his voice in check because he is standing here *talking to a fashion photographer who's wearing a thousand-dollar Patrick Kelly jacket like it's a thrift store special. Get it together*, he tells himself.

"So I hear. Gil says you're turning his place into a fire hazard with all your back issues. I can relate. I have them piled floor to ceiling in my place."

A town car speeds past, blaring Bell Biv DeVoe from its windows, singing about poison.

"Are you busy?" Rebecca's tone is suddenly urgent. She looks at her watch, a plain black Timex.

"Right now?"

"Yes. Now." She slips her sunglasses back over her eyes and starts walking across Great Jones toward Broadway, watching the street for an empty cab. "Well?"

"Not really." Ben trots after her, magnetized.

"Good. What say you be my photo assistant today. I need to be at Paradiso Studios like twenty minutes ago to shoot Davina da Silva in six different winter jackets and my usual last-minute assistant can't make it. It's for *Elle*'s November issue. We'll have to skip lunch but there's always candy at the studio. How does a handful of fun-sized Three Musketeers sound?"

Ben can't believe the words falling out of her mouth. *Elle*? Photo shoot? Davina da Silva?

"Are you kidding?" he asks.

"One thing to know about me, Ben, is that I don't bullshit. Your shift starts now. We need a cab."

Ben ducks behind her and into the street. He spots a taxi and throws up his hand.

"Good work," she says. She pushes him into the back seat, then piles in behind. "Washington and Bethune," she says to the driver. "And we're late."

Despite her sharp directive, the trip across Houston Street and up Bedford is slow. Rebecca taps her foot impatiently against the floor of the cab.

"What does a photo assistant do?" Ben asks.

"Whatever I tell you to do," she says. "It's not hard. Move shit around the set, hold up light reflectors, reload cameras. You just have to pay attention to me, and only to me, and do exactly what I say. I'll pay you sixty bucks and you'll be done by six. Got it?"

"Got it," Ben says, vibrating inside.

Their taxi pauses at a stop sign on the corner of Bedford and Grove. While they wait for passing traffic, Ben watches a boy about his age, with floppy hair and a Mount Rushmore T-shirt, approach a taller guy, much taller. He just walks straight into him like he belongs there, like he's coming home. The boy closes his eyes. The taller one curls himself around the boy, protective, hugging him. Ben sees the muscles in his lean arms twitch as he hugs the boy even closer.

The boy opens his eyes. They are pale green, like weathered bronze, and they catch Ben's just before the taxi pulls away.

Tell me what you wished for.

When I was in first and second grade my mother would do this thing in the car where she'd say, "I love you," and then wait for me to say it back to her. If I didn't answer right away she'd say it again. "I love you." Only she'd make it sound like a question, so that I knew I should answer. "I love you?" And if I still didn't say it back she'd keep trying, again and again, and then she'd start to get pissed, like, "I SAID I love you," and I'd just stare out the window. I hated the way it made me feel like a vending machine. She'd put in a coin, "I love you," and expect me to spit out a candy bar. "I love you, too." Like a transaction.

One day traffic was bad and it took forever, so by the time we got home she was so mad that I wasn't playing her game that she shut herself in her bedroom. I would be alone for dinner.

I didn't care. I knew there was a box of Stouffer's French bread pizzas in the freezer. They come two to a package, and I was hungry, so I made both. They just barely fit into the toaster oven. They got so hot in there! I burned the top of my mouth on the first bite, so I had to let them cool. But it tasted so good.

I took both pizzas and a can of Squirt down to the television and ate them while I watched The Love Boat and Fantasy Island.

I wanted to go to Fantasy Island so bad. I would tell Mr. Roarke that my fantasy was to meet Cher. And then she'd show up to take me to her dressing room and let me pick out her clothes and she'd only say "I love you" once, at the very end, and she would mean it.

ADAM

After Adam's shift, Callum leads him over to Rebel Rebel, the little music shop on Bleecker Street. They each grab a spot at the "Try It Out" turntables and slip on a pair of headphones. Adam puts on Sinéad O'Connor to see if she has any other good songs besides "Nothing Compares 2 U," but he doesn't really pay attention while it plays. He's busy watching Callum listen to Bach. The way his face transforms after he drops the needle is mesmerizing to Adam. The way his hands move with a visible rhythm, but also in unpredictable swirls. Callum becomes so focused, so serious and intense, closing his eyes and drawing his hands through the air. He extends his neck as if he's enduring a deep and profound pain, then drives one arm downward in a violent thrust. And then, as if pierced by an arrow, he lowers his head slowly and draws his hands inward, graceful, soft, like a dancer. Adam could watch him forever.

"Sorry," Callum whispers when he notices Adam's stare. He pulls off the headphones.

"Bach?" Adam asks.

"Did I embarrass myself?"

"A little," Adam teases.

"In my defense," Callum says, holding up his headphones. "Listen."

The quick, delicate notes unfurl into Adam's head, creating a bouncy, light, almost spastic melody. "What is that instrument?"

"Harpsichord. It's a keyboard, like a piano, but with two levels of keys. Inside, it plucks the strings instead of striking them, so you get more reverberation. I love it. It sounds so alive, you know? Like the weather or something. Do you hear it?"

Adam pictures the scene in *The Heart Is a Lonely Hunter* when Sondra Locke tries to describe Beethoven to Alan Arkin. *It's like water running down a hill. Like the leaves just before it starts to rain.*

"How can anyone move their fingers that fast?" he asks.

"This guy, Scott Ross, was an incredible musician. He recorded tons of pieces before he died last year. Every time I hear them, it reminds me that there's so much in Bach. There's the technical side of things, and Bach's structures and forms are tight and clean and so smart. But there's also all this meaning in there, you know? All this human emotion. Beauty, conflict, joy, dissonance, resolution. He makes it all so clear."

"Like a story," Adam says. *Beauty, conflict, joy, dissonance, resolution.*

"Yes," Callum says. "Like a story. You get it."

They listen to a few more records, then Callum buys the cassette version of the harpsichord concertos, and Adam buys a four-dollar cassingle of the new Madonna song, "Vogue." He's only heard bits and pieces of it, once at the Duane Reade when he was buying a package of Trident, and then again last night, when the guy who rides his boom-box-rigged bike rode past his window, blasting the movie-star roll call in the middle of the song. Gene Kelly, Fred Astaire, and all that.

Callum holds out his hand. "Give me that."

"Huh?"

"Madonna. Hand it over. You give me your music, and I'll give you mine. What a person picks out at the record store says something about them, and I want to know more about you."

"But I barely know this song," Adam says, worried what "Vogue" might say about him.

"You know enough to buy it. That means something."

"If you say so." They trade tapes.

"Hungry?"

"Starving."

"Mamoun's?"

Just a few weeks ago they'd determined that Mamoun's has the best falafel, and it's only two-fifty for a pita stuffed with three falafels, vegetables, tahini, and as much hot sauce as you want. They collect their lunch and carry it down to Sullivan Street in SoHo. There's a little park on the corner of Spring where Adam used to go with Lily because there was a guy who played basketball there who Lily had a crush on. It's one of the million perfect little nowhere spots in the city.

They straddle a backless concrete bench, facing each other. Adam attacks his pita with giant, ravenous bites. He finishes half of it before he notices that Callum hasn't even touched his.

"Not hungry?"

Callum smiles with just half his mouth, an incongruously wistful expression. "I really like being with you," he says. "Mr. Mount Rushmore."

Adam puts down the rest of his pita, suddenly nervous. "I do, too," he says. "I mean, with you. You know what I mean."

Callum brushes a crumb from Adam's shoulder.

Kiss me, Adam thinks, hoping to will it to happen. *Kiss me.*

And then, instead of waiting, Adam harnesses a flash of courage. He takes Callum's chin in his hand. He leans closer, so close that Callum's face goes blurry in his vision. He tilts his head and pulls Callum to him, pressing his lips into Callum's, gently at first, and then, his boldness building, with force. Callum takes Adam's hand

and soon they are kissing, *really* kissing, right out here at the little park on Spring Street, and Adam's eyes are closing and his lips are opening and he's pushing his tongue against Callum's, and he can feel Callum's hand around the back of his neck now, pulling him even closer. It's like he's melting into Callum, osmosing into his warmth, into the safety of him. Their lips separate just enough for Adam to draw a new breath, and then there is another kiss. And another. The feeling spreads across his skin and he wants to jump onto Callum, to push him down on the bench and lie on top of him, to connect every piece of their bodies. Adam wants more, and more, a million more.

And then, abrupt and sharp, Callum retreats. He drops his hands and turns away, breaking the spell.

Adam's heart sinks. What happened? Did he do something wrong? He looks into Callum's eyes, which are so different from a moment ago. Glazed. Distant. The shine is gone. Adam searches them for a clue. *Say something. Please. What did I do?*

BEN

When Ben and Rebecca step out of the cab at Paradiso Studios, a woman in wraparound sunglasses and a Bad Brains T-shirt waves a walkie-talkie at them from the front door.

"Disaster," the woman is saying.

"Siobhán," Rebecca says, hugging her. "Let's talk about it."

"Davina's plane never took off from São Paulo. Catrine is upstairs having a cow, saying that *Elle* needs the photos by the end of the day today or their entire production schedule will fall apart. She keeps shouting 'Fix this!' and I'm like, fix what? The plane? I'm a studio manager. I don't book models."

"Did anyone call the agency?"

"I did. I made them promise to send someone or else I'd take out their kneecaps. But the bottom line is we have a studio full of winter coats, but we have no model. Not yet."

"You are an angel, Siobhán. Meet my assistant, Ben."

"Nice to meet you," Ben says.

"He's a genius," Rebecca says.

Siobhán shakes his hand. "Got any ideas, genius?"

Me? Ben shakes his head, but as Siobhán leads them up the stairs to the studio, he starts to think. He scans the trillion images in his brain. Among them, he finds a series of photographs he saw several months ago in a German fashion magazine.

"Are the coats really fitted?" he asks. "Or are they kind of bulky and loose?"

"Not fitted," Siobhán says. "Gigantic. Also, crazy bright colors."

"Hmm. What if—" He cuts himself off. "Never mind."

"What if what?" Rebecca asks.

"Nothing. It's a dumb idea."

Rebecca stops on the stairs, blocking the way. "Okay, Ben, listen. As my assistant, you don't get to decide if your idea is dumb. I decide. You tell me your idea, I tell you if it's dumb or not. Get it?"

Ben swallows. "Well. Do you even need a famous model like Davina? She's amazing, but if the coats are big and bright, maybe they can carry the shots without her."

"You mean a still life?"

"No, I mean on people. Just not on Davina."

"*Elle* wants big-name models," Siobhán says.

"Yes, usually," Rebecca says. "Go on, Ben."

"Maybe you could shoot three or four coats at a time, rather than one after the other on Davina. What if you have more than one person in the shot, and if they're kind of moving around, kind of blurry. You'd lose detail, like facial features, but you'd get, like, an Ellen von Unwerth mood."

Rebecca jerks her head backward. "You know Ellen von Unwerth?"

"She's one of my favorite photographers."

"*Elle* doesn't do blurry and moody," Siobhán says.

"Don't they?" Rebecca asks. "Let's go look at the coats."

Ben follows them up the rest of the stairs and into a giant room with two-story high ceilings and rows of dirty, square-paned windows at each end. The brick walls alternate red and white. Little clusters of furniture spot the floor, laid with knotted wooden planks covered in layers of shellac. Rebecca's boots echo as she walks through. It feels rough, industrial, like an empty warehouse, like someone turned on the lights in the middle of "The Pleasure Principle" video. All that's missing is Janet Jackson.

"Thank god they haven't washed the windows," Rebecca says.

"Why?"

"It's easier to work with fuzzy light. Makes the colors pop more. More room for layers."

"More control," he says, still thinking about Janet Jackson.

"You get it," she says.

At the far end of the room, two young women in white jeans and white T-shirts are tugging on a massive sheet of white paper, twelve feet wide, that's hanging from a roll on the ceiling. Like a shade, they pull the paper down to the floor and across the wooden planks, creating a clean white backdrop and floor. They clip the paper to a pair of temporary poles set up on either side to keep it in place. "Listen to Your Heart" is playing quietly from speakers set into the ceiling.

"Are we sure about the white seamless?" Rebecca says, then under her breath, "And the Roxette?"

"Catrine said she needs the white space for copy on the page," Siobhán whispers. "And you know she loves the Lite FM lifestyle."

"Oy, all right. Show me the coats."

Siobhán points to three large wheeled clothing racks packed full of parkas, at least three dozen, puffy and quilted and shiny. The colors are brilliant: red and blue and green and orange and purple.

Two guys in denim shirts and tinted glasses lean against the wall by the racks, looking equal parts stressed and bored. "Hallelujah, you're here," one says to Rebecca. "Are we doing this or not?"

"Believe it, Derek," Rebecca says. "We're doing it and it's going to be great. This is Ben, my muse and good luck charm. Ben, meet Derek and Charles. The best hair-and-makeup team in the city, and the cutest couple of all time."

"Hello, muse," Charles says. "No pressure."

"Don't listen to my bitchy boyfriend," Derek says. "It's great to meet you."

"Listen," Rebecca says. "Davina's still in Brazil. Don't be sad. I have her booked for another shoot in two weeks for *Tatler*. I promise I'll get you on that job."

"What's the shoot?"

"Jewels."

"As in Julie Jewels?"

"No, darling. Julie Jewels is still stuck in the bathroom at Limelight. I'm talking about rocks. Big, fat, juicy rocks. Bulgari, Van Cleef, Tiffany."

"Harry Winston, tell me all about it," Derek says. Charles snickers.

"But today I need lemonade. We'll have models here in twenty minutes, and we'll have to jam because we only have the studio until six."

"What models?"

"All in good time, Charlie Charles. Where's Catrine?"

Charles gestures behind the clothing rack, where a woman in a violet cardigan sits in front of a makeshift vanity, inspecting her reflection.

Rebecca turns to Ben. "That's the client. Everything depends on her being happy. Stay close and let me do the talking."

"Got it," Ben says.

Rebecca's voice changes into a singsong tone. "Catrine! Look at you. Love that color on you. I want you to meet my assistant, Ben. Ben, this is Catrine Jericho, visionary fashion director."

"I'm very pleased to meet you, Ms. Jericho," Ben says.

Catrine gives him a chilly look, then turns to Rebecca. "Well?"

"Don't worry. We have some great ideas that I think you're going to love. We're going to turn the beat around."

Catrine huffs and returns to her mirror. "We'll see about that."

"Come meet Jorge," Rebecca says, pointing Ben toward a slim man in a black leather blazer and purple suede Chelsea boots. "He's our stylist, and my favorite person anywhere."

"Hello, doll," Jorge says. His loose curls bounce as he kisses Rebecca's cheek.

Ben spies a Keith Haring T-shirt underneath Jorge's jacket. "I like your shirt," he says.

"Thank you, doll number two," Jorge says. "I got it at Pop Shop."

"His name is Ben," Rebecca says. "Now tell me everything."

Jorge mouths *Catrine* and makes a circle around his ear with his finger. "Bananas," he whispers. "Bananas *foster.*"

"That bad?"

"Ovah. And this music. I feel like I'm at the dentist."

"We've seen worse," Rebecca says, high-fiving Jorge. "So, what's the mood?"

"Snow globe chic," Jorge says. "Not ski bunny or *Doctor Zhivago*, nothing tired like that. More fashion. More Paris. Like an Antonio Lopez illustration, but athletic."

"I love Antonio Lopez," Ben says. "The best."

Jorge points at Ben and says to Rebecca, "Keep him. He gets it."

"I'm glad someone does. I'm already lost."

"Okay. It's cold, right? Winter. Like, arctic. Like, *brr, it's cold in here. There must be some fashion in the atmosphere.* Like, my nipples are hard. Like, send a Saint Bernard. But I'm also at the disco. Those little lights coming off the disco ball? That's actual snow. You with me?" He takes a shocking-green jacket from the rack and drapes it over his shoulders, posing and pouting. "Work!"

"Jorge, I desperately want to live in your world," Rebecca says. "It's the only place I want to be."

"Come on in anytime," Jorge says. "And your friend Ben, too."

Catrine strolls over, pointedly unrushed. "The idea is not a disco," she says flatly, not addressing anyone in particular. "Bright coats when the world is gray. Simple. Get it?"

"And just look at these colors," Rebecca says. "And the way they're cut! Look at this orange one with the foot-high collar. It's designed to completely cover the face. And the hoods! Gigantic. Let's highlight these shapes. How many pages, Catrine?"

"A spread and a page," she says. "And the story is *color*. Shapes are secondary."

"A spread and a page," Rebecca repeats. "Okay. A gutter-jumper for the spread? Or all singles?"

"Get both," Catrine says. "And I'll need a lot of room for copy."

"Of course." Rebecca smiles. Ben can see how hard she's straining.

As Catrine walks back to her seat by the mirror, Ben notices that her patent leather slides don't fit. Her heels are hanging off the back and spilling over the edge. Jorge leans in and whispers, "We call that serving biscuits. As opposed to when your toes hang off the front. That's serving shrimp."

"Okay," Rebecca says sharply. "Let's crack. Ben. Ask Jordana at the front desk downstairs to come up here. Then go over to Tortilla Flats on Twelfth Street and ask for Nicola. Tell her I need her here as soon as she can. We only need her for thirty minutes, and I'll make it worth her time."

"Got it."

"Siobhán, come here. Jorge, grab that blue coat. I want to see what it looks like on Siobhán."

"On me?" Siobhán says.

"On her?" Jorge says.

"Yes. The blue one."

"Ultramarine," Jorge says.

"That's what I said. Ultramarine. Ben, I told you to go. Go!"

Ben races downstairs and delivers the message to Jordana, then runs up the street to Tortilla Flats. Nicola is right there at the host stand.

"Anything for Rebecca," she says. "I'll be there in ten."

Ben races back to the studio, where Siobhán and Jordana are standing in front of the white seamless. Siobhán is wearing a bright yellow parka with the collar turned up past her eyes. Jordana's purple hood is pulled all the way over. The two women in white jeans and T-shirts, Rita and Amy, are trying on coats.

Rebecca drapes her Patrick Kelly jacket over the back of a chair, wearing just her tank top now.

"Ten minutes," Ben says.

"Perfect. If I know Nicola, that means she'll be here in three . . . two . . ."

Nicola comes bursting in. Rebecca kisses her on both cheeks, points at Jorge, and shouts, "What do you think, Jorge, the blue for Nicola? Ultramarine, I mean."

Jorge glances at Nicola. "You're gorgeous," he says.

"Derek, I need you on Amy's hair."

Soon Amy is in orange and Rita is in green and all five non-models are standing on the seamless, facing away from the camera. Rebecca shoots them, shouting orders. "Taller! Switch places! Siobhán on the end, Nicola in the middle! Catrine, what do you think? Are the colors doing it for you?"

Catrine shrugs and turns away.

Rebecca winks at Ben. "Okay, she's happy. Now, tell me the truth. What do you think?"

"It's great," Ben says.

"You're a shitty liar. Try again."

Ben blinks. "Okay. It's colorful. But it's a little static. Feels like Benetton, 1986."

"I agree. How can I make it better?"

"Do you see Jordana's purple coat? When she stands still, it's just Grape Ape. But when she moves into the light that's coming in from above, look, see? Squint your eyes so she's a little blurry. The nylon, like, it streaks through the air, like it has a tail, like a comet. There are so many more colors in that coat but you can't see them when she stands still. The blue one does the same thing."

"Ultramarine," Rebecca says. She shouts, "Nicola! Do me a favor and spin around."

"Look!" Ben says. "Did you see that? Like her coat is painting the air or something. Is that because of the light? Can you imagine them dancing? Could you get that in a still picture?"

Rebecca stares at Jordana, then slowly turns back at Ben. "Painting the air?"

Ben flushes red. "I'm sorry. I don't really know that much about photography."

She stares at him for a moment, expressionless, before her face begins to pull itself into a smile. She fiddles with her camera for a moment, adjusting the controls to new settings, then walks over to the stereo system in the corner and swaps in a new CD.

"Does everyone love house music? Say yes!" She hits PLAY and turns the volume all the way up. A bouncing house beat fills the room, deep bass drums with tight snaps on top. She starts dancing back toward Ben, biting her lip and bobbing her head.

"I love this song!" Jorge yells. He throws an arm into the air. "LNR, baby! *Work it to the bone bone bone!*"

Soon Ben is bobbing his head, and Derek and Charles are dancing with Jorge, and Rebecca hoists her camera to her eye and yells, "Okay, supermodels! I need you to move! Dance! Spin! Jump! Cabbage Patch! Smurf! Hit that Running Man!"

Ben squints his eyes and watches as the purple, orange, yellow, green, and ultramarine begin to swirl and spin and jump and bounce and swoosh and wave and play across the plain white seamless, and the five colors become five hundred colors, five thousand colors, five million colors, every one different, every one alive, every one dancing.

ADAM

After they finish their falafels and Callum gathers the trash and puts it in the bin by the gate, he asks, "Want to come uptown? I need to go to the sheet music store." He sounds weary when he asks it. Distracted. Derailed. It's been a few minutes since their kiss, and his eyes still haven't snapped back to true.

Yes. Of course, Adam will go uptown. Adam will go any-where with Callum right now. To separate in this moment, with the uncertainty he feels, would be unbearable. "Sure!" he says, as brightly as he can. *Come back, Callum*, he thinks.

They walk up to the West Fourth Street station to catch the F train, they sit side by side and ride in silence, staring at their feet. When the train stops at Fourteenth Street, Callum shifts his eyes from his own shoes to Adam's and says, in a low voice, "You kissed me."

Is it an accusation? A complaint? Just a statement of fact? Adam clamps down on the inside of his cheek. "Yes," he says. Should he also say *I'm sorry*?

"Well," Callum says.

Adam waits for him to say more, but Callum stays quiet while passengers shuffle around them, some getting on the train, others getting off. A man in an Adidas tracksuit and wing tips stands fac-ing them, uncomfortably close.

"I really liked it," Callum says, and the certainty in his voice sinks through Adam like warm water. Adam lets go of his cheek. Maybe he didn't do anything wrong after all.

The train starts up again, but quickly stalls between Fourteenth and Twenty-Third Street. The lights flicker off, leaving the car dark. No one reacts. Adam wouldn't expect them to, unless the outage lasted more than a minute or two, or if it happened twice in a row. A single blip doesn't merit notice in New York. It's normal. Everyone's used to it. No one's afraid.

When the lights struggle back on, Callum is facing Adam. "Can I ask you a question?" he says.

"You just did," Adam replies. It's an old Pop joke.

Callum offers a half smile. "Good one."

"Thanks. I've been workshopping it."

"Am I a good kisser?"

Adam is taken aback by the question. Callum, confident Callum, is really asking this? "Are you kidding?" he answers.

"No. Seriously. How would you rank me? Against your priors."

The train pulls into the Twenty-Third Street station. The doors open, and a young woman with a toddler in one hand and a shopping bag in the other gets off. An older woman in cutoff jeans and a yellow sweater takes her seat. The doors close and the train starts rolling again.

"I don't really have any priors," Adam says. "I've only kissed one person before today, but I wouldn't count that." It was a boy from Xavier who kissed Adam at a house party in Chelsea a year ago. Adam freaked out and left the party.

Callum nods and lowers his eyes back to his shoes. "Well, you should probably know that I've had, you know, priors. I've been around the block."

Adam isn't surprised; he'd always assumed Callum was more experienced. But he isn't sure what to say in response.

"Actually," Callum continues, "I've been around a couple blocks. A few blocks. A lot of blocks."

There are thousands of things about Callum that Adam doesn't know, has never asked about. Callum's mentioned his family, his three older sisters, his hard-core Catholic parents. He's joked about his big suburban *Breakfast Club*–style high school, with its jocks and nerds and freaks and prom queens. But he's only ever mentioned these things in passing, like they don't really matter anymore, like they belong to a place and time that Callum no longer inhabits. Callum's past seems very far away, unlike Adam's, which is all piled onto his bookshelves and stuffed into his bedroom closet.

"There's more," Callum says. He makes fists with both of his hands, balancing them on his knees. He looks up at Adam, and then beyond, into the crowd pouring into the car at Thirty-Fourth Street. "Dammit. I never imagined having this conversation on the train."

A terror races through Adam. He's never seen Callum's face so serious, so dark. What could it be? He takes shallow, anxious breaths. He worries.

The train doors close, and they sit silently again until Times Square. "Let's get off," Callum says. "We can walk from here."

They emerge onto Forty-Second Street and Sixth Avenue, across from Bryant Park, which is still behind a wall of plywood. It's been closed for two years already, the kind of big civic renovation project that drives Pop crazy. *What's taking so long? Put down some grass, plant a few trees, done! What's the big deal?* He brings it up all the time, and Mom always has to remind him that they're also revamping the public library's underground stacks beneath the park. *Oh yeah*, he says. *It's all coming back to me now. As the skunk said when the wind changed.*

"I have a better idea than sheet music," Callum says. "Let's go sit in the sun on the library steps. The lion statues are good luck, and I wouldn't mind a little luck today."

Luck? What does he need luck for? Adam is saturated with anxiety now. "Okay," he says. "Sure." He forces a smile.

"Did you know they have names?" Callum asks. "The lions, I mean."

"Patience and Fortitude," Adam says. Every New York City public school kid knows that.

"Very good," Callum says.

They round the corner onto the busy Fifth Avenue sidewalk and pass long flowerbeds glowing vibrant red with springtime tulips. The library looms above them, its facade regal and grand, more like a museum than a library. Fountains, pillars, the two giant lions, and a massive sweep of steps lead up to the imposing front doors. Pop loves this building. *It's a Beaux-Arts masterpiece*, he always says before smiling smugly at his ease with sophisticated architectural terms. *That's right, I said* Beaux-Arts. *Not bad for a bozo like me, huh?*

They sit in the very middle of the stairway, halfway up from the street. People in ones and twos and threes sit scattered around the steps, taking breaks, soaking in the sun, looking at one another. Down on the sidewalk, a middle-aged couple stops in front of the tulips. She grabs his arm with both hands and leans her head on his shoulder. He turns to kiss her on the forehead.

Adam is impatient. "Callum, what—"

"Okay, listen," Callum says, cutting him off. "If you and I are going where I think we're going, there's something I want you to know. Something I *need* you to know."

Adam nods.

"But no one else, okay? Only you."

Only you. "I promise," Adam says.

If Adam were able to stop time right here and search deep inside his brain, he would find that he already knows what he's about to learn. He's felt it gathering, like a storm.

"Well," Callum starts, then stops. He inhales again. "I need you to know that I'm positive. I have HIV." He says it quickly, like he's racing, like there's a clock to beat.

The words burrow slowly into Adam's ears, each a weight pressing into his brain. *I . . . have . . . HIV.* A short string of words. A simple sentence. Declarative and clear. Adam understands it perfectly. And yet, he can't make sense of it. All he can do is stare at the couple by the tulips.

"Holy shit, that feels weird to say out loud," Callum says.

No, Adam thinks. *No*. HIV is for other people. HIV is for people who are going to die. It can't be here now. It's not for Callum. Callum is not going to die.

"Okay," Adam says. He clasps his hands in his lap.

"Okay?"

Adam's head fills with words and half words, flashing and darting and spinning before him like a school of uncatchable fish. They dive and snap and change shape as they swirl, mocking him as he grasps clumsily for something to say. *Why? How? When? Who?* He can't catch one, not even one. *Are you sick? Are you dying? What about us? What about me?* A riptide tugs at his feet, dragging him out to sea. *Fight, Adam. Breathe.* He bows his chin to his chest.

"I don't know what else to—"

Callum interrupts. "I'm not sick. I want you to know that. I'm healthy."

Adam can hear the strain in Callum's voice. He's trying to sound optimistic, to coach Adam through the moment, just like Adam's grandmother did when she was in the last stages of cancer. *Don't worry, sweetie*, she'd say. *I'm strong as a bull.* She was more worried about him than herself. She died when Adam was nine.

"I should have told you before now," Callum is saying.

Adam stares at Callum's knee, at that perfect rip in his jeans, right at the cap. His eyes shift to Callum's hand, to the freckled spot just below the wristbone, so smooth, so young. He sees its pulse, its soft rhythm tapping against the skin from inside, *tap, tap*. His blood.

His mind sweeps back to his neighborhood, where he's watched so many men suffer, himself at a safe distance. He's seen the sharp faces. The hanging mouths. The misshapen necks, the unseeing eyes, the bruises, the angularity, the pace, the bloodlessness, the shadows. *No. Not Callum.* He squeezes his eyes shut, trying to erase the visions.

"Adam?"

Adam shakes his head. He is afraid to try and speak now. All he feels is density. Weight.

"Well," Callum says. "Now you know."

Adam should say something reassuring. He should say it's all right. He should say that Callum will be fine. He should turn to Callum and take his head in his arms and hold him and say it's going to be okay. He should make Callum feel better, secure, comforted, contented. But something inside isn't working. He can't turn his body. He can't move, except to wring his hands in his lap, over and over.

Callum speaks again, more solemn now. "I know this is a lot. If you want to end this here, if you want to take off, if you want to cut your losses and go, I would understand."

"Is that what you want me to do?" The words spill out involuntarily, as if from somewhere else.

"No, Adam. It isn't. I just know that this is a lot and I . . ."

Callum's voice fades. Maybe he stops talking, or maybe Adam just stops hearing. It's impossible to know. Everything in this moment is strange, out of reach, alien. And quiet. The traffic on Fifth Avenue speeds by soundlessly. The people all around them make no noise. The whole city is deadly silent.

Eventually, Callum stands up. "I'm going to go now," he says. He pauses for a moment, as if waiting for Adam to answer, and then he's stepping down and away, first one slow step, then another, and then he begins to speed up, trotting down the stairs, getting smaller and smaller as he goes.

Adam sits, frozen.

This is the scene where the audience expects Adam to leap up and run after Callum. If he's swift, he can catch him next to the flower beds. He can grab him, and hold him, and tell him right there on Fifth Avenue in front of a thousand tulips that it doesn't matter, that nothing matters but being together, in sickness and in health, come what may, together forever. And he can throw his arms around Callum and kiss him, and the camera can pan in close, capturing the devotion in his eyes, and the gratitude in Callum's, and the strength of their embrace, and the music will come up and the crowd on the steps will erupt into cheers because they don't know what's coming, and the audience in the theater will cry because they *do* know what's coming, but everyone cheers for the same reason. They cheer because they believe, or they want to believe, that love conquers all.

Doesn't it?

Adam won't leap up and run. He will just sit, halfway between Patience and Fortitude, and watch Callum walk away.

BEN

After the shoot, Rebecca sits on the floor in the middle of the studio and lays out all of her photography equipment. Cameras, film cases, lenses, filters, light meters, cartridges. It looks to Ben like twice as much stuff as the little bag could possibly accommodate.

"I do this six times a week and I still can't figure out how everything fits," she says. "Why can't I be like Bill Cunningham and just wear a little point-and-shoot around my neck?"

"Who?

"Bill Cunningham. He photographs the collections for *Details* and also works for the *New York Times*. He doesn't do studio shoots like this one for the *Times*, more like 'on the street' stuff, you know? Rich people in designer clothes mostly, because that's what the paper wants, but also everyday people in the park or wherever. He looks for ideas in what people wear. Like it could be an expensive Yves Saint Laurent suit on a fancy uptown lady or a pair of sneakers modified by a skate rat. He's one of the few people in this business who actually acknowledges where the ideas come from. To him, if it's interesting, it's interesting. He reminds you that ideas are everywhere, not just in fancy ateliers. The best designers think that way, too."

"What do you mean?"

"Like, you see a collection from Vivienne Westwood or Isabel Toledo or Stephen Sprouse or Mugler or"—she points at her jacket, still draped over the chair—"or Patrick Kelly. They don't think only about fashion. They think about art, music, what's going on in the world. They think about ideas. They go out and look around. Do you know what I mean?"

"I love Patrick Kelly."

She inhales sharply. "He died a few months ago, you know."

"I didn't know."

"Yes. And just last month, Tseng Kwong Chi. I love his photographs. He died like three weeks after Keith Haring. Remember that book they did together, *Art in Transit*? And Way Bandy, Angel Estrada, Willi Smith, Joe MacDonald. So many more. So many."

"Antonio Lopez," Ben says.

"It's relentless. I keep wondering what this little world will look like if this doesn't stop." She takes a sharp breath and looks up at the ceiling. "Jesus, Rebecca. Hold it together."

"What about you?" he asks, carefully changing the subject. "Where do you go out and look around?"

"Everywhere," she says. "I'm always looking. Lately I've been finding a lot to look at in the East Village. It's full of ideas. You should hang out there."

They finish packing up, then carry everything down to the curb on Washington Street. Ben looks for a cab to hail for Rebecca, but the street is empty.

She lights a cigarette. "That's okay. I'm not in a rush. And I want to ask you something."

"Okay."

"I want to know where you'll be in ten years."

Ben tries to imagine himself at twenty-eight. It seems a thousand years away. What will he look like? What will he work at? Who will he love?

"Here, I guess," he says. "In the city."

"That's not what I mean. You know what I mean. *Who* will you be in ten years?"

He shrugs. "Me, I guess."

"Who is that?"

"What do you mean? Me is me."

Rebecca takes a long drag on her cigarette. She studies his eyes. "Are you sure about that?"

"I don't know what you mean."

She laughs. "I'm not sure I do, either," she says. "I just think about me ten years ago, when I first got here on a Greyhound bus from Pueblo, Colorado, and how little I knew about who I was. You seem way more self-aware than that. Way more confident."

Oh, how wrong she is. "What did you do when you got here?" he asks.

"I got me a job as a barback at CBGB. I carried a camera and took pictures of the bands on my break. Talking Heads, Blondie, Ramones, Patti Smith, the Fleshtones. Talk about terrible pictures.

I had no idea how to deal with the lighting in there. It was dark and it stank, and every surface was sticky. I threw away so much film back then. I wish I'd made at least one or two good images. Do you know how cool people would think I was if I had a huge photograph of Mink DeVille hanging in a gallery in SoHo?"

"Who's that?"

"Punk band. That whole scene is over for me now. Those late nights make it too hard to hustle the next day, and if you want to make it in this fashion racket, you have to hustle nonstop." She stamps out her cigarette. "I bet CBGB ends up as a boutique or something. A restaurant. Something safe like that. But, that's New York. Nothing here lasts forever."

Ben looks past her shoulder toward the World Trade Center towers downtown. They seem so tall from here, but also weightless in the sunshine.

"Shit, I owe you sixty bucks," she says.

"No, that's okay."

"Wrong response." She hands him three twenties. "Important rule about this business: Never turn down money. You did a great job today. Oh, and take this CD, too. It's a newish English band, Saint Etienne. I'm supposed to shoot them in a week or so. Let me know what you think. If you like it, I'll hire you to assist."

"What if I don't like it?"

"I'll hire you anyway. You saved this shoot today, you know."

"I doubt that," Ben says.

"Another rule: Take the compliments when they come. They don't come often enough." She turns to the street. "Here comes my cab." Ben waves it down.

They say goodbye, and she climbs into the taxi. He pulls on his headphones and turns east. He won't go down to Tribeca yet. He's still buzzing from the shoot. He'll walk over to the East Village.

But before he gets there, when he's right at the edge of Washington Square Park, he will see the boy in the Mount Rushmore T-shirt again. He'll just be standing there, alone this time, looking up at the sky. Ben will stop and stare from across the street and wonder what he's thinking.

ADAM

Adam stands at the edge of Washington Square Park. Something has stopped him here on his long, blurry walk downtown. It's a feeling, a recognition, a sudden awareness of something familiar. It's not quite déjà vu, more like a code finally cracked. The virus is no longer an abstraction. It's next to him now, facing him. He sees now that he's been preparing for Callum's revelation for years. Every public service ad in the subway, every pamphlet handed to him at school, every news story on television, every neighbor who's vanished—it's all been a campaign to prepare him. It carried the guise of safe sex, but now Adam sees that message was always just a smokescreen. The real message for Adam has always been: There is no way out. There is no protection. This virus will take its fee, one way or another. Be prepared to pay. Maybe with everything you have.

He looks up at the sky. It's all so clear now. He knows what to do. He sprints home.

"Hey, pal!" Pop shouts, cheerful, when Adam unlatches the door. He's standing at the counter, clanking plates.

"Shoes!" Mom yells from the TV room. She's watching a Knicks game.

"Where ya been?"

"Nowhere."

"Fast?"

"Something like that," Adam says.

"We got you a chicken parm sub at the deli. Why don't you bring it in and join us? Your mother says it's an important game."

"That's okay, I'm not really hungry."

"But I went all the way to the deli on Fifteenth Street, the one with the good bread!"

Adam calculates. If he refuses the sandwich, something he's never done before, they'll be on his case for days trying to figure out what's wrong. But if he eats some sandwich and watches fifteen minutes of the game, they'll think everything's fine. They'll leave him alone.

"Okay," he says.

"Quiet," his mother says as Adam settles on the floor by the couch. "Everyone, concentrate. Ewing needs to make this free throw or we're out of the playoffs. Hold your breath and imagine glory."

Adam holds his breath until Patrick Ewing makes the shot.

He wasn't lying to Pop, he really isn't hungry, but he manages to finish half his sandwich. When he stands up to excuse himself, Mom's too focused on the game to notice and Pop's already asleep next to her. Adam wraps up the uneaten half of his sandwich, then washes his plate and puts it in the dish rack to dry. He takes the phone from the kitchen table and slips into his room. He burrows under the covers and dials Callum in the dark, using his fingers to feel for the buttons. They know the pattern of Callum's number by now.

"Hello?" Callum sounds so close when he answers.

The words fly out of Adam, a rapid-fire string of sounds that he can barely control.

"I want you to know that it doesn't matter to me. What you told me earlier. It's not too much. I don't want to end it. I don't want to take off. I want to stick around."

"It doesn't matter?"

"No, of course it matters. It matters a lot. But it doesn't change my mind. I want to stick around. I'm not afraid." This last part is a lie. "But I have questions."

"Okay," Callum says, sounding tentative.

"You said you are healthy. What does that mean?"

"It means that right now, I feel good. I don't have any infections."

"Have you had infections before?"

"Yes. I spent a few days in the hospital. I got better. No big deal."

"The hospital is a big deal," Adam says.

"I got better."

"Was it only one time?"

Silence.

"What about last month? Remember? We didn't get to hang out that week."

"Yes," Callum says quietly.

"Were you in the hospital that time, too?"

Silence.

"Callum?"

"I hate talking about this stuff," Callum says. "It's not fair to dump this all on you."

"The only thing that isn't fair is if you don't tell me the truth. Start at the beginning."

"All right," Callum says. He takes a deep breath. "After high school I started working at a record store in Jersey, a couple of towns over from mine. When our shifts ended, my manager Randy would invite his friends to the store to blast twelve-inch singles and pass around airplane bottles of vodka and dance. Randy's friends were older than me, but I kept up. They were the first gay guys

I knew, and we partied a lot. I was popular, if you know what I mean. But a few months later Randy got sick and then another friend of his got sick. I got scared. I'd had a flu that summer, too. So I stopped partying so much. I kept my job, but I didn't carry on after work anymore. That winter, I had what felt like the flu again. It took me a few months to get up my courage, but I finally went for an anonymous test. When I went back two weeks later for my results, they handed me sheet of paper that said *REACTIVE*. A counselor told me I was lucky. I was young, he said. I could count on at least a couple of years if I stayed healthy."

"A couple of years?" Adam tries to swallow but his throat is too dry.

"He didn't know what he was talking about. It's already been three since that test."

Adam does the math in his head. If that first flu was a signal, it's been almost four years since Callum was exposed.

"The weird thing was, I felt really calm after I got my result. As soon as I had that piece of paper, I got focused. I realized I wanted to be in the city, and I wanted to study music. I quit my job at the record store and found a room to sublet over on Avenue C for four hundred bucks. Once I got my job, I moved to Horatio Street. I started going to the clinic regularly. I found a doctor."

"How many times have you been sick since then?"

"What do you mean by sick?"

"Like, in the hospital."

"A few."

"Doesn't that mean you have full-blown AIDS?"

"I hate that term. It's creepy. But I suppose it's the only one we've got right now."

"Sorry."

"Not your fault. But your question is harder to answer than

you would think. The official definition has changed a couple of times. It will probably change again as things progress. You can drive yourself crazy trying to keep up. But yes, I've been told that I have AIDS."

"I have a lot to learn," Adam says. *I'm going to learn all of it.*

"All I really know is how I feel, and I feel good. I'm going with that."

"Aren't you scared?"

"Yes. But being afraid only makes things harder, so I try to keep it all in a box, you know? I try to focus on other things, like music. But sometimes, yeah. It smacks me in the face and I get terrified. But that counselor was right. I am lucky. I keep bouncing back."

"Did anyone visit you those times you were in the hospital?"

"No one really knew I was there."

"Not even your family?"

"Oh, no way. I've never told them about any of this. They would just freak out. You should have seen it when they found out I was gay. It was the biggest tragedy ever. If they knew about this, everything would be worse, especially for me. There's nothing they could do about it anyway."

"I hate thinking about you being alone," Adam says.

"It wasn't so bad. The truth is, I don't like people knowing about it, because as soon as they do, they treat you differently. They start saying things like, 'How are you? No, how are you *really*? Are you *sure* you're fine?' It's like they won't let it go, and then you have to try and make *them* feel better. I hate that. I'd rather not tell them at all."

"Is that why you didn't tell me?"

"No. I didn't tell you because I didn't want to bring all this into your world, you know? You shouldn't have to deal with this."

"But it's part of you."

"Yeah. I guess it is. I'm sorry about that."

"I don't accept your apology. There is nothing to apologize for."

"There is so much to apologize for. I'm not an angel."

"Shut up."

"For a while I thought it would be easier to just stop seeing you. To just break up, stop coming around on Saturdays. It would be cold, but people get dumped all the time, you know? You'd think I was a jerk, you'd be pissed, you'd be sad, and then you'd move on. But I couldn't do it. I couldn't walk away from this, Adam. Not from you."

"No more secrets. From now on you have to tell me everything. Everything."

"Okay."

"I'm serious."

"I know."

"Promise me. No more secrets. Say it."

Callum's voice cracks. "No more secrets."

Adam buries deeper under the covers.

"Say it again."

"No more secrets. I promise."

More breathing.

"They're going to figure this thing out, you know," Callum says.

"I know they will," Adam lies. He doesn't know. No one knows. "But we're doing this together."

Callum doesn't answer.

"Did you hear me?"

"I never thought anyone would say anything like that to me," Callum whispers.

Adam blinks back the tears, even though there's no one to see them. He bites the inside of his cheek. He feels his body turn, pulled as if a compass, pointing toward Horatio Street. Callum's pull is irresistible now. He needs him. Adam is falling desperately, physically, finally in love, and suddenly it feels like a very long way to fall. *Please catch me*, he thinks. *Please be there when I land.*

After a moment, Adam speaks. "I've never been alone with you. Not really alone. You know?"

"No, you haven't."

"Is this why? I mean, all of this."

"Maybe. I guess I've wanted to keep it away from us."

"Can't do that forever."

"No. Probably not."

"I think about it a lot," Adam says. "About being with you."

Callum doesn't answer.

"Do you? Ever think about it, I mean."

"All the time," Callum says. "Every day."

Adam inhales the words. They swell in his chest, pressing against his ribs. Oh, this ache.

"Will I see you again on Saturday?" Callum asks.

"Yes. One o'clock."

"Good."

"It's going to be a long week."

"I know," Callum says, and Adam can hear that he means it.

"Well," Adam says.

"Wait. I have a present for you. Hold on."

Adam hears Callum put the phone down. A shuffle, then the squeak of furniture on the floor. And then, a chord on the piano. And then another, and another, each bouncing in after the one before . . . *bomp, bomp, bomp-bomp-bomp.*

"Strike a pose!" Callum yells, and the chords continue. And even though Adam is under the covers in a dark basement bedroom four blocks away, he draws a hand up to cover his mouth. Callum is playing "Vogue." In the hours since they parted, Callum listened to Adam's cassingle, and learned it, and practiced it, and now he's playing it for Adam, getting every note right, as careful and attentive as he'd be with any piece by Bach. Adam's eyes begin to sting. He whispers along with the only part he knows, the Hollywood roll call: *Greta Garbo and Monroe—*

When the song ends, Adam asks, "How would you rank me against your priors?"

Callum whispers, "Oh, baby. You have no idea."

"Tell me."

Tell me about your first love.

Whenever we were on winter break in grade school, the local television station would show movies in the afternoons to keep kids busy because their parents still had to go to work. They would show stuff like The Black Stallion and The Bad News Bears. But the best was when they showed Ice Castles because of Robby Benson.

I loved him. With those big eyes that always made him look like he was just about to cry, or else just finished crying. Remember? I just wanted to hug him and make him feel better.

I used to go to the library and find pictures of him in magazines. You know, Tiger Beat and Teen Beat and all of those. I would tear the pages out, super slowly so I didn't make a ripping sound. I'd put them in my Pee-Chee and bring them home to look at. I never put them on my bulletin board or anything like that. I kept them behind my encyclopedia set and only took them out after it was bedtime and I could hide under the covers with my flashlight.

Later I switched to Christopher Atkins, and then Matt Dillon, and then Ralph Macchio and Greg Louganis.

We had these little mini lockers in sixth grade and I always kept pictures of Kristy McNichol and Brooke Shields and Nancy McKeon in there. I don't think anyone even paid attention, but I had them there just in case. Looking back, though, I probably got that wrong, too. If I wanted people to think I was normal or whatever, I should have put up pictures of Evel Knievel or the "Miracle on Ice" hockey team or John Belushi. That's what all the normal guys had.

BEN

Ben walks for hours, long past dark, listening to the CD that Rebecca gave him. Saint Etienne. The first song asks how it feels to be alone, and right now, Ben doesn't mind it at all. He likes the anonymity of the city. It's funny how much freer he feels on a crowded city sidewalk than in a small town. How much less scrutinized. He can be himself, and no one thinks it's weird, because no matter where you are in New York, there's always someone or something weirder than you right up the block.

His route, if you can call it that, is a zigzag through the streets of the East Village. He walks up Second Avenue, down First Avenue, across East Fifth Street, and back on East Fourth. He walks past the Crowbar on Tenth, the Wonder Bar on Sixth, the Pyramid Club on Avenue A. On St. Mark's Place he passes a group of rockabilly girls, all crimson lipstick and sleeveless gingham. At Tompkins Square Park he watches a towering drag queen trade wigs with her much smaller companion, a pink bob for a blond beehive. On Third Street, a balding man in a gray overcoat locks the door to a tiny laundromat with a giant picture of Linda Evangelista in the window. "We close at eleven," he says to the skinny boy in the Iron Maiden sweatshirt carrying a basket of dirty clothes. A pair of women in ACT UP T-shirts with their arms around each other pass by, arguing passionately. A young man in frayed jeans stops a young woman in a puffy silver parka to ask, in Spanish, for a light. She doesn't have one, but the old woman in the HOW'M I DOIN'? T-shirt does. A muscled guy in a denim jacket with the sleeves cut off kisses both cheeks of an older man in a rumpled brown suit, then hails a cab and speeds off. A shiny sports car rolls by with speakers booming Biz Markie. The bass rattles windows all the way up the block.

If Ben doesn't know who he'll be in ten years, at least he knows where he'll be. He'll be here.

ADAM

Lily holds up a black tuxedo jacket with a giant embroidered skull and crossbones design on the back, stitched in red metallic thread with multicolored rhinestones for eyes.

"This is the one," she says. "This is *definitely* the one. Glam rock metal punk couture. Perfect for the Mirror Ball tomorrow night. Try this on and take me down to paradise city."

Adam tugs at the price tag. "Are you kidding? Three hundred dollars? No way."

"This is Century 21, Best. Nothing is full price here. It's the whole point of this place. Look again, where it says YOUR PRICE. See? It's only one eighty."

"Only one eighty, says Cinderella Rockefella."

"Oh, come on, Eileen. This is the perfect complement to my Trash and Vaudeville number. It's sleek. It's ironic. It's got layers. It's fashion. Brains, looks, and money. Put it on."

Adam sighs but lets Lily help him with the jacket. He's relieved that it's far too small. "Thank god," he says. "Why am I buying a new jacket anyway? Can't I just wear something I already own?"

"I know every article of clothing you own, and I promise, you do not have a look for this party. Oh, that reminds me, we need to strategize about your hair."

"My hair?"

"And makeup."

"Hair and makeup. How much is that going to cost me? I already had to borrow a hundred bucks from my mother for the ticket, and have you met my mother? She charges interest."

"What's money, anyway?"

"Says the girl who has an endless supply."

"You promised," she says.

"Under duress. And without all the information."

"Why are you being such a bitch about this?" She uses a pinkie to detangle a lock of hair from her earring. "It's going to be fun."

"I'm not being a bitch," he answers, but maybe she's right. This feels like a chore. For the last few weeks all he can think about—all he wants to think about—is Callum. He spent every afternoon this week at the public library learning about T cells and PCP. He scours bookstores and record shops for safe-sex pamphlets. He bought a used copy of *And the Band Played On.* But none of it gives him confidence or courage or hope. Only fear, and each day it grows. Each day it weighs more. Each day it tricks him into thinking about how long it will be before Callum gets really sick. But he can't show his fear to Callum. He has to hold it inside. It's hard to do.

"Yes, you are being a bitch." She hands him a pair of patent leather loafers. "Try these on."

"No way. Too shiny. I can see my reflection in those. Can't I wear my sneakers? Wouldn't that be kind of punk? Or metal? Or whatever you said the look is supposed to be?"

She shakes her head. "You're just giving up. Let's take a break over in ladies' underwear. I need bras for Greece. Then we can go up to Star Struck on Greenwich Avenue. I saw a jacket in the window that would be perfect for you. Gray and black tiger stripe, very 1984 new romantic, but with an edge. It's only forty dollars, if it's still there."

Greece. In his worry over Callum, Adam forgot about her trip. "When do you leave again?"

"Day after tomorrow. I have my hangover sunglasses all ready for the plane. You should see them. I look like the love child of Jackie O and *Tron*. Impenetrable. The flight staff will think I'm dead."

Adam follows her through the labyrinth of merchandise in the famously messy store, through gowns and overcoats and luggage, past belts and designer jeans and sweater sets, up a flight of stairs, down a flight, deeper and deeper.

"I hope you know the way back out," he says. "It's like *Streets of Fire* down here."

"Ooh, remember Diane Lane's haircut in that? I should bring that look back. Or maybe I should do this," she says, pointing at a model on a box of tank tops. "A bob like the girl from Swing Out Sister."

"Who?"

"You know, the one who looks like Louise Brooks meets Isabella Rossellini in Martika's kitchen. Fooled by a smile, and all that."

"I love it," he says, too distracted to conjure the image she's suggesting.

Lily puts down the box. "Okay, Best. Time to cut the shit. What is going on with you? Are you depressed or something? I'm worried about you, and it's getting on my nerves."

"I'm fine," Adam says. What else can he say? He can't tell her the truth. He promised.

"When something's wrong, you're supposed to talk to your best friend about it. That's how it works. Don't I tell you everything?"

"There's nothing to tell," he lies. "I hate shopping, that's all."

She leans against a bin of tousled bras. She picks one up, folds it neatly, and lays it on top of the pile. She picks up another. "You never tell me anything about him," she says. "It's like you have a whole other life that I know nothing about."

The guilt sinks through him, from the back of his throat, to his stomach, to the floor. This is the last place he wants to be, caught between Lily and Callum. "I'm sorry."

"My best friend doesn't trust me," she says.

"That's not true," Adam says, but it is true, sort of.

She folds another bra. "I bet you trust Callum. I bet he knows what's wrong."

"Lily," he says. "Stop."

She folds another bra, and another, moving quicker with each one. "Well, does he know?"

"Lily, stop."

She stares at him for a long moment. "I see. It's all so clear now. He's more important."

"Are you being serious?" he asks, his tone incredulous.

"Just tell me, Adam. Just rip off the bandage. Who comes first? Me or Callum?"

The question shocks him. He wants to yell back. But he keeps his voice low. "I would never ask you a question like that. Never."

"Because you wouldn't need to," she says. "You've always known exactly where you stand."

"Really?" he snaps, angry now. "Where do I stand right now, Lily? Because you're making me feel like shit because I won't break a promise."

She looks up. "Promise? What promise? To Callum?"

"Forget it," Adam says, regretting using that word because to her, *promise* means *secret*. She'll never let it go now.

"Well, how about that," she says. "I was right. Callum comes first."

"That's right, Lily," he hisses. "Make everything about you. It's what you always do."

She freezes, like she's been shocked. "I guess I'm a bad friend. I guess I'm a bad person."

"I didn't say that."

"Yes, you pretty much did," she says. "Thank you for being honest. Thank you for finally telling the truth about what you think of me."

"That is not fair!" Adam is yelling now. He can't hold back his anger. "I have always been there for you! Always! And I have never forced you to talk about anything you didn't want to talk about. Never. Not once!"

"Because I've always told you everything," she says, infuriatingly calm. She folds another bra, and then another. "Do you even want to go to the Mirror Ball?"

Adam stares at his hands.

"Your silence speaks volumes," Lily says after he doesn't answer. She tucks her hair behind her ear. "You know what? Let's forget the whole thing. The ball is a dumb idea."

"No, it isn't," Adam says, repentant. He picks up a bra to fold. "You've been looking forward to it for months. I want us to go. I just need to find a jacket, that's all. And shoes."

"Nah," she singsongs. "The ball sounds stupid anyway. I don't want to go. I just decided."

And then, for the first time in their lives, Adam's best friend in the world turns and walks away from him without saying another word. No double kiss. No smile. No *call me later* or *don't do anything I wouldn't do* or *I love you*. Not even a backward wave. Nothing. She just goes, vanishes, leaving him jilted and lost in the basement of the great Century 21 discount department store, his hands buried in a bin of cut-rate bras.

BEN

Ben turned in his independent history project early, and today Mrs. Clovis told him that "Dior, Balenciaga, and the New Garment Economy," earned him an A. He'll have an *almost* perfect average this semester. Leave it to English to drag him down to a 3.7 average. But it's still good, and a major boost if he decides to apply to FIT after all. He only has two more weeks of school and nothing real to do in them. It's all performance now, perfunctory, a show. The results are locked in. He'll honor Gil's attendance rule until the end, but after that, it's goodbye, high school. Goodbye, Metro-North. Goodbye, past. Moving on.

Back at the loft, he collapses onto the couch. Elsa Klensch is on CNN interviewing Rifat Ozbek about his collection inspired by *One Thousand and One Nights*. It takes Ben only two seconds to see that this is an Elsa Klensch rerun. *Nights* was Ozbek's inspiration for last year's show, and he would never repeat a theme.

Ben closes his eyes, just for a minute.

It's almost ten when he jolts awake, ravenous. Gil is at work. Ben finds some leftover shrimp fried rice in the fridge and reheats it in a skillet with a little bit of water and an extra beaten egg that he stirs around with chopsticks. He scrapes it into a bowl and squeezes on a little soy sauce from a packet he finds in the drawer. Down in a dozen bites. That's better.

He won't go back to the couch now. It's warm out. It's spring. He's buoyant about being finished with school. He's eighteen. He's restless. He is compelled to go out, like it's a requirement. Ben, reporting for duty.

He brushes his teeth, slips on a plain black T-shirt, hides his hair under his baseball cap, and heads out. East Village, here he comes.

Ben walks swiftly. Not because he's in a rush, but because he's on a wave, a current underfoot, like a moving conveyor belt that spirits him along, an inch above the ground. Faces flash past him, one by one, as if he were a television camera panning through a crowd, each person visible for only a split second. Ben marvels at his speed. He rides the belt, losing track of time, until, without warning, it stops, depositing him at the corner of Second Avenue and Fourth Street. Just outside The Bar.

That's the name of it. The Bar. Ben's read about it in *GXE*. By now, he's read about a million bars and clubs. The Bar, Wonder Bar, Boy Bar, Crowbar, Boots & Saddle, Two Potato, the Stonewall, Uncle Charlie's, Ty's, Rounds, Townhouse, Candle Bar, Limelight, Palladium, the Spike, the Eagle, Barbary Coast, Save the Robots, the World, Mars, the Roxy, Barracuda, and on and on and on. Only, he's never been inside any of them. Not a single one. Not yet.

The door of The Bar swings open right in front of him, and tinny jukebox music pours out. *Pump up the jam. Pump it up.* Ben cranes his neck to peer inside, but before he can see anything, three men push through the door, blocking his view. One is crying violently, his eyes red and angry. He swipes at his face, mopping tears with his palms. The other two are holding his shoulders, comforting him. The taller one is wearing a Yankees baseball cap. The other is in a plaid shirt with the sleeves rolled up beyond his biceps. Ben guesses they are in their twenties. Early twenties.

"Take it easy," Yankee Cap is saying to Crying Guy. "It's okay."

"Shut up!" Crying Guy shouts. "You don't know what it's like!"

"We all miss him, too, you know," Plaid Shirt says.

"Then where were you for the last month? I was the only one with him! Me!"

"That's a load of crap. We came when we could."

"Leave me alone!"

Yankee Cap pulls Crying Guy closer. "Hey. We love you, okay? He is gone but we are here. Look, look at me. See? We are here."

Crying Guy buries his head in Yankee Cap's shoulder and starts sobbing loudly. Plaid Shirt wraps his arms around both of them. "We won't let you go," he says.

Ben backs up a few steps, embarrassed to be caught right here in this emotional moment that isn't his. Someone is gone, someone Crying Guy loves, and these are his friends. Ben doesn't belong here. Plaid Shirt's muscles twitch with purpose as he squeezes them closer.

We won't let you go.

Ben looks at the open door. The jukebox is playing Deee-Lite now. Should he step in? Does he dare? Two more guys come out, laughing. One is waving an unlit cigarette and chanting along with Lady Miss Kier about supper dishes and succotash wishes.

His companion swings an imaginary ponytail behind his shoulder. "Sing it, baby!"

Cigarette Guy says, to no one in particular, "Anyone got a light out here?"

Yankee Cap leads Crying Guy and Plaid Shirt down the block and away. Ben starts to step away, too, but Cigarette Guy shouts after him, "Hey, you! You're cute! Got a light?"

Ben mumbles, "I have to go."

"Aw, hold on," Cigarette Guy says, smiling. He seems drunk.

Ben shakes his head and takes a step backward.

"C'mere a minute," Cigarette Guy says. "What's your name?"

Ben takes another step, missing the curb with his foot and tumbling onto the street.

"Hey! Are you okay?"

Imaginary Hair Guy reaches down to help Ben up, but Ben scrambles to his feet unassisted. "I'm fine," he says.

"You're bleeding," Cigarette Guy says. He points at Ben's elbow, shiny and red with a nasty scrape. He shouts, "He's bleeding!"

"I'm fine," Ben says. He clasps his hand over the wound to hide it. "It doesn't hurt."

"Come inside," Imaginary Hair Guy says, his voice kind and measured. He smiles and reaches for Ben. "We'll get you a Band-Aid and buy you a drink."

"I need to go," Ben says. He pulls his cap down and steps away again.

"Wait," Imaginary Hair Guys says. He hands Ben a flyer with two shirtless guys on it. "Here. My friend is DJing downstairs at the Monster tomorrow night. You should come. I think you'd fit right in."

Ben offers a nervous smile, folds the flyer into his back pocket, and quickly crosses the street. A taxi speeds past, blasting Black Box. Ben keeps walking, his hand covering his elbow. He'll come back to The Bar sometime. Maybe he'll have the guts to go inside.

ADAM

Now. Tonight. It's time. The first day of May. Adam's fears have assembled. They're in formation. The ones he's always anticipated (insecurity, humiliation) and the ones he knows he's not prepared for (illness, death). Even the ones he doesn't know about yet (regret, remorse). They're all waiting for him, and if he doesn't find and face them now, he fears he never will. They'll take hold and take over and seal themselves inside, where they will live forever. No. It is time to be brave.

"Can I come over?" Adam asks. It's after eleven, too late to call, but he's calling anyway.

"Right now?"

"Yes."

"Are you sure?" Callum asks.

"Yes," Adam says again.

Yes.

It takes only five minutes to run up to Horatio Street. He buzzes number 4A—*as in 4 A good time!* Callum joked—and takes the stairs two at a time. He tries to catch his breath, then knocks on the door. He chews the inside of his cheek while he waits to hear the deadbolt unlock.

Callum peeks through a crack in the door. With a raspy, old-man voice he says, "I gave at the office," but Adam doesn't have the patience to play along. He pushes against the door with both hands, and walks straight into Callum.

"Whoa!" Callum shouts, stumbling backward. He's wearing nothing but gray sweatpants, his torso covered in exquisite freckles even more beautiful than Adam imagined. His hair is wet from the shower, and he has a black tank top hanging from his fingers. "Give me a chance to get dressed?"

Adam ignores his plea, reaching his arms around Callum's neck. He raises himself up on tiptoe, pulling Callum down, smashing their lips together. He drops his hands and tugs at Callum's waistband, pressing forward, driving Callum backward toward the single bed in the corner. He doesn't see the piano bench underneath Callum's legs, and suddenly they're falling, Callum onto his back, and Adam down with him, their crash on the pine floor rattling the silverware in the sink.

"Easy!" Callum laughs. "I'm breakable!"

Adam scrambles up and onto the piano bench, his face searing hot. He sits on his hands and bows his head, embarrassed. "Are you okay?"

Callum is still on the floor, still laughing. "You sure know how to make an entrance," he says.

"I'm stupid," Adam says, feeling small.

"Hey. Don't tell lies like that," Callum says. He gets up, pulls on his tank top, and opens the window. He climbs out onto the fire escape and holds his hand out to Adam. "Come. Sit out here with me. It's warm, and if you crane your neck just right, you can almost see Midtown. There's a moon tonight, too. It's just a half moon, but that's enough for fools like us, don't you think?"

Adam climbs out the window and they sit for a while, not talking, until Callum points at the moon. "Did you hear about the restaurant up there?"

"On the moon?"

"Yeah. It has great food, but no atmosphere."

"You're worse than my father," Adam says, smiling weakly.

Callum drapes his arm around him, pulling his head into his shoulder. Adam leans closer.

"Did I blow it?" Adam asks.

Callum kisses the top of Adam's head. He seems so calm. "Not even close."

"I don't know what happened," Adam says.

"I can relate," Callum says. "What do you say we talk things through a little bit? I know it would put my mind at ease."

"Talk about what?"

Callum reaches back through the window, stretching to grab a shoebox that's been tucked just under the foot of the bed. "Look here."

"What's that?"

"Stuff." Callum opens the box. "Stuff we might need. Just in case."

He takes out a small plastic packet that looks like it should contain ketchup. He tears open a corner and squeezes a bead of gel onto Adam's finger.

"Feel that?"

"Smooth."

"Water-based," Callum says.

"Compatible with latex," Adam says.

"Very good."

"I studied the pamphlet," Adam says, and he feels a sense of relief seeping into his chest, pushing out the worry.

"You mean one of these?" Callum pulls a stack of safe-sex pamphlets from the box.

"Probably." Adam smiles.

"Wanna see what else is in the box?"

Adam nods, and together they poke through the other contents. Some latex condoms, more packages of lube, a couple of squares of terry cloth.

"Let's only do what we want to do, and nothing else, okay?" Callum says. He puts the box back inside. "And if we change our minds and decide to do nothing at all, I'd love to sit out here and hold hands with you all night. Or we can go for a walk. Or play songs on the piano. Or make out with our clothes on. We can do anything we want, and nothing we don't want."

Adam takes Callum's hands in his lap. He studies them, running his fingers over Callum's palm, his knuckles, his wrist.

"I want to do everything," Adam says. "I want to do everything with you."

"Well," Callum says. He draws his finger along the inside of

Adam's elbow, resting it on the blue vein that's just visible where it bends, raising goosebumps across Adam's arm. He presses gently against it. "Let's start here. This soft part, the inside part, right here. Can I have this part?"

Adam's body vibrates, entranced by Callum's touch. "It's yours."

Callum brings it to his lips, and kisses it, softly, just once. He stands up and leads Adam back in through the window. He takes off his tank top, then pulls Adam's T-shirt over his head. "Look at you," he says, tracing the back of his hand down Adam's chest. "Look at you, beautiful boy."

Adam leans into Callum, pressing his cheek against the freckles on his chest. Callum unbuttons the top button of Adam's jeans, and then the second. Adam moves closer. Soon they're naked together, face-to-face on Callum's bed. They begin to move.

Everything happens slowly at first, with Callum leading the way because Callum knows the way. Callum is so much bigger, so much stronger, and when he takes Adam's head between his hands, smiling gently into his eyes, and kisses him so slowly, Adam wants to disappear into him.

Callum whispers as they go. *Yes*, he breathes when Adam finds him, and *not yet* when Adam moves too fast. *Let me show you.* He trains his eyes on Adam's, presses his thumb on Adam's lips. Adam stares into him, releasing himself. *Stay there*, Callum whispers, calming Adam's worry. *Breathe. That's it. Right there. I've got you. Kiss me again. Oh, you are so beautiful. So beautiful.*

Callum never closes his eyes, never leaves Adam, and soon Adam's body starts to feel so good, so startlingly, enormously good that he stops thinking, stops wondering, stops being anything but here, with Callum, connected, only connected. *I'm yours*, Callum whispers, not letting go, never letting go. *I'm yours.*

Afterward, Callum stays very close, steering their descent,

catching them both. He slows his breath, setting a rhythm for them both. He holds Adam's hands, guiding him back into himself, a shared space now. He wraps his body around Adam's, protecting him from every direction. *Adam*, he whispers. *Adam*. He says it again and again, reassuring him, naming him, not letting go. *Adam*.

Soon Callum is quiet, lost in a deep and steady and calm sleep.

A streetlight flickers outside, dappling the room with unsettled shadows. Adam is unsettled, too. How childish he was when he got here. How desperate, how foolish. How small and stupid and fearful.

But Callum knew what to do. Callum knew the words, and the way. Beautiful, endless Callum carried them there.

When Callum stirs, raising his arm away to tend to a distant itch, it's as if a wall's been breached and Adam feels the cold. He wants to cry out. *Come back!* Oh, this moment is so fragile. Just an itch, a tiny movement changes everything. *I'm too small without you*, Adam thinks. *Come back. Don't let go.*

As if in response, Callum silently returns his arm. He surrounds Adam again and coils his body even closer, every part of them connected again.

Callum's breathing steadies again, the even tempo of a conductor keeping time with the sounds from the open window—the thump of taxi tires on the cobblestones downstairs, the peal of laughter from across the street, the siren disappearing uptown. His rhythm coaxes the sounds of the city into a lullaby for Adam. *Rest now*, the sounds say. *You are safe.*

Adam closes his eyes.

Yes. He'll sleep now.

Three

MAY 1990

It just takes a beat to turn it around.

—Cyndi Lauper, "Change of Heart"

ADAM

Adam wakes up slowly, the soft rustling of paper nudging him into the morning. He's alone in the bed now, but Callum isn't far, just a few feet away, sitting at the piano and studying his sheet music. He's wearing only his sweatpants again, the same outfit he greeted Adam with last night, if you can call it a greeting. He's also wearing his Walkman, swaying to music that Adam can't hear, stopping every now and then to make notes. Adam watches Callum's naked back. The muscles tense and twitch and spring, as if he's concentrating not just with his mind, but with everything. He remembers the shapes Callum's body made last night, the curves and angles and expansions. He remembers his skin, the sweat that beaded on its freckled surface, the sheen reflecting the dappled city light, the salty taste of it, its tautness on his lips. The discovery of it. What he knows now.

Last night, he'd barely noticed how tiny Callum's studio apartment is, no bigger than Adam's bedroom at home. It's crowded with furniture: a dresser, a pair of stools, an orphaned ottoman, a stepladder. Nothing matches or seems anchored anywhere in particular except for big, boxy Clara, with yellow keys and a boom box on top. A tiny kitchen in the corner sits just in front of an even tinier bathroom. The bathroom has no sink. Callum has to wash his hands in the kitchen.

Posters from Lincoln Center cover the only open wall: MOSTLY

MOZART, 1989. CHAMBER MUSIC SERIES, 1988. And a movie poster, too, *Amadeus.* The library sits on top of the fridge, music textbooks mostly, a biography of Beethoven, an anthology of *Peanuts* comic strips, a dictionary.

On the floor next to Clara is a pair of shoes, beautiful deep brown oxfords with elegant broguing. Adam's never seen those shoes before. They look worn, but not too much, and impeccably cared for, as if Callum dusts them every night with a soft cloth and takes them for a professional polish once a month.

Adam sneezes, and Callum turns around. "Hey," he says gently, pulling off his headphones.

"What are you listening to?"

"Mozart. Mornings are for Mozart." Callum ejects the tape from his Walkman and drops it in the boom box. It's a light, quick, almost playful melody that Adam faintly recognizes.

"I like it," he says. *I like you.*

"It's even better when you hear it live. Have you ever been to a show at Lincoln Center?"

"No."

"I'll take you. We'll go."

"I wish you could call in sick today," Adam says. "We could go see *Cry-Baby.* I love John Waters."

"Not a chance. Mandatory staff meeting at one and I have to stop by Colony first. They're holding a copy of a Chopin étude for me. So I need to get going." He musses Adam's hair like a father would. No kiss. "You want to borrow a toothbrush?"

Adam remembers reading in one of his pamphlets that sharing toothbrushes is dangerous. Same with razors. But how can he say no? How can he fake it, just wetting the toothbrush and rubbing toothpaste on his teeth, when the only sink is out in the open? Won't Callum see? Won't it make him feel bad, infectious, different? Won't it create space between them? How can Adam say no?

His mind somersaults with what to say when Callum holds out a brand-new toothbrush, still in the package. "Here you go," he says. "They were two for one at the Duane Reade."

Adam exhales.

He pulls on his jeans and brushes his teeth at the kitchen sink while Callum gets dressed. First a maroon shirt, a little too loose on him, then a pair of black pants and a black leather belt with a brass buckle. Over his shirt, a charcoal vest with five buttons in the front. Callum buttons all five, then smooths his vest across his stomach. "What do you think?"

"Sexiest usher of all time. I'd follow you to any seat you took me to."

Callum smiles. He picks up his brogues and slips them into a little velvet bag, and then into his backpack.

"Where are you taking your shoes?" Adam asks as he ties on his Sambas.

"These are my work shoes. I don't want them to get trashed on the subway, so I carry them in my bag and change when I get to work. Gotta look sharp at Lincoln Center or else they toss you out." He hoists his backpack over his shoulder. "All set?"

"I still think you should call in sick."

"You're cute," Callum says, with only half a smile. He unbolts the door. It breaks a seal, and Adam can feel the world rush in.

"Can I walk to you to the subway?"

"Free country," Callum says, and the words feel cold in Adam's ears.

He trots to keep up with Callum's long, urgent strides, across Horatio and up Eighth Avenue, just two blocks to the Fourteenth Street subway. The deli next to the entrance sells flowers, and today they are particularly beautiful—daffodils, tulips, branches of forsythia and pussy willow, all the May flowers promised by the nursery rhyme, all fastened into bunches with rubber bands. Adam pulls four crumpled dollar bills out of his back pocket and trades them for a clutch of daisies, white petals with yellow eyes. He holds them out to Callum at the edge of the subway stairs.

"For you," he says.

"Me? Aw." Callum's smile seems troubled. "But I don't have anywhere to put them at work. They'll just die in my locker. Will you keep them for me?"

Adam's stomach sinks with embarrassment. Of course Callum can't take flowers to work. What was he thinking?

"Okay," he says, stepping closer. "I'll keep them for you."

"I'll call you later."

"Later?"

"I have to go."

Adam waits for a hug, a kiss, even a squeeze on the shoulder. Nothing comes. He watches Callum descend quickly out of sight, not looking back, as if he's escaping. He drops his hand, letting the flowers hang upside down in his grasp.

He imagines this scene for the movie. He'd mount a camera on a rig high above him. The shot starts as a close-up of Adam's face, sinking from childlike hopefulness to puzzlement to shame, then pulls back and away to reveal a busy sidewalk, pedestrians hustling in every direction, pushing past him like he's little more than an obstacle. The music moves into a minor, melancholy key, sweet but unresolved. A slow rain begins to fall, soaking his hair and matting it to his forehead as he turns away from the stairwell and begins to walk downtown.

But the rain only happens in the movie. Today, here, in real life, there is only sunshine.

BEN

Ben's deep in a dream. He's inside a bar, squeezing through a crowd of men all smiling and laughing and flirting and drinking and dancing. The music is so loud, heavy beats rattling his eardrums and feet. Ben stands by a wall, watching the men dance toward him, one after the other catching his eye, spinning and swaying before him, enticing him to join, to touch, each face coming closer, closer, but staying just beyond his focus. One, and then the next, and then the next, just out of reach. Soon everyone is facing him, beckoning. *Come dance!*

He feels their eyes, senses their sweat, absorbs their expectation. He tries to move, to dance with them, but his legs are like stones, calcified, trapped in cement. He can't make them respond. He can't dance. Can't follow. Eventually the men's faces turn away, looking at one another instead of at him, and soon they've forgotten him, because he is invisible now. *Wait!* he wants to yell. *I'm right here!* He tries to wave, knocking his injured elbow against the wall, wincing at the pain. When he looks up, everyone has disappeared. Gone. Only darkness now.

"Ben? Wake up."

Ben's eyes jerk open. For a panicked moment, he's not sure where he is. Everything is still dark.

"Are you in there?"

He peeks out from under a pillow to see Gil standing in the doorway in a rumpled T-shirt, with a messenger bag across his chest and a set of keys dangling from his hand. He just got home from his shift. Ben pulls the pillow back over his face. How long has Gil been there? "What time is it?" Ben mumbles.

"Almost eight. What happened to you?"

"What do you mean?"

Gil holds up a bloody washcloth. "This."

Last night comes cascading back into Ben's groggy consciousness. The walk up to the East Village, the crying man outside the Bar. The stumble off the sidewalk. The scraped elbow. The swift walk home. The stinging shower, the collapse onto the couch, the descent into a dancing dream.

Ben points at the three Band-Aids that barely cover the wound. "It's nothing. Just a scrape."

"Uh-huh," Gil says. "Let me see."

Ben sits up and holds out his arm. Gil peels back the Band-Aids.

"That looks worse than the road rash on the skateboarder I treated last night. What happened?"

"It's fine. I just tripped and fell. I missed the curb with my foot."

"Where were you?"

"In the East Village."

"Were you drinking or something? How do you miss the curb?"

"I don't know. I just did."

"You cleaned it?"

"Yeah. There was gravel stuck in it."

"You did a pretty good job. But I want to take a closer look at it. Why don't you have a shower and give it another good rinse and meet me in the kitchen. I want to talk to you."

When Ben finds his glasses, he sees the flyer from last night on the coffee table. A black-and-white photograph of two very muscular guys, shirts off, abs ripped, staring straight at the camera with borderline menacing smiles. One stands behind the other, with his hand reaching around and down into the jeans of the guy in front. GO DEEPER AT THE MONSTER, it reads in gold gothic letters.

ADAM

"Daisies? For me?" Adam's mother beams from the kitchen table. "What did I do to deserve daisies? I haven't even finished the cross-word puzzle."

For a moment, Adam is perplexed because Adam has forgotten he's even carrying a bunch of flowers. Then he remembers. "Yes, for you."

"An early Mother's Day bouquet from my adoring son. Did you go all the way up to Central Park to pick them? I woke up at six thirty and you were already gone."

"Couldn't sleep," he says, which isn't exactly a lie.

"Welcome to adulthood," she says, reaching for his hand. "How can it be that you're eighteen? You're all grown-up now."

"Something like that," he says, biting the inside of his cheek.

She leans back and pulls a vase from a cabinet under the sink. "Fill this halfway with water, will you? I'll snip the ends of the flowers. We'll put them in your room for now. This table is way too crowded with my crap."

After she arranges them, Adam takes the flowers into his room and closes the door. He sits on the edge of his bed with the vase in his lap and wonders where Callum is now. He pictures him riding the subway, visiting the music shop, changing his shoes at Lincoln Center. It was so dumb to buy these flowers. Did he really think Callum would take them all the way uptown?

His atlas is on the bed next to him. He turns to a map of the world, then a map of the United States, then New York State, then Manhattan. He runs a finger from the Village to Sixty-Fourth Street, Lincoln Center. Just a few inches away on the page. But it seems so far.

BEN

Gil snips two squares of gauze off his roll, then carefully places them over Ben's scrape and secures them with medical tape. "Keep it covered until you get a scab, all right? Maybe a day or two. I'll leave some extra gauze for you."

"Thanks." Ben takes a sip of coffee. It's bitter. He checks the fridge for cream, but there is none. He stirs in some sugar. Still bitter.

Gil gets up to wash his hands. "I have a strong feeling there is more to the story of this scrape."

"What do you mean?"

Gil places the flyer on the counter. GO DEEPER AT THE MONSTER.

Ben stares at it like it's an inkblot test. "It's just a flyer."

"That's true," Gil says. "And the copies of *GXE* by the television are just magazines."

Ben covers his scraped elbow with his hand.

"Look, Ben. You don't have to tell me anything you don't want to tell me. I know we've never talked about any of this, and that's okay. That's your call. But I need to know that you're being careful."

"I know. Condoms."

"Yes. Condoms. Always. Do you need some?"

"No."

"You already have some?"

"No. I just, I don't—" Ben hunches his shoulders, compressing himself. He doesn't want to talk with his brother about condoms. He doesn't want to talk to his brother about his sex life. He doesn't even have a sex life to discuss. "Do we really have to talk about this? I took Health class."

"We don't have to talk about sex. But we do have to talk about the rest of it."

"The rest of it?"

"Day before yesterday, I had a patient come in who'd been beaten up outside a bar in Chelsea after kissing his boyfriend good-bye. Some punk saw them and took the opportunity to follow this kid and kick out two of his teeth."

"I didn't get beat up."

"That's not my point. My point is it happens all the time, and it's on the increase. Maybe it's because of AIDS, I don't know. But I'm seeing it more and more often. If you're going to be hanging out around places like this"—he points to the flyer—"like the Monster, you have to be careful."

"I've never been to the Monster."

"Still not my point."

"Everyone has to be careful," Ben says, growing defensive. "You could get hit by a bus."

Gil puts his palms on the table. "Yes. I could get hit by a bus. But that's not the same. You could get hit by a bus *in addition* to every threat that I don't have to face. I'm not a target for gay bashers. My risk for HIV is nowhere near as high as yours. Things are different for people like you."

"People like me," Ben repeats. "Targets. HIV risks. Okay."

"I just don't ever want to see you in the hospital. I don't know what I'd do."

Ben digs his thumb and forefinger into his eyes. *Don't cry*, he thinks. No matter what, don't cry. "People like me," he says again.

"Ben."

"You want me to be someone else."

"I don't."

"I'm in the way."

The words hang in the air like an accusation.

"That isn't what I said," Gil says.

Ben looks at his feet. *Don't cry.*

Gil leans forward and speaks in an infuriatingly measured, grown-up tone. "Ben. You're eighteen. You can make your own decisions. I just want you to make smart ones."

Ben's words come too fast to stop. "Decisions? Decisions about what? About who I am? Do you think I *decided* to be—" He feels a sob rising in his throat. He desperately swallows it back. *Do not cry. Do not give him that. No.*

"Come on, Ben. Don't do that."

Ben stares into his cup of bitter coffee, anger and despair churning through his chest. He can't say any more. If he speaks, he'll break. He contracts every muscle he can feel, tenses every fiber. *Don't break, Ben. Don't break.*

After a long silence, Gil gets up. "I don't enjoy being an asshole, you know."

Ben scoffs.

Once he's sure Gil's gone to sleep, he will let himself cry. But only very quietly, and only for a minute or two.

Tell me what you hide.

I've been renting all these movies from the Gay and Lesbian section of the video store, like Querelle and My Beautiful Laundrette. I always wear a backpack when I go so that I can hide what I rent on the way home. You never know who you're going to run into. Imagine bumping into your next-door neighbor and she asks you what you're renting. If it's Batman or Uncle Buck she'd be like, "Oh." But if it's Making Love or The Boys in the Band, she'd have follow-up questions. You know? I hate follow-up questions.

My favorite gay one is Maurice. Have you seen it? It made me cry. That one scene at the end where Rupert Graves is like, "Now, we shan't never be parted." Even the second time I saw it I cried. Also it takes place like eighty years ago so there's no AIDS in it or anything, like in Longtime Companion or Parting Glances. Those are good movies but they still freak me out. I like Maurice better because even though it's kind of sad it's mostly a love story and the ending is pretty much happy. Complicated, but happy. Sorry, did I just ruin it for you?

I guess it's stupid that I think about hiding them in my backpack. But it's just more efficient that way. You get home faster.

It only took a few weeks to rent every tape in that section. I wish there were more. By the way, have you seen Querelle and My Beautiful Laundrette? They are about as different as two movies can be. They don't belong in the same section at all.

ADAM

Callum still hasn't called.

On the first day, a couple of petals on the daisies started to brown, just at the tips. Adam removed them, and the bunch looked like new. On the second day, even though Adam trimmed the stems and changed the water, several more petals turned. He pulled them off. On the third day, he found twenty-seven fallen petals on his desk.

Today, the fourth day, the petals are falling steadily, silently fluttering as they go like little desiccated wings, twirling through the air and onto his desk and the floor beneath.

Adam lies in bed and watches them. All flowers do is die, Adam thinks. You buy them because they are beautiful, but as soon as you bring them home, you realize that they have already begun to die. Swiftly, or slowly, it doesn't matter. They only die, and all you can do is watch.

He's tried to call Callum a dozen times this week. He's only left three messages on the machine, though, and he's used an upbeat voice, casual and light like nothing's wrong at all. But Callum hasn't called back. If only Adam knew what he did wrong. Then maybe he could fix it.

He imagines what Lily would say if she weren't in Greece. *Okay, pull it together. A day of pining was cute. A second day of pining was weird. But now? This is just pathetic and your room is starting to smell funny. Boys are boys, they come and go. Now get up and bring over some movies to watch. Maybe* Mahogany. *We haven't seen that one in almost a year.*

Imaginary Lily is right. Boys come and go.

Adam ties up his Sambas and heads outside. He walks up Eighth Avenue, past the deli, past the burger bar, past the magazine shop. At the diner, the owner stops him to say hello. She asks him where his tall friend is. Adam says he doesn't know.

He walks east, over to Greenwich Avenue, then down toward Seventh. Adam watches his feet while he walks, not paying attention. Just outside Two Boots Pizza, he bumps awkwardly into another pedestrian.

"Hey, buster! Watch where you're going!"

The voice, gravelly and loud and familiar, erupts into laughter. It's his godfather, Jack, big and broad with a denim shirt and a new goatee. Next to Jack, his other godfather, Victor, smiles as he refastens the black-and-gray ponytail that bursts into curls at the back of his head.

"Come here, my boy," Jack says, his beefy arms oustretched. "Gimme a hug."

Victor hugs him, too, then reaches over to adjust Adam's crooked collar. "There, you were crooked. Where are you off to, sweetheart?"

"Nowhere."

"*Nowhere*," Victor repeats. He casts a skeptical expression at Adam. "Oh, honey. I see it in your face. What's his name? And don't tell me it's *nobody*."

"Victor!" Jack snaps.

"What?" Victor throws his hands up in surrender. "I'm just asking."

Jack turns to Adam. "Ignore him."

"What about you guys? Where are you going?" Adam asks, eager to change the subject.

"We're making the rounds. We were just upstairs to see Albert." He points across the street to St. Vincent's, the giant red brick hospital that's been there forever. Adam knows it well. He was born there. He had his leg set there when he broke it in fifth grade. Pop had his gall bladder out there.

"Would you believe, we got hissed at by a security guard," Victor says. "For taking the back stairs. Can you imagine? Hissed! Like an alley cat! As if we don't know every square inch of St. Vincent's better than he ever could. I wanted to push him down the stairs."

"It's a good thing you didn't because we don't have money or time to bail you out. We still have to get to Mount Sinai to see Joe-Joe."

"Don't forget Ron," Victor says.

"I thought he was discharged."

"Yes, he's home. We're doing groceries. And we need to pick up his prescriptions at the pharmacy on Eighth Avenue. Oh, and what about Timo?"

"I thought Timo wasn't speaking to us. Didn't he blow us off for drinks last week?"

"No, Jack. He didn't blow us off. He's back in."

"You're kidding. When?"

"A few days after Jay's party."

Jack takes a deep breath. "He seemed fine that night. He's what, twenty-four? Way too young for this. Where is he?"

"Twenty-three. Eastview."

Jack checks his watch. "We won't make it today. We'll go tomorrow afternoon." He turns to Adam and shrugs. "Like I said, the rounds. They never end. But you gotta show up for family, right?"

Adam nods like he understands, which he doesn't. Not yet.

"You feeling all right, kid? You look worn out."

"Oh, leave him alone," Victor says. "He's probably been up all night. Don't you remember being eighteen? I didn't sleep for a year. Adam, honey, you go out and shake that tush all you want. Sleep when you're old, like us."

Jack and Victor say goodbye and cross the street, making it to the other side just before a cab hits a pothole in the intersection, dislodging a hubcap and sending it rolling, racing toward Adam. It jumps the curb and he spins out of the way, losing his balance and nearly falling onto the sidewalk. The cab speeds on.

Albert. Joe-Joe. Ron. Timo. Albert. Joe-Joe. Ron. Timo.

Adam feels the next name take shape in his brain. He says it aloud. "Callum."

BEN

Ben is being careful.

He leans up against the scaffolding surrounding Gil's building. Behind him, a checkerboard of posters for new albums from Concrete Blonde and Kylie Minogue. Last week, this same temporary wall was advertising Sonic Youth and Tony! Toni! Toné! The week before it was Heavy D and Curious (Yellow) and the Church.

Ben wonders how many layers of posters a piece of plywood can carry before the posters outweigh the walls and no one remembers what was inside in the first place. Ten layers? A hundred? A thousand? Maybe that's what Gil wants Ben to do. Build scaffolding around himself for protection, then slap on a bunch of layers, more and more, until his core is totally obscured. Until it dissolves.

He's managed to avoid Gil almost completely this week. But he can't stop thinking about what Gil said, about what he meant.

I don't ever want to see you in the emergency room. I don't know what I'd do. It sounds a lot like their mother. A lot like *I'm not equipped.*

Ben knows he has to be careful. He isn't blind. Remember Marco? They stuffed him in a closet. Remember that boy up in Maine a few years ago, Charlie Howard? They threw him in a river. Ben's always known about the dangers. That's why he's careful about how he walks, the way he talks, the way he laughs and smiles. He's always tried hard not to be conspicuous.

But this is New York, and Ben is eighteen, and things should be different.

Across the street, a car radio is playing a song from the new Depeche Mode album. It booms under a heavy, aggressive drum, warning him against a policy of truth. He'll hide what he has to hide, just as the song directs.

ADAM

Adam is careful not to pass under the ladder leaning up against St. Vincent's. Ladders are bad luck. Although, he thinks sarcastically, if the guy up there repairing the second-floor window drops a tool on him, the good news is he's already at the hospital. He steps inside.

The woman at the information desk is wearing a white pullover with peach flowers on it. Her square-frame eyeglasses are huge, covering half her face.

"Can you tell me where Callum Keane's room is?" The question comes out so easily.

She glances at her clipboard. "Which floor?"

"I don't know."

"Date of admission?"

"I'm not sure."

"Nature of condition?" She speaks in a monotone, like she's reading from a script.

"I don't know."

She puts her pen down and looks up. "What is your relationship to the patient?"

"He's—we're friends."

"Friends," she repeats.

"Yes."

"I see." She straightens her glasses and pushes the clipboard aside. "I'm afraid I can't help you. Policy. I'm sure your friend is fine."

Adam nods, wanting to believe her. He stands there for a moment, and then says, "Thanks."

He exits the building and lingers on the sidewalk out front. He looks uptown, toward the Empire State Building, then downtown, toward the World Trade Center. He likes the sense of balance the landmarks create, like they're keeping the island of Manhattan steady, preventing it from capsizing. If one went missing, he thinks, the whole island would just tip into the harbor.

He walks up to Fourteenth Street, lined with budget retailers, porn shops, and storefronts selling window fans and umbrellas and pot pipes in the back. He walks toward Union Square, where skateboarders gather to do tricks on the concrete steps and artists set up tables to sell small paintings of the skyline to tourists. He finds an all-day breakfast cart. "One egg and cheese, please," he says.

The cook cracks an egg onto the hot griddle, breaking its yolk with the corner of his spatula. He splits a deli roll to toast next to the egg. When it's light brown, he lays a slice of yellow cheese on the bottom bun, slides the fried egg on top, adds another slice of cheese, and then the top bun. He wraps it tightly in foil lined with wax paper, dancing to Taylor Dayne on his transistor radio as he works.

"Thanks," Adam says, handing the man a dollar bill and a quarter.

"Tell it to my heart." The man smiles.

Adam walks as he eats, chastising himself. Stop being so stupid, he thinks. Callum is not in the hospital. He said he's healthy. The only reason you think he's sick is because you don't want to believe the truth, that he just doesn't want to see you anymore, that's all. You blew it. You're not what he wants after all. He's just doing what he probably thinks he should have done in the first place. He's walking away. He's making it easy for you. People get dumped all the time, he said. Remember? They get over it. Now it's your turn. Get over it. Your movie isn't in the romance section anymore.

BEN

Ben is dazzled by the restaurant. Beautiful people everywhere, each made more beautiful by the flattering amber light that floods the bustling room. Waiters in waist aprons dart between tables draped with white bistro tablecloths. Bursts of laughter flare up from this corner, then that corner, all tempered by the clinks and clangs of silverware and wineglasses. Conversations wind through the air like wisps of weather. De La Soul plays in the background below the din, going on about me, myself, and I.

He's never been anywhere like this before. It's a long way from TGI Fridays and the Chicken Hut up in Gideon. Ben's eyes race around the room, tallying labels. He sees a Donna Karan stretch bodysuit, black of course. He sees a shiny belted raincoat by Marc Jacobs for Perry Ellis, the one Naomi wore in the runway show. He sees a Martin Margiela deconstructed blazer, an Elsa Peretti bone cuff bracelet, at least three different pairs of Manolo Blahnik stilettos. A Versace bomber jacket, a Todd Oldham hammock dress, a Christian Lacroix pencil skirt overlayed with black fringe so long it tickles the floor.

When the waiter comes to offer menus, Rebecca holds up her hand. She orders three steak frites, medium-rare, and a martini for herself. Ben asks for a glass of red wine and Gil tells the waiter to make it a bottle.

"I remember the first time I came here to the Odeon," Rebecca says. "I think it was 1986? I sat at the bar with my roommate Antonia for, like, three hours, sucking on the same drink the whole time because that's all we could afford. See those mirrors over the bar? You can use them to spy on people and they'll have no idea that you're watching them. Brooke Shields was here that night with Nicolas Cage. Grace Jones was at a table in the corner in sunglasses. I swear I saw Talisa Soto and Jessica Lange that night, too, but Antonia didn't believe me."

"I can't believe this place is three blocks from my loft," Gil says. "All this time I could have been hanging out with Nicolas Cage."

Rebecca waves at a man wearing a navy blazer over a white V-neck T-shirt. "That's Ross Bleckner," she says. "I shot a portrait of him recently and he paid me in art. I'll show you the painting sometime. It's trippy, like this mess of oddly shaped blobs across a gray canvas that seem to move with you when you walk past it. He said it was inspired by Kaposi's sarcoma lesions."

Ben pretends not to notice when Gil glances at him when Rebecca mentions KS. He keeps his eyes on the woman in the Chloé palazzo pants passing by their table. He'd restyle her, he thinks. Swap out that blousy top for a slim tank. The proportions would be better.

Their drinks arrive. The wine is sharp on Ben's tongue, a feeling he likes.

"How did you two meet?" he asks.

"At the hospital," she says.

"Were you a patient?"

"I don't date patients," Gil says. "That would be unethical."

"I was there to visit my friend Sean in the ICU," Rebecca says. "They wouldn't let me in because I wasn't on his list, and I wasn't family. Dr. Gil here overheard me trying to bribe the orderly with cigarettes. He recognized me because it was my third day in a row there."

"She was the only one visiting Sean," Gil says.

"His family disowned him when they found out he was gay. And Sean didn't really tell a lot of friends that he was sick. He said he didn't want to bother them with it because they all had enough people to worry about already. He felt guilty. But Gil saw that Sean needed a hand to hold, so he broke the rule and snuck me in."

"I didn't sneak you in," Gil says. "I evaluated the situation, and in my judgment as a medical professional, I believed that her visit would be palliative for Sean. In my opinion he needed a friendly face. Yours seemed friendly enough. I prescribed you to him."

She cups his chin in her hand and kisses his cheek. "Dr. Feelgood."

"Is he okay?" Ben asks. "Your friend."

"He had AIDS, Ben," Gil says, a hint of dismissiveness in his voice.

"Oh," Ben says. He turns to Rebecca. "I'm sorry."

"Sean was great. He was one of the best stylists in the city. Do you remember that spread in British *Vogue* last winter where all the models were naked except for Burberry coats and those insanely amazing Vivienne Westwood boots?"

Ben nods. Of course he saw it. It was incredible.

"Sean did that. You could say that it wasn't that much styling, because they were barely wearing anything. But it was his vision, and it was so much more than fashion. It was art. Sean was an artist. The absolute best." She takes a big, solemn sip from her martini. "Twenty-five years old. Didn't do anything wrong. But he's gone now."

Gil looks at Ben.

"Do you see what I mean?"

Ben pulls his arms into his body, shrinking himself.

"What are you talking about?" Rebecca asks.

Gil takes a gulp of wine. "I just don't want to see Ben in the hospital. That's all."

"Why would Ben be in the hospital? Why would you say that?"

Gil doesn't answer.

She puts her hand on Ben's knee under the table.

"Gil?"

"He just needs to know what he's getting into," Gil says. "If he's going to be gay, he needs to know the risks. That's all." He holds his hands up when he says it, as if he's simply stating a truth that only he is brave enough to say out loud. As if to say, *don't blame me for pointing out the obvious.*

"*If* he's going to be gay? That is a hell of a thing to say, Gil." She clears her throat and imitates his voice. "*I'm a medical professional, and in my medical opinion, if you choose to live your life honestly, then you will only have yourself to blame when terrible things happen to you, up to and including death. I prescribe not being gay.*"

"That's not what I meant."

"No?" She drains the last of her martini. "You said *if.* You implied a choice. As though Ben should *choose* to be someone else. To hide himself away. To deny who he really is, to live half a life, to be afraid. To be alone."

"Look," Gil says. "I don't have a problem with gay people. I didn't create this world we live in."

"Didn't you?" Her tone is icy, piercing. Ben draws his knee away from her hand.

Gil takes a long breath and clasps his hands on the table. He speaks slowly. "He is my brother, Bec. I'm only trying to protect him. I only want him to be safe."

Rebecca's glare is as cold as her voice. "For a guy who's supposed to be so smart, you know so much less than you think you do." A waiter reaches for her martini glass. "I'll do that again," she says, tapping its rim. The waiter nods and slips away.

"So you're saying I shouldn't look out for him?"

"Jesus, Gil."

Ben's eyes are fixed on his empty place setting. They're talking about him like he's not even here, so maybe he shouldn't be. He stands up, letting his napkin fall to the floor, and snakes through the beautiful people to the back of the restaurant, to the door marked MEN. It closes behind him, dulling the din of the restaurant. He doesn't have to pee. He stands in front of the mirror, but doesn't look at himself. He washes his hands, rinses, and then washes them again. He doesn't rush.

After a while, he returns to the table. Gil and Rebecca are silent. At his place is a plate of steak, sliced into pink strips and showered with chopped parsley. Beside it, a big pile of thin French fries still glistening with oil. Ramekins of mayonnaise and ketchup sit in the center of the table. When he sits, Rebecca begins to eat.

Ben's steak is delicious, tender and meaty and charred on the outside, with a faint flavor of blood. He takes a few salty fries, then another bite of steak. He doesn't look at Gil or Rebecca, and they don't speak, to him or to each other. He takes another bite, and then another.

Outside, a fog has settled over the city, reflecting the restaurant's amber light in the windows, a golden glow. Ross Bleckner's table empties out and is quickly repopulated with a group of young businessmen. A woman in a blindingly white shirt dribbles wine on her chest but doesn't notice. A pair of beautiful men in baroque Gaultier T-shirts take corner stools at the bar. A tall, beautiful woman settles into a banquette in the back. Is it Anh Duong from the Lacroix shows? A busboy drops a plate on the floor near the kitchen. No one turns to look.

As they pick at the last of their French fries, Rebecca lights a cigarette and says, "Ben, are you free tomorrow? I have a denim story to shoot for *Mademoiselle*. We're shooting on a roof down in the Financial District. I don't know why. I guess they want the Trade Center in the background or something. Derek and Charles will be there. And Jorge. Remember them?"

"Yes."

"I'll pay you a hundred bucks. You're worth more, but that's what I have in the budget."

"I'll be there," he says.

"Great. Then why don't you stay over at my place in the Lower East Side and help me haul everything over in the morning. Maybe we can go through the shot list tonight and sketch out some concepts. What do you say? I have an extra toothbrush."

"I say yes." Ben doesn't look at Gil. He won't look at Gil for the rest of the evening.

ADAM

The city is foggy tonight. Ground fog, they called it on the news, due to a temperature inversion. It's like a cloud just dropped from the sky and wrapped itself around the city. Landmarks emerge from the soft, squishy glow, taking shape as Adam walks uptown.

The Flatiron Building. The Empire State Building. The Pan Am. He waves them away. They don't have the answers he needs.

Adam enters Grand Central Station. Inside, the main concourse feels airy, expansive, a million times bigger than you'd think from outside. It's not busy at this hour, just some after-work drinkers catching trains back to Westchester and a few bridge-and-tunnel revelers arriving for a night out. He circles the massive room, climbing and descending the stairways on both ends. He crosses to the clock in the center. Pop says it's the only clock in New York that's always right. Ten thirty, it says.

The giant split-flap display above the ticket windows clicks through its list of destinations, departure times, track numbers. White Plains, 10:40, Track 9. Albany, 10:55, Track 6. Poughkeepsie, 11:10, Track 4. Every minute or two, the display refreshes. *Click . . . click . . . clickclickclick.* Percussion. Syncopation. Music.

He looks up at the ceiling, pale green with golden stars painted into constellations. Orion, the Big Dipper, Ursa Major and Ursa Minor. Adam reaches up to trace them, like freckles on a lover.

He imagines this scene in his movie, how he'd rig a camera from the ceiling to take in the full vastness of the room, the echoes of the rushed footsteps, his stillness by the clock, his solitude. He imagines a closer shot, just his sneakers, on the left side of the frame. He imagines a pair of brogues approaching, stopping just in front of his shoes, toes almost touching his. *Here you are*, the man in the brogues will say. *I've been looking everywhere for you.* The camera pulls up to their arms, and the man touches the inside of Adam's elbow. *Everything is okay.*

Adam sits down on the floor, hugging his knees, making himself smaller. He'll stay here for a little while. No one will look twice at him. He's just another kid with messy hair and nowhere special to go. You see them all the time around New York. They don't really matter.

Tell me how you made it through.

I know I'm too old for it but Frog and Toad Are Friends by Arnold Lobel is still my favorite book. I used to sleep with that book like it was a teddy bear. I always wanted a friendship like Frog and Toad have.

I remember this one time, when I was six or seven. It was dark, an hour after bedtime, and I was in bed with my book but I wasn't asleep yet. My father came in, which was strange, because I hadn't seen him for a few days. He was staying somewhere else.

"Why don't you get up," he said. "I want you to come for a drive with me. We're going to see the field where Jimi Hendrix played, and Janis Joplin, and Creedence. I want to pull up a piece of grass from that field. Don't you want one, too?"

I didn't know what he was talking about, but I could tell that I shouldn't ask any questions, I should just get out of bed and follow him. I brought my book with me even though he shook his head at me when he saw it. I got in the back seat of his old sedan with the bench seats, right behind him. That was always my place to sit so that I wouldn't be in the way of the rearview mirror. I felt myself getting fidgety so I sat on my hands. That was the rule for fidgeting.

Once we were on the highway, he said, "It's not in Woodstock, you know. It's in Bethel." I still had no idea what he meant.

We were on the highway for a really long time. The radio played songs about hotels in California and peaceful easy feelings, and he kept singing along at the top of his lungs. I just looked out the window at the headlights from oncoming cars that kept sweeping past in brilliant flashes. My father kept saying, "Isn't this great! Just a dad and his son out for a drive!" but I never answered. I just stayed quiet. The flashing headlights made me sleepy.

After a while I lay down on the seat and curled up like a ball. I could feel the springs in the bench poking through. I leaned my head on Frog and Toad. The jacket felt so cool on my face. I fell asleep.

When I woke up we were back in the driveway and my father was shaking his head at me. "You missed it," he said. "You missed the whole thing." I could tell he was upset but I didn't care. I went back inside and got in bed with Frog and Toad and hoped my father wouldn't come in, too.

BEN

Rebecca's apartment is ten feet wide and a million feet long, like a railroad car wedged into a building four stories up. White walls reach twelve feet high, nearly every inch tacked with pages torn from magazines, set sketches on graph paper, endless headshots and test shots of models and movie stars and artists and music icons, faces Ben recognizes. Long flat file cabinets and light boxes line both sides of the room, leading from a small kitchen and sleeping area near the entrance all the way to a distant pair of floor-to-ceiling windows overlooking the foggy lights out on Delancey Street.

A string of studio worktables runs the length of the room, right down the center, end to end to end. Glossy stacks of thick magazines, dozens of them, cover the surface of the tables. *Grazia. Femina. So-En. Flare. Fame. Aperture. Artforum. Bomb.* Fashion magazines, art, design magazines, magazines filled with ideas. Everything smells like paper and ink. Ben walks the length of the table, touching every issue. He could spend a year in here, reading, absorbing, imagining, believing. He sits down on a bench by the windows.

"I know it's in here somewhere," Rebecca is saying as she flips through a crate of records underneath a clamp light by the kitchen. "I need to organize this vinyl one day. I inherited it from a friend last year, on the condition that I would play at least one song every day in his memory. But I never seem to put them back in any useful order. Ah! Here it is. Chaka Khan. You'll know this song, but it's a remix. Frankie Knuckles gave it an update."

Tentative, untethered synthesizer notes seep into the room from speakers under the worktables. They build in volume, steady, mellow, welcoming a soft house beat that comes in from a distance, unrushed but insistent. Every note is an echo, reverberating into layers that last for several minutes. When Chaka's voice finally comes through, it's like she's emerging from the fog outdoors, floating under and into and around the music.

Yes, Ben knows this song. Everybody knows "Ain't Nobody."

"No one sings like Chaka," she says.

"I love that bounce," Ben says. "I've never heard this mix."

"Frankie's a genius."

"Do you know him? I mean, have you met him?"

"Once or twice," she says. She draws two glasses of water from the sink and brings one to Ben.

"Your kitchen is so small," he says. "Do you even have a stove?"

"This isn't really an apartment. It's not officially zoned for residential. I tell people I'm just staying here while I look for a new place but I've been here almost two years now. No one in the building cares. There's a ceramicist named Alex living downstairs on a blow-up mattress between her pottery wheels. We look out for each other, you know? Outlaws."

Ben smiles. "I love it here."

"You're welcome anytime."

"Do you want to go over the shot list for tomorrow?"

"Not really." She sits down across from him. "You know, Ben. You remind me of Sean. You know, the guy I mentioned at dinner."

"I do?"

"Yeah. I could tell when we were on set with the winter coats.

That could have been a throwaway shoot and the client would have been happy enough. But you made it different. The way you talked about how those coats should move, the way you saw all those colors in that purple parka. You thought about how those coats would sound if they spoke. How they'd come alive if they danced. Sean had the same instincts. I think it's an artist thing."

Ben shakes his head. He doesn't believe her. He takes a magazine from a stack in front of him, a copy of *Vogue Italia* with Linda Evangelista on the cover. It's a black-and-white closeup, her hair tousled and tangled into her hoop earrings, her neck extended in a retro movie-star pose.

"She looks incredible," he says.

"Steven Meisel shot that," she says. "I would kill to work with Linda one day."

"That would be a dream."

"If I ever get that job, I'm calling you first."

"Deal. I'll work free that day."

"What did I tell you about money?" She takes a different magazine from the stack, the *World of Interiors*, and starts paging past luxurious kitchens and crisp gardens and living rooms heavy with fabric. She pauses on a photograph of a bathroom with scarlet walls and a claw-foot tub.

"Gil sure was a prick tonight," she says, not looking up. "Don't you think?"

"I was kind of a prick to him the other day."

"Well, he's a bigger prick. No offense."

"I thought you liked him," Ben says cautiously.

"I do, usually. Not tonight."

"He likes you."

"Did he tell you that?" She flips another page. "I wish he would tell me that. Sometimes I don't know what's going on in his brain.

Sometimes I don't *like* what's going on in there. Like tonight, for example. It's like, he just launches words out of his mouth without caring about how they land. If he hurts someone, that's not his fault, that's *their* fault. They should understand that his point of view is more correct, more important. And they should thank him for carrying the heavy burden of having to know everything all the time. Classic control freak, you know? It's really just fear though."

"Fear? Of what?"

"Of everything beyond his reach. The world spins on its own schedule and doesn't give a shit about him and he hates that. He resents everything and everyone who doesn't need him. But, you know, *need* is a big word." She downs the rest of her water. "And I'm in love with him anyway."

Ben hears the words and wonders what it feels like. To really be in love, even with someone who makes you mad.

"Oy, now I'm wound up," she says. "It's time for new music. Roxy Music I think."

She goes to change the record, and the first smooth notes of "Avalon" come up. Soon, Bryan Ferry's moody, haunting voice. *Now the party's over . . .*

"This song," he says, memories flooding into him.

"You like?"

"Gil left behind a Roxy Music record once when he was visiting. I must have been eleven."

"I didn't know he was into Roxy Music."

"Maybe he wasn't. Maybe that's why he left it behind. But I went through a whole Roxy Music phase after that. I always went through a phase whenever he left anything behind. Books, music. I even tried to like *Caddyshack* after he said it was his favorite movie. I spent a lot of time trying to be like him."

She turns out the light by the record player, then walks over to stand in front of the window, looking out at Delancey Street. The blinking traffic lights pulse in the mist like glowworms. "Come here."

Ben goes to stand by her.

"You see that building?" she asks, pointing through the fog to a skinny structure on the corner of Eldridge Street. "If it wasn't there, I'd have a perfect view of the Williamsburg Bridge."

"Maybe we should burn it down."

"I like you, Ben," she says.

After a minute, Ben says, "He thinks I'm going to die, you know. He thinks I'm going to die because I'm gay."

"Wait. You're gay?" She elbows him.

"I am," he says. *I am.* He's never said it so clearly before. So unambiguously, unapologetically, definitively, confidently. So out loud. So fearlessly. *I am.*

She slips her hand into his.

"We're going to be all right," she says, and they stand there at the window, watching the fog churn, until long after the song ends. In the quiet he can hear the crackle of her cigarette.

ADAM

Adam is standing in front of Eastview Medical Center, squinting at people coming and going through the main entrance. He wishes he brought his sunglasses, because the clouds from last night have cleared and now the early afternoon daylight is relentless.

Is he in the right place? This is where Jack and Victor said they were coming to visit Timo, right? It's so hard to be sure of things when you don't sleep. Adam's mind is a set of gears with faulty teeth that won't catch. Memory and logic just slip around inside, confused. If he could think clearly, he'd wonder what he's even doing here in the first place, looking for someone who doesn't want to be found.

There's a pay phone on the corner. Maybe he'll try Callum again. Maybe this time he'll pick up.

No, he won't. Slippery logic again.

He sees Jack and Victor approaching before they see him. Jack's in a pair of cargo pants, Victor's in a pale-blue V-neck T-shirt with a sunburst pendant nestled right in the middle. They appear grim, until Jack looks up and sees Adam and his face lights up.

"What's this?" he bellows. "Second time this week! How'd we get so lucky?"

Victor smiles. "You divine creature. What are you doing here?"

"Hi," Adam responds, but his voice cracks, so he clears his throat and tries again. "Hey." Still scratchy. One more time. "Hey, guys."

Jack and Victor glance at each other, then back at Adam.

"You all right, kiddo? Sore throat or something?" Jack asks.

Adam rubs his eyes. "No, I'm just tired. Didn't sleep much."

Victor smooths Adam's hair away from his eyes. "Oh, he's all right, Jack. He's probably just been out at the disco all night, like we used to do, remember? Those nights at the Saint? Oh, I miss those days. But what on earth are you doing here, darling?"

"I guess I'm looking for someone," Adam says. "I don't know. I'm just not sure—"

Jack cuts him off. "You're worried about someone."

"Yes."

"And you think they might be at the hospital."

When Jack says it aloud, Adam hears how silly it sounds. "I'm just being paranoid or something."

"Who is it?"

Adam clears his throat again. "Just someone I know. I don't

know. He's probably not here. They probably wouldn't tell me even if he was, since I'm not family. It's a rule or something."

"I hate that rule," Victor says. "Half of the patients we know end up completely isolated because their quote, unquote legal families don't bother to visit and their friends can't get in."

"Some quote, unquote legal families are pretty good," Jack says. "And patient privacy is important. Especially for AIDS."

"I still hate the rule. It's full of holes, never consistent one day to the next. It's a crapshoot depending on who's at the desk. The whole thing is friggin' ridiculous."

"Well," Jack says, smiling at Adam. "I hope you enjoyed today's episode of *Vic Rants*."

"Are you guys going in to see your friend Timo?" Adam asks.

"Yes. We brought fresh undies and the new issue of *People*."

"Pot brownies, too," Victor whispers, tapping his tote bag. "For the nausea. AZT is a bitch."

"Can you look for Callum when you're up there?"

"Callum?"

"Yeah. Callum Keane. He's super tall, with freckles all over."

Jack studies Adam's face. He looks at Victor, who nods. He looks back at Adam. "I have a better idea. Why don't you come up with us?"

"I don't want to get in trouble."

"If you can't get what you need by following the rules," Victor says, "you have to find a way around them. It's a lesson they don't teach you in school. We learned it when our friend Anton was gone before we could get to him."

"Let's give it a shot," Jack says. He gestures to the entrance, and the three step inside.

The lobby bustles with people. Medical staff in pale scrubs, visitors carrying armfuls of fresh flowers, an older couple standing by the window leaning into each other. A few kids playing tag underneath a sign that reads EMERGENCY ROOM, laughing and squealing like they're at the park. An announcement over the PA system calls a doctor to an operating room.

"Are you sure this is okay?" Adam asks.

"Worst that can happen is they'll tell you to leave," Victor says. "Did you ever see *9 to 5*?"

"I love that movie."

"Good. Pretend you're Lily Tomlin in a fake lab coat and name tag. Pretend you belong here."

They approach the reception desk. "We're here to see Timo Luz on six," Jack announces.

The distracted attendant, busy with a telephone call, points to a sign-in sheet on the counter. Jack scribbles something illegible, grabs three VISITOR stickers, and leads them to the elevators.

"Strict policy," he says, slapping his sticker over his AIDS WALK '88 T-shirt.

In the elevator, Victor turns to Adam. "Don't expect the sixth floor to be like a maternity ward. No one's up in the AIDS ward high-fiving each other and trading cigars. It's better than it was a few years ago, when they'd seal people into rooms and slide food under the door, but you won't see a lot of balloon bouquets up there."

"Adam gets it," Jack says. "He knows it's not Disneyland."

The elevator doors open to a quiet hospital hallway. Linoleum floors, pastel walls, fluorescent lights. A balding man with a stethoscope around his neck brushes past them into the elevator, not looking up.

"This way," Jack says, pointing to a second passageway, just beyond a nurse's station. "I don't think anyone will bother you if you want to look around. We'll be in with Timo. Don't go far."

They disappear into room 602, which has two pieces of copy paper taped to the door. One reads *Luz*, Timo's last name. The other reads *Johnson*. It doesn't say *Keane*.

Adam steps down the hallway. He reads the signs on room 604. *Velez. Sweet.* Room 606. *Pantaeva. Mori.* 608. *Jones. Carter.* He wonders how often these signs are swapped out. How often a sign comes down because a patient got well enough to go home. How often a sign comes down because a patient didn't.

The door to room 610 is ajar, so Adam glances in, smiling. He sees a man in an awkward twist, a skinny leg sticking out from a sheet and a blanket pulled up under his chin. Adam can see he is sleeping. It's not Callum.

In the next room, a man with rounded, veined biceps stands next to an IV pole, staring out the window. Another man, very thin with long hair pulled into a lazy ponytail, sits in bed listening to a Walkman.

He turns away before the man sees him. It feels weird looking in the rooms. Invasive. He'll just read the names on the doors instead. If Callum's here, his name will be posted. He continues down the hall. *Donahue. Kaya. Mariani. Kelso. Moskowitz. Smith. Torres.* He makes it all the way to the end of the wing, and back again. No Keane.

He rides the elevator back downstairs. He doesn't tell Jack and Victor.

The sunshine outside is warm, unlike the cold fluorescent lights upstairs. The air is fresh, not stale. It's better down here, he thinks, where you can pretend that the sixth floor at Eastview Medical Center isn't even a real place. He closes his eyes, listening for the comforting sounds of the city.

After some time, he feels a tap on his shoulder. "There you are, kiddo. Any luck?"

Luck? Would it be lucky to find Callum here? Adam shakes his head no.

"Well," Victor says, "personally, I'm starving."

"Me too," Jack says. "Let's get cheeseburgers. Adam, you come, too. We'll get a burger in you and then send you home for some beauty sleep."

Adam, mostly because he doesn't know what else to do now, follows them to the corner. They hail a cab and crowd into the back seat, Victor in the middle.

On the way to wherever they're going, Adam stares out at the sidewalk full of people. They've been out all day, working, shopping, laughing, bickering, being. Do they even care about the patients up on the sixth floor? *Did you even care, Adam, before now?* He leans his head against the window, letting the city blur past him. He's so tired.

BEN

Ben's arms are filled with equipment. Gel filters, camera stands, rig clips, and strobes. He can barely balance it all and nearly drops them when Rebecca shouts his name.

"Ben! Take the light reflectors up, too. I'll need them for the group shot."

"I can't carry any more," he says.

"Just figure it out, Ben, all right?" Rebecca sounds pissed, but Ben knows she's just focused, hunched over a table in the top-floor studio studying the creative brief. "I'll be up in five minutes with three models and I don't want to wait. We're already so far behind schedule. So be ready. Hear me?"

He wedges the reflectors under his arm and scales the stairs to the roof. It's an eleven-story building with a perfect view of the

Twin Towers and the harbor. He hopes there's no wind today, because the light reflectors—big hoops stretched with nylon to help reflect or soften the sunlight—are like kites without strings on windy days. If you don't have a good grip, they'll fly out of your hands. Or carry you into the sky.

Sluggish, puffy afternoon clouds coast slowly overhead, obscuring the sun every minute or two. Ben wishes the models had been on time so they could have shot earlier in the day, when the light was consistent. It's not their fault, not this time, but still. He organizes all of the equipment in a shady corner, near the section of roof that Rebecca's taped off for the set and waits.

He doesn't wait long before Rebecca bursts onto the roof with three models behind her. Veronica in a black maxi skirt and slim white denim jacket, Beverly in a faded chambray shirt tied at the waist over black denim shorts, and Irina in a sleeveless denim vest and torn jeans. All three are taller than Ben, sharp and serious and stunningly beautiful.

"Where's Derek?" Rebecca shouts. "Charles?"

"Right here," Derek says.

"Good. Stay close. Watch the breeze. They'll never print a picture if the hair's obscuring the face. Keep it casual. Intentionally messy, but not a rat's nest. Got it?"

Just then a smiling young guy with an unlit cigarette behind his ear emerges from the doorway. His bleached hair is buzzed short and he has a chain-link choker around his neck. "Hello," he says.

"Who are you?" Rebecca demands.

"I'm Jorge's assistant. We shot together last week, remember?" He holds out his hand. "I'm Justin."

"Where's Jorge?" she asks, scowling as she shakes his hand.

"His pager went off. Some kind of emergency and he had to go. Anyway, I'm here."

"Yeah, but I didn't hire you. I hired Jorge. Is he coming back?"

"No, but he asked me to cover for him."

"Shit," she says. "Are you any good at this?"

He grins. "I guess we'll see."

"I guess so," she says, irritated. "Why don't you start by swapping out Veronica's skirt. There's no way we can shoot it in this wind. Put her in the white clamdiggers. Oh, this is my assistant Ben."

"Hi," Ben says.

Justin offers a conspiratorial assistant-to-assistant smile that says *Ugh, bossy photographers, know what I mean?* His tank top is tight on his lean torso. Ben wonders what he looks like underneath.

Justin takes Veronica's elbow. "Let's go, my love. The skirt is too much look. We can't handle the fierceness. Let's put you in something sleeker, chicer, mystique-r." They disappear downstairs.

"Honestly, I feel like kicking him out and having you style," Rebecca says. "But I need you up here for test Polaroids. Go position Beverly and Irina along the edge there and get me a light reading."

Ben helps the models find their marks, then unclips a light meter from his waistband and holds it between them. "F4!" he shouts.

"Higher," Rebecca responds. "I need their faces."

"Same. F4." Ben steps away and Rebecca hoists her Polaroid camera and shoots. The camera buzzes and whirs and spits out an undeveloped photo. She hands it to Ben, who slips it under his arm while loading Rebecca's Nikon, the camera she'll use when she shoots real film.

"I need a body in Veronica's spot until she gets back. Ben, stand there, to the right of Beverly."

"Me?"

"Now."

Ben positions himself next to the models, feeling ragged and silly next to their extreme beauty. Rebecca takes two more test shots before Justin returns with Veronica, now in calf-length denim jeans.

"Perfect," Rebecca says. "You look great. Okay, let's do this. Veronica, next to Beverly. Ben, I need you four feet in front of Irina, reflector at your waist, light side up. Give me forty-five degrees. Get that glow onto their necks."

Ben crouches, angling the nylon disc just enough to cast a soft light onto the models.

"Perfect," Rebecca says. "Don't move. What do we think?"

"Cloud approaching," Ben says. "You should shoot."

"Let's go!" Rebecca shouts. "Smile! Happy! Let me see those necks!"

The models aim enormous smiles at Rebecca. She starts clicking, and Ben starts counting. When he reaches thirty-six, he takes her camera and quickly replaces the cartridge with a fresh roll. He slips it into her hand and bounces back to his spot.

"Beautiful!" she shouts. "Angels! Irina, relax your shoulders! Beverly, open up that smile! More neck! Veronica, where is your neck?"

She shoots a second roll of thirty-six, hands the camera to Ben to reload, and repositions the models. Derek and Charles swarm with hairbrushes and lipliners, Justin dives in to smooth wrinkles and straighten collars, and everyone's back in place within a minute. It begins again.

"Gorgeous! Yes! Find that sun! Smiles! Show me teeth!"

On the next reload, Ben loses his grip on the light reflector tucked between his legs.

"Do you want me to hold that?" Justin asks, pointing at the reflector.

"Thanks," Ben says, flustered.

"Anytime." Justin takes the reflector. His sleepy eyes are smiling at Ben.

After two more rolls, Rebecca announces, "We got this one! Let's rinse and repeat, and hurry. We're losing the light." Justin hustles the models back downstairs for new outfits, and Derek and Charles follow for touch-ups. Rebecca shoots several more rolls of film. After two more outfit changes, the shoot finally wraps. Everyone helps to carry the equipment back downstairs.

"How'd I do?" Justin asks as Rebecca packs the film into her shoulder bag.

"Not bad," Rebecca says. "Not Jorge, but not bad."

"I'll take that."

She turns to Ben. "I have to bolt if I'm going to get these rolls up to B&H for processing before they close. Pack all my shit up and leave it in the lobby. I'll send a messenger to pick it up later. Label it clearly, okay?" She kisses him on both cheeks. "Everything good?"

"Everything," he says.

"You're the best."

Rebecca leaves. The models finish changing back into their tank tops and boot-cut jeans and file out. Derek and Charles load up their bags and follow, waving at Ben on the way out.

Ben carefully organizes Rebecca's lenses and filters into their padded cases. He twists the light reflectors into their carrying satchel and gathers the clamps into a drawstring bag. He stacks everything carefully by the security desk, labeling each piece of baggage with Rebecca's address. He goes back upstairs to make sure he's got everything.

Only Justin is still here, organizing his garment bags.

"The worst part of every shoot," Justin says, straining to zip up an overstuffed bag. Ben stares at the raised vein running down his bicep. What would it feel like to touch?

"Can I help?" Ben asks.

"That's okay," Justin says. He bites his lower lip and smiles, melting Ben. "I'm just about done. Are you going to the subway?"

"No, I'm walking."

"I'll walk with you," Justin says. Not a question, a declaration. Ben's stomach jumps.

"Sure," he answers as casually as he can.

ADAM

"Welcome to Julius', the unflashiest bar in the Village," Jack says as they step out of the cab. "If you want flashy, you gotta go to Uncle Charlie's up on Greenwich."

"Isn't Uncle Charlie's the place where—" Adam asks.

Victor interrupts. "Where someone set off a pipe bomb last month? Yes. That's the place. A bombing in a gay bar. And the cops say it was, ahem, *not bias related*. Idiots. Thank god no one was killed."

"All the more reason to keep going out," Jack says. "To show we're not scared."

"As if he needs another reason to go out," Victor mumbles.

"You sure I can be here?" Adam says. "Drinking age is twenty-one."

Victor pushes him inside. "Please. This is New York."

Inside, sunlight struggles through the dusty windows, casting splotchy light across the room. Three middle-aged men, two in baseball caps and one in a tan suit, chat on barstools. Another man, younger, sits a few seats away leafing through a magazine. A quiet jukebox spits out an old Cyndi Lauper song.

A guy in a white SILENCE=DEATH T-shirt and black leather vest waves from behind the bar. "Hello, handsomes," he says. "I haven't seen you since the Love Ball up at Roseland."

"Oh, babe," Jack says. "We're still recuperating from that night."

"You two had more fun than anyone."

"I deny everything," Victor says.

"We saw Timo today," Jack says.

"How is he?"

"He's been better. Toxo."

"Toxo," the bartender repeats. "Not great."

Toxo. Adam recognizes that one. Callum mentioned that.

"Could be worse," Victor says.

"Always the optimist, Victoria." The bartender nods at Adam. "Who's your friend?"

"This is Adam," Jack says. "He's family."

"I'm Angus," the bartender says. He shakes Adam's hand. "You guys eating? Or just drinking."

"Yes," Jack says. "Both."

Angus points them to a table across the room. "Three cheeseburgers? And three beers?"

"Sounds good to me. Okay with you, Adam?"

"What else do you have?"

"Just cheeseburgers. Easiest menu in town." Angus winks at Adam.

"Okay, but I'll have a Coke instead of a beer."

"You got it."

Jack leads them to a little table by a window. He takes three napkins from the dispenser and sets them around the table. "So," he says to Adam. "Feel like talking about it?"

Adam takes a deep breath. It's time to tell them what's going on. "I'm not sure where to start."

"Well, we could start with who's Callum?"

"He's my—I don't know. I thought we were boyfriends."

"What do you mean?"

"I mean we met in January. We see each other every Saturday. And now I don't know where he is. I can't reach him. He won't answer. It's like he's just vanished."

Victor rolls his eyes. "Men."

"What makes you think he'd be at the hospital?" Jack asks.

"I just—" Adam stalls. "You just hear about things, you know?"

Jack and Victor lean forward, their expressions inquisitive. Adam's promise to Callum snaps back into view. He can't tell. Not even them.

"I have to pee," Adam says, needing a way out of this moment.

"It's back that way." Jack points toward the hallway at the end of the bar.

On his way to the bathroom, Adam sees a man with white hair standing in front of the jukebox, punching spastically at the buttons. "Sister Sledge!" he shouts at the machine, tugging at the cotton scarf around his neck. He looks up at Adam with glossy, wet eyes. "What happened to Sister Sledge?"

Adam shrugs.

The man narrows his eyes at Adam. "You are young," he says. "Very young. Good for you."

Adam goes into the bathroom. When he comes out, the old man is gone.

Back at the table, Adam asks, "How many of your friends have died from AIDS?"

"That's a hell of a subject change," Jack says.

"Half," Victor says. Jack shrugs and nods.

Half. Adam pictures his own friends at school. Lily, of course. But also Cara, Tyson, Hyun, Andrej, Roberta. What if half of them got sick? What if half of them died? What if just one of them died? What if Lily died? Just imagining it feels heavy.

"How do you deal with that?" Adam asks. "I would be so sad every day."

"Funny thing," Victor says. "After seven, eight years, you kind of get used to it."

"How could you get used to it?"

"Victor doesn't mean it gets easier," Jack says. "He means it gets more familiar. Back when this thing was first getting going, we were flat-out terrified. It just started happening, everywhere. We looked up and suddenly we knew five, ten people who were so sick they couldn't leave their apartments. No one knew why. No one knew anything. That was truly terrifying."

"Remember how mad everyone was at us?" Victor asks. "At all the gays? As if they didn't already hate us enough, now we were infectious. They thought we were the problem. Not the disease, not the virus. The people. I don't know why I'm using the past tense. They still feel that way."

"Not everyone," Jack says. "Things are starting to change. I hate to say it, but when people like Rock Hudson and Ian Charleson die, it unlocks some compassion in people."

"I don't know about that," Victor says. "Let's not forget all the *how do you turn a fruit into a vegetable* jokes. Let's not forget how patients who got it from blood transfusions are considered 'innocent victims' as if everyone else who has it deserves it. Let's not forget how you and I were spit on and refused service at restaurants in our own neighborhood because we looked gay. *You make the other customers nervous*, they would say."

"Victor." Jack's tone is tense, warning.

Victor turns to Adam. "I'm telling you, kid. The straight world wouldn't mind a bit if we all just disappeared. You, me, Jack, Angus, all of us. We are an inconvenience to them. That's why there will never be a cure. Not enough people think it's important to help us, and too many people think we're getting what we deserve."

"You don't really believe that," Jack says.

"I don't?" Victor's tone rises. "People don't want to be associated with deviants. They want to consider themselves morally superior. Think about it. Shunning us makes them feel better about themselves. *Well, they shouldn't be having that weird sex*, they say, as if straight people don't have weird sex every day. Adam needs to understand bigotry."

"Do you really think Adam doesn't know about bigotry?"

Victor glares at Jack. They lock eyes, deadly serious. This is the first time Adam's seen them go at it like this, and it's over him. He stares at the tabletop.

Jack breaks first. He sighs. "I'm sorry, babe."

"Me too," Victor says. "Amor."

Jack turns back to Adam. "It's true. Bigotry is everywhere, even in New York, even in the Village. But there are more than a million gays in this town. Things have to get better."

"Not by themselves," Victor says. "No one is going to fix this except us. We can try and shame straight people into doing the right thing, but they won't. So we stand up and shout, we overrun the stock market with protestors, we lie on the floor of St. Patrick's Cathedral during mass, we petition the FDA, we call out the drug companies, we bring lawsuits against discriminatory laws. We have to fight on a hundred fronts if we want anything done. We can't trust anyone else to do it but ourselves."

"Ourselves, and Elizabeth Taylor," Jack says. "Oh, thank god for Elizabeth Taylor."

"And Liza. Don't forget Liza. And Joan Rivers. And Princess Diana. And Dionne Warwick. And thank god for Madonna, too. Our divas are the exceptions. They make people listen. They insist."

"Remember when Liz went after Congress? That hearing was amazing. She's a warrior."

"But our friends keep dying," Victor says.

"Yes," Jack says quietly. His eyes begin to well up. He squeezes Victor's hand. "They keep dying. Year after year after year."

"But we keep fighting," Victor whispers.

"Yes, we keep fighting." A tear falls to his cheek. "Goddammit, it's hard sometimes."

Victor puts his hand on Jack's chin. "My love," he says.

To see the big man cry makes Adam want to turn away. Sorrow is so hard to watch. They both bear so much. He's known this for a long time. But he's never seen it on display. Not like this.

Jack kisses Victor's hand and turns back to Adam. "Sorry about the tears, kid. You'd think I just won Miss America. The point is, you don't get used to it. But you do learn some things. You learn how to sit with someone when they're scared. You figure out what someone recovering from pneumonia might want in their fridge. You learn about thrush, and meningitis, and toxoplasmosis."

"Toxo," Adam says.

"Yep. It's not a good thing to get. It can lead to brain infections."

"Did you know you can get it from cat shit?" Victor says. "I mean cat *feces* of course. Where are my manners?"

Adam thinks about Clarence. "Really?"

"Don't worry," Jack says. "You're healthy, so your immune system would take care of it. But if your T cells are down, it can be real trouble."

"You know a lot."

"Believe me, we'd rather not know so much. We'd rather fill our brains with vacation plans and Academy Award predictions and good old-fashioned gossip about who's doing who."

"Don't lie to the boy," Victor says. "There's plenty of room for gossip."

"Good point," Jack says. "We can walk and chew gum at the same time. Besides, a dish of hot gossip is just as restorative as a bowl of chicken soup. Scientific fact."

Victor smiles. "The part I hate the most is when you're helping take care of a friend, you never know if you're helping them get better, or just helping them die a little less miserably. Usually it's the latter. You always know that no matter how much you do, it won't be enough."

Angus yells over. "Three cheeseburgers for three sexy men!"

Victor jumps up. "I'll get them. Just have to wash up first." He disappears into the back.

Jack puts a hand on Adam's shoulder. "Did we overwhelm you?"

Adam shrugs and looks at his hands. "I love him," he says.

"Victor?"

"Callum."

Jack leans forward. "Does he love you, too?"

The question curls around Adam's neck. "I don't know. I thought so. Maybe I was wrong."

"It's hard to know for sure."

"Does Victor love you?"

"I believe so. Not because he tells me, which he does every day, but because I know him so well now. It's been twelve years together, and we've just grown into each other, you know?"

"How did you meet?"

"Out of the blue, like in that old Sister Sledge song about the greatest dancer at the disco. Only, we weren't on the outskirts of Frisco, we were at the Paradise Garage downtown. I don't think either one of us was looking for it. Maybe that's why it worked. No preconceived notions. We just saw each other, grabbed on, and we never let go."

Never let go, Adam thinks. He looks past Jack, to the bar behind him. The two men in Yankees caps and the guy in the tan suit are all embracing one another and laughing uncontrollably.

"Adam, why do you think Callum could be at the hospital?"

Adam shakes his head. "I can't," he says, keeping his promise. "I can't say."

"I see," Jack says, clearly understanding. His face turns darker. "Were you careful together?"

"We followed the rules," Adam says, but even as he says it, he wonders. Did they? Does anyone really even know what the rules are? They keep changing. He bites the inside of his cheek.

"That's good," Jack says. "Do your parents know about him?"

"No. Why?"

"I bet they wonder."

"I just don't want to talk to them about it. I don't know why." The laughter at the bar has subsided, but the three men are still leaning on one another. Adam recognizes the limp, satisfied exhaustion that comes after an extraordinary bout of laughter. He's felt that way with Lily before. But it's been a long time.

"You know," Jack says. "It's hard for me to imagine having parents like yours. My folks haven't spoken to me in twenty years. Your parents are the opposite of that. But I know it's complicated. Gay children are always a mystery to their families. Always."

"What do you mean?"

"Because we can't tell them everything."

"I don't get it."

"Adam, have you ever been called names at school? Like queer, or fag, or whatever?"

"Yes," Adam says softly, unsurprised by how acknowledging this makes him feel ashamed.

"Did you tell your parents?"

"No way. That would be embarrassing."

"Why? You didn't do anything wrong."

"I don't know. They just wouldn't get it."

"Exactly. They wouldn't get it. They'd tell you to square up and be brave, or maybe they'd even call the school and complain, but they wouldn't get it. Not really. It's not their fault. They've never walked in your shoes, and they can't. But you know, they love you to the ends of the earth."

Adam bows his head. "Everything is so confusing."

"You can't do this alone, Adam."

"Do what?"

"Life."

"I have you and Victor."

"Yes," Jack says. "You have us. You will always have us."

Adam nods stiffly, but he wonders. *Will I?*

The three men at the bar are laughing again. Victor appears with three cheeseburgers. Angus follows with three beers. "Bottoms up," he says.

Adam wanted a Coke. But he doesn't say anything. He'll have the beer instead. Maybe two.

Tell me why you felt so small.

I was, like, twelve and I was listening to the radio while I was doing the dishes, and Cyndi Lauper came on. You know that song "She Bop"? I was singing along at the top of my lungs and shaking my ass all over the kitchen. I didn't even hear my father come in until he started cheering and clapping behind me. He was like "turn it up!" but I turned it off instead. Wait, that's not even the embarrassing part.

He asked who the singer was and I said Cyndi Lauper, and he said it was a great song. I was so surprised, because he was always more of a Paul Simon and Fleetwood Mac kind of guy.

The next week was his birthday, so I went to the record shop and spent eight dollars and fifty-six cents, almost a month's allowance, on the new Cyndi Lauper album and wrapped it in the funny pages for him. It was the first time I knew for sure what to get him for his birthday. I was confident. I already knew he liked it.

Mom had to go out of town so when it was time to celebrate his birthday, he was like, "Guys' night!" We rented an Indiana Jones movie and got submarine sandwiches from the deli. Mom left me money to go buy him a cake from the supermarket, so I got him a frozen Sara Lee pound cake and some vanilla ice cream and a can of Hershey's syrup. That was his favorite.

I was so excited when I handed him his present, because I

knew for sure he was going to love it. But when he unwrapped the funny pages and saw the record, his face collapsed. He looked like he didn't want to be there. He turned the record over, looking at Cyndi Lauper with her wild hairdo, and said, "Kind of a strange choice for guys' night, don't you think?"

I said I thought he liked her and he said, "Well, then, I guess I do. Thanks, buddy."

Buddy. There was something about the way he said that word. He'd never called me that before. Not once. It was like he was reading the word from a script someone just handed him. Like he'd just been informed that "buddy" is what a father is supposed to call his son. A real father. A real son. He looked ashamed, as if by not knowing this code until now, he'd failed us both. As if I wasn't his son, but his fault.

He asked if he should play the record and I said no, let's just watch the movie. Later on when he cut the cake I took a slice, but I didn't want it. I tipped it into the trash when he was in the bathroom. I just wanted to forget the whole day.

BEN

Ben plans to say goodbye to Justin at Canal Street and turn back toward Gil's, but when they get to the intersection, Justin is in the middle of a story, so Ben keeps walking with him.

"I only had five bucks left after paying the cover," Justin is saying, "so I flirted with this guy who bought me a vodka tonic, but it turned out that he was there with his boyfriend so I ditched him. Anyway, Candis Cayne and Girlina performed, and Mona Foot. She was so fierce. Connie Girl was supposed to be there, too, but I didn't see her. I didn't get home until five and of course I had to be at a shoot by nine. I wanted to die. But a drag show at Boy Bar is worth it. You know what I mean?"

"I've never been there."

"Really?" Justin sounds surprised. "How old are you, anyway?"

"Eighteen."

"Really? I thought you were my age. I'm twenty-one. But sometimes I feel like I'm thirty."

"What do you mean?"

"I mean, I feel like I've done everything already. I've been going out every night since I was, like, fifteen. Since the Private Eyes days. Danceteria. I just get tired of it, you know? But then I'm like, you know what? I'm young. I'm supposed to be going out! And so I go back out."

"I know what you mean," Ben lies. He doesn't know what Justin means at all.

They walk all the way up the west side to the Christopher Street pier. They stop and look across the river, out toward Jersey City, glowing in the last rays of the sun. A group of guys is gathered way out at the end of the pier, spinning and vogueing to music Ben can't hear.

Justin leans up against a concrete road divider a little farther up. "Do you want to smoke a joint? I have pinner in my wallet. Just keep your backpack on in case we have to run."

Justin lights the joint, inhales, and hands it to Ben. Ben takes a puff and feels a tingle in his feet. It travels up to his head. The warm breeze coming off the river feels nice.

"Where are you from?" Justin asks.

"I live in Tribeca," Ben says.

"Are you kidding? No one lives in Tribeca."

"I do. But I want to move to the East Village." He takes another puff, stifling a shallow cough as he exhales.

"I live on Avenue C and Second Street. Right next door to the World. You know that club? You should go there one of these days, too."

He hands the joint back to Justin. "I've never really been to any clubs at all."

"Why not?"

"I don't know."

"This is New York," Justin says. "If you want to do something, all you have to do is do it."

Ben isn't sure what Justin means, but he likes the sound of it. He likes being here with Justin.

"Shit," Justin says, looking at his watch. "I have to jump. See you at another shoot soon, okay?"

"Okay," Ben says, smiling dreamily at Justin.

"You're cute," Justin says, and it's like a gust of warm wind sweeps through Ben's body. He opens his mouth to say something back, but what? It doesn't matter. Justin is already gone.

You're cute lingers in Ben's ears. Right now, he almost believes it. It feels good.

ADAM

After their beers—Adam has three—Jack and Victor invite him for a show-tune sing-along session at Marie's Crisis, the piano bar over on Grove Street, but Adam says no thanks. He's buzzed from the beers, unsettled, and would rather go sit by the river. It's his favorite place to be on summer evenings.

He stumbles down Christopher Street, past the string of gay bars that line it. Music follows him. First Jody Watley, whose voice spills out from Boots & Saddle, then Alannah Myles, singing about black velvet at Ty's. Lisa Lisa is wondering about taking you home from the Two Potato, while Madonna's busy expressing herself at the Dugout. Adam sings along with all of them.

He crosses the West Side Highway and scrambles over a barrier. He crosses a stretch of potholed asphalt to the head of the Christopher Street pier. It's crowded as it always is on warm evenings, people talking and dancing and cruising, radios playing La India and Ten City.

Adam is happy to be outside but he wants solitude. He walks up to the Jane Street pier, where no one ever goes because it's not paved over. He slips through an opening in the chain-link fence set up to keep people off—he doesn't care because no one cares—and steps onto the crumbling structure, a tumble of rotting wooden planks and pocked concrete riddled with holes that open straight down to the water. He walks carefully to avoid falling through, but also to keep from squishing the little weeds growing between the planks. They work so hard to survive out here. In the fading light, they seem almost beautiful to Adam.

He scoffs at the thought. It's no wonder Callum disappeared. Who'd want to go out with a boy who cares about weeds? What a joke.

He reaches the end of the pier just as the last band of orange fades from the horizon. He sits at the edge with the city at his back. He fixes his gaze on the current in the river, watching its lumbering, powerful crawl downstream to the harbor, and into the ocean beyond. Adam tries to imagine a power strong enough to stop it. What would it take to reverse the Hudson River? What would it take to stop the tide? What would it take to change everything?

Thoughts bounce like pinballs through his head, crashing and knocking against his skull. *I love him. He hates me. I want him. He ditched me.* They multiply, swell, press painfully against his brain. If only he could crack the bone of his skull, he thinks. Just a little, just enough to relieve some pressure. If only he could open an exit. If only he could force them all out.

The sound surprises him. It comes slow at first, like gathering clouds in his chest, but when it hits his throat, it explodes, like thunder. *AAAAAAHHHHHHHH!*

It feels good to shout, to empty his lungs. So he does it again. *AAAAAHHHHHHH!*

And again, and again, each time releasing another thought, another image, another stupid fantasy, another useless wish, another humiliating regret. One by one, shout by shout, he blasts them out and away. No more Callum! Shout! No more love! Shout! No more sex! Shout! No more anything! Be empty! Shout!

AAAAAHHHHHHHH!!

BEN

Ben is watching the boy at the end of the pier, shouting. They aren't threatening shouts, or frightening shouts. They are mournful, sorrowful shouts. Barbaric yawps over the roofs of the world, to quote Walt Whitman, who Ben had a little phase with when *Dead Poets Society* first came out last year. (In retrospect, it was mostly just a crush on Ethan Hawke.) Ben listens until the shouts subside and the boy is quiet again. Ben remembers, through the haze of Justin's joint, the last line of Whitman's yawp poem: *I stop somewhere waiting for you.*

I stop somewhere waiting for you.

It's getting harder to see him in the dark. Is the boy leaning over the water? Is he leaning too far? Ben walks carefully toward him, watching his feet on the uneven, splintery planks.

You shouldn't be doing this, he thinks. That guy is none of your business. Turn around.

But Ben ignores his thoughts. They sound too much like Gil.

Soon he's near enough to see the boy's shoulders moving up and down. Is he crying? Ben stops a few feet away. He waits a moment. He looks around. No one else is out this far. No one else has heard the boy. No one else is paying attention. He really should go. He should leave this boy alone. But no. Wait. There's something familiar here. He looks around again. No one is near.

He turns back to the boy, startled to see that the boy is staring at him now, with angry eyes. Ben blinks in recognition. He knows those eyes. The eyes of the boy in the Mount Rushmore T-shirt. He's seen this boy before. He knows this boy.

"Who are you?" the boy demands. "What do you want?"

Ben points at himself. "Me? No one. I'm no one."

The boy turns back to the river. "Same here."

Ben takes another tentative step forward. "I thought I heard you yelling."

The boy doesn't answer.

You should be careful, Ben tells himself. You don't know this boy. You don't know this pier. It's dark out here. He imagines Gil, shaking his head in disappointment. He decides to stay.

But look at him. He's hurting. Even in the dark, you can see that. He's hurting, and he's alone. Maybe he needs something. Maybe it's something you have.

"You can sit if you want," the boy says.

Ben sits.

ADAM

The boy in the black baseball cap is still sitting here next to Adam. He wonders why, but he doesn't ask. He keeps his eyes on the river, watching it darken, first deep green, then charcoal, then black. Its swirls reflect flickers of light from the city behind them.

The boy's presence should bother him, Adam thinks, but it doesn't. It feels something like natural, like his arrival here is logical, planned, scripted. Like it has a reason.

"I'm Ben," the boy says after a while.

But what is the reason?

"Adam," Adam says. "What are you doing out here?"

"Nothing." The boy, Ben, takes off his glasses. Adam glances over. He sees a flash of light in his eyes, like a glint in the river.

"What are you listening to?" Adam asks, pointing at the headphones around his neck.

"The Cure."

"Which one?"

"'Lovesong,'" the boy says. He hands Adam his headphones. "Here."

Adam positions the scratchy speaker pads over his ears and Ben presses PLAY. Guitar, keyboards, drums all start at once, a resolute beat under a minor-key melody. And then Robert Smith's voice, so full of sadness, or madness, singing about love holding true across distance and time and complications. Adam lies back on the concrete. He closes his eyes and lets it seep into him.

The music fills the spaces he'd emptied out with his shouts. It creates shapes, colors, a vision, Callum. He's behind Adam's eyes now, listening with him, here. Adam watches him sway forward, and back, and forward again, measured and deliberate with the music. Adam reaches for him, and Callum reaches back, touching his hair, smoothing it, tending him.

The touch is so warm. Adam closes his eyes even tighter, grasping for Callum's shoulder, neck, beautiful face. *Come*, he thinks, cradling his hand around Callum's head, pulling him close. *Come. Be with me.* He leans closer, closer, closer.

Kiss him, Adam. Feel his lips on yours. Tighter. Tighter. Again.

Silence. The song is over. Adam opens his eyes. He sees his hand around the boy's neck, feels his head in the boy's lap, and his mind is suddenly, searingly, desperately clear again. This is not Callum. No. No!

Adam tears off the headphones and leaps to his feet.

"That did not just happen. No. That did not happen."

The boy whispers, "Are you okay?"

"No!" Adam swats his hand away.

"I'm sorry," the boy says.

Adam turns and starts to run, fast, faster than he's ever run before. He stumbles over a split beam, losing his balance, rolling onto a patch, crushing them. *Get up*, he thinks. *Move!* Up to the head of the pier, through the chain-link fence, over the barriers and up to the edge of the busy West Side Highway. Don't stop. Faster! He darts into the road. A car screeches, and another swerves, but Adam doesn't slow. He races forward, sprinting through the traffic and across the street and into the city. Keep running. Keep running. It doesn't matter where you run to. It doesn't matter where you go.

BEN

Ben only follows for a few steps before Adam disappears up Jane Street and into the shadows of the city. In seconds, he's gone. Just like that. Ben is alone again.

He picks up his backpack and wipes his glasses on the hem of his shirt to clean them. He pulls on his headphones and turns toward the city, watching his feet as he walks, careful not to trip on the crumbled surface. The last thing he needs is another scrape for Gil to be concerned about.

He turns up the music in his ears, which is why he doesn't hear them coming. He doesn't see them coming. He doesn't know even what's happening when he's already falling, spinning through the air, his hands outstretched. His forehead glances off the concrete barrier, and he twists onto the pocked concrete, landing hard on the ground. The sharp, intense disorientation of pain takes his breath. Panic shoots through him. What's happening?

Instinctively, he coils into himself, hiding his head in his arms. The men above him, two of them, no, three of them, prod at his body with their feet.

Is he alive? They laugh. He coils tighter.

Dunno, man, you might have killed a queer. They laugh louder. They prod again.

Dude, you killed him! They laugh.

It's not my fault! He was in the way. They laugh some more. And then they turn and walk off, forgetting him, leaving him behind like litter. Like trash. Like nothing.

Ben doesn't move. He wonders how far away Adam is. Probably just a couple of blocks. He hopes he's farther. He hopes he didn't see what just happened. He hopes he didn't hear them laughing.

In a minute or two, Ben will feel the wetness on his forehead. It will be blood, of course, seeping across the bridge of his nose and into the corner of his eye. He'll taste the blood when it reaches his lip and he'll think it doesn't taste so bad. He won't stand up. He'll just move a little closer to the barrier. He'll lean up against it and sit for a while. He'll be all right here in its shadow. He won't be in the way.

Four

MAY/JUNE 1990

What I feel has got to be real.
—Jomanda, "Don't You Want My Love"

ADAM

Adam checks the Post-it note in his hand one more time. Scrawled in his own jittery writing, it says, *Callum, Room 707, St. Hugh's*. He'd written it with shaky hands when Callum called this morning.

Room 707 isn't hard to find. It's right there, the fourth room on the right after you step off the elevator, and inside is Callum. Beautiful Callum, propped up in a bed that Adam can already see is too short for him. He has dark circles around his eyes and his curls are matted on one side. He's got an IV in one arm and hospital bracelets on both wrists, and his gown is lopsided, bunched on one side as if he'd twisted it while sleeping but hasn't bothered to fix it. He doesn't even seem to notice. His face is pulled into an expression of intense concentration as he makes marks on a notepad, as if he's not in a hospital at all, but in a classroom. Is he writing words, or music? Adam can hear the scratches of his pencil against the paper. They echo off the hard floors and walls. It's funny how such tiny noises—the squishy footsteps of an orderly, the distant chime of an intercom—can sound so much louder in a place like this.

Callum looks up, and his face brightens. "Adam," he says lazily. "You brought my flowers."

"I promised," Adam says, laying the fresh bunch in Callum's lap. He wants to yell, and shout, and scream about how Callum made a promise, too. How Callum promised no more secrets. But he's in a hospital bed. How can you yell at someone in a hospital bed?

Adam grasps the aluminum guardrail that keeps Callum from falling out of bed, and jerks it up and out to lower it. He leans down and rests his cheek on Callum's chest. He listens for his heart.

"I thought you didn't want to see me anymore."

Callum rests his hand on Adam's head. "I'm sorry," he whispers.

"You promised no more secrets."

"I know."

"Tell me what happened," Adam says.

"Shh," Callum whispers.

"Why are you whispering?"

Callum points to the curtain hanging from a track in the middle of the ceiling, pulled across to divide the room. There's another patient on the other side.

"Same old story," Callum repeats. "PCP."

"But it came on so fast."

"Maybe it had been building up for a while and I didn't pay attention. I had a headache that morning but I didn't start feeling really bad until I was uptown. I took some aspirin and finished my shift but when I got back home, I could tell something was wrong."

"Why didn't you call me? I could have brought you here."

"It was so late. I didn't want to wake you. I thought they would just give me something to take and then send me home, or maybe just keep me for a night. But in the ER, I had a bad reaction to the antibiotic they gave me. It made my fever worse and screwed up my breathing. That's when they moved me to Intensive Care. I've mostly been asleep since then."

A thought grips Adam. "Did you catch it from me?"

Callum smiles. "No, sweet boy. Not from you. It's caused by a fungus in the air. In other words, there is a fungus among us."

"I hate you."

"No you don't. By the way, you don't have to fear the fungus. You have a strong immune system, so you can knock it out without even noticing it."

"When can you get out of here?"

"It won't be long. My doctor had me take some tests earlier. I just have to wait for the results."

"What kind of tests?"

"The usual. They want to see if I'm pregnant."

Adam stands up and swats him on the shoulder. "I'm serious. What did they do to you?"

"A bunch of stuff. Blood tests, X-rays, I can't remember. I tried to tell my doctor that I'm fine but she wouldn't listen. She wants more tests."

"I'm on her side," Adam says. He unwraps the flowers and drops them into the plastic pitcher on the windowsill. "I will stay here with you until you get out. I can sleep right here." He drops into the chair next to Callum's bed, landing with a *whoosh* on its yellow vinyl upholstery. He curls his legs underneath him, leans his head back, and pretends to snore.

"You'll get a crick in your neck," Callum says.

"I don't care."

Adam takes Callum's hand and for the next hour or two or three they talk softly about nothing. Someone brings a lunch tray of macaroni salad and applesauce and cheesecake. When Callum wheels his IV into the bathroom so he can pee, Adam remakes his bed. "I gave you hospital corners," he says, and they laugh, but quietly so they don't disturb the patient behind the curtain.

Callum falls asleep and Adam sits and watches. It will be all right, he tells himself. Callum won't be here long. He's been down this road before. He'll be better by Saturday. He'll be well enough to go to the movies. Maybe even Central Park.

Later they bring Callum's dinner, mashed potatoes and creamed chicken. Callum makes a face at the creamed chicken, but Adam makes him eat it.

"I miss my music," Callum says after he finishes.

"I'll go get it for you. I'll go get it right now. I'll get all of it."

"No. You can bring it tomorrow if you want, but just a couple of tapes. And when you come, you can't stay long, okay? I don't want you to be around all of this."

"All of what?"

"This." Callum points at his IV. "And this." He points at his chart. "And that." He points at the bedpan on the hook. He points at the curtain divider. He points at the doorway to the hall, and to the man wandering down it in bare feet, pulling an IV pole behind him. "All of it."

"I don't care," Adam says.

"I do, and I'm bigger than you. You have to do what I say. And I say it's time for you to go home to bed. Let a man get some sleep, would ya?"

"I'm shaking, Stretch Armstrong," Adam says. "By the way, what's my phone number?"

Callum recites it perfectly.

"If you move to a different room or anything, call me. No excuses."

"Yes, sir."

"I'll be back in the morning."

"There's a key to my apartment in my backpack there."

"Say my phone number again."

Callum says it backward.

"Smart guy."

"You won't forget my music, right?"

Adam takes Callum's fingers and presses them against the inside of his elbow, Callum's spot. "I won't forget anything."

He kisses Callum's cheek, and his forehead, and his nose. At the door, he smiles and waves goodbye. At the elevator, he smiles and says thank you to the nurses standing there. Downstairs, he says thank you to the attendant at the information desk. It's not until he's back out on the sidewalk that his body convulses and doubles over, and he has to steady himself on a NO PARKING sign to keep from falling.

BEN

Gil's movements are precise and confident as he sits across from Ben in the bathroom and sews the stitches into Ben's forehead, just above the eyebrow. He'd applied an analgesic to dull the pain, but each stitch feels like a snakebite to Ben. He balls his fists as tightly as he can, digging his fingernails into his palms to distract from the sting on his face. He doesn't complain. Not with the mood Gil's in.

"What were you doing over there in the first place?" Gil asks. His voice is stiff and severe.

"Walking," Ben says.

"Walking," Gil repeats.

"Yes. Walking. After the shoot with Rebecca."

"The shoot was in the Financial District. That's nowhere near the piers."

Ben doesn't respond. He glances over at the mirror to look at his wound, but without his glasses he can't see himself.

"Keep your head still," Gil says.

Ben can't explain everything that happened last night because he is still trying to understand it himself. After he got home and cleaned himself up, he sat on the floor watching *Headbangers Ball* with the sound off, blotting his forehead over and over with paper towels, hoping that the split would scab over on its own.

"If you weren't on the pier, this wouldn't have happened," Gil says. "They go looking for trouble on the piers."

"It could have happened to anyone," Ben says.

"I wonder," Gil says, and it sounds like an accusation. He snips the final thread. "Thirteen stitches. Unlucky number, but you're lucky as hell that this is the worst of it. No concussion."

Ben touches his fingers to the fresh stitches, testing the tender flesh. He winces.

"Don't touch it," Gil says. He tapes a clean square of gauze over the wound. "Change this in twelve hours. I can trust you to do that, at least. You've had practice."

"Yes," Ben says, ashamed. His head throbs.

"Take a Tylenol if it hurts. Try to sleep. Don't get it wet today. I have to go to work."

Gil zips up his little home medical kit, washes his hands, grabs his messenger bag, and leaves for work without another word.

Ben won't go out today. He won't go out tomorrow, either, or the next day. He'll stay in his room. He'll watch television in the dark. He'll fall asleep reading magazines. He'll wonder who he's going to be in ten years. He'll think about Adam. He'll think about Adam a lot.

ADAM

Adam studies his reflection in the mirrored walls of the elevator at St. Hugh's. He's wearing a black ACT UP T-shirt with a pink triangle on the front, over the words SILENCE=DEATH. Jack and Victor gave it to him when he told them he'd found Callum. *Wear it and you'll feel brave*, they'd said.

He can't tell, from visit to visit, what to expect when he gets here. Sometimes Callum seems better, sometimes worse.

"How are you feeling?" he asks this morning.

"I'm all right, for a Monday."

"It's Tuesday," Adam says, trying to sound cheerful. It's not easy. Callum looks dull today, like his blood's been drained away.

"What happened to Monday?"

"You slept through it."

"You were here?"

Yes, Adam was here. Of course Adam was here. He's here every day now. This is what he meant when he said he wanted to stick around. He didn't know it then, but sticking around means trying to cut Callum's hair with a pair of scissors borrowed from the nurses' station. It means getting a BLT for him on the days the cafeteria is serving that creamed chicken. It means becoming deeply involved with the characters on *Days of Our Lives,* wondering if Bo and Hope would survive the shipwreck of the *Loretta*, and then, when they did, whether they'd ever escape the evil clutches of Ernesto Toscano.

There's a knock at the doorway and a woman in a white lab coat enters the room. She has curly hair and a stethoscope around her neck, and short fingernails painted deep purple. She nods quickly at Adam, who steps out of the way.

"Good afternoon, Mr. Keane." She pulls back the curtain in the middle of the room to reveal an empty bed. "How about this single room? Nice to have a little extra space, isn't it?"

"Hi, Dr. Nieves," Callum says. "It's great. Can I go home now?"

Dr. Nieves takes Callum's wrist in her hand, then feels his

forehead. She disconnects his IV bag and replaces it with a fresh one.

"That's not something he's allergic to, is it?" Adam says.

Dr. Nieves doesn't answer Adam, but stays focused on Callum. "Friend of yours?" she asks.

"Better than that," Callum says.

"Okay to talk freely?"

Callum nods.

"Don't worry, Mr. Keane." She speaks slightly louder than before. "Your allergies are noted on that glamorous wristband you're wearing. This is just a mild sedative to help you rest. I want you to knock this thing out once and for all. Best way to do that is sleep."

She feels under his chin. Callum winces.

"Tender?" she asks.

He nods.

"Stubborn things," she says. She pulls his blanket over his bare feet. "Don't you have socks?"

"Yes," Adam says from behind her. "I got him three new pairs on Fourteenth Street."

"Looks like I'm covered," Callum says to her. "When can I go home?"

"Let's see how things look tomorrow when we have your test results. Oh, wait. I won't see you tomorrow. It's my day off. I'm going to the shore with my girlfriend. Or as she calls it, the Dinah Shore."

"That sounds fun."

"Too early in the season, if you ask me. I'll probably spend the day shivering in sweats."

"Don't get hypothermia," Callum says.

"Deal." She turns to Adam, finally making eye contact. "I'm Dr. Nieves. What's your name?"

"Adam."

She clicks her pen and gestures to the door. "Can I see you in the hallway for a moment, Adam?"

Adam follows her out, feeling like he's just been asked to stay after class.

"It was very good of you to speak up about the antibiotic," she says. "Patients always do better when they have an advocate. Keep it up."

"He told me about what happened last time. He said it made him really sick."

"Did he?"

"What is that about?"

"I'm not able to discuss any specifics of Mr. Keane's case with you," Dr. Nieves says.

"But you just did. In there."

"No, I only spoke to him, and only after making sure he was cool with it. Remember?"

"Oh," Adam says.

"He can tell you anything he wants, but not me. That's a line I won't cross. If you've got questions about his treatment or status or anything related to his health, the best person to ask is him. Make sense?"

"I understand."

"Cool shirt, by the way. I have one just like it. Do you know the story behind the pink triangle?"

"I never thought about it," Adam says.

"You should look it up." She nods, tucks her pen behind her ear, glances at her clipboard, and enters the next room. "Mr. Jacobi, how are you? Great tiara."

Adam returns to Callum's bed.

"What test results was she talking about?" Adam asks.

"Did you know that you're the cutest boy in the universe?"

Adam can't help beaming. He'll press more about the scan later, but right now he just kisses Callum's forehead. "Why don't you sleep for a while?"

"I'm not sure I have a choice with whatever she just shellacked me with."

Adam slides the new socks onto Callum's feet, then sits in the yellow chair and takes his hand. They rub their thumbs together until Callum's eyes close. After a minute, he shudders, and his eyes pop open again, startled. He stares at Adam for a moment, then the ceiling.

"He wasn't here when I woke up this morning," Callum says.

"Who?"

Callum points at the empty bed. "They took him away in the middle of the night. I don't know where. He's just gone."

"Shh," Adam says, leaning forward and resting his chin on the guardrail. "They're not going to take you away in the middle of the night. I'll beat them up if they try."

There's a tear on Callum's lower eyelid. It shines.

"You should go," Callum says. He closes his eyes again. The tear squeezes out onto his cheek.

"Not yet," Adam whispers. He gathers Callum's tear on his finger, to save it.

Tell me about the heart you broke.

It was in seventh grade when I took Monica to Skate City. Actually, if you want to get technical, Monica took me. I didn't want to go, but it was Sadie Hawkins day or whatever they call it, and you didn't want to be the only person who didn't go on a date. You never wanted to be conspicuous that way.

I already knew how to roller skate pretty well because I had a secondhand pair of skates, bright blue with orange wheels and a brake on the toe. Remember those? I taught myself how to skate in the carport. I could spin, do crossovers, you name it. Then one day these ninth graders rode up on their BMXs and started laughing at me. They told me that I must be a girl because boys don't roller-skate for fun. They only do it if they think they can get in a girl's pants that way. One of them pretended to be Eddie Murphy doing that one skit about how he has nightmares about gay people. You know, the one where he imitates Mr. T? Hey boy, you look mighty cute in them jeans. I laughed, because I wanted them to think that I liked Eddie Murphy, too, but they just rode off, laughing and yelling "fag" as they went.

Anyway, I said yes to Monica and we went to Skate City. I didn't bring my own skates. I rented the crappy ones there and pretended that I didn't know how to skate. After a few laps, the fog machine started up for couples' skate. Monica said we were supposed to hold hands. A couple of times she skated backward in front of me and put her arms around my neck like we were supposed to kiss.

So I kissed her and she got this big, excited smile on her face. I freaked out and let go of her and told her that it didn't mean that we were dating or anything. Maybe that was mean but I didn't want her to think something was true when it wasn't. She skated off the rink and went to the pay phone to call her father. I felt bad all the rest of that weekend but when I went to apologize to her on Monday, she said she didn't care. But that was the last time we ever talked.

Maybe I didn't break her heart after all.

BEN

Ben stands outside Charivari on Fifty-Seventh Street. He's come uptown to apply for a stockroom assistant position at the famous high-end clothing store because he knows he'll never be free of Gil until he gets a regular job. Shoots with Rebecca won't cut it, and when he saw the ad in the *Village Voice* classifieds this morning, he decided to come uptown and apply. Maybe they'll look past the patch of gauze on his forehead and give him a chance. He puts on a black button-down shirt and wrestles his hair into a clean side part.

The storefront spans several large windows, and before he goes inside, Ben takes his time studying the merchandise on display. He sees an acid-green Versace raincoat, a striped yellow-and-black Issey Miyake suit, a lace Moschino bustier, a pair of Gaultier track jackets with giant chevrons. He lingers longest over a boxy black neoprene suit by Helmut Lang. He recognizes it from this month's *L'Uomo Vogue*. He'd love to try it on.

But then he sees his own reflection in the window. The gauze on his forehead is discolored, like dried blood. He can't go into Charivari like this. He could name every label on every item of clothing in the shop but it wouldn't matter. He looks like a skinny, strung-out teenager who doesn't know anything. He takes his baseball cap from his backpack and pulls it down low, wincing when it pinches his stitches. He heads back toward the subway.

At the corner Ben sees two men, one in jeans and a sleeveless T-shirt, the other in a pale blue business suit. They're kissing. Right there in the middle of the busy sidewalk. And not just a peck on the cheek. A real kiss, a romantic kiss, the kind of kiss that suggests there was much more happening before it, and there will be much more after. Their fingers are intertwined at their sides, the suited man on tiptoe to reach the taller man in jeans. They kiss so comfortably, so confidently, so utterly unworried about the pedestrians on the sidewalk who have to walk around them.

After a moment they part, and the man in the jeans hurries off. Ben stands and waits. This man in the suit just kissed another man in public. Surely someone will say something. Someone will shout at him. Any minute, a group of guys will come running around the corner and push him to the ground shout and whoop and *laugh* and leave him bleeding on the sidewalk. Isn't that how this works? He draws his shoulders up to his ears, bracing himself.

But no one shouts. No one comes running. No one seems to take any notice at all. The man in the suit just descends into the subway and New York City just carries on, shiny and busy and hopeful and alive.

ADAM

Adam received a postcard today.

> *Greece is beautiful. I'm eating too much food. I met a boy from Crete. He has the longest eyelashes I've ever seen and a moped.*

You don't have to wear helmets here. You should be here. Greek boys are better at you-know-what. Anyway, I hope you aren't having too much fun without me. Just kidding.

Your Best,
Best

PS: Brains, looks, money. I still love you.

The front of the postcard shows a brilliant orange sunset over a jade-green sea. *Naxos*, it reads. Adam looks it up in his atlas and lays his finger on the island. There, he thinks. There is a place where things are fine. Right there, see? Not like New York. Not like St. Hugh's. Callum is back in the ICU.

What would she say if she were here now? Their lives seem so different now. Adam spends every day at a hospital, chewing the inside of his cheek. Lily's on a beach.

Adam pins the postcard to his bulletin board, next to an eighth-grade photograph of Lily in a Boy George bowler hat and oversized I'LL TUMBLE 4 YA T-shirt. *I still love you, too, Lily*, he thinks.

It's late, but he can't sleep. He opens the copy of the *New York Mainstay* on his desk. Some guy on the corner was handing them out this afternoon and Adam never refuses a freebie on the street. You never know. It could be something useful. And even if it's not, well, you looked another person in the eye and said thank you, and that's worth something to you both.

The *Mainstay* is one of the more serious gay newspapers in the city. Adam usually sees it at work, where they keep a stack by the door next to the flyers and announcements and Learning Annex catalogs. He can't concentrate on it tonight, though. It's just a jumble of words. *Housing discrimination. Pharmaceutical gridlock. Viatical settlements. Queer Nation. Domestic partnership initiatives. National Institutes of Health. Needle exchanges. Patient rights. C. Difficile. Opportunistic infections. Cryptococcal meningitis. Wasting. Cytomegalovirus. Comorbidities. Power of attorney. Mathilde Krim. Maria Maggenti. Joseph Sonnabend. Douglas Crimp. T cells. AIDS. AIDS. AIDS. AIDS.* It dizzies him, but he will learn them all. Just as soon as he can concentrate. Just as soon as Callum is better.

In the back of the *Mainstay*, Adam finds a whole section of classified ads promising miracle treatments. There's an herbalist on Fourteenth Street advertising immune-boosting teas. An acupuncturist in Midtown who promises increased T cell counts after just three treatments. A specialist on East Twentieth Street promoting a medieval drink-your-own-urine therapy. A hypnotist on Second Avenue. A physical therapist in Hell's Kitchen. A "free-thinking, sex-positive virology enthusiast" in Turtle Bay. Adam knows better than to believe any of these. He knows there are no miracles.

But what about this ad here? It says that some vitamins can help boost immunity. Extra-potent zinc, or double doses of magnesium, or "pure" vitamin B6. Combine them just right, and you can change your prognosis. Exclusive consultation: $100.

Vitamins aren't so weird, Adam thinks. Maybe vitamins could help Callum. He counts the money in his top drawer, but he only has sixty-four dollars. He'll save up.

BEN

At the far end of the studio, two models Ben doesn't recognize are sitting at the vanity mirrors, deep *in process* with Derek and

Charles. A young woman is organizing a table of necklaces off to one side, and another is setting up a black seamless backdrop.

Rebecca sees him and sprints over. She's wearing a loose DAY WITHOUT ART/VISUAL AIDS T-shirt.

"I'm so goddamned happy to see you. The stylist is stuck on the Hampton Jitney. I already have the gowns here, but they look like hell and need steaming. I need shoes for each dress, but don't sweat the jewelry. The accessories editor is back there and she's handling that. Just, please, tell me which of these Speedy bags is from the newest Vuitton collection. No one can tell them apart and we can't fuck up this job. It's for the December issue and there's no time to reshoot. We have exactly seventy-five minutes before we lose the studio, so we need to jam." She takes his chin in her hand and turns his head to the side. "How is your face? Gil told me about the stitches."

"It's fine," Ben says, squirming out of her grasp. "December issue of what?"

"*Vogue*, baby. Motherfucking *Vogue*."

Ben's mouth drops. *Vogue* is the hardest magazine to break into, and the editors are notoriously finicky and tough. But everyone sees *Vogue*. Everyone sees every picture in *Vogue*. Everyone. This is a huge chance for Rebecca. He peels off his backpack and rubs his hands together.

She lowers her voice. "Listen, it's just a filler photo for a trend roundup in those few pages right before the well. The news is backless dresses. Not groundbreaking. But if we nail this, maybe we'll get a bigger job."

Ben points confidently at the Vuitton bags. "The one on the left is last year, 1989. The one on the right is new. You can tell by the rivets on the handle base. See? In relation to the stitching. Personally, I think the '89 version is chicer."

"Great," Rebecca says, pushing the 1989 bag aside. "Now, gowns. Go steam them. I can't shoot naked models."

Ben starts walking toward the dresses.

"Wait!" Rebecca shouts.

He turns back to her.

"The rivets? Really?"

"Yeah. The rivets."

"Thank sweet baby Jesus for you, Ben. I'm paying you double today."

Ben plugs in the steamer and goes to work on the gowns. One is an elegant satin sheath with a cowl back. It's pale gray, almost pewter in color. The other is a deep green chiffon minidress with a windowpane back. A little flimsy for a December issue, Ben thinks, but that's what couture overcoats are for. He's so glad neither dress has pleats or intentional creases, because that would take much longer. He runs the steamer gently across the fabric from inside, and the wrinkles fall away quickly.

Ben helps the models, Danica and Miwa, into the dresses. He chooses shoes for them. A silver stiletto for the gray dress, an oxblood mule for the mini. The oxblood will bring out the detail in the Vuitton clutch, Ben thinks, and jewel tones are perfect for a December issue.

The accessories editor, Brett, introduces herself and begins to hang necklaces over the models' necks, overloading them with chains and pearls and pendants in a way that would never happen in real life. It's a fantasy look, *editorial* as they say, and it emphasizes the way the dresses drape.

"I love that look," Ben says.

"Thanks," Brett says. "I'm ambivalent about it myself, but layering this stuff on gets more visibility for advertisers in the issue.

The sales team flips out whenever their accounts don't make it into the spreads."

Ben leads the models over to the set where Rebecca positions them for a few Polaroid tests.

"Backs to me, ladies, but look at each other so I get your beautiful profiles. And Danica, hold that bag where I can see it," Rebecca says. "Perfect. Ben, fix Miwa's shoulder strap, would you? It's twisted at the shoulder."

Rebecca clicks speedily through her roll, then repositions the models and clicks through a second. Brett asks for one more take, with fewer accessories. Soon Rebecca announces, "We've got it. Great work, everyone."

"Already?" Charles asks.

"Fastest shooter in town," Derek says.

"I'm not going to touch that one," Charles says.

Danica and Miwa change back into street clothes and say goodbye, leaving comp cards with Rebecca and Brett. Charles and Derek pack up and follow them. Soon it's just Ben and Rebecca left in the studio.

"Not yet," Rebecca says when Ben starts fitting her camera into the carrying case.

"What?"

"I want to test something. See where the light is coming in through the window? It looks like a sunbeam but it's actually a reflection off the building across the street. I want to see how it behaves on film. Go stand in it."

"Me?"

"Yes. Right there. No, a little more to your left."

He finds the spot. She raises her camera. He turns his face away, embarrassed.

"Oh, come on. Just look at me. Open your eyes. You don't have to smile." She snaps the shutter a few times, adjusts a setting, then snaps again. "Okay. Thank you. You're released."

Ben exhales, and they go back to packing up.

"So are you going to tell me about what happened? With your face I mean. Gil sort of told me, but no details."

It would feel good to tell Rebecca. There's no one else he knows who might listen. And so, while they fit the cameras and lenses into their little foam slots in their carrying cases, he tells her everything about that night, from the walk home with Justin to the strange, shouting boy, to his long trip back to Tribeca holding a wad of Kleenexes to his head the whole way down on the subway to keep from bleeding everywhere. He dripped on the floor of the train anyway. He felt bad about that. She doesn't interrupt, not even once.

"I shouldn't have talked to that boy," Ben says. "None of this would have happened if I hadn't sat down next to a complete stranger."

"Oh, screw that. You saw a human being in pain, and you sat down to help. I want to believe I would have done the same thing. And I would have kissed him, too, if he was cute. Was he cute?"

Ben shrugs.

"It wasn't your fault. You know that, right?"

He doesn't answer.

"Right?"

Ben starts to laugh. "I'm sorry," he says, covering his mouth.

"What's so funny?"

"I just—" He snorts. "I just can't believe—"

"Can't believe what? You can't fall out laughing and not share. What?"

"It was my first kiss," he says.

"Are you kidding me?"

"Ever!"

She leans back and looks up at the ceiling. "Pardon my French, but that fucking sucks!" She throws an arm around Ben and yells, "That! Fucking! Suuuuuuccckkks!"

Together, they crack up, wiping tears as they laugh.

When they catch their breath again, Ben says, "But, whatever. It doesn't matter. It's not like I'll see him again."

"Would you even want to?"

Yes, Ben thinks. *Oh, yes.*

ADAM

"Oh, thank god it's you," Victor says when Adam calls. "I need you. I'm flat on my back and we have people coming for drinks in two hours. Jack sashayed off to Jefferson Market for god knows what, and of course as soon as he shut the door behind him I threw out my back doing dishes and now I can't move. Doing dishes for god's sakes! How are you? Is everything okay?"

"I'll be right over," Adam says, seizing the opportunity to fill an empty Saturday afternoon.

"Bless you, my child."

Victor is true to his word. When Adam arrives, he is on the floor next to a glass coffee table, his head next to a faded pony-print chair with scratched chrome legs.

"I hate these popcorn ceilings," Victor is saying. "From down here it looks like we're in the claims department of a low-rent insurance office. Honestly, who invented these? Hello, darling."

"Are you all right?" Adam asks.

"Never better. Listen, babycakes. I need you to finish the dishes and put them away. I need you to take the trash downstairs and grab some folding chairs from the closet in the basement. The keys are on the counter. Oh, wait, first come give your Auntie Mame a good morning kiss."

It's after four in the afternoon, but Adam says, "Good morning," and kisses Victor's cheek.

"That's lovely," Victor says. "Now dishes." He points to the kitchen, separated from the main room by a clean but shabby island cluttered with dishes, a rotary telephone, and a stack of newspapers—the *Times*, the *Post*, the *Daily News*, the *Native*, the *Voice*, and the *Mainstay*.

Adam dives into the dishes, scrubbing and drying the plates, pots, pans, and coffee mugs and putting them away. He refills the sink with fresh water and soap to do the glasses, so they don't come out greasy. Then he wraps up the garbage and relines the bin with a new bag. He carries the refuse downstairs to the bin out front, and retrieves four folding chairs from the basement storage closet.

Jack arrives soon after Adam finishes his tasks, six plastic grocery bags hanging from his wrists.

"Adam!" he shouts, his deep, rich voice vibrating through the flat. Adam remembers being young, when Jack would sing to him whenever he and Victor were babysitting. He'd always wanted to be a musical theater star, but turned to public school administration after one too many failed auditions. "Good to see you, friend."

"Hi," Adam says, waving from the kitchen island, where he is straightening the newspapers.

"Six bags of groceries?" Victor asks from the floor. "Aren't we just doing drinks?"

"I thought I'd make my grandmother's smothered pork chops," Jack says. "Everyone loves them. Why are you on the floor?"

"Don't ask. But ixnay on the opschay. Half of these queens

coming over are on pre-Pride diets so they can take their shirts off at the march next month. Just nibbles and bits."

"Wait, that means you're on a diet, doesn't it? You didn't tell me."

"Are you saying I'm fat?" Victor rolls onto his hands and knees, then pulls himself up the side of the couch. "I need a shower. See you kids in a little while, when I'm gorgeous."

Jack watches Victor go, then turns to Adam. "Okay. People are coming at six. If we can't have pork chops, we can at least have meatballs. Some cheese and crackers. And I have a peach pie in the freezer. We'll bake that, too. Hit the oven for me, will you? Three-fifty. I'm glad you're here. Is everything okay?"

"Everything is fine," Adam says, not making eye contact.

Jack stops for a half moment to study Adam's expression. "Hm," he says. He hands Adam a carton of eggs. "Fridge, please."

"Who's coming over?"

"Oh, you know. Just family."

"Your family? I thought—"

"No. I mean our real family," Jack says. "You're staying, right?"

"No, that's okay. You have plans with your friends. Family I mean."

"You're staying," Jack says. "Let's start with the meatballs. Get me the big mixing bowl from the cupboard down there, would you? Throw the ground pork and ground beef in there. Oh, and I need two eggs, and the Parmesan cheese."

Jack orders Adam around the kitchen for the next forty-five minutes, and Adam's happy to have the direction. Occupying his mind and his hands keeps him from worrying too much about Callum. But oh, he is worried.

When the meatballs are finishing in the oven, Victor emerges from their bedroom, freshly showered and wearing only a pair of jeans. He holds up two shirts. "Blue or yellow?"

"Blue," Jack says without even looking up. "And how about some music, maestro?"

"Aye, captain," Victor says. He buttons up the blue shirt and slips a Sade CD into the player.

"Oh, Victor," Jack says at the first notes of "Smooth Operator." "You know I love Sade, but as Dorothy Zbornak said, how about something with a little octane? It's a party. Maybe some Janet? Whitney? Madonna?"

"Fine," Victor says, and soon Madonna is singing about how the sidewalks talk and how you better watch what you say. Jack bobs his head and swings his hips in time.

"Adam, you see that side table by the bookshelf? Do me a favor and move all the photographs off of it. You can tuck them onto the bookshelf for now. We need that tabletop free for drinks."

Adam starts picking up the photos, all framed snapshots of smiling young men. They're dancing at parties, playing paddleball at the beach, blowing out candles. A dozen photos, maybe more. "Are any of these guys coming today?" he asks.

"This is our memory corner," Victor says, picking up one of the photos. "This is Hector. I knew him growing up. He always wore leis to parties. And this one is Levi, who started every evening in a terrible mood but always ended it happier than anyone else. Over here is Martin, in the turtleneck. So handsy, that one. Remember, Jack?"

"Like an octopus."

Adam shivers, realizing that every photo is a dead man.

"Here's Kevin," Victor says. "Cuddly Kevin with the two dachshunds, and his boyfriend Joaquin, in the pinstripes. Joaquin was our Wall Street working girl. You should have seen his Celia Cruz drag. Oh, and look at Tony. Sweet little Tony who could barely grow a mustache. He knew Barbra Streisand's entire *Broadway Album* by heart. Not just the words, but all the little inflections and key changes."

"He looks so happy."

"We only save the happy pictures," Victor says. "I believe that angels smile."

Jack points to another photograph. "You see Michael there? In the balloon hat? He made an entire career for himself twisting balloons into animals at kids' birthday parties. He was crazy about kids. But when he tested positive, he quit. He was always afraid to be around kids after that, even though the science said that he was safe. Everyone wore a balloon hat to his funeral."

"That wasn't a funeral," Victor says. "That was a celebration of his life. We weren't invited to the *real* funeral, remember? None of us were."

"Well, it was a hell of a party. Adam, can you fill this bucket with ice from the freezer, and put these cocktail napkins over by the cheeses on the coffee table. People will be here any minute."

"Our friends are annoyingly prompt," Victor says. "Drives me bananas."

And then, just like that, the buzzer sounds. The first arrival is a slender man in a cabled pullover and long white scarf, which surprises Adam given how warm the day is. Next, a pair of bulging muscle boys in tight jean shorts. A young man in nerd glasses enters arm in arm with a man with salt-and-pepper twists. Everyone is hugging everyone else, double kissing cheeks, asking *how are you* like they mean it.

"Family," Jack whispers in Adam's ear. "Just like I told you."

The man in the long white scarf takes Victor's shoulder. "Vickie Sue, be a plum and bring me another sweater, would you? A cardigan perhaps, to drape over my shoulders? You know, just *so*."

"At once, your majesty. I'll fetch the ermine stole from the fur closet. Meanwhile, say hello to my beloved Adam. He's eighteen, so behave."

"Hello," the man says. "I'm Joe-Joe." He smiles from behind a pair of thick round glasses.

Adam recognizes the name. He'd been on Jack and Victor's list of people to visit in the hospital not too long ago. He shakes Joe-Joe's hand, surprised by how cold it feels. "I am very pleased to meet you," he says.

"The feeling is mutual, I'm sure," Joe-Joe says with a coy smile. He turns to Jack. "What lovely manners. Where did he learn them? I know it can't be from you."

"Oh, Adam," Jack says. "Don't be too polite to this one. Joe-Joe is a devil and he doesn't deserve it." He wraps his arms around Joe-Joe's pointed shoulders and squeezes so tight Adam's afraid he'll snap.

Victor returns with a sweater for Joe-Joe, then introduces Adam to Dennis, with the twists. He says, "Hello, young man," with an English accent. Carlos and Alexey, the muscle guys, say "hey" and smile.

Robert, with the nerd glasses, grins goofily and says, "Howdy-do." He hands Adam a flyer. "We're organizing a zap down at City Hall in a few weeks. Tell your friends, will you? The more the merrier."

"A zap?" Adam reads the flyer. *Demand fair housing for all! ACT UP, fight back! June 13.*

"Like a demonstration," Robert says. "Oh, if any of your friends are cops, don't tell them."

The buzzer sounds again, and Victor welcomes three women. Diane, with close-cropped hair and six earrings on each side; Lalita, with the brightest red lipstick Adam's ever seen; and Caryn, whose braids are tied back with a strip of black leather.

"Are we late?" Diane asks. "We were at squish-squish."

"You're right on time," Jack says. "But what is squish-squish? Sounds kinky."

"It's our volunteer gig," Lalita says. "We go to the Center every week to put together safe sex packets for distribution at clubs and bars and stuff. You know, little pouches with condoms, dental dams, how-to instructions. And squishy little packets of lube. Squish-squish."

"Is there any wine in this apartment or did you queens drink it all?" Caryn asks. "Lushes, every one of you."

"Oh, are we reading already?" Victor asks. "Jack, get this beauty some vino."

"We've been reading. The library is *open* today."

"Oh, honey, your books are overdue," Victor says.

Caryn throws her arms around Victor's neck. "You're my number one, you know that?"

Joe-Joe sits down on the couch next to Carlos and Alexey. "Did you two go out last night? Or did you spend the whole night at World Gym? Look at your pecs!"

"Oh, stop," Carlos teases, flexing. "We were at Sound Factory until seven or seven thirty."

"Baby, we didn't get home until nine," Alexey says.

"Ah, the Factory," Joe-Joe says wistfully. "You get there before two, you're too early. You leave before sunrise, you miss out on the best part."

"I thought nightclubs had to close at four," Diane says.

"Only if they sell booze," Alexey says. "You can only get water at the Factory, so they can stay open as long as they want. We never buy water though. It's like four bucks a bottle. We just drink from the fountain."

"Was Madonna there?" Victor asks.

"No, she's still on tour," Carlos says. "Blond Ambition, you know. Gaultier Gaultier Gaultier."

"I hear she's making a behind-the-scenes documentary of the tour," Caryn says. "I'd be psyched to see that."

"I haven't seen her at the Factory since that night Junior let her up into the DJ booth and she spent the whole set shining his flashlight on the voguers on the floor. Remember, Alexey? José and Luis were turning it *out* that night."

"Oh, Junior," Dennis says. "I want to like him. But he's no Larry Levan at Paradise Garage."

"Paradise Garage was sacred ground," Jack says. "Sacred *underground*. But that ride is over. Larry is in a class by himself, but he's off in Japan or someplace, so now we have Junior Vasquez."

"And Frankie Knuckles and Tony Humphries and François K," Dennis says. "Et cetera."

"All good," Joe-Joe says. "But you have to admit, there's nothing like the Factory right now. Have you been there, young Adam?"

Everyone turns to Adam. Their attention makes him timid. He shakes his head. "I haven't really been anywhere," he says.

"Is that my cue?" Joe-Joe asks. "Shall we go to the Factory?"

"Here we go again," Lalita says, smiling as she refills her glass.

Jack whispers to Adam. "Time for the Joe-Joe show. Just go with it."

"I'll get the lights," Victor says. "Eyes closed, everyone."

Adam closes his eyes, and Joe-Joe begins to speak.

"It's Saturday night," Joe-Joe says. "One or two in the morning. You've said goodbye to the friends you were hanging out with, and they've gone home to bed. But you're not done. What is sleep, when you can dance?"

"For inspiration," Robert says, and everyone giggles. "Get into the groove."

Joe-Joe continues. "You run home for a quick costume change and you head up to that unnamed neighborhood above Chelsea. You see a doorway there, and a small crowd. Downtown boys in baggy T-shirts, mustache men in camo tops, club kids in cartoon costumes, disco boys in disco shorts. No clones. Not many circuit queens. No one's here to cruise.

"You walk through a dim hallway toward the ticket window. You can feel a deep *thump, thump* coming up from the floor. It's not in your ears yet, it's under your feet, in your legs, creeping up your spine. You pay fourteen dollars at the window. If you have a jacket, you check it for two dollars more. You pass through a second door and follow a ramp down, trusting your instinct because it's almost too dark to see. The music grows louder, closer, deeper. You pass through a small room where you can barely see little groups of boys and girls in twos and threes and fours, just sitting, bobbing their heads, rubbing each other's shoulders.

"You press forward, turn another corner and BOOM, the music explodes around you, heavy industrial house beats that you feel in your bones, your blood, your cells. *THUMP THUMP THUMP THUMP.* You're almost knocked backward. Your eyes begin to adjust to the dark and you see you're in a vast space now, filled with pulsing crowd, people in every direction, every color, young and old, uptown and downtown, all stepping and jumping and moving in sync with the beat. You push into them, swaying, twisting, dancing. They make room for you, because there is always room.

"The lights above you flash, and the drums pull you deeper. You feel hands, bodies, breath, sweat, beautiful freaks in every direction, freaks like you, everyone dancing, posing, releasing, belonging. The song begins to crescendo and the strobe lights flash and Junior sets off a siren, and everyone's hands are in the air in defiance and determination and gratitude and sex and joy, and there's another crescendo, and another, and you just dance, emotion pouring like sweat because you know you're all here together, everyone, the living and the dead, tight, united, because if we all just dance together, feel together, rage together, release together, then maybe this place, this dark, beautiful place can become the only place in the world. Maybe, *maybe* we can survive together, no matter what they want to do to us out there. They don't know that their world is fake and ours is real. There is nothing but here, nothing but now, nothing but us, nothing but the music . . ."

Joe-Joe's voice begins to trail off.

"Nothing but the music," Dennis says.

"Nothing but the music!" Caryn shouts.

"The music!" Everyone raises their glasses.

After a minute, Victor turns a light on. Adam looks around. Joe-Joe has cast off his cardigan and is mopping his brow with the end of his scarf. Jack and Lalita are hugging. Dennis is wiping his eyes.

"Still got it, Joey Joe-Joe," Diane says.

"Oh, I miss the Factory," he says. "And the Garage. And the Saint. I miss all of them. Even the Roxy, and you know I never had the kind of hairlessness required for the Roxy."

"Why don't you come out with us next Saturday?" Alexey says.

"No, my Factory days are on hold. Can you imagine my walk of shame on these legs?"

"It was quite the walk home down Ninth Avenue this morning," Carlos says. "The parade of churchgoers in pastel sundresses was thick. The glares we got, honey. The *glares.*"

"In their defense, we looked like hell," Alexey says. "And the only name we got called was *goo-gobblers.* I honestly can't even take offense at that one. It's so goofy."

"I don't care about any of the slurs anymore," Dennis says.

"Like, do they think we haven't heard them all? The bigots need fresh material, if you ask me. But that would require creativity. Bigots don't have much of that. If they did, they wouldn't be so bigotty. There, see? I just created a new word. Creativity in action."

"Did you lose your shirt at the Factory again?" Robert asks.

"How did you know? Buzz ripped it off me during that Adeva song."

"Oh, I used to love those Sunday morning dirty looks," Joe-Joe says. "A badge of honor."

"I hope we never lose that outlaw feeling," Dennis says. "I know we all want progress, we all want gay rights, but I still want to hold on to that outsider vibe. It's so energizing, you know?"

"Double edges," Jack says. "It's complicated."

Victor puts in a new CD, Luther Vandross this time, and everyone goes back to chatting. But Adam is still lost in the Factory. He wonders if Callum's ever been there. Maybe they could go together sometime. After he gets better.

"Hey, by the way, where's Tim Ado?" Caryn asks. "He should be here."

"You didn't hear?" Robert says. "He went back to Detroit to stay with his sister."

The room is silent for a moment, and then Joe-Joe says, solemnly, "I didn't know."

"Oh, I hate that tired routine," Victor says. "The whole 'maybe it will be easier on my friends if I just disappear quietly so they don't have to watch me die' routine. The 'I want them to remember me when I was cute' routine."

"We don't know if that's why Tim went to Detroit," Jack says. "Maybe he's just more comfortable there. There are lots of reasons to go home, you know."

"Fine. if that's what Tim needs, all right. But I hate it when people disappear. I *want* to be there for them, you know? I want to help."

"It's better than the 'I'm going to dump my boyfriend because I feel guilty for being such a burden' routine," Robert says. "That's what Tim's boyfriend did to him before *he* died, remember?"

"The only routine I'm participating in is the 'running up my credit card on the way out' routine," Joe-Joe says. "This scarf? Barneys. Cashmere. And not from the sample sale, either. Full price."

"My routine is going to blow everyone's mind," Dennis says. "I'm gonna get that tattoo that William F. Buckley says everyone with HIV should be required by law to get."

"Now that's what I call bigotry," Diane says. "Let's go together. I'll get one, too."

They all laugh, except Adam. His head is spinning. He tries to raise his glass of ginger ale to his mouth, but his hand is shaking and he dribbles his drink on Joe-Joe's trousers. "Sorry," he says.

"Don't worry, sweetheart," Joe-Joe says. "But fetch me a napkin, will you?"

"Here you go," Jack says, handing him a paper towel.

Adam tries to help Joe-Joe blot the liquid, but when he shifts around he knocks the rest of his ginger ale onto the carpet. "Oh no," he says, his heart racing now. "I'm sorry."

"It's all right," Jack says. "That carpet's seen worse."

Adam picks up his glass and puts it on the kitchen counter. His face is hot, flushed with embarrassment. Everyone is looking at him. "I'm gonna get going," he mumbles.

"Are you sure?" Joe-Joe asks.

"Yes, I, um, I have some things I need to do," he lies.

Caryn walks across the room to give Adam a double kiss. "I hope to see you soon," she says.

"It was really nice to meet you," Adam says. "All of you."

"Come to the Factory with us one night!" Carlos says.

Adam nods, nervously. He offers a shallow wave and steps toward the door.

"I'll walk you out," Jack says. He smiles at the room, then follows Adam out into the hallway. "Are you all right, kiddo?"

Adam isn't sure how to answer. He doesn't know how he feels. Everything is a blur. Is Tim Ado going to end up in a framed snapshot on the bookshelf? Is Joe-Joe? Are Dennis and Robert and Carlos and Alexey and Jack and Victor? Is that what's going to happen Callum? Is that what's going to happen to Adam, too? He balls his hands into fists and stares at his shoes.

"I don't think he's getting better and I don't know what to—" Adam says. He won't look up. He doesn't want to cry. He whispers. "I don't know what to do. I don't know."

Jack takes Adam into his arms, pulling his head into his shoulders and surrounding him with his warmth. He sways from foot to foot, rocking Adam as the tears stream down.

"I know, Adam. I know. I've got you. I've got you."

Tell me a secret you never told anyone.

In sixth grade we had lunch period at 11:10 a.m. and it lasted for twenty-four minutes. I knew all the cafeteria staff by name. Ms. Slovinsky, Ms. Benedetto, Mr. Cordon. None of the other kids ever said hello. But I did, every time. "Here comes my favorite customer," Ms. Benedetto would say as I pushed my tray along the line. "I saved this dish of cobbler for you, because it's the biggest one."

My favorite was Ms. Johnson, because sometimes on pizza day, she'd only pretend to punch my free lunch card. "In case you need to come back for seconds," she'd whisper, and then she'd squeeze my elbow. "Such skinny little arms."

Once, Ms. Johnson brought me a paper bag filled with brownies that she'd made at home. "I put chocolate chips in them so that they'd taste good," she said.

But I forgot the bag of brownies on the bus. I felt so bad because I knew she made them special for me. I worried that the bus driver would tell her, even though they probably didn't even know each other.

I wrote Ms. Johnson a thank you note anyway, in a blue felt-tip pen on lined paper. "Thank you for the delicious brownies, Ms. Johnson. They were the best brownies I ever ate in my life." It was a lie because I hadn't even tasted a single brownie. I don't think she ever found out. I hope she didn't.

The next year I went to a new school for junior high. The first time I went through the lunch line I found out my mother hadn't registered me for free lunch. They took my tray away. All these girls in line behind me laughed.

I stopped going to lunch after that. I just went to the library during that period to wait it out. I don't think anyone ever noticed. None of my teachers said anything. I would be so hungry when I got home, so I would microwave a tortilla with cheese sprinkled on top. I put Lawry's Seasoned Salt all over it and then folded it over to eat while I watched General Hospital. I was really into Frisco and Felicia.

I never told my mother that she forgot to sign me up for the free lunch program. It would only make her mad.

BEN

Ben pulls on a pair of black jeans and a red T-shirt with a silk-screen on the front of David Bowie in full Ziggy Stardust glam makeup and spiky wig. He hooks his wallet to the new belt-loop chain he picked up on St. Mark's Place and slides it into his back pocket, letting the chain drop to the side. He lines his lids, grabs his backpack and baseball cap, and heads out. His destination is St. Hugh's, where Gil's finally going to take out his stitches. But first he wants to stop by Tower Records for the new Cocteau Twins CD.

He studies the shop windows in SoHo as he heads uptown. The bandage dresses at Alaïa, the checkerboard capes at Comme des Garçons, the band collar snap jackets at Agnès B. One day he'll have the money to shop in these stores. One day. He turns east on Prince Street.

The sidewalks get busier as Ben approaches Broadway, a mix of neat young women in black sleeveless turtlenecks, scruffy bike messengers with heavy chains around their shoulders, street vendors sitting at tables displaying sunglasses, sheets, socks, incense. Delivery drivers throw open the back doors of their trucks for offloading, dropping ramps with metallic thunderclaps onto the asphalt, loud enough to make Ben jump.

A taxi stops just in front of him on the corner, blocking his way across the street. He steps backward, out of the way. The door opens, and *oh my god*, is that Cindy Crawford getting out?

It is. Ben stares, gobsmacked. She's wearing a blindingly white oxford shirt with the collar turned up, its crisp edge just grazing her razor-like jaw. Her hair is pulled back into a sloppy chignon, sunglasses stacked on top. She's wearing faded jeans and even from here, several feet away and in the middle of busy lower Broadway, Ben can smell jasmine on her. She sees Ben gawking, and smiles.

"I love Bowie, too," she says, nodding at his shirt. Before he can answer she darts across the street and into Dean & DeLuca.

Holy shit. Ben just saw Cindy Crawford. The most famous model in the world. Right here. In person. It takes two cycles of walk signals before he's able to move on but when he does, it's with a new buoyancy. Today is a good day. Distracted, he forgets to stop by Tower Records.

He makes his way uptown, not rushing. What if Linda Evangelista or Karen Alexander is next? Good things happen in threes, right? He doesn't want to miss them.

When he's about a block away from St. Hugh's, he begins to hear the shouts. They're coming from a group of people gathered by the hospital's front door. Ben counts ten or a dozen of them, carrying signs on colorful posterboard and chanting something he can't quite make out. Is it a labor strike? You see those around every now and then.

As he gets closer, the slogans on the posterboards come into view. HOMOSEXUALITY IS SIN! LEVITICUS 18:22! MAN SHALL NOT LIE WITH MAN! AIDS IS GOD'S MERCY!

The chanting grows louder. "Dir-ty! Dir-ty! Dir-ty!"

They're blocking the way into the hospital. So annoying. Ben wonders if there's another door he should use, but decides that the best way in is straight through the shouters, so without stopping, he squares his shoulders and walks into them. They surround him as he walks through in his David Bowie T-shirt and eyeliner.

"Dir-ty! Dir-ty!"

They're protesting him. They're protesting Ben.

A woman, about Ben's mother's age with bottle-blond hair thrusts her pointer finger into Ben's face. "Dir-ty! Dir-ty!" Her expression is pure disgust, and she's screaming so hard she's spitting. A glob of saliva lands on Ben's chin, wet and gross. He flicks it off, then flips her off. He steps around her, elbows away a poster that reads ABOMINATION! and enters through the front door.

Gil is standing just inside at the window, watching the protestors from inside.

"Hey," he says.

"I just saw Cindy Crawford in SoHo," Ben says. "She looked amazing."

"Who?" Gil's still watching the shouting people.

"Cindy Crawford! She's a supermodel?"

"Okay," Gil says. "Sounds cool."

"Do you even know who she is?"

Gil puts his arm around Ben and leads him away from the window. He hands Ben a ten-dollar bill.

"Why don't you pick us up a couple of sandwiches in the cafeteria. I'll meet you in my office. You know where it is, right? Get a visitor tag first." Gil waves over to the receptionist, then points at Ben and makes a thumbs-up sign.

Ben brings two egg salad sandwiches up to Gil's office, where they eat in silence while Gil flips through a medical journal. When they finish, Gil takes Ben into a treatment room. Gil pulls a fresh sheet of paper from the roll above the treatment table. It crinkles under Ben when he hops up.

"I have been doing a lot of thinking," Gil says, snapping on a pair of latex gloves.

"Oh?" Ben says, cautiously, bracing himself for Gil to tell him he needs to move out.

"I want to tell you a story. It's not a story I'm proud of."

"Okay." Still tentative.

Gil removes the gauze from Ben's forehead, then dabs on a bit of analgesic gel. "When I was in tenth grade, I got suspended from school for fighting."

"Fighting?" Ben is surprised. Gil's always seemed strong and intimidating, sure. But not a fighter.

"*Fighting* isn't the right word. It was more like an attack. Me and two other guys cornered this kid Gordon in the school gym. We beat him up pretty bad." He takes a pair of steel scissors and carefully snips a stitch from Ben's face, removing it with a tiny tug.

Ben stares at the bridge of Gil's nose, just inches from his eyes. "I never knew that."

"We beat up Gordon because we thought he was different. We thought he was gay."

Ben narrows his eyes. "What?"

Gil snips another stitch.

"Like I said, I'm not proud. What we did was really, really bad. We got suspended for a week. But when my father, *our* father, found out about the suspension, he raised hell. He got a bunch of other parents to sign a petition to reverse the punishment. He told the administration that the real threat wasn't me or my friends, it was boys like Gordon. He was a bad element, and our reaction to him was natural. The school agreed. We went back with clean records. People high-fived us in the halls."

"Are you kidding?"

Snip.

"No, I'm not. And you know what? If that suspension had held up, if I'd had that stain on my transcript, I would never have gotten the scholarships that put me through college and medical school. I probably wouldn't even be a doctor right now."

"I don't believe that."

"It's true. You know those scholarships were the only way I could afford school. I deserved that punishment. The fact that I am sitting here right now, able to treat you or anyone else, is fucked up in a hundred thousand ways."

Snip. Each time Gil removes a stitch, it tugs at Ben's skin. It doesn't hurt, but it unsettles him, like Gil can see inside.

"Gordon knew what was happening that day and he knew he was going to have to endure it. He knew he couldn't win. But it wasn't because he was outnumbered, or because we were all bigger than him. It was because we didn't care. That's what the look on his face said. We were going to beat the shit out of him and *we didn't care*."

Ben struggles to hold his head still. Gil snips another stitch.

"Can I ask you something?" Ben says.

"Sure."

"When you were beating up Gordon, were you laughing?"

Gil drops his hands into his lap and lowers his head.

"It's okay," Ben says. "It doesn't matter."

"I have a lot to apologize for," Gil says. "But I want you to know that I believe in you. Even when I don't get it, or when we disagree, or when I'm just being a dick and can't admit it. I believe in you."

"I can be a dick sometimes, too," Ben says quietly.

"Look at me. As long as I have a home, you have a home. Okay? I love you, Ben."

I love you. Ben hasn't heard those words in a very long time and it's like they open a tap inside. He doesn't even feel the tears coming until they're already slicking down his cheeks and dripping off his chin. They come before he can stop them. *Stop them*, he thinks, turning away to hide his face from Gil. *Stop crying. Not here. Not in front of Gil. Never in front of Gil.* But the tears won't stop.

Gil drops his scissors to the floor and wraps his arms around Ben.

"Hey," he says. "Hey. It's okay, brother. It's okay."

After Ben quiets, he looks up to see that Gil's eyes are wet, too.

"I don't think I've ever admired anyone as much as I admired you today, Ben."

"Me?"

"And I bet you don't even know why. Which makes me admire you even more."

"What are you talking about?"

"I'm talking about the way you just walked right through those assholes at the front door. The way that woman was screaming in your face. I saw the spit. And you didn't even break stride. You just stepped through her like she was nothing. You just walked right in and started talking about Cathy Crawford."

"Cindy."

"What?"

"Nothing."

"And you flipped that woman the bird for a little flourish. Ben, do you even know how cool that was?"

Ben shrugs. "I had to get through."

Gil takes a new pair of scissors from the sterilizer and snips the last remaining stitch. He applies a little more gel, then places a fresh square of gauze over the scar.

"I'll change the dressing when I get home tonight. No peeking until then, all right? Tomorrow, no more bandage. You'll be as good as new."

Later, after Gil goes back to work, Ben peels back the bandage in the men's room to peek. He sees the scar over his eye. It will fade eventually, but it will never disappear. It will never be as good as new. Maybe that's okay. Maybe being good as new is overrated.

ADAM

"Good morning, sweetie," Adam's mother says when he shuffles out of his bedroom just after ten. "If you want coffee, you should brew a new pot. That one's been there since six thirty."

"Okay." Adam fills the Mr. Coffee pitcher with water and pours it into the machine.

"You've been scarce lately," she says.

"End of senior year. You remember how it is."

"That's what worries me," she says. "Listen, your father and I are going upstate this afternoon."

"For how long?"

"A few days. Pop has decided we need to take advantage of my parents' old camp up near Margaretville, which he insists on calling Margaritaville, because he thinks he's Jimmy Buffett. I told him if I was going to marry a rock star it wouldn't be Jimmy Buffett. It would be Jon Bon Jovi and we'd be living on a prayer."

Adam squeezes his eyes shut to banish the image of his mother in a wedding dress, kissing Jon Bon Jovi. "Is Margaretville the place with the mosquitoes?"

"That's the one. He wants to spend more time up there this summer, so I have a feeling we'll be away a lot over the next few months. He's working through some kind of fantasy outdoorsman phase. Hiking and fishing and god knows what else. Another city boy who's read *Call of the Wild* one too many times, you know?

234

Anyway, I hope it passes soon. You all right holding the fort while we're gone?"

"Sure."

"Frankie!" Pop yells from the TV room. "I'm about to press PLAY!"

She rolls her eyes at Adam. "He's on another home video workout kick, too. Getting in shape for the rigors of the backwoods, I suppose."

"Jane Fonda?"

"*Buns of Steel.* Pray for me." She kisses his forehead. "Oh, your friend Callum called. He said something about going home today? I wasn't sure what he meant." She disappears into the TV room.

It takes Adam less than twenty minutes to get to St. Hugh's. He pushes through a crowd of people chanting about AIDS being God's punishment against perverts or something, but he doesn't even bother looking at the signs they're holding. The attendant at the reception desk finds Adam's name on the list and hands him a visitor sticker. He slaps it on and sprints to the elevators. He dives out on the seventh floor and rounds the corner into Callum's room, breathless.

But Callum isn't here. Instead, there's a man in a wheelchair next to Callum's bed. The man is bald, with a jet-black beard. Adam stares at him, disoriented.

"Who are you?"

The man looks at Adam but says nothing.

"Where is Callum? Where has he gone?"

The man looks away.

Adam darts back into the hallway. He looks in the room next door and the room across the hall. No Callum. He runs over to the nurses' station, relieved to see a nurse he recognizes. He wears two small studs in one ear, with bloodred stones in them. They always say hello to each other.

"Hi," Adam says. "Did Callum leave?"

"I'm sorry?" the nurse says.

"Callum Keane. He's not in his room."

"I can't give out any patient information."

"It's okay, I'm on his list."

"I don't have a list for a patient with that name."

"Has he been discharged?" Adam feels the anxiety begin to spin. He can't lose Callum again. He barely made it through the last time Callum disappeared. No. Not again. "Has he left the hospital?"

"I can't share that information."

"But you know me," Adam says, forcing a smile. "Remember? I'm here all the time."

The nurse shakes his head, eyes downcast. "Rules."

"He doesn't have cab fare!" Adam says, his voice rising. "Is he just supposed to walk home?"

The nurse still doesn't look up.

Adam begins to panic. Why won't the nurse look at him? Did something bad happen to Callum? Is he back in the ICU? He looks up the hallway, and down. He spins around. He shouts blindly into the hallway. "Dr. Nieves!" Several people look around, but quickly go back to what they were doing. "Dr. Nieves!" he shouts again.

"She's not even on this floor right now," the nurse says, maddeningly calm. "If you shout again, I will call down to security."

Adam lowers his voice. "Please," he says. "Callum is counting on me. I'm the one who's supposed to take him home. I'm the one who knows about his new diet. I'm going to make him fat. Where is he? Dr. Nieves!"

The nurse puts his hand on the phone.

"I'm the one who's supposed to take care of him!" Adam shouts.

"Then why didn't he wait for you?" the nurse asks, just loud enough for Adam to hear.

Adam is stunned at the question. It cuts him deeply. His body convulses with anger and panic. He spins around and bursts through the first exit door he comes to, into a stairwell. He has no idea where it leads, but he takes the stairs two at a time, dangerously fast. On the second landing down, he nearly collides with someone walking up.

"Hey!" the guy yells. "Watch it!"

Adam looks up, his eyes thick with tears.

"Adam?"

The memory comes racing into Adam's consciousness. It's the boy from the piers, from that strange nightmare by the river. Remember him? The shouting, the Cure, the kiss. It's Ben, that's his name, and he's standing in Adam's way.

"Are you okay?" Ben is asking.

No, Adam thinks. No. Don't stop. This boy doesn't matter. The only thing that matters is Callum. He elbows Ben out of the way and jumps down the next flight of stairs. He hears Ben shouting after him, but he doesn't stop. He can't stop. He has to get downstairs. He has to get to Callum.

BEN

"Wait!" Ben yells.

"No!"

Ben can't believe he's seen the boy again. And here, in a maintenance stairwell at St. Hugh's, where neither of them is supposed to be.

Adam leaps down another flight, and then another. At the

ground floor, he pushes through an exit door. It slams behind him with a cold thud.

Ben hesitates. He looks up the stairs, then down. No one here. If it were anyone else, Ben wouldn't even give the encounter another thought. He'd just turn around and move on with his day. But Adam's voice, even just that one syllable *No!* feels so familiar to Ben, like it's someone he's known forever. It compels him to follow.

He pushes through the same heavy door, exiting into a small, fenced-in area outside the building. It's filled with garbage bins. Two are metal, with padlocks sealing them, marked TOXIC. The rest are big, blue plastic bins. All are filled, and the aroma of stale garbage hangs over them.

"Don't let it shut!" Adam shouts from behind the door.

Ben thrusts his hand back to catch the handle, but he's too late. The door slams again. Ben hears the latch slide into place. They're locked out.

"Nice going," Adam hisses. He pounds at the door. "Open!"

Ben stands back. "Are you okay?"

"Leave me alone," Adam says, slamming his hand against the door. His hair hangs in wayward clumps, and his eyes are bloodshot. He scratches at them. His movements are jerky, desperate.

Ben backs up against the gate that must lead to the street. It, too, is locked tight. He looks up, where chicken wire crisscrosses the sky. There's no way out. Not without a key. They're trapped.

"Open!" Adam slams his hand against the door again. "Hello!" He rushes up against the gate and kicks it. His eyes dart around the enclosure.

"Are you okay?" Ben asks again.

Adam glares at Ben for a moment, then slumps to the ground,

his back against the door. He puts his hands over his face. "No! I am not okay. I am locked into this trash heap. With *you*."

The way he spits the word *you*, spiked with disdain, stings Ben.

"Someone will come soon," Ben says quietly, hoping Adam will quiet, too. "They're always emptying trash here."

"How would you know? What are you even doing here?"

"My brother works here. He's a doctor."

"Good for him." Adam jumps up and slams his hand against the door again.

"Don't worry," Ben says. The words sound soothing to him, so he says them again. "Don't worry."

Adam turns to Ben and narrows his eyes, as if he's searching for something. Ben stares back, unblinking.

"Don't worry," he says, one more time.

"What happened to your face?" Adam asks.

Ben touches his bandage.

"Nothing," he says, but it's a lie. Something did happen. Something that connects Adam to Ben. The scar will always remind Ben of that night. The scar will always belong, in part, to Adam. But he can't tell Adam that. Not now.

Adam's face falls from fury to something more like desolation, like hopelessness. He sinks to the ground again. "I don't know where Callum is," he whispers.

"Callum?"

Adam looks up at Ben with pleading eyes. "I have to find him. He's disappeared."

"I'm sure he's not far," Ben says.

"You don't understand. I love him."

"Oh," Ben says, and things begin to fall into place. The embrace on the corner. The shouting on the pier. The escape after the kiss.

The panicked pounding at the door. The desperation in him, the fire. Ben's been caught in someone else's love story.

Just then the door opens and a man in green coveralls steps out. "Who the hell are you? You aren't supposed to be here!"

"We got lost," Ben says.

"Well, how about you get lost again," the man says, pointing to the stairs. "Now, punks."

With astonishing speed, Adam leaps at the door, past the man, into the stairwell, and away. Ben watches him go, wondering what it must feel like to be so in love.

ADAM

Adam, out of breath, crashes through the door to see Callum sitting at the piano in his hospital gown and jeans. "You're here! How did you? When did you—"

Callum plays a pair of major chords. "I walked."

"You walked? All the way? In a hospital gown?"

"No one even looked twice. I love that about New York. You can be the weirdest weirdo walking down the street, and no one cares."

"Why didn't you wait?"

He plays a minor chord. "I'm sorry. I wanted to get out of there before they changed their minds. Did you worry?"

Inside, Adam shouts, *Did I worry? I got in a fight with a nurse! I got stuck in the garbage! I almost punched a kid who didn't deserve it!*

But instead he says, "I'm just glad you're here. Are you hungry?"

"I'm starving."

"That's great! I'll go to Rocco's and get the cake."

"No," Callum says. "Let's get Grand Sichuan instead. I want the spiciest noodles on the menu. Double order. And soup dumplings. I love those. And fried rice. Can we have fried rice, too?"

"Slow down!" Adam dials Grand Sichuan. He adds a large tub of egg drop soup to the order, to stash in Callum's fridge for later. He asks for extra soy sauce, extra spicy mustard, extra napkins and chopsticks. After he hangs up, he shouts at the ceiling, "CALLUM IS HOME!"

"Shh," Callum says. "I have brain swelling."

"You do not."

"Oh, right. I forgot." He plays another chord. "I've missed you."

"I've missed you, too," Adam says.

"I was talking to Clara."

Adam sits next to him on the bench and softly punches him on the arm. "Jerk."

Callum is back. Playful, perfect Callum is back, and he is so happy. He watches Callum's hands as they start a new melody.

"Bach?" Adam asks.

"Very good."

Adam leans his head on Callum's shoulder. His body feels different than it did before. Thinner, bonier. He really is delicate. But Adam will feed him and Callum's shoulders will be round and strong again, and his smile will be full again, and Callum will be the big one again, and Adam will be the small one, and they will both be back where they belong.

When the food arrives, they sit at the piano and eat noodles straight from the containers. Callum makes up silly songs between bites, poking at the keys to create melodies. *You gotta use your noodle / to make such delicious foodle / Kiss me, my poodle / Mwah.*

Adam laughs as Callum sings. He's so happy to be here, in this room, together with Callum, again. *I love you*, Adam thinks. But he won't say it aloud. It all feels too fragile. What if Callum doesn't say it back? Even now, even after all that's happened, Adam is afraid of the gamble.

He opens a fortune cookie and reads it. "*Your heart is kind, your mind is clear, your soul is pure.*"

"Wow," Callum says. "Deep."

"What does yours say?"

Callum cracks open his cookie. "*Welcome change.*"

"That's it?"

"That's it." He plays another chord. "*Welcome change / Don't be a strange-er!*"

"I feel like a nap," Adam says. "You?"

"Not me. I want to play." And Callum plays all afternoon. First just scales and chords, then as he loosens up, Mozart and Bach. He plays with his whole body, leaning close for the quiet notes, stretching backward for the loud ones, smiling when he nails a complicated sequence. Adam watches from the bed. He could watch forever.

Later, after they eat the leftovers, Callum plays "Clair de Lune," chastising himself for making two mistakes along the way. "Debussy would be appalled at me," he says. "I guess I'm tired."

"It's late," Adam says.

"Ten is not late. Ten is halfway through my shift."

"You should get in bed, old man."

"Okay." Callum brushes his teeth and climbs under the covers. "It is so nice to be here."

"In a bed you actually fit into."

"Oh, I need to take my pills. Are you staying over?"

"Where are they? I'll stay if you want me to." *For as long as you want me to.*

"Over on the counter. I do want you to."

Adam finds the prescriptions. "It says you need to take it every eight hours. And this one is twice a day."

"That's right. That's for the *C. diff.*"

242

"The what?"

"*C. difficile.* It's a bacterial thing. Too gross to talk about. But I'm almost done with the course of antibiotics. It's almost gone."

"I'll set the alarm," Adam says. He'll look up *C. difficile* in his encyclopedia tomorrow when he goes home for a change of clothes.

"You don't have to. I'll wake up in time."

"I'm setting the alarm," Adam says, and he does.

"Put this on," Callum says, handing Adam a cassette of Beethoven's Sixth Symphony.

They lie on their sides, facing each other, their noses nearly touching, while Callum narrates the whole symphony as it plays, explaining every movement from the awakening of cheerful feelings to the shepherd's song. Adam listens intently, watching Callum's mouth as he speaks. He's been starving for Callum. Again he thinks, *I love you.* Again he won't risk saying it. Not in this perfect moment.

"That was as good as a movie," Adam says when the music ends. "Intense."

"Like the fire at the campground," Callum says. "Get it?"

Adam rolls his eyes. Then he kisses Callum on the cheek, and then on the lips, and then, unafraid, everywhere else.

BEN

"*Vogue España* came in," Ali says, gesturing at a display.

Ben picks up a copy. It's Madonna on the cover, in a pearlescent Alaïa raincoat, open nearly to her belly button with nothing underneath except a gigantic Harry Winston diamond necklace. She's smiling strenuously, like the shoot was taking too long, like she didn't want to be there. She looks tired. Ben doesn't blame her. Imagine being Madonna all the time, how exhausting it must be. There she is again, on the cover of *Bazaar*. And on the cover of *Interview*. On *Premiere*, French *Glamour*, *Cosmopolitan*. She's everywhere this summer.

The shop door opens, and an old couple shuffles in. She's wearing a plastic rain bonnet, even though it's not raining outside.

"Hello, Doris," Ali says. "Hello, Francis."

"Where is last Sunday's *Times*?" Doris asks. "Francis here doesn't believe they gave a good review to that Italian place over on Thirteenth Street. Have you been there? It's terrible."

"Terrible," Francis repeats. His eyeglasses are tinted blue.

"All the leftover Sundays got picked up by recycling this afternoon," Ali says. "Sorry."

Doris scoffs. "Recycling. Pfft. Who ever heard of it?"

Francis shrugs and smiles. "It's the future," he says. "I've been recycling our newspapers for three months now."

Doris looks at him, appalled. She shakes her head. "Forty-four years. Forty-four years and still you surprise me."

"I need to keep my best girl on her toes, so she doesn't get tired of me," Francis says.

She pats his cheek, tenderly, then straightens his collar. "What will I ever do with you?" They exit the shop. Ben says good night to Ali, takes a copy of *GXE*, and follows them out.

Out on Hudson Street, Ben watches Doris and Francis walk slowly down the sidewalk, their steps matching perfectly. Forty-four years, Ben thinks. Forty-four. How does that happen? How did they meet? How did they know? What does it feel like to be forty-four years entwined together?

The cover of *GXE* is a photograph of a headless male torso, over the words *DO IT*. It reminds Ben of Justin. Not the torso, the words. *All you have to do is do it.* He opens the magazine to an ad for Boy Bar, the place Justin told him about. But he'd said to go on Thursday, and it's not Thursday.

The next listing is for Crowbar. *Best music in the East Village*, it says. *Friendliest guys.* Maybe he'll walk over to the East Village. It's warm out. Soon he's standing on Tenth Street, near a crowd of guys by the entrance to Crowbar, a gaggle of Onitsuka Tigers and camouflage tank tops and leather wrist cuffs. They smoke and laugh, draping their arms over one another.

One guy looks over at Ben, then whispers something in the ear next to him. Soon another guy looks over, and another. Ben feels their scrutiny. It's not a hostile assessment. The smiles are earnest. But it doesn't matter when the anxiety in his chest won't let him smile back. Ben feels scrawny and awkward and childish. He pulls his baseball cap lower to hide more of his face, then turns around to leave.

ADAM

It's Callum's third morning at home, and he's sleeping. But his breathing is funny.

It's been that way since they woke up for his six o'clock pills yesterday. Adam wanted to call Dr. Nieves but Callum said no, he was all right, this happens sometimes. Callum said Adam should go home and just let him sleep. Adam said no, he wanted to stay. They argued about it. Adam won and they stayed in and listened to music all day, and every time Adam got worried because it seemed like Callum couldn't catch his breath, like he was losing his rhythm, he got it back. He spent a lot of time in the bathroom but he didn't have a fever. And he slept through most of the night. Adam knows, because he watched him.

He touches Callum's chest. It's much warmer this morning. They should go to see Dr. Nieves. Adam knows they should. But he doesn't want to fight again.

Callum's eyes flicker and he pushes Adam's hand away. "I need to go to the bathroom," he says.

He sits up on the edge of the bed, then clears his throat. He pushes himself up to his feet and takes two wobbly steps, but on the third step he stumbles, catching himself on Clara.

Adam stands up and holds his breath as Callum shuffles to the bathroom. Adam can see the stain, now, running down the leg of Callum's sweatpants, a stain that has also soiled the sheets.

When the bathroom door closes behind Callum, Adam quickly strips the sheets from the bed. He rolls them up in a ball in the corner. He'll take them to the laundromat later. He stands still, listening but hearing nothing.

"Can I come in? I can help you."

"No. I don't need you."

"But I can—"

"I said I don't need you!"

Adam watches the bathroom door. What is going on? Has he picked up a new infection? Is the *C. diff* back? What did he eat last night? Think, Adam. Think.

Just then he hears a loud thud from the bathroom.

"Callum?" he asks, pressing his ear against the door. "Are you okay?"

No answer.

Fear surges through Adam. He looks around, as if there's an answer somewhere in this tiny studio apartment. Grow up, he tells himself. He needs you.

"I'm coming in."

He opens the door to see Callum sitting on the floor next to the toilet, leaning against the plastic door to the standing shower. His head hangs from his neck, as if he's lost the strength to hold it up.

"Leave me alone," Callum slurs. "I'm okay."

But Adam can see that he is not okay. He is not okay at all. He has to get him up off the floor. He reaches down, but freezes before touching Callum. A distant voice warns him. Are you sure this is safe? Is this mix of sweat and saliva and phlegm and diarrhea safe? Think, Adam. What did the most recent pamphlets say? What did you learn from the *Mainstay*?

No, he thinks. It doesn't matter. He's not going to leave Callum here on the floor, no matter the risk. Adam is responsible now. He's the one who's going to help him. Isn't that what he yelled at the nurse the other day? Isn't that what he promised after their afternoon on the library steps?

He begins to move with steadiness and purpose. He plants his feet and takes Callum's arm, but his hand slips and Callum slumps back against the wall. No. Too slippery. Think, Adam.

He removes Callum's sweatpants and tosses them into the pile of sheets. He wets a washcloth and cleans up every part of Callum he can reach. He pats him dry with a towel.

"I'm cold," Callum says.

"I know," Adam says. "Let's try again." He grasps Callum under the arms and, with all of his strength, pulls Callum to his feet. He guides him slowly to the piano bench. Callum feels very warm. The fever is back in a big way. "Sit here."

He finds another pair of sweatpants at the bottom of a stack of clothes, and, with Callum lifting one foot and then the other, he manages to get them on. Adam slips a T-shirt over Callum's head, then zips him into a hooded sweatshirt.

"I'm going to take you up to St. Hugh's now," Adam says, hiking up Callum's socks.

"No. I just need sleep." Callum's voice is slow and wobbly. "I don't want to go back there."

Adam gets a glass of water and holds it to Callum's lips. "Can you take a little sip?"

Callum tries, but most of the water dribbles onto his sweatshirt.

Adam kneels down in front of him. "Listen. I know you don't want to go to St. Hugh's. I don't blame you. But let's just go up there for a minute. They'll look at you and see that you're fine, and they'll laugh at me for being such a worrier. You can make fun of me the whole way home in the taxi. I have enough money for cab fare, both ways."

Callum looks at the bed, which Adam has stripped, then at the pile of sheets. He sighs. "Okay."

Adam helps Callum tie on his sneakers then dresses himself in a flash, and together they find a way down to the street. The journey down the stairs is slow, but with one hand on the banister and his arm around Adam, Callum makes it safely.

"Wait here," Adam says, helping Callum sit on the front steps. "I'll get a taxi."

He runs over to the corner of Greenwich. By luck, a free cab is just a block away. Adam puts up his hand and climbs in. He points at Callum on the stoop. "First pick him up, then to St. Hugh's hospital."

The cabbie turns around to look at Adam. "Is he sick or something?"

"Yes, he needs a doctor. Please hurry."

"Is he your boyfriend?"

"What does that have to do with anything?"

The cabbie turns off the meter. "Get out of my car. I don't need that shit in here."

Adam glares at him in the rearview mirror.

"I said get out."

Adam wants to yell, to fight, but there's no time for that. He jumps out and slams the door as hard as he can. "Shithead," he says, as the taxi speeds off.

He looks for another cab but the street is empty. Hurry, Adam. Callum is leaning against the railing at an odd angle, and his head is slumping again.

There's a pay phone on the corner. Before talking himself out of it, Adam dials 911 and gives the dispatcher the address. "Please come right away. No, he's not on drugs. Please hurry. Please."

He sprints back to Callum, catching his head just before it knocks against the railing. "Don't worry," Adam whispers. "Okay? Don't worry. Our ride is coming."

After a time, a much longer time than Adam expects, an ambulance rounds the corner and pulls up. No siren, no lights. It doesn't seem to be in a rush at all.

"No," Callum groans. "Not that."

"I'm sorry," Adam whispers. "There was no other way."

Three EMTs get out of the ambulance. Two of them crouch down next to Callum. The third asks Adam what happened.

"I don't know. He is dizzy. He can't walk very well."

"Has he been sick before this morning?"

"He has HIV," Adam says. "He has AIDS."

The EMT looks at her coworkers. They all nod and tighten their medical gloves.

Callum winces as they lift him onto the wheeled stretcher. Adam can see that these sweatpants are dirty now, too, but it's too late to change. They load the stretcher into the back of the ambulance. Adam starts to climb in, too, but an EMT blocks his way.

"No companions," he says.

"But he'll be alone!"

"Protocol," he says.

"Where are you taking him?"

"Wherever dispatch tells us."

"His physician is at St. Hugh's. Her name is Dr. Nieves."

"That's good to know."

"Please be careful with him."

"Sir, we are always careful," the EMT says, his voice sharp and dismissive. He slams the door and the ambulance pulls away.

BEN

All you have to do is do it.

Justin's words repeat in Ben's head as he steps up to the door of Boy Bar on Thursday night, determined this time. He's going to go into the first gay bar of his life, and it's going to happen tonight. He's chosen his outfit carefully—a Book of Love concert T-shirt, dark denim jeans, black Converse sneakers, and his baseball cap. He chose the T-shirt because it fits just right, making his chest appear more muscular than it really is.

He hands the attendant a five-dollar bill and steps inside. The space, large and echoey with a long bar in the back and a small stage at one end, is still sparsely populated. A few guys in groups of two and three dance to a Cathy Dennis track, a lazy disco ball spins slowly overhead. It's early still, not yet midnight. The "Boy Bar Beauties" drag show, which *GXE* says will include Perfidia and Codie Ravioli tonight—won't start until at least one.

Ben approaches the bar. The bartender looks just like the go-go boys in *GXE* magazine. Rounded shoulders, washboard stomach, perfect teeth. Ben asks nervously for a Coke.

"Just Coke?" the bartender asks. "No rum?"

Ben shakes his head.

"Okay, sexy. Here you go. This one's on me." He winks, then turns away to help another patron.

Ben slides two dollars across the bar anyway, then tightens his baseball cap and finds a dark corner at the end of the bar, with his back to the wall. Over the next few songs—Lil Louis, 49ers, Jomanda, and a Hi-NRG remix of "I Should Be So Lucky" by Kylie Minogue—the room fills up, and soon it's packed tight with people laughing, dancing, carrying on. They crowd the bar, trying to get the bartender's attention. Nobody notices Ben.

Sometime after one, the music slows and the disco lights go dark. A single spotlight shines onto the curtain at the center of the stage. A few isolated whoops pierce the air, and a fog machine shoots mist across the floor. A voice from the DJ booth announces, "Codie Ravioli!" just as the curtains part to reveal the glamorous drag star in a spaghetti-strap mermaid dress and satin choker, red hair piled high and cascading down her back. She drops a fierce look over the crowd, then strolls, slowly, to "I Am Woman" by Helen Reddy, and a chorus of whistles from the crowd. A twirl, a pose, another pass, and another. *Work! Work, Codie!*

Codie exits. She's followed by Connie Girl, who switches her hips seductively as she walks. Then Candis Cayne, Girlina, Princess Diandra, Miss Guy, Perfidia. One after another, in gowns and corsets and chic evening suits, dancing and walking and working the stage. Ben is captivated by their glamour. They are supermodels.

Eventually the beauties finish their walks, and the dancing begins again. A boy in an inside-out Stacey Q T-shirt and combat boots jumps up and down next to Ben, dancing feverishly. Ben avoids looking at his face—eye contact with a stranger is one step further than he'll go tonight—instead watching a tiny glow-in-the-dark dog, hanging from a lanyard around his neck, bounce against the boy's chest. He throws his body carelessly into the music, moving closer to Ben as he bounces. He loses his balance on a downbeat and falls into Ben, knocking him sideways.

"Sorry!" the boy shouts.

"That's okay," Ben mutters, knowing the boy can't hear him. It's time for him to go anyway. He puts his empty Coke cup on the bar and starts to step away.

"Hey!" the boy yells. "Wait, is that you? It *is* you! Ben!"

It's Justin, from the photo shoot. Ben smiles. "Hey," he says, half hiding his face behind the bill of his baseball cap.

"Where are you going?"

"Heading out!" Ben says, pointing at the exit.

"No way! It's just getting started!" Justin slides his drink onto the bar and grabs Ben by the wrists. "Come on!"

He pulls Ben into the middle of the room, spinning and twirling in front of him. Ben steps side to side, too self-conscious to dance, too self-conscious to stand still. The music changes to a baseline Ben knows. The strobes flash overhead and a vocal comes in over the bass. It's "Into the Groove."

Justin throws up his hands ecstatically. "I haven't heard this song in forever!" he shouts. "Madoooonnnnna!"

The beat rolls forward. Ben looks around. No one is watching. Everyone is dancing. He twists his hips, bobs his head, moves his shoulders to the beat, steps forward and back. He taps the base of his stomach with his thumbs to keep the beat.

Justin leans forward into Ben's ear. "That is so sexy," he says, his breath warm on Ben's neck "The way you drum your body like that." He bites his lower lip and wraps a hand around Ben's waist, pulling him closer.

Ben keeps a blank expression, despite the thrill of Justin's touch.

He dances closer. The air in here is hot, rich with cigarette smoke and sweat. The good kind of sweat, the kind that comes from dancing. He mouths along with the words, *now I know you're mine*, and drums his stomach.

Justin spins away, then back. He reaches over and takes Ben's face in his hands, and leans up to kiss him. Justin holds the kiss for several beats, stroking Ben's jaw with his thumbs and opening his mouth. Ben closes his eyes, finds Justin's rhythm, and moves with him. They kiss some more. Justin's taste is smoky, alcoholic, sexual. Ben wants more. He puts a hand on Justin's hip. Soon they're swaying together, feeling, grinding. Justin's body, Justin's lips, Justin's waist. Yes, he thinks. More.

Ben leans in for another kiss, but Justin just smiles and yells, "You're so cute!"

Madonna gives way to "Let There Be House" by Deskee. Ben closes his eyes again to find the beat. When he opens them, Justin is gone.

Ben searches the crowd for a moment, then winds his way back to his spot at the end of the bar. From there he sees Justin, just a few feet away, making out with someone else now. Joyously, vigorously kissing a different boy. Ben watches them. Somewhere in his mind, he knows he should be upset by this. That he should be deflated, somehow, or even hurt.

But he isn't. Ben is just as electrified as he was moments ago, when Justin's hands were on him. He watches Justin move from boy to boy, spinning, dancing, kissing, flirting. He grins as he goes, and Ben grins watching him be so free. What does that feel like, Ben wonders, to be so free?

After a few more songs, he decides it's time to go. He finds his way out of the club and back onto the sidewalk and floats all the way back to Tribeca, tasting Justin on his tongue.

Tell me where you want to go.

I would love to go to Paris or Tokyo or Australia or Morocco but the place I want to go the most is the Arctic. I don't know where, exactly. Maybe Greenland. As far north as you can go. Every time I see a photograph of the Arctic, or see a documentary on television or something, I am mesmerized. I don't know why. I don't even really like the cold that much.

But there's something about all that space, all that quiet. I feel like if you're way up in the Arctic, you can look a million miles in every direction and only see gray, white, maybe a little bit of blue in the sky, maybe some black if the ocean isn't iced over. No colors, you think. No life.

But that's an illusion because if you wait, if you stand still, if you watch and maybe listen, too, then you start to see all layers and textures and movements and messages. You see all these colors start to emerge from the grayness. Vibrant, alive, just waiting to be seen. I love that idea, of things hiding in plain sight, you know? Like if you look closely, and wait patiently, you'll see that nothing's truly empty. Things are always more complicated than you think at first. Well, maybe not always, but usually.

I don't know. Maybe the Arctic is nothing like that. I have never been any farther north than Albany. But that's how I imagine it.

ADAM

Adam sits in the yellow vinyl chair next to Callum's bed and watches him sleep. He's knocked out, thanks to whatever's in the IV bag hanging above him, but Adam can see it's not peaceful. His restless hands lie across his chest, twitching with each uneven breath. Why can't he find a rhythm?

"There you are," the nurse says when he enters the room. It's the man with the bloodred studs in his ear, the one Adam yelled at.

Adam stands up. "I'm sorry about the other day. I freaked out and—"

"Shh," the nurse says. "I'm just glad you're here." He touches Adam's shoulder, and leaves.

Adam leans closer to Callum. "Breathe," he says. "Like a musician. One two. One two. One two."

He has a sip of Snapple. Out next to the vending machine earlier, Adam overheard two nurses talking about the tall, young patient who'd had a spinal tap and brain scan today. *So young*, one of the nurses said. *Just so young.* How can this be happening? Everything was so good yesterday, the day before, the day before that. What changed?

He takes Callum's hand and brings the knuckles to his lips. His fingers are so cold, so sharp. Like twigs. Like kindling. In Adam's palm, he feels the bones and twisted tendons inside, the veins and nerves underneath the skin. The complexity of this hand, the rigidity of it, the *anatomy* of it overwhelms him and unleashes a wave of nausea in him. Whose hand is this? Where are Callum's beautiful, musical hands? He drops it back onto Callum's chest, momentarily repulsed. He wants to run out of here, out the door and down the stairs and away, far away, so far away.

He turns to the window, ashamed, hating himself for his selfishness. He looks up at the ceiling to blink back the remorseful, guilty tears. This is what you committed to, he thinks. Grow up.

He turns back to Callum, whose eyes are open now.

"You're here," Callum says, his voice low and scratchy.

"Yes," he says, forcing a soft smile onto his face. "I'm here."

"I have to pee," Callum says. He reaches for the edge of his blanket to pull it aside, but with the movement, he tugs at the IV tube in his arm and winces. "Ouch."

"No," Adam says. "Stay where you are. We can do it here."

"I can walk," Callum says.

"I know. But I've always wanted to try this," he says. "Will you let me? As a favor. Turn on your side."

Adam takes the plastic urinal cup from a hook next to the bed. He helps Callum open the fly on his underwear and guides his penis into the opening.

"Holy cannoli. Do you have a license for that thing?" he jokes, reaching desperately for levity. Failing to find it.

When Callum is finished, he leans back in bed. Adam takes the urinal cup and empties it in the bathroom. He washes it out and dries it with paper towels. Soon Callum is asleep again.

An hour passes, and another. Adam counts the dust bunnies under Callum's bed. At least a dozen. Why are they there? Aren't hospitals supposed to be clean? He waves his foot at them to create a breeze and make them dance. He'll get some 409. He'll scour this place, just like he scoured Callum's apartment earlier. The mess was so much worse than he thought. He shakes his head to erase the image. It doesn't work.

After dark, Dr. Nieves comes in.

"Callum is sleeping," Adam says.

"Good. Good things happen in sleep."

Adam watches her work. She feels under Callum's throat, under his arms. She listens to his lungs with her stethoscope, feels his forehead, inspects his IV bag. She makes notes in her chart. She moves in a methodical manner. Not cold, but clinical.

"What are spinal taps for?" he asks.

"Spinal taps are used for many things."

"But for him, what about for him?" he says. "Why did he have one today?"

"You know I won't answer that, Adam." She smiles. "You can ask him. Not me. All right?"

She turns to go. He jumps out of the chair and follows her into the hallway.

"But Dr. Nieves, I need to know," he says, agitated.

"Adam," she says. "I understand how frustrating this must be for you."

"I don't think you do," he says sharply.

"Adam."

"He's not getting better!" he shouts. "This place is full of doctors and nurses and equipment and medicine and he just gets sicker!"

"You need to lower your voice, right now."

"Why can't you fix him?" He chokes back a sob. "What kind of doctor are you?"

She takes a short step back and squares her shoulders, her face drawn tight. Her voice is low and stern. "Don't speak to me that way. Ever. Do you understand?"

He scowls at the floor, fists clenched. Don't cry, he thinks. Don't cry.

"Do you understand?" she repeats.

He narrows his eyes and nods. "Yes."

"I have three things to tell you," she says. "First thing. Callum is lucky. He is lucky to be at this hospital. He is lucky to be covered by insurance. He is lucky that it's not 1983. He is extremely lucky to be white. And so are you. You are both very lucky. That is the first thing."

Adam begins to regain his breath. "I—"

"Second thing. AIDS is one of the most complex and confusing diseases we have ever seen. Not a single doctor or scientist in the world knows how to fix him. Not one. You can't hang that on me."

"I'm sorry," Adam whispers. "Dr. Nieves, I'm so sor—"

"Third thing. Look at me. You are a hell of a partner for him. I see it. We all see it. A hell of a partner. The difference that makes is massive. You have no idea how much it matters."

Adam slides down the wall to the floor.

"You should have seen him at his apartment," he says.

She crouches down next to him to listen.

"Everything was so great. He played the piano and told dumb jokes and we laughed all day and we ate so much, just like you told him to, and then, I don't know what happened. He was someone different. He wasn't making sense. He wouldn't let me help. I didn't know how to help him. I didn't know—" He's gasping for air now. "I didn't know what to do."

She puts a hand on his shoulder. "No, Adam. You did know what to do. You brought him here. I thank you for that."

Adam puts his face in his hands.

"Dr. Nieves, I'm very sorry for what I said."

"I accept your apology. But I want you to think about what *I* said."

"I will," he says. "I promise I will."

Her pager beeps. She glances at it and sighs. "Look, Adam. I would tell you to go home and get some sleep but I know you won't listen."

He shakes his head.

She stands up and holds out her hand for him to grasp. She pulls him to his feet.

"You have a lot to learn, Adam," she says. "But you are already a good man. Remember that. A good man." She turns and goes.

A good man.

Adam goes back into Callum's room and closes the door. He takes off his shoes and lowers the guard on Callum's bed. Carefully, mindful of the IV tube and other devices, he sits on the edge of the bed for a moment, then turns and lies down, slowly, nudging his body next to Callum's, curling around him like a spoon. He closes his eyes and tries to remember the first night they spent together. How close they were. How tightly connected. So warm, so safe. Together. Just like this. Forever like this. *I am yours.*

Callum shivers, and Adam curls closer.

"Sleep," the good man whispers. "I'm here."

BEN

It's finally cooling off after a muggy day. Ben's spent most of it indoors watching cable—*Club MTV* (which is nothing like Boy Bar), a CNN report on the pending reunification of East and West Germany, that new soap opera on NBC, *Generations*. Nothing special. Ben didn't really pay attention to any of it. All he could think about was last night. He went to a gay bar! He danced! He made out with a cute boy! Imagine! He can't wait to do it again.

Now that the sun is down, he's back out in the city, walking with the Pet Shop Boys and Dusty Springfield in his ears, singing about what they've done to deserve this. When the Waverly Diner comes into view, he suddenly realizes how hungry he is. He hasn't eaten all day, unless you count a package of Nerds. He checks his back pocket for the ten-dollar bill he folded into it earlier. Maybe a sandwich would be nice.

He peeks in the window. It's after nine, and the diner is uncrowded. Just a waitress pushing through the swinging doors to the kitchen, a pair of women drinking coffee and flipping through a newspaper at one end of the counter, and a boy in a booth by the window. He's sitting alone, his head bent over a glass of water. He looks like—

No, Ben thinks. It can't be him. It must be an illusion. He didn't sleep that much last night so his mind is playing tricks on him. But then the boy in the booth looks up.

It *is* him. Adam.

They lock eyes for an instant, then Ben jerks away. Just keep walking, he thinks. The last two times you've seen this boy haven't gone well. Don't court more disaster. Just walk. Maybe he didn't recognize you.

He strides quickly up the block, but he doesn't get far before he hears, "Hey! Ben!"

He turns to see Adam, standing in the soft neon light of the diner's OPEN sign. His hands are stuffed in his pockets and his shoulders are hunched up to his ears, like a shy boy would stand at a party where he doesn't know anyone. So different from the frightened boy on the pier, so different from the angry boy at St. Hugh's. His eyes are tired now, not angry. Lonely. Soft.

Ben lowers his headphones, securing them around his neck. Go say hello, he thinks. That's all. Then keep going. Tell him you are late for something. He walks back toward Adam.

"Are you hungry?" Adam asks.

"I'm—" Ben starts. "That's okay."

"Come eat with me," Adam says. "I won't be weird. I promise."

Ben is disarmed. "I guess I am hungry."

He follows Adam inside and slides into the booth across from him. A waitress in a waist apron and a BROADWAY CARES T-shirt offers two giant, multipage plastic menus. "You boys want coffee?"

"Yes please," Ben says.

"Can we have cream, too?"

"You got it," she says, scribbling on her notepad. "Do you know what you want to eat?"

Ben adjusts his glasses. The menu is several pages long. Overwhelming. He shrugs at Adam.

"Two grilled cheese sandwiches," Adam says. "Deluxe. And can you make the fries extra crispy?"

She scribbles it down, slips her pen into her apron pocket, and tucks the menus under her arm. "I love Crowded House," she says, pointing at Ben's T-shirt. She begins to sing, "*Hey now, hey now—*" Her voice fades as she walks back to the kitchen.

"Music everywhere," Adam says.

"What?"

"Nothing."

"Oh." Ben feels Adam's eyes on him. He wants to ask a hundred thousand questions, about the pier, about the hospital. Mostly about the kiss. But he won't.

"Are you a fan?" Adam asks. "Of Crowded House, I mean."

"I only know that one song," Ben says. "It's my brother's shirt."

The waitress returns with two mugs of coffee with spoons sticking out, and a tiny aluminum pitcher of cream. She's still singing.

"Free concert with every meal," Adam says when she walks away.

"So that's what you meant when you ordered our sandwiches 'Deluxe.'"

Adam laughs. Ben laughs, too. They've never laughed together before. It feels good.

"What kind of music *are* you into?" Adam asks.

"A lot of stuff. It changes."

"What's in your Discman right now?"

"Pet Shop Boys," Ben says.

"Which one?"

"*Actually.*"

"Is that the one with 'It's a Sin'?"

"Yeah."

Their sandwiches arrive. Ben immediately grabs the salt shaker.

"You have to salt them right away," he says, showering his fries. "If you wait too long, the salt won't stick. Here." He hands the shaker to Adam, but Adam's already got both hands filled with a triangle of sandwich. Adam nods, and Ben shakes salt over Adam's fries, too.

Ben pours a glug of ketchup onto his plate and dips the corner of his grilled cheese into it.

Adam stops chewing. "You eat grilled cheese with ketchup?" he asks with playful indignation. "That's nuts."

"I love it," Ben says. "You should try."

"I'm scared."

"Be brave."

Ben pushes his plate toward Adam, who dips the corner of his sandwich into the pool of ketchup.

"Not bad," Adam says. He dips again, then pours some ketchup onto his own plate.

"How old are you?" Ben asks.

"Eighteen. I just graduated."

"Same here. What are you doing next year?"

"NYU. I'm going to study film."

"You must be really into movies."

"Yeah, I guess so. I work at a video shop just so I can get free rentals."

"What's your favorite?"

Adam remembers how worried he was the last time someone asked him this question. He won't panic now. He just won't answer. "I have too many favorites. What about you?"

"I don't know," Ben says. "I don't really see that many movies. The other day I saw *Desperately Seeking Susan* on cable at my brother's. It was better than I remembered."

"Susan Seidelman is a great director," Adam says. "Have you seen *Smithereens*?"

"No."

"It's very East Village–ish."

"I love the East Village."

Adam picks up a French fry and drags it through the ketchup on his plate, writing *EV* in the pool. He draws a heart around the letters.

"Nice," Ben says.

Adam swipes his fry through it and eats it. "What about you? What's your grand plan for life?

"I don't know. I applied to FIT but I missed the deadline for fall. Maybe I'll get accepted for January."

"Do you want to be a designer or something?"

"I'm not sure. Maybe a stylist. Maybe a photographer."

"Like Laura Mars," Adam says.

"Who?"

"It's this movie from the seventies, *Eyes of Laura Mars*. It's about a fashion photographer who gets caught up in this whole serial killer plot. It's completely unhinged and so great. You should rent it sometime."

Outside it starts to rain. Thick, heavy drops *thwack* against the glass, each one exploding like a tiny water balloon.

"I didn't know we were getting a storm," Ben says.

"Janice Huff on Channel Four said it would push through quickly. She said it would be violent but short-lived."

"Violent?"

"But short-lived. Don't worry, the subway's right over there." Adam points across the street to the West Fourth station. He picks up a fry, then puts it back down. "I owe you an apology for the other day. In the stairs. In the garbage."

Ben drops his hands to his lap. He never expected Adam to mention that day. "Did you ever find him?"

Adam pushes his plate to the side of the table and leans back in his seat. "He's going to be all right," he says. "He'll be all right."

Ben can't tell if Adam wants to talk about it or not. He won't risk it. He doesn't want to drive Adam away again. The last two times they've met, Adam's run off. He looks out the window again. "It's really coming down out there."

"How is your face?" Adam asks. He is pointing at Ben's forehead.

Ben presses at the faint red scar with his forefinger. "It's fine. It doesn't hurt anymore."

"How did it happen anyway?"

Ben clenches his jaw. How should he answer? Should he tell the truth? Does he want Adam to know? It would be so easy just to say that he tripped and fell. They could go back to talking about movies or the weather or their futures or the singing waitress. But Adam was there that night. He's part of the story. Maybe he should know.

"It happened out on the pier," Ben says. "That night that, you know."

Adam's eyes return to the scar. Ben watches them change, as recognition seeps in.

"You mean—"

"I didn't even see them coming," Ben says. "I was watching you."

Adam lowers his eyes. Already Ben regrets telling him. He should have kept it to himself. What difference would it have made?

"It's fine," Ben says. "It was no big deal."

"It's my fault," Adam says, looking out the window again.

"No."

"Yes."

"I don't want you to—" Ben cuts himself off. "It's not your fault. It's my fault."

The waitress, still humming, approaches with the coffeepot. "Don't dream your coffee's over," she says. "Can I top you up?"

"No thanks," Adam says. "I think we're done."

"All right. I'll bring the check."

After she walks away, Ben says, "I'm sorry."

"For what? You didn't do anything."

"Neither did you," Ben says. "It's old news now."

They don't say anything more until the waitress brings the check. They do the math to split it. They decide to leave a little extra for the song. They step out into the rain. It is steady and strong, but not violent.

"I'll see you around," Adam says.

"Yeah," Ben says.

"Okay," Adam says.

Adam turns uptown and walks into the rain with his shoulders hunched. He doesn't have an umbrella. Ben watches his hair slowly mat to his head. Ben wants to run after him, to apologize for saying anything about that night, to ask him to sit and drink more coffee together, to be friends. But he knows, now, that Adam is already gone.

ADAM

Nelson Mandela is on the television in Callum's hospital room. He's visiting Amsterdam, part of a world tour following his release from prison a few months ago. Next week he's coming to New York, and the city is planning big ticker-tape parade down on Wall Street. They expect a million people to show up.

"I think we should go," Adam says. "It would be so cool to see him."

Callum's spoon lands with a clang on the floor. His hands have been bothering him and eating is hard for him. Dr. Nieves told him she suspects reactive arthritis but Callum said he can't have it. You can't have reactive arthritis and be a conductor, he said. He won't let Adam help.

"Dammit," Callum says.

Adam picks up the spoon, then takes it into the bathroom to wash it with soap and water. He takes his time. He fills a cup with water and rinses out his mouth. He looks in the mirror. He is so, so tired. Just keep moving, he thinks. Pick up the spoon. Smile at Callum. Wait for what's next.

When he hands the spoon back to Callum, Callum waves it away, knocking over his cup of water. Adam picks up the cup, takes a stack of paper towels from the dispenser in the bathroom, and starts to gently mop up Callum's lap.

"It's time for you to go," Callum says. "This is humiliating."

"It's okay. I can stick around," Adam says. *I promised to stick around.*

"When are you going to stop pretending?" Callum asks. He swats at Adam's hand, sending the paper towels scattering. "You need to go."

Please go back to sleep, Adam thinks. Everything is better when Callum sleeps.

He remembers back to when his grandmother was sick. His mother coached him to make her feel needed. *Tell her that you need her advice on something*, she said. *Tell her that you can't remember that one story she used to tell, and that you'd really like it if she reminded you how it goes.*

"Remember when we listened to Beethoven's Sixth?" Adam asks. "I can't remember which comes first, the part with the rushing water, by the brook, or the thunderstorm."

Callum presses the button to return his bed to flat, then rolls onto his side, away from Adam. He covers his face with his arm, exposing his back. "I don't know."

Adam wants to shout. He wants to throw the pitcher of flowers, new ones today, across the room. He wants to break a window. He feels gutless, so useless, so weak. He hates this. He hates everything.

But instead Adam stares at Callum's spine, the spiky ridge of vertebrae that moves and twists against the skin with each shallow breath. It's as if they're unconnected to each other or to anything else, rearranging themselves inside, slipping across each other like stones. He watches the freckles stretch and distort as they stretch across the bones. Is he in pain? Would he say so if he was?

"I love you," he whispers.

He knows he's said it loud enough for Callum to hear, but Callum doesn't respond. The silence closes around Adam.

He crouches down to collect the scattered paper towels. He bunches them up and drops them in the bin by the bathroom door. He refills the cup of water next to Callum's bed, then pulls Callum's blanket up to cover his back.

"I love you, too," Callum whispers. "Adam."

Adam nearly loses his balance at the impact of the words. He inhales them, holds them in his lungs. He stands there for a very long time, listening. When the silence creeps back around him, he wonders if he imagined them. No. He didn't.

He takes Callum's tray to leave outside the door. When he steps into the hallway, he sees Dr. Nieves in the cold fluorescence of the corridor.

She clicks her pen and smiles at him. "You all right? You look like you just ran a marathon."

Adam looks at his shoes.

"What is it?" she asks.

"He said, um—" Don't cry, Adam. "He said he wants me to go. I don't think he wants me to be here anymore."

She pushes her glasses up onto the top of her head, and exhales. "Ah."

"Why would he say that?" he asks.

"Listen. No one can know what Callum is thinking except Callum. But I have seen many patients try to push away people they love. It's almost a protective reaction. They want to protect the people they love from having to go through this. They don't want you to have to carry the load."

"But I told him it doesn't matter to me," Adam says. He feels his throat closing, his voice rising. "I told him that we were doing this together. He agreed. He promised."

"Shh," she says. "Be patient, Adam."

"Fuck!" Adam says, shocking himself. He looks at her with wide eyes. "I'm sorry."

She smiles and whispers, "Fuck fuck fuck. Feels good to say that sometimes, you know?"

Adam presses his thumbs into his eyes. He is chewing violently on his cheek now.

It's time for him to ask the question. It's time for him to know. He needs to ask it, fast, before he loses his nerve. He puts his hands on his hips.

"Is he going to die?"

She draws a deep breath. "Adam. You know I won't—"

He interrupts. "Please," he says. "Dr. Nieves, please tell me. How much longer?"

The doctor's body takes on a stillness that Adam's never seen in her before. Her posture changes, her expression, even the way her hands fall limp at her sides, depleted. He wonders how many angry, terrified people like Adam she has to deal with every day. How many people she has to carry through this same hideous journey. How many hopes she has to kill, how many rules she has to follow, how much empathy she has to gin up when all anyone wants from her is something that doesn't exist: a cure. She's tired, too, he sees. So tired.

"I don't know," she says. "And that's the truth. I'm not dodging your question. I just don't have the answer. I'm sorry, Adam."

Her answer makes him queasy, because he knows it's the only answer she has.

"There's so much about him that I don't know yet," he says.

"I know," she says.

She takes Adam's hand and they stand quietly for a moment. An orderly in a green cardigan pushes a wheelchair past them, its seat filled with crumpled-up bed linens. He nods to Dr. Nieves, and she nods back.

"What's the last thing he said to you?" she asks. "Just before you came out here. The very last thing."

"He said—" Adam gasps for air. "He said *I love you, too.* He said my name. He said *Adam.*"

She squeezes his hand. "Do you believe him? Do you believe he loves you?"

It takes Adam a long time to answer. "Yes," he says.

"Then that's the part I want you to remember, okay? That's the important part."

Adam looks up at her with wide eyes. She holds them with her own. They study each other for a minute, and then Adam pulls his hand free. "I need to go back in. I don't want him to be alone."

"Why don't you let him sleep a bit," she says. "He knows you're here. Go for a walk. It's a beautiful night."

It takes a monumental effort for him to respond. "Okay," he says.

"Okay," she answers.

He feels his body turn away from her and walk, steadily, almost mechanically, toward the elevators. He rides down to the first floor, walks straight through the lobby and out the front doors and onto the sidewalk. He crosses the street and starts walking uptown. He doesn't know where he's going. He tries hard to remember the important part, like she told him to. He tries to hold on to it, to wrap it in his fists, to press it into his flesh. But it's so slippery. He can barely keep his grip.

BEN

Ben is back on the couch at Gil's, thinking about a boy, about Justin. Justin in his inside-out T-shirt on the dance floor at Boy Bar, Justin's shoulders snaking forward and back with the music, Justin's torso making confident, sexual circles, moving closer and closer to Ben, enticing him. Justin's eyes, his chest, his waist, hands, lips. Justin grasping Ben's hips, holding him, pulling him closer. Justin's back, pressing into Ben. Justin drawing Ben's hands around his body, daring him to move closer. Ben feels the image physically, in his bones and in his flesh. He closes his eyes to see it better, to feel its insistence and danger. Soon he's out of breath, a sheen of sweat across his body. He keeps his eyes closed while his heartbeat settles into a slower, more steady rhythm. Justin's image fades from his mind. It's replaced by Adam's.

ADAM

Adam touches Callum's wrist softly, staring at the freckles, the stars. To see Callum sleeping, even here, even in this crappy bed with itchy sheets, even stuck with tubes and plastered with sensors, gives Adam a sense of calm. Callum is quiet. I am beside him. We are here. We are safe.

It's dark now, after midnight. Callum's chest rises, falls, pauses, and rises again. Adam counts. Two breaths. Three. Four. A hundred.

He picks up Callum's Walkman. "Do you want to listen to some music?" he whispers. He tries to fit the headphones over Callum's ears, but he is leaning at an awkward angle and Adam doesn't want to move it for fear of waking him. He reaches over to cover Callum's feet with the blanket.

He turns his chair to face the window. He slips the headphones onto his own ears and pushes PLAY. It's Bach, of course. The storyteller.

Reflected in the window, Adam can see the little blips of yellow-green on the monitor next to the bed, competing with the lights of the city beyond. *Blip, blip, blip.* They keep time with the music, syncopate with the flashing traffic lights. *Blip, blip, blip.* Adam's body is heavy. His eyelids are heavy. He reaches for the sweatshirt on the windowsill and pulls it up to his chin. He tucks his legs underneath himself and leans his head against the back of the chair.

Bach unfurls his story. Every piece is there, every quality, every emotion just like Callum said it was. Beauty, conflict, joy, dissonance—what was the last one? Adam can't remember. He turns up the volume to listen for it. He closes his eyes.

Soft clouds of gold and purple and gray fill the space behind his eyelids. They flow around his body, and through the room, then out the window and into the city. Adam sinks deeper into his chair. He dissolves into the music. He forgets where he is. He falls into sleep.

Later that night, when Callum's breathing loses its rhythm again, Adam won't hear. When the blips begin to slow, Adam won't see. He won't sense anything at all. He will only sleep, peaceful and still, until the sky falls and the nurse comes running.

Resolution.

Five

JUNE/JULY/AUGUST 1990

Come and pour your heart out to me.
—Erasure, "Weight of the World"

BEN

It's the last Sunday in June, and Ben's mind and body are firing with anticipation. He's seen the Gay Pride march on television before, but Rebecca said there's no way a news report could ever do it justice. It's a thousand times bigger than you're imagining, she'd said. And a thousand times more fun.

What should he wear? It's going to be warm, but there's no way Ben's wearing shorts. His legs are way too skinny and sad. The slate gray jeans will work. And on top, a black T-shirt with a stained-glass window printed on the front, panes of faded orange, red, yellow, green. He got this shirt from the three-for-ten bin over at Cheap Jack's on Broadway, and he likes how the decal has started to peel, like the windows are cracked. In the mirror, he considers cutting off the sleeves to look a little more punk. If only he had biceps. Maybe next year.

The parade route runs from Central Park all the way down Fifth Avenue to the Village, and then across to the west side, ending at Christopher Street and Hudson. He'll watch from Fifteenth Street and Fifth Avenue, outside the Paul Smith store, because Rebecca says it's the perfect spot. "Meet me at 12:30 so we can catch Dykes on Bikes," she'd said. "They're always first in the parade."

Ben slips on his baseball cap, grabs a pair of Gil's Ray-Bans, and heads out. He walks up West Broadway and through Washington Square to Fifth Avenue. The crowds get thicker as he goes. People in groups of two and three and ten, holding hands, hugging, laughing, posing for pictures snapped by disposable cameras. Plump clouds pass slowly across the sun overhead. A beautiful New York City summer day.

So much fashion! Multicolored tank tops, neon fanny packs, flannel bandeaus. Leather vests, leather captain's caps, leather jeans, leather cuffs. Glittery wigs, bikini tops, Daisy Dukes, bowler shirts, Speedos, muscle shirts, crinoline tutus. A woman with two nose rings holds hands with a pair of older men in golf pants waving a flag with Judy Garland's face on it. A young man in a leather harness and full face of makeup including at least three layers of fake lashes walks a ferret on a leash. A group of six girls in matching T-shirts that all read, I'M NOT GAY BUT MY GIRLFRIENDS ARE.

Ben finds the Paul Smith store. The shop window displays a row of sleek, tightly tailored men's suits and colorful shirts. Ben is intrigued but not today. Besides, the sign in the window says CLOSED FOR THE HOLIDAY. This is the spot.

Competing boom boxes blare dance music in every direction. On this side of the street, En Vogue. Across the way, Black Box. Up the block, Dead or Alive.

"Ben!" Rebecca almost knocks him over when she grabs him from behind and wraps her arms around his waist. She's wearing aviator sunglasses and a leopard-print tank top with the words MY KITTY BITES scrawled across the front.

"Do you like my lip?" she asks, puckering her bloodred mouth at Ben. "I triple applied."

Ben lowers his sunglasses. "Flawless."

"I did it for you," she says, and presses them against his neck, leaving a perfect lip mark. "There. A kiss for my favorite boy in the world. Are you so excited?"

"I can't believe all of these people!" he says.

A man next to them points up Fifth Avenue and shouts. "Here they come!"

Ben cranes his head to see two dozen or more women in torn jeans and leather vests rumble past on big fat motorcycles, rolling three across in perfect formation, rainbow flags and pink triangle flags fluttering from their handlebars. The crowd cheers. Rebecca shouts, "Goddesses!"

Behind them, as far as Ben can see, Fifth Avenue is packed solid. Groups of marchers begin to file past, waving and carrying banners that read BROOKLYN GAY YOUTH and BRONX POLITICAL ACTION GROUP and FRONT RUNNERS NEW YORK and DRAG DRILL TEAM. Drums beat, whistles sound, people whoop and clap. It's just getting started.

Here comes a float for the Roxy, a flatbed decked out like a disco, giant speakers thumping Ultra Naté for a dozen go-go boys in sequined short-shorts and combat boots dancing and singing along. Behind it, a group of men in leather jackets ride in a pickup truck, waving flags for the Spike. *Yes, daddy!* shouts a group of guys gathered by the police barricade. Behind them, the Imperial Court of New York, carrying a throne occupied by Camille Beauchamps, aka the Forbidden Empress. She waves to the crowd like a pageant queen, short, short, long, long, pearls. Behind her, the House of Africa float, its deep beats rattling windows in the buildings above. Ben throws up his arms and cheers.

They keep coming, group after group, each with its own soundtrack, each eliciting a new cheer from the crowd. *Yessss!* the crowd screams at a pair of drag queens on roller skates, one dressed as the Statue of Liberty and one as Barbara Bush, both wearing sashes that read I LOVE LESBIANS. Here's the Lesbian and Gay Teachers Association, throwing plastic beads and number two pencils into the crowd. Here comes Parents and Friends of Lesbians and Gays, a bigger group than Ben would have thought, waving signs that read I LOVE MY GAY KID. Ben scoffs to think of his mother marching.

Here comes a marching band, horns blaring skyward, percussion shaking the ground. Six men flank them on each side, twirling batons and stopping every few steps for a high kick or cartwheel. A gay double Dutch team follows, skipping two ropes to Lisa Stansfield singing about the right time to believe in love. It goes on and on. A man with two standard poodles dyed pink to match his wig. A pair of women holding hands, each with a child on her shoulders. A double column of people in wheelchairs wearing tiaras and passing a basketball between them. Another pickup truck filled with men in cowboy hats and rodeo buckles holding hands and kissing. Everyone is smiling. Everyone is happy. Ben's never seen, never even imagined, so much color and music and energy.

Rebecca leans into his ear. "This is for you, Ben. Everyone is here for you. Happy Pride, baby."

Ben just beams back at her, too spellbound by the spectacle to even speak.

"Oh my god," Rebecca says. She grabs his wrist and drags him through the crush to two women dressed in identical overalls, identical K-Swiss sneakers, and identical but opposite asymmetrical bobs. "Tania! Gabby!" Rebecca shouts. She hugs them both simultaneously, then gives each one a kiss on the mouth, tongue and all.

"Yum," Rebecca says after Gabby's kiss. "Ben, these are the sho-longs!"

"Heeeey!" they say in unison. They each pinch one of his cheeks, then move on.

Ben asks, "The sho-longs?"

"That's right. Short hair on one side, long on the other. Sho-longs. I love them."

"I could tell," Ben says, raising an eyebrow.

She shrugs. "We have a lot to talk about. One of these days."

Ben turns back to the parade. A group of men and women in old-time boater hats marches slowly next to a double-decker bus with a banner that reads SAGE: SENIORS ACTIVE IN A GAY ENVIRONMENT. Several white-haired men and women wave at the crowd from the windows. One man with a Santa Claus beard and rainbow suspenders locks eyes with Ben from inside the bus. He blinks slowly, almost like he's in a daze, but his smile is enormous. Ben wonders how old he is, how much he's seen.

Ben feels an arm around his chest from behind, holding him. He looks around to see Gil in a white T-shirt with a sticker of two men in sailor's suits kissing. READ MY LIPS, it says.

Ben punches him. "I didn't know you were coming!" he yells.

"Are you kidding? I wouldn't miss it! Gotta show up and be counted!" He leans over and mumbles something into Ben's ear.

"What?" Ben shouts.

Gil cups his hand around his mouth to say it louder. "I am so proud of you."

Ben smiles so hard his face hurts. No one's ever said that to him before. Not once. He tries to think of something to say back, but it's too late, he's drowned out by another float, this one blasting Janet Jackson, and Gil is already singing along. *We are a part of a rhythm nation!*

Abruptly, a whistle sounds and then another, and another farther up Fifth Avenue. The music slows, then stops. The crowd quiets. Suddenly everything is still. Ben looks around. "What's happening?" he whispers.

"It's two o'clock," Rebecca says. "Moment of silence for everyone who isn't here."

Rebecca takes both of his hands and bows her head. Ben keeps looking up and down the avenue. There are thousands of people in each direction, hundreds of thousands, maybe a million if the news reports later are to be believed, but the air is still. He can hear a bird across the street scolding another. How can a city, *this* city, so boisterous and alive a moment ago, be so utterly quiet now? It's as if every person here has retreated inside themselves, to find a memory, to grasp a sorrow, to honor their grief. Here, together. The weight of it all, the gravity of this massive display of mourning, amazes him. It's a hundred times more powerful than the loudest music all day.

After two minutes, exactly two minutes, a distant whistle sounds downtown, and shouts begin to roll up the avenue, washing over the crowd like a wave. The silence is giving way to an ecstatic cheer, everyone clapping and cheering a shouting at the sky, releasing the moment.

"Remember the dead! Remember the living! Remember the dead! Remember the living!"

"Never forget! Never forget!"

Ben shouts with them, over and over again. "Never forget! Never forget!"

Soon the music comes back up and the march resumes. More groups. The Lavender Light Gospel Choir. The AIDS Bereavement Support Group. Gay Men's Health Crisis. The mayor, David Dinkins. And on, and on, and on.

And then ACT UP, the loudest group yet, hundreds of people deep, marching behind a massive banner that reads ONE AIDS DEATH EVERY TEN MINUTES. The marchers carry placards that read WHERE IS YOUR RAGE, and SILENCE=DEATH. They chant in unison. "*How many more! How many more! How many more!*"

When the cops stop the march for cross traffic, the ACT UP marchers begin to lay down in the street, still chanting. "*How many more! How many more!*"

"What are they doing?"

"They lie down to represent the dead," Rebecca says. "Although they'd need thousands more for it to be accurate."

Their chant morphs into "*ACT UP! Fight back! Fight AIDS! ACT UP! Fight back! Fight AIDS!*" Ben chants with them, pumping his fist in the air. Rebecca and Gil chant, too, and everyone around them. Ben's voice breaks as he shouts, louder and louder, "*FIGHT BACK! FIGHT AIDS!*"

When the marchers scramble back to their feet to resume walking, Gil taps Ben on the shoulder. "We're going over to Two Boots for a slice. Wanna come?"

Rebecca is standing behind Gil, shaking her head and mouthing, *No. Stay here.*

"I'm going to stay," Ben says.

"Good call," Rebecca says. She and Gil head west, holding hands.

The next float rolls up. It must have sixty people on its flatbed, dancing, posing, voguing, walking, waving. It stops right in front of the Paul Smith shop, right in front of Ben's spot, just as Madonna's voice filters through its speakers. She's so right, he thinks. Life *is* a mystery.

Ben looks around expectantly. Everyone's listening, coiling up in readiness, preparing for this little prayer.

And then, *boom boom boom boom*, the music opens up and "Like a Prayer" fills the street, driving every other thought out of his head, every feeling out of his body, filling him with music. Everyone knows this song. Everyone sings. Everyone dances. Everyone jumps and swirls and thrusts and spins and sweats and jumps and smiles and shouts—Ben the loudest of all. His feet don't touch the ground.

ADAM

Adam's forgotten that today is Pride Day. He's forgotten what day it is at all. He's forgotten the difference between day and night, the difference between hours and minutes, the difference between together and apart, up and down, safe and unprotected, living and dead. His parents have been upstate for a couple of weeks now. He's glad they're away. He can just wander around his bedroom, looking blankly at books and staring at Callum's backpack.

Everything confuses him. The clothes on his floor. Whose are those? The pictures on his bulletin board, who are they? The food in the refrigerator, what is it? Even his mother's giant calendar is indecipherable. What could these markings mean?

If only he could sleep. But someone is outside his bedroom window blasting "So Many Men, So Little Time" and he doesn't even have to pull back the curtain to know that the march has spilled out from the end of Christopher Street and flooded Hudson, as it does every year. There will be hours and hours and hours of music and laughter and drunken partying outside his window for the rest of the day and night. It's going to be so loud down here today. He'll never be able to sleep now.

Maybe he'll go see what's happening.

BEN

The end of the parade route is at the intersection of Christopher and Hudson Streets, and marchers and partiers spill out across the neighborhood like a delta at the end of a rushing river. Thousands of people still buzzing from the march mill around, chatting, laughing, drinking, flirting, screaming with uncontained delight when they recognize friends in the crowd. Ben wanders among them, grinning stupidly at every face he sees. Every face grins back.

He buys a Coke for a dollar from a guy dragging a cooler behind him, then finds a stretch of open curb under a gingko tree. He'll sit here in the shade for a while, to rest his feet and watch.

He's wiping his sunglasses with the hem of his shirt when the boy, who he doesn't see coming, trips on the curb just a couple of feet away. By the time Ben is aware of him, the boy is already glancing off Ben's shoulder and collapsing onto the sidewalk beside him.

"Watch out," the boy says from the ground, as he's remembering what he meant to say before he fell. Ben scrambles out of the way.

Adam blinks up from the sidewalk with glazy eyes. His mouth moves but doesn't open, like he's chewing the insides of his cheeks. His white T-shirt is dirty and torn. Slowly, with visible effort, he fixes his eyes on Ben. When they land, they widen in recognition.

"Ben!" he shouts in a gravelly voice. "Ben boy! Benny! Private Benjamin. Benzoyl Peroxide. Happy peroxide, Ben! I mean, happy Pride!" He rolls toward Ben's feet, giggling to himself.

Ben stands up, then reaches a hand down to help Adam stand, too. Adam swats it away.

"It's a beautiful day!" Adam shouts, pulling himself up the trunk of the gingko tree. "Pride in the sunshine!"

Ben can see Adam's knee is freshly scraped, a raw, red wound embedded with pebbles, blood slowly collecting. Adam doesn't even seem to notice it.

He looks around. Is Adam here with someone?

Adam falls again, tugging Ben's shirt on the way down,

tackling him to the sidewalk. He starts laughing again. "Let's get some beers," he says. "We need more beers. Do you want beers? Beers!"

Ben scrambles up and looks around again. Where did Adam come from? Who is he here with? What should Ben do?

Adam sits up, suddenly serious. "Look at that," he says, pointing to his knee. "That looks bad. That looks fatal. I am going to die. Maybe I will just die right here."

"Take my hand," Ben says. Adam grabs it but loses his grip, falling again.

"Whoopsie!" he laughs. "Gotta use both hands, Benedict!"

Instead of trying again, Ben sits down next to Adam, scanning the crowd. If only he knew where Adam lived. He could walk him home. Should he take him down to Tribeca? His mind lurches from worry to panic, while Adam laughs on.

Suddenly, a voice. "Adam!"

It comes from a big man in a baseball T-shirt at the edge of the crowd. He approaches with another man who adjusts his curly black ponytail as he walks. Together they reach down, grasp Adam under the arms, and lift him to his feet. "You okay, kiddo?"

Adam slurs his answer. "Hi, guys! Happy Pride!" He leans against Baseball Shirt.

Ponytail turns to Ben. "Are you all right?"

Ben nods.

"This is Benjamin Franklin!" Adam shouts. "He knows me from the hospital. Isn't that right, Eggs Benedict? Hey, Ben! Who works at the hospital? Is it your father or what?"

"My brother is a doctor at St. Hugh's," Ben says to the two men.

Adam is still talking. "I almost got Ben here killed. Remember that, Ben? Remember when that happened? You almost died."

"No," Ben says. "That's not true."

Adam pats Baseball Shirt's chest. "He was nice to me. Why were you so nice to me, Gentle Ben?"

Because you were hurting, Ben thinks. *Because I care about you. Because—*

"We should get you home," Baseball Shirt says.

"Wait," Ben says, unsure who these men are, unsure if he should let Adam go. "How do you know Adam?"

"Where are my manners?" Ponytail says. He holds out his hand. "My name is Victor. This is Jack. We've known Adam since he was a baby."

"These are my gayfathers!" Adam shouts. He buries his head in Jack's shoulders. Several people look around to see who's yelling. They quickly turn away.

"He means godfathers," Jack says, smiling reassuringly. "We don't have any godfather ID on us, but if you'd like, you can walk with us to make sure we deliver him home safely. He lives right up the street."

"On Bank Street!" Adam shouts, pointing north. He grabs Victor's hand. "I love you guys."

"His scrape looks pretty bad," Ben says, pointing at Adam's knee.

"We'll get it cleaned up," Victor says.

"You sure you're okay?" Ben asks Adam one more time.

Adam touches Ben's cheek. "Do you see what I mean? He's nice to me. Why are people nice to me? I don't deserve it. I'm not nice. Don't be so nice, Ben!"

Jack takes both of Adam's shoulders. "We better go," he says.

Victor turns to Ben. "Are you okay? It looked like you got tackled."

"I'm fine," Ben says, brushing dust from his jeans. "Just worried about Adam."

"He'll be all right," Jack says. "He's having a hard time. He lost his boyfriend not long ago."

Ben swallows. "You mean Callum?"

"Yes. Did you know him?"

"No," Ben says. "I just heard about him from Adam. I think he loved him."

"Yes. I believe he did," Victor says. He smiles. "Have fun."

The two men turn Adam around and guide him away. Adam leans his head on Jack's shoulder as they walk. "Happy Pride!" Adam yells as he goes. "Everyone be proud!"

After they disappear up the street, Ben throws away his empty can of Coke and surveys the crowd. From somewhere deep inside it, he hears Soul II Soul, telling him to keep on moving. Ben takes a deep breath and dives back into the sea of smiling strangers, swimming toward the music.

ADAM

Adam stirs in the darkness. He is disoriented in that way that deep rest can render you, unmoored, suspended between wakefulness and sleep. His grandmother described the feeling to him once after a childhood nightmare. *You've been out in dreamland but you haven't found your way back yet. Don't be afraid. You can call yourself back. Use your name.*

Come back, he calls silently. *Adam. Come back.*

Slowly, his senses return. He hears rain falling outside his window. He sees a glass of water on his desk. He feels his shoes still on his feet. He doesn't remember coming home.

His body is heavy with a thick, physical pain that he can't isolate. It simply exists along the length of him, an ache gripping every bone inside. Everything hurts.

His clock radio says four fifteen. His stomach is rotten. He gets up, shaky, and goes into the bathroom to throw up. Nothing comes.

Back in bed, Clarence nuzzles into Adam's arm. When's the last time Adam fed him? He doesn't remember. He pushes the cat onto the floor. Clarence jumps back up. Adam decides to ignore him. If he was hungry, he would whine. Just let the dumb cat cuddle, if that's what he wants to do.

Slowly, pieces of yesterday slump back into view. He remembers stepping out of the apartment and into the crowd on Hudson Street. He remembers the disorienting energy, the noise, the bright colors in every direction. He remembers the smiles and laughter. He remembers the feeling of walking through them as if he were walking through a cartoon forest. None of it seemed real.

He remembers a man he didn't know handing him a can of beer in a tiny paper bag. He remembers drinking it quickly, then walking away. He remembers how the sun felt hot on his neck. He remembers asking another man for another beer, and then another. He kept asking for beer. He had no money, but it was easy. Smile, ask sweetly, get a beer, find another man. Over and over.

He remembers being down on Eighth Street and up on Fourteenth Street. He remembers a group of skinny young boys sticking pink triangle stickers all over his T-shirt, their hands touching every part of his body. He remembers a man in an acid green tank top removing the stickers and applying them to his own shirt. His hands went everywhere, too. He remembers a woman in leather jeans grabbing his butt and proclaiming, "Firm flesh!" He remembers drinking more beer. He remembers becoming confused in a scrum on Hudson Street and losing his breath. He remembers pushing through to the edge of the crowd. And then he doesn't remember any more.

Adam turns onto his side and stares at nothing. He shouldn't have gone out. He only did it to make the day go faster. That's all he wants now. For the days to go faster. He wants them to come and go and go and go and go. He wants no trace of them to linger, no memory, nothing.

But his wish goes unanswered and when he closes his eyes again, a different memory appears.

The nurse shook him awake that night. "They're on their way," she'd said, and he knew what she meant. He stood up from the yellow vinyl chair and carefully gathered Callum's things. His Walkman and his notebook and his sweatshirt and his Chapstick and the sunglasses he wore when the fluorescent lights gave him a headache. He put everything in the backpack as if it were all his own. He slung it over his shoulder and calmly thanked the nurse, even holding out his hand for her to shake. He did not look at Callum. It didn't even occur to him.

He moved as if he were a machine, controlled by a faraway joy-stick. No thought. No emotion. Just an empty journey down the stairs and out into a city that felt neither familiar nor strange, its neutral grid of sidewalks and streets leading nowhere. He walked, seeing nothing and hearing nothing, no traffic, no voices, no lights, no stimuli at all. No music. He did not wait for walk signals to favor him. He did not acknowledge rules or people or cars or convention. He just walked. Daylight came, and then went away again, and then returned. He walked.

He found himself in Grand Central Station sometime just before the second dawn. It was quiet then, just a few early commuters echoing through the concourse. He lay down on the floor, right there next to the clock, staring up at the ceiling of stars. He pointed at them, a million miles up, tracing his finger from star to star to star. From freckle to freckle to freckle. No one bothered him. They just walked around him on their way to somewhere else. He stayed there a long time. He doesn't know how long. He'll never know.

Adam gets up and goes back to the bathroom. He throws up this time, but it's only liquid and acid, and it's not enough. He's not empty enough. He returns to bed.

Beside him is Callum's backpack, still tightly zipped. Adam hasn't opened it once. He holds it to his chest and inhales its warm canvas smell, stained with spilled coffee and Callum's sweat. He won't look inside, maybe not ever. Callum is inside this bag, safe and warm, right here in his arms.

He runs a finger over the inside of his elbow. Callum's spot. It soothes him. He'll sleep again.

Tell me what makes you wonder.

For the longest time I hardly saw any music videos because we didn't have cable. The only place I could watch them was at the electronics store, where the wall of televisions was always tuned to MTV. I used to camp out there for hours.

Back then my favorites were the ones that were like little movies, like "Take on Me" by a-ha. Do you remember that one? With the animation and everything? I still have dreams about that one. Sometimes nightmares, about being stuck in a world you don't belong in.

I ended up buying a-ha's album and I listened to it a lot. There's this one song on there called "The Blue Sky" and it has this one lyric where he sings, "I used to be confused but now I just don't know."

I think about that line all the time. Like, is he saying that life gets more confusing as you go? You get so confused that you're not even sure when you're confused? Because I always thought that life was supposed to get less confusing. I always thought that you're supposed to get a grip on it at some point. But maybe that's not the case. Maybe that's just something everyone pretends to do. Maybe no one really has any grip at all, and the planet just spins and people just grow older and some of them get lucky and some of them don't. I wonder about that.

BEN

"Have you thought about calling our mother?" Gil asks, scooping another spoonful of Life cereal from his bowl. Life is Gil's favorite. Regular, not cinnamon. Ben likes it, too, but only at the end of the box, all the little broken pieces at the bottom where the sugar-to-cereal ratio is highest. Ben's favorite is Frosted Flakes. This is the kind of things that brothers should know about each other, he thinks. Can't we talk about cereal instead?

Ben crosses his arms. "Why?"

"Because," Gil says with his mouth full. "She's your mother."

"She doesn't act like it."

"I won't disagree."

"So why would I call her?"

"Because she deserves it. She hasn't had it easy, you know."

"Neither have I."

"No, you haven't. But you're on a new path now. You're an adult. You're not going back. You're safe. So why not be bigger than she is? Why not reach out?"

Ben sighs. "There's nothing to talk about. Besides, if she wanted to talk to me, she would call."

"Look," Gil says. "We both know that I'm not the smartest person in the world when it comes to feelings. But I know that if you don't put the bad shit behind you, it never goes away. So if you call her, you wouldn't be doing it for her sake. You'd be doing it for your own sake."

Ben considers for a moment before answering. "She'll never understand me."

"So what? Do you really need that if you know who you are?"

Ben shrugs.

Gil takes another bite. "It's not up to me. You do what you want. But I think you should think about it."

ADAM

Lily is standing at Adam's bedroom mirror, fluffing her hair. "What do we think? I got new layers. They're supposed to give me volume. As if I need more volume. I'm loud enough, don't you think?"

Adam lies in bed, watching her. "Your face looks different," he says.

"It's the eyeliner. Do you love it? Say you love it. I perfected it in Greece. You have to use this special eyeliner that you can only get in Europe. Dramatic, no? Kind of Maria Callas meets Debi Mazar on a date with Endora from *Bewitched*. A whole entire look." She spins, showing off her flowy black sundress. "Mediterranean chic. I'm thinking of moving there. What do you think?"

Adam struggles to keep up with Lily's narration. "Okay," he says.

"The gladiator sandals are killing me though. Who invented these? And someone please explain to me why I saw fit to break my no-sandals-in-New-York rule. Open shoes in this town? Gross. But they are cute, no?" She points her toe at Adam.

"When did you get back?"

"Night before last," she says. "I've called here like seventy-five times. Haven't you even checked the machine? Honestly, it's a good thing you gave me a key to this place, or I'd have had to pound on your shoe window like we were in sixth grade again."

He rubs his eyes. "What time is it?"

"And what day is it?" she responds, completing the quote from *Auntie Mame*, their favorite movie to watch together. Lily's greatest ambition in life is to grow up to be Auntie Mame, with costume changes throughout the day and a foot-long cigarette holder.

Adam coughs. "I'm thirsty."

She hands him a mug, one of Mom's old *Mad Magazine* mugs, with a goofy Alfred E. Neuman on the side. "I knew you would be. I brought you some Pepsi. Or would you prefer *a black coffee and a sidecar*?" More Auntie Mame.

He drinks greedily, then puts the empty mug on the floor. Clarence sniffs at it disdainfully.

"Your hair is a mess," she says.

"Sorry." Adam runs his hands through it.

"Are you hungry? Do you want to go to the Bus Stop? We could get patty melts. Which, I have to say, would be a great name for a drag queen. Ladies and gentlemen, *Patty Melt*!"

"No," he says, swallowing the nausea brought on by the mention of food. "How was your trip?"

She sits on the bed next to him. "We will be discussing my trip in excruciating detail over the next several weeks, and I promise, it will be excruciating. But right now, we are going to talk about you."

"What about me?"

"Cut the shit, Best. I ran into Victor at the dry cleaners and he told me that Callum—well, you know. He didn't tell me everything. But he told me the big part."

"Oh."

She pulls his head into her lap. "I came straight here."

"I'm sorry that we fought," he says.

"Shut up," she says. "Tell me about Callum."

"He told me not to worry," he says, his voice scratchy and slow. "He thought he would get better. And I believed him. I really believed him. I'm so stupid."

"I don't think that's stupid. I think that's love."

"I couldn't stop it," he says. "No one could stop it."

She strokes his hair, brushing it off his forehead.

Adam stares at the ceiling. "How did it all happen so fast?"

"Tell me the story," she says.

He holds his breath for a moment that feels like forever, then covers his face with his hands.

"I said yes," he says, and he begins to cry.

He cries for a long time. Slowly, quietly, an exhausted and unrushed stream of sorrow. He takes his time, soaking her dress with his tears. When the crying slows, she lies down next to him in her sundress and holds him.

"Sweet baby," she says softly. "My sweet, sweet baby."

He tells her everything, from the beginning to the end. He doesn't rush, and she listens to every word. When he starts to fade and fall back into something like sleep, she holds him tighter. She doesn't let go. They stay all day, and all night, just like that, just there.

Shortly after daybreak, she gets up to go. She'll be back in a little while, she says. She'll bring something to eat. He doesn't want anything, he says. She'll bring it anyway. Don't move. Okay, he says.

When the door closes behind her, he begins to cry again. Not softly this time, but violently, recklessly, a keening so desperate and expansive that he fears—no, he *knows*—that it will never end.

BEN

Rebecca tugs Ben deeper into the crowd that's gathered in the East River Park. Two or three hundred people, every color, every size, every age and shape and style. Punks and indie kids and lipstick lesbians and B-Boys and gym rats and hippies and blue hairs, all gathered around a ramshackle platform under a pair of sycamore trees. Rebecca leads them closer to the stage where they stand next to a skinny boy in a QUEER NATION T-shirt and a pair of women in hoop earrings draping their arms around each other. "This House" by Tracie Spencer plays over the scratchy speakers.

Ben is happy for his sunglasses today. Rebecca woke him up before he was ready. Yes, it was eleven when she rousted him, but he'd been out late again, dancing.

"Eric is next," she says. "He's an old friend from my days back at CBGB. I want you to hear him."

Just then, a young man in faded jeans and a blue bandanna round his neck steps up, swinging a bullhorn. He's welcomed with a few isolated whoops before raising the bullhorn to his lips.

"My name is Eric Flores," he begins. A few more whoops. He smiles and waves. "My name is Eric Flores, and I am mad as hell."

A few people applaud.

"Did you hear me in the back?" he asks. He takes a dramatic breath and shouts, "I SAID I AM MAD AS HELL!"

The crowd shouts in response, so loudly that Ben puts his hands up to his ears. Rebecca grabs them and yanks them down. "You should hear this," she says.

Eric Flores continues. "Ahh, it feels good to shout. It feels good to get it out. But I am not here today only to shout. I am not here today only to be angry. I am here today to talk about love."

The crowd murmurs.

"I hear you groaning," he says. "I know this sappy shit isn't what you came here for. But let me tell you a story. Last year, I had a beautiful young man in my arms outside a hospital uptown. He was in mourning. He said to me, Eric, I can't be your friend anymore. Every friend I have just disappears, withers away, vanishes. My heart is too broken now. I can't have friends. He tried to walk away but I held on. No, I said. Don't go. Please stay. I begged. I demanded. I threatened, and he stayed. I took him home and held him all night."

"Don't let go, Eric!"

"I didn't let go, but I didn't change his mind. He stopped calling me. Stopped answering when I called him. I didn't see him for months. But then one day, he did call, because he himself was in the hospital now. Meningitis, KS, wasting, the full nine. He couldn't get out of bed. Couldn't eat. Could barely speak. But when he spoke, he chose the greatest words in the world."

The crowd is silent.

"He said: I love you, Eric. And then he said it again. I love you. He said it over and over, *I love you, I love you,* and each time he said it, his voice became stronger, braver, drawing power from the words. He began to say more words. I see you, he said. I cherish you. I am grateful to you. I respect you. I believe you. You are my friend, he said. You are my friend. And then I was the one crying in his arms, and he was comforting me. Imagine. My beautiful, dying friend was comforting me."

"We love you, too, Eric!"

"I don't need to tell you how his story ended. You already know. But I am here to tell you, my—*MY FRIENDS*—that I love you. Every single one of you beautiful motherfuckers. I love you. My love for you feeds my determination, my commitment, even my fury. My love *is* my fight. Yes, we need attention. Yes, we need money. Yes, we need leadership. We need policy. And we need to attack the

296

damn power until we get all of it. We need to put our bodies in the streets and shout until we can't breathe and then shout some more."

"Keep shouting, Eric!"

"But most of all, we need love, because nothing else is strong enough to hold us together. Anger can't do it. Hate can't do it. Money can't do it. Only love. Only love is strong enough to carry us." His voice quiets, and the crowd is silent. He whispers into the bullhorn, "Only love."

He steps to the side of the stage and puts down the bullhorn. He clasps his hands at his waist and bows, as if praying. And then someone in the middle of the crowd shouts, "Only love!" and then another person repeats it, "Only love!" and then another, and another, and soon the whole crowd is chanting. "On-ly love! On-ly love! On-ly love!"

After some time, the crowd loses the rhythm and the chant subsides, a few whoops and whistles in its wake as they await the next speaker. Rebecca wipes her eyes.

"I'm a mess," she says, laughing against her tears. "Every time I see him speak. Let's go backstage and say hi."

But Ben shakes his head no. The day has turned muggy and he's too warm here in the crowd. He says goodbye and winds through the back of the crowd to a sparser section of the park. He finds a patch of grass with no one else on it, big enough to lie down and stretch out his arms. His heartbeat throbs in his ears. He thinks about friendship. He thinks about love.

ADAM

Saturdays are the worst days now. The emptiest days. He tries his best to sleep through them, but when he can't, he wanders.

Today he's wandered into the waiting room at St. Hugh's

Hospital. He chooses his chair carefully, the only one with uphol-stery that isn't split, the only one whose foam filling isn't spilling out. He sits, and waits, for something. It's not crowded in here today, just a few people sitting, a few people walking around in circles, worried. He pulls his feet up underneath himself and tips his head onto the armrest. He closes his eyes.

"Adam?"

The voice startles him awake. It's Dr. Nieves, standing over him, clicking her pen.

He presses his palms into his eyes, straining to remember where he is. How long has he been asleep? He pulls himself up from his contorted state.

"Adam? Is everything all right?"

"What did they do with him?" he asks softly.

She studies him for a moment, not speaking.

"Where is he, Dr. Nieves?"

"I'm on my way to the deli to get a coffee," she says. "Walk with me?"

She turns toward the main doors. Adam gets up and follows behind her. On the way out of the lobby, they pass the nurse with the red stud earrings. He nods at Adam and says, "I'm sorry."

Across the street, inside Gotham's Apple Deli & Beer, Dr. Nieves asks for two coffees with two sugars and two creams. "My usual, only twice," she says.

The man behind the counter nods.

"They didn't take him to Hart Island, did they?" Adam's read about the city's burial grounds, where they take unclaimed remains.

Dr. Nieves turns to Adam. "No," she says. "His sisters came to sign for him."

His sisters. He's glad for that. Better than no one coming.

"Where did they take him?"

"I don't know."

"Did they have a funeral?"

"I don't know. It's not like they'd invite me."

The man slides the two coffees across the counter, then takes her bill and makes change.

"How long did you know Callum?" she asks.

Did. Past tense.

"Since January," he says.

She nods and sips her coffee, then asks the man for more sugar packets. "Bitter today," she says. The man shrugs.

"Have you ever had a patient like him?" Adam asks.

"What do you mean?" She stirs more sugar into her coffee and tastes it again. "That's better."

"I mean young like him."

"I've treated a lot of people," she says. "A lot of ages. Most are older. Some are younger. Callum was on the young side."

Was. Past tense.

She steps outside, holding the door for Adam. The street is filled with yellow cabs and city buses, brave delivery guys weaving through on bicycles. Up the street, an ambulance siren blares, trying to blast away the traffic that keeps it from the St. Hugh's emergency room entrance. He wonders if it's ever quiet here.

"Adam, can I give you some advice?"

"You don't have to," he says. "I'll get tested."

"Good, but that's not what I mean. I'm talking about your heart."

"My heart?"

"It is broken. I can see it from here. It's been shattered and ground down to dust."

"Oh," he says.

"It won't stay that way, you know. Good hearts never do. They rebuild themselves. But only if you let it. You have to let it."

"I don't understand."

"One day you're going to wake up and the world won't be so dark."

"I like the dark," he says.

"I get it. I do. I felt the same way after my—" She cuts herself off. "Look. You'll never forget Callum, okay? No matter what happens in your life, no matter what you do or where you go, he'll be with you. But one day the air will change, and the sun will feel good on your face again, and when it does, I want you to let it. It won't be a betrayal. It won't mean you've stopped caring. I promise, you'll never stop caring. I promise. You won't ever forget him."

He lowers his eyes. How did she know that forgetting is the thing he fears the most? How did she know that every time he finds himself thinking about something else, like brushing his teeth or watching a movie, that he wants to punish himself? That he's afraid to fall asleep because he might dream about something other than Callum? That just days ago he went to Callum's apartment to gather Callum's things to keep forever, only to find the locks had been changed? That the reason he came here today was because he felt guilty for not being closer to Callum, closer to the place where he last saw Callum, last watched him breathe, last heard him say his name? How did she know?

You won't ever forget him.

"I won't ever forget you either, Dr. Nieves," he says. "Never."

She puts her coffee down on the sidewalk and opens her arms to him. They embrace, and Adam feels her warmth. He lays his head on her shoulder. He lets her hold him.

"Listen," she says. "The last time I told you to get some sleep, you ignored me. This time, doctor's orders. Okay?"

"Okay," he says, and then very carefully, very quietly, with great intention, he says, "Thank you, Dr. Nieves."

On his way downtown, he steps into the crosswalk just as a speeding bike messenger swipes past, dangerously close, yelling "*Watch it, punk!*" Adam drops his coffee and it splashes all over his sneakers. He leaves the cup where it lies. He crosses the street and ducks into a phone booth, where he sinks to the ground and rests his head on his knees. He won't cry. Not now. He's tired of crying. He just wants to be safe inside this phone booth, just for a minute, just until he can walk again.

BEN

A young man peels off from the crowd in the East River Park and approaches Ben's patch of grass. He's taller than Ben, with brown skin and perfect jeans. He has one crooked tooth in the front that Ben sees right away because he is smiling. *Smile back*, Ben tells himself, but the young man is very, very handsome, like a model, and his beauty makes Ben nervous. He watches the young man's grin grow bigger. *Smile back!* He steels himself, and smiles.

The young man is standing above him now. He speaks. "I, um. My friend over there dared me to come tell you that I think you're cute." He points at a group of people under a tree not too far away. They're all watching intently. "So, I took the dare and here I am. I think you're cute."

Ben's cheeks get hot. He knows he's blushing. He doesn't know what to say. What are you supposed to say when someone so beautiful says something like that?

"I saw you earlier and then I saw you again and I, well, my name is Elián."

"Hi," Ben says. "I'm Ben."

"I've never seen you at an ACT UP meeting, have I?"

"No," Ben says.

"You should come sometime. We have meetings on Monday nights." He hands Ben a flyer.

Ben deflates, just a little. He's recruiting him, not flirting. "Thanks," he says.

Elián turns to go, then stops. "Even if you don't come, I'd still love to see you sometime. Can I give you my number?"

"Okay," Ben manages to say. He hands the flyer back to Elián, who scrawls in the margin with a ballpoint pen, then returns to his friends.

Ben looks down at the number. It's incomplete. Elián only printed six digits. Ben thinks for a moment about chasing after him, but he doesn't get up. Right now, it just feels good to be out here on the grass. The scratchy speakers over by the stage play the B-52's. Roam, if you want to.

ADAM

It's beautiful out this morning. Clear and dry and a quiet breeze. Jolly cotton-puff clouds float lazily above, intermittently obscuring the early August sun. The woman who runs the Bus Stop diner is out walking her new puppy, a scrappy little mutt with floppy ears. She smiles and waves at Adam. A cab rolls smoothly up Eighth Avenue playing that sentimental new song by Wilson Phillips about holding on for one more day. It's all perfect, picture perfect. Adam hates it.

He trips as he plods along the sidewalk because he isn't paying attention. Adam used to know every plank of concrete in the Village, every tilt and crack. He knew them in his feet, because this is where he learned to walk. But now, every step is a surprise. Like he is a stranger here.

He stops at the newsstand on Sheridan Square. It's one of the big ones, with rows and rows of magazines and newspapers, every kind of candy bar and cigarette, a glass-front fridge filled with bottles of iced tea and soda.

A headline on the *New York Times* reads:

CUT DOWN AS THEY GROW UP: AIDS STALKS GAY TEEN-AGERS.

Nelson Mandela is on the cover of *Time*. "A Hero in America," it reads. Adam remembers wanting to go see him on his visit to New York. Was that a week ago? A month? A lifetime?

Above Mandela's photo, he sees a smaller inset picture of ACT UP demonstrators, above a coverline that reads, "AIDS: The Losing Battle."

He stares at the words. *The losing battle.*

Losing.

Lost.

He closes his eyes.

"Adam?" The voice from behind him is familiar. He turns slowly and blinks twice. It's Ben. He hasn't seen Ben since their grilled cheeses at the Waverly Diner, right? That was a nice time.

Ben's hands are in his pockets. When Adam looks at his eyes, they dart away. Adam watches them flit across the magazines like a grasshopper, landing everywhere but on Adam. He wishes they would settle, so he could study their colors more closely.

After a moment, Ben speaks. "Weird how we keep running into each other."

Adam nods, but he knows that's how New York works. You run into people all the time. Usually when you don't want to, and almost never when you *do* want to.

"I was worried about you," Ben says. "After Pride."

Adam's chin sinks to his chest. They must have seen each other that day, but he doesn't remember. "That was a strange day," he says.

"Yeah," Ben says. His voice is faintly melancholy. It matches his looks, Adam thinks. Broody and complicated.

"Your face is healed," Adam says.

"Almost," Ben says. "I'll probably have a permanent scar though."

"I've always wanted a scar."

"I don't recommend it."

Adam chastises himself. *Why aren't you thinking about Callum?* They stand side by side looking at the magazine covers. Famous faces stare back. Gloria Estefan on *People*. Madonna on *Cosmopolitan*. Julia Roberts on *Rolling Stone*. Denzel Washington, Johnny Depp, Whitney Houston, Winona Ryder, Demi Moore. Adam likes the feeling of Ben's presence. It calms him.

"Well, I'm going to get a slice at Ray's," Ben says. "I'll see you around."

Adam's throat catches. He doesn't want Ben to go. What is this surprising sense of panic? He doesn't want to be alone. For the first time in weeks, he doesn't want to be alone.

"Joe's is better," he says.

Ben raises his eyebrows. "Are you sure? I'm very picky about pizza."

"Trust me. I've lived here my whole life and—" He cuts himself off. He remembers saying these words before, to someone else, a long time ago. They belong to the past.

"Where is Joe's?"

"Carmine Street."

"Are you hungry?"

Adam is, and together, without talking, they walk the few blocks over to Joe's tiny storefront. Despite the dozen different pies under the glass—plain, sausage, pepperoni, mushroom, deluxe, and so on—Adam orders two plain slices, one for each of them.

The pizza guy lays out four paper plates, the flimsy kind with dimples around the perimeter. He'll use two for each slice, doubling up so that the grease doesn't soak through. He drops a big triangle of pizza on each set. Adam digs through his pockets for money but Ben beats him to it.

"And two Cokes," Ben says. The pizza guy slides two cans across the counter.

Adam showers his slice with red pepper flakes, then hands the jar to Ben. Ben uses even more than Adam does. Adam likes that.

They walk across the street to the little park, Father Demo Square. There's an open bench facing the Our Lady of Pompeii Church, so they sit. A pair of nuns walk by, smiling at the boys. Adam smiles back.

"This looks good," Ben says, lifting his slice to his mouth. Before he can take a bite, the tip of his slice droops, sending a splatter of grease onto the ground.

"No," Adam says. "Look. First you have to dab your slice with a paper napkin, to sop up the excess grease. See? Then, you fold it lengthwise to keep it from flopping around." He demonstrates for Ben, folding his slice over into a torpedo. He aims the tip at his mouth and takes a clean bite.

Ben follows suit. "I never knew that," he says.

"Now you're a New Yorker," Adam says.

After they finish their slices, Ben says, "I met your friends Jack and Victor at Pride. They told me about Callum. I'm really sorry."

Adam looks down to see a bee on his shoe, just nosing around. Adam watches it. What is it looking for? Adam's sneaker holds no nectar. Is it lost? Has it forgotten where it belongs?

"Hey," Ben says. He's waving his hand in front of Adam's face. "Are you in there?"

Adam snaps back to Ben. He hears himself ask, "Have you ever been in love?"

"No," Ben says.

Adam crunches his empty Coke can on the bench. "That's smart. Love is stupid."

Ben doesn't answer.

They sit silently for another few minutes. Adam's bee flies away. Is it going home? How does it know where home is?

Eventually, Ben says, "Well, I guess I should get going."

No, Adam thinks. *Not yet.* He opens his mouth to say something like *wait* or *not yet* or—something. But nothing comes out. He watches helplessly as Ben gets up and takes a few steps toward Sixth Avenue. *Don't go!*

As if Ben hears his silent plea, he abruptly turns back to Adam. "Would you ever want to do something sometime?"

Adam is startled by the question. He cocks his head to one side.

"Not like a date," Ben says, apparently reading what must be a confused expression on Adam's face. "Just, you know, like friends."

Friends. Adam's mind fills with a vision of Jack and Victor's apartment, filled with friends.

"Okay," he says.

Ben digs through his backpack for a pen and a scrap of paper.

Adam writes down his number. Ben folds it into his back pocket, then writes down his own number for Adam.

"I'll see you," Ben says.

"See you."

As Ben begins to walk away again, the panic of separation presses harder against his chest, and Adam blurts out, not thinking, "Where are you going now?"

Ben shrugs. "Nowhere."

"Can I come?"

Tell me how no one underrtood.

In eighth grade we all had a choice. We could take metal shop, home economics, or arts and crafts. I chose arts and crafts. Our first assignment was to make a piece of pottery out of clay. It could be a cookie jar, or a mug, or an ashtray, whatever we wanted. It just had to be quote, unquote "something people can use." In other words, not just decorative.

I was obsessed with ancient Rome at the time so I decided to make a lacrimarium. Do you know what that is? It's a little vessel that they supposedly would pass around at funerals to collect the tears of the mourners, and then seal it up and bury it with the dead.

I have no idea if people really did this or if it's just a legend but I thought the idea was perfectly morbid. Right up my alley in eighth grade.

After our projects were fired in the kiln, we each had to tell the rest of the class what it was. When I tried to explain my lacrimarium, everyone just stared at me with these blank expressions. They didn't even snicker or laugh, which is what I expected. They just stared and waited for me to finish so they could talk about their ashtrays and mugs.

I took it home and tried to make myself cry to see if it would work, but I couldn't get any tears flowing, no matter what sad or horrible things I thought about. I guess by eighth grade I'd pretty much stopped crying.

BEN

"Nowhere" turns out to be Union Square Park. Ben and Adam wander through the hot dog carts and sidewalk artists to sit on the concrete steps at the south end of the park, where a musical theater troupe has set up bongo drums and tambourines and an open guitar case. They're singing that Age of Aquarius song from *Hair* when a stray riderless skateboard comes careening down the steps, crashing into Adam's foot.

Adam grabs his foot. "Ow!"

Ben picks up the skateboard and stands up. "Hey!"

"That's mine!" A kid in a Beastie Boys T-shirt comes running. He grabs the board from Ben's hand. "Give me that."

"You should be careful," Ben says. "You could hurt someone."

"I don't care," the kid says. "You don't like it, you should take your boyfriend somewhere else."

Adam springs up. "Get out of here," he snarls.

The kid stares at Adam, incredulous.

"I said get out of here," Adam repeats.

The kid looks back at his friends, then at Adam. "Fag," he says.

Adam steps forward, standing face-to-face with the kid, squaring his shoulders. "Say it again."

The kid takes a half step back. His eyes widen.

"What?" Adam demands. "No one told you that fags fight back?"

Ben sees Adam's hands forming into fists. *No*, he thinks, his mind flashing back to that night on the piers. *Don't*. He puts his hand on Adam's shoulder.

But Adam shakes it off and takes another step forward. "You have something to say?"

The kid takes two steps backward, then trips on a stair and falls over onto his side, dropping his skateboard and scraping the side of his face on the concrete. A couple of girls in baggy jeans with the waistbands folded over point and laugh. Ben steps forward, next to Adam. They stand shoulder to shoulder over the kid on the ground, casting shadows across his body. Ben feels ten feet tall next to Adam.

The kid scrambles up and away, back to where his buddies are standing, waiting for him, jeering him now. *You scared of those queers?* They punch him on the arm in solidarity, then they all skate away. The girls in the baggy jeans cheer, giving thumbs-up signs to Ben and Adam. "Yes!"

Adam's angry scowl gives way to a broad, triumphant smile, and his eyes fill with light. Ben holds his hand up for a high five, but instead of clapping it, Adam furrows his brow, drops his chin to his chest, and walks straight into Ben, wrapping his hands around Ben's waist and pressing his head into Ben's neck. His body softens against Ben's like a child's. Ben wraps his arms around Adam, locking his hands behind Adam's back and squeezing. Is everyone watching them? Are they laughing, or pointing, or snickering? Let them. It doesn't matter. They aren't real.

"That was great," Ben says. He tightens his grip.

"Yeah, it was," Adam says, but Ben can feel him trembling. Is it fear?

A siren sounds, but like everything else right now, it's a million miles away.

ADAM

Adam inhales Ben's warmth as they stand, embracing, in Union Square. It's not the mature warmth that Callum exuded, the warmth that sparked a desire in Adam, a yearning. This is a different warmth, nascent and uncertain, a soft glow of kindness. Adam takes it in, like a language he understands. He takes a step back from Ben and puts his hand on Ben's jaw, feeling the warmth there, too.

"Are you going to be all right?" Ben asks, touching Adam's hand.

Adam answers, with a sliver of confidence, "Yeah. I am."

Ben smiles.

"I'm going to go," Adam says.

"Okay," Ben says.

"I'll see you," Adam says. "I will." He means it.

He looks down at his shoes, puts his hands in his pockets, and turns downtown.

BEN

It is so hard not to follow Adam, but he doesn't. He stands still until Adam has disappeared down Broadway, absorbed back into the city.

I'll see you, he said. *I will.*

But when?

Ben feels for Adam's phone number in his back pocket. He reads it ten times, memorizing it, then moves it to the safety of his backpack. There's an inside pocket that holds the most important things. Ben zips it tightly inside.

ADAM

You can hear the conversation in the kitchen through the transom window over the door to Adam's bathroom if the transom window is left ajar. Adam's known this forever, but for most of his life, he's ignored it, because whatever's going on in the kitchen is usually uninteresting—his mother conversing with a client, Pop singing songs from *Godspell* while he packs his lunch. But today he listens.

"I'm worried," his mother is whispering. "He missed work again today. I poked my head into his bedroom and there he was, curled around his atlas like he was eleven. He's barely spoken in weeks."

"He just needs time, Frankie," Pop says. Adam can picture him hugging her, resting his chin on her head. "Remember what Jack said?"

"Yeah, that we'll never understand our own kid."

"That's not what he said. He said that the most important thing we can do, maybe the only thing we can do that's real, is to make sure he knows we love him and respect him. The worst thing we can do is pretend we know how he feels, or force him to explain or justify how he feels. Beyond that, the rest is up to him. If he wants to share, he'll share. If not, he won't. But it's not our call, it's his call. He has to know that our love is unconditional, not transactional. He has to know he owes us nothing. I promise he knows that. He's a good kid. Mourning isn't easy. It's different for everyone. Give it time, okay? Time."

Adam stares at his image in the mirror. He looks so tired. He hasn't gotten a haircut all summer. Pop calls him a hippie.

"But do you think he was safe?" she is asking Pop. "Do you think he protected himself?"

"He knows as much about all of that as we do. Maybe more."

"He's a baby."

"He's not a baby, Frankie. He's eighteen."

"Jesus. What does that make us?"

"Jurassic," he says, and their voices disappear into the TV room.

What if he wasn't safe enough, he wonders. What if he didn't protect himself? What if he gets sick next? What would he look like if he did get sick? What *will* he look like *when he does* get sick? He imagines how difficult it will be on his parents. How disappointed they'll be when he dies young. How they'll blame themselves. How they'll blame him, even if they pretend not to.

He stands in front of his desk and methodically untacks every photograph from his bulletin board. There are layers and layers of pictures, dozens of tacks. He works carefully, neatly stacking the pictures of Lily in one pile, the pictures of Mom and Pop in another, and everything else in a third. There's a picture of the cat he adopted from the shelter in seventh grade, the charcoal cat he named Dave. Dave disappeared after just two weeks, and even when Adam papered the entire West Village with notices offering a ten-dollar reward, Dave never came back. That's when they got Clarence.

Soon all that's left on the bulletin board is the top half of the strip of photos of Callum and Adam from the day they met. Callum's face dominates the frames, his smile wide and happy. Adam peeks from behind Callum's shoulders like a child. He's smiling, but Adam sees the anxiety in his eyes.

He tears the strip in two. He stacks the two pieces on top of each other and tears them again. And then again. He tears, methodically and dispassionately, until his desk is covered in tiny little squares of photo paper. Confetti. Litter. He brushes it all into the wastebasket.

It won't be until later, much later, that Adam will realize that he's torn up the only photographs of Callum he had. For the rest of his life, he'll wonder why he did it.

BEN

Ben takes Gil's new cordless phone into his room and dials his mother in Gideon. It takes him a minute to remember the number even though he grew up with it. Was it really just eight months ago that this number was his own?

"Hello?"

Her voice raises the hairs on his arms. He's tempted to hang up.

"Hello?" she says again.

"It's Ben," he says. "It's your son."

"Oh," she says dully. She sounds like she's been interrupted by something unimportant, like that little bell that goes off when the dryer is finished. "What time is it?"

"Five thirty."

"In the afternoon?"

"Yes. Did I wake you?"

She clears her throat. "No."

"Well, I—" He stops and starts again. "I just wanted you to know that I'm fine."

"Okay," she says. She sounds very small, and it makes him feel rotten. "There are still a couple of birthday cards here for you. One is from your aunt and uncle in Worcester. It's probably a check. Didn't they send you twenty dollars last year?"

"I don't remember."

"I'll keep it for you."

"You don't have to."

"Are you coming back?" she asks.

The line is silent. He feels the distance between them, all sixty thick miles of it. He's the one who created that distance, on his eighteenth birthday. He remembers how brave he felt that morning. How unkind he'd been to her, and her to him. Nothing is simple.

"Not now," he says, knowing he means *not ever*. He's pretty sure she knows it, too.

"Okay," she says.

"I'm sorry," he says. "For everything."

He waits for a response—an acceptance, a refusal, an apology in return—but nothing comes. Not a word. She simply hangs up. *Click.*

He stares at the ground. Maybe he should call back. Maybe they were disconnected by accident. Maybe she had more to say. Maybe he has more to say. But he doesn't call back. He'll consider it again, but not until later.

He looks at the clock. He should start dinner in case Gil's shift miraculously ends on time. He puts on his new Adamski CD and cues up "Killer." He loves the singer, whose name is Seal.

Soon the familiar spaghetti sauce is simmering, and Ben has a pot of water boiling and ready. He's got all the rest of the ingredients out on the counter: dried noodles, grated Parmesan cheese, red pepper flakes. He even bought some fresh basil at Angelino's because it looked good. He'll chop it and throw it on top of the pasta. Gil will laugh and say it counts as a salad.

Gil calls to tell Ben he won't be home. He's going out with Rebecca tonight. He invites Ben to come along, but Ben says no thanks. He boils the spaghetti and eats it while reading his new issue of *Vogue Paris*, the haute couture special with Christy Turlington on the cover, wearing Dior.

ADAM

When Victor calls to invite Adam over for brunch, he warns him to have a snack first.

"You know how these BGBs are. These big gay brunches. Everyone chats too much or drinks too much and you never end up eating until five."

Adam asks who else is coming and Victor says just family, so Adam expects to see Joe-Joe, Dennis, Alexey and Carlos, Caryn, and some of the others from last time.

He chooses his Mount Rushmore T-shirt. He hears an echo of Callum's voice. *Look at you*, he's saying. *Cutie*. Adam wonders if anyone will ever say anything like it to him again. He decides to change.

"Where you off to, kid?" Pop asks as Adam ties up his Sambas.

"Jack and Victor's."

"Will you be back for dinner?"

Adam can tell that Pop's question is genuine. A year ago, it would have disguised Pop's real meaning—*I expect you to be home for dinner*—but now Adam knows he's honestly curious.

"Not sure," he says.

"Okay either way. By the way, I'm going to the laundromat in a few minutes. Do you need anything done?"

"That's okay. I'll do my stuff tomorrow."

"All right."

"I'll see you."

"Wait," Pop says. "Give your old man a hug."

Adam complies. He expects a normal hug, the quick embrace they usually share. He pats Pop on the back. But Pop holds on to him for much longer than he expects. "I'm proud of you," he says.

"Thanks, Pop," Adam says.

By the time he gets to Jack and Victor's place, several others are already there. Dennis is there, and Alexey and Carlos and Caryn and Diane and Lalita. But not Joe-Joe. Everyone greets Adam with a hug and a kiss on the cheek. They seem honestly happy to see him. It makes Adam feel good. The stereo is set to Z100, where Anita Baker is singing about the rapture of love.

Jack hands him a glass of champagne.

"I don't think I should drink," Adam whispers.

"You sure? We're celebrating today."

"Celebrating what?"

Jack winks. "Tell you what. I'll fill your glass with ginger ale for the toast."

Victor is setting dishes onto the kitchen island, creating a buffet. There's a fat lasagna, still bubbling under a cap of browned mozzarella. There's a basket of glistening fried chicken. A glazed ham. Biscuits, dinner rolls, garlic knots, cornbread, a platter of cheese.

"And my grandmother's Okie-style smothered pork chops," Jack says, pointing to a baking dish filled with browned pork chops in a pool of thick, peppery gravy.

"Lord, give me strength," Alexey says. "We've been invited to Fire Island this weekend. I will never squeeze myself into a Speedo after this."

"Oh, please, Slim Goodbody," Victor says, squeezing Alexey's bicep.

Jack straightens his spine and taps his champagne glass. "Attention, everyone! Victor and I have an announcement to make."

"What, are you getting married?" Dennis says, snickering.

"Yeah, right," Carlos says. "Gays can get married, and in other news, I'm Princess Diana."

"Wrong," Jack says. He takes Victor's hand. "We are officially retirees!"

"Cheers to us!" Victor shouts, raising his glass.

But no one else raises a glass. Everyone just stares at the couple.

"But you, wait, how are you—why?" Dennis asks. "Did you win the lotto?"

"No, darling," Victor says. "We're tired of it all. We're tired of the rat race. Life is too short, and we have things we want to do. We want to see the world!"

"That's right," Jack says. "Machu Picchu, the Great Barrier Reef, the Eiffel Tower, Fiji. We have a long list."

"I had no idea you were secretly rich," Alexey says. "Are you actually Leona Helmsley?"

"Rich? Hardly," Jack says. "We just cashed in our retirement plans, that's all."

"Wait, you can do that?"

"Don't you pay a penalty?"

"But what about—?"

Jack interrupts the questions. "The future is now! We're so excited. Let's drink."

No one drinks. The silence is heavy as the truth sinks in. Adam understands the code now. When people cash in their retirement plans at Jack and Victor's age, it means they don't see any reason to save it. It means they don't want to wait to spend it. It means—his knees begin to buckle. He moves to the wall to keep from falling. Maybe he's wrong. Maybe he misunderstood.

"So," Dennis says, his tone a solemn contrast to Jack and Victor's buoyancy. "Whose name did it call this time? Just one of you? Both of you?"

"Just Jack this time," Victor says.

"Oh, Jack," Caryn says. "When?"

"Hey, listen," Jack says. "Today is about good news, okay? And I believe I proposed a toast. Can we please drink to us?"

Everyone looks around, at one another, at nothing. Finally, Dennis raises his glass. "Here's to the happy couple!" he shouts. "And to the High Calorie Gay Buffet!"

Everyone drinks except Adam. He is disoriented. Don't they all know what this means?

Jack hands a plate to Carlos and another to Alexey. "Start eating, queens. I'm going to force all of you to get fat with me."

"My dream come true," Alexey says. He kisses Jack on the cheek. "I love you, Papa."

"We all love you," Carlos says.

Soon everyone's filling their plates and chatting animatedly about Jack and Victor's travel plans. Everyone except Adam. Adam is hugging the wall. The air around him has started to close in. He doesn't understand. How can they all be so cheerful? How can anyone be anything but devastated? He sets his glass on a console by the door and slips out the door. No one will notice.

Tell me why you don't sleep.

I didn't say goodbye. I knew what was happening, but I didn't say goodbye. I didn't even try to.

BEN

Ben's deep in a new issue of the *Face*, studying a haphazard fashion spread of quirky boho looks—sweaters, shorts, sandals—all shot on a hazy beach. He's not crazy about the clothes, which seem like they could be from any old mall, but the model is stunning. Freckles, a goofy smile, incredible eyes. She's not glitzy like Linda or Naomi. She's different, more laid-back looking, more relaxed. He finds her name in the credits: Kate Moss. He'll have to ask Rebecca if she's heard of her.

The phone rings. He lets the answering machine pick up.

"Hi, um, this is a message for—"

That voice. It's Adam. Ben grabs for the phone. "Hello?"

"Ben?"

Ben has been replaying that moment with the skateboarder at Union Square over and over in his mind for days. He hasn't been able to stop thinking about Adam. The way he embraced Ben so forcefully. The way he said *I'll see you.* The mysterious way he walked away.

"Hi," Ben says.

"What are you up to?"

"Nothing."

"Oh."

"What about you?"

"Um, I was thinking about going over to the movie theater on Broadway to see what's playing."

Ben can't tell if it's a statement or a question. Is Adam asking Ben to come, too? It's hard to tell.

Adam speaks again. "I mean, it's so hot and muggy today and the theater has the best air-conditioning."

"That's for sure."

"Anyway, I don't know what's playing, but—"

Ben can hear Adam's voice wobble, a sound of sadness or anxiety or something. He sounds small, tentative.

"What time are you going over?" Ben asks.

"Pretty soon. Maybe now?"

Now. Now!

"Okay," Ben says, as cool as he can. "I'm all the way in Tribeca. Forty-five minutes?"

"Okay," Adam says.

Ben races to his room to change. What should he wear? This is not a date, he reminds himself. Just a friend calling a friend to see if he wants to go to a movie. Nothing special. Nothing surprising. Nothing weird. White T-shirt and gray jeans. Baseball cap. He flies uptown to the movie theater.

He keeps one eye on his watch the whole way up, but by the time he arrives, Ben is five minutes late. He looks around for Adam but doesn't see him. Has he already gone in? Did he give up and leave?

Ben approaches the ticket booth. "Did you see a guy here? About my age?"

The attendant shakes her head. "I see a lot of people. Do you need a ticket?"

Dick Tracy, with Madonna and Warren Beatty, is playing in ten minutes. Ben decides to buy two five-dollar tickets. He goes inside to see if Adam is in the lobby. He comes back out. He looks up Broadway, then down. No Adam.

Five more minutes. The movie's starting soon. Is Adam blowing him off? He tugs at his T-shirt, which is sticking to him in the humidity.

Ten minutes now. No Adam. He's stuck on the subway, Ben thinks. He's gone to a different movie theater. He's been hit by a taxi. He's been kidnapped. Ben thinks of every possible elaborate scenario to avoid the most obvious: Adam's changed his mind. He's not coming.

And then, before Ben can accept this disheartening explanation, Adam rounds the corner, sweat dripping from his temple. "I'm sorry," he says, breathless. "I got halfway here and realized I didn't have any money. I had to run back home to grab ten bucks from my mother's stash."

"We just missed it," Ben says, pointing at the *Dick Tracy* poster. He won't tell Adam that he bought tickets. Too embarrassing. "Do you want to see *Gremlins 2* instead? It might suck but, you know, air-conditioning."

"What else is there?"

"*Another 48 Hours*, *The Adventures of Ford Fairlane*, and *Arachnophobia*."

"Ugh. Nothing good," Adam says.

"Sorry," Ben says, only slightly crestfallen.

"It's my fault. I'm really sorry I was so late. Can I buy you a FrozFruit or something?" He points at a deli across the street. "It's my favorite thing to eat in the summertime."

"Okay."

Ben chooses cherry and Adam chooses lime, and together they

walk down to Washington Square. Adam sits on the edge of the fountain, then kicks off his shoes and rolls up his jeans. He swings around to dunk his feet in the water.

"Really?" Ben asks. The water doesn't *look* dirty, but still.

"We used to do this all the time. It feels good. You should try."

Ben unties his shoes and slips his feet into the water. It's colder than he expects. When he shivers, he dripples cherry FrozFruit onto his T-shirt.

Adam points at the stain. "Bleeding heart," he says. He smiles, and Ben smiles, too.

The park is full of people today, couples sprawled out on the grass, clusters of friends playing cards, a group of drama students running lines. A teenage boy pushes a dachshund in a baby carriage. Three old men laugh uproariously on a bench. A pair of women plays "Dueling Banjos" on ukulele.

"This is my second favorite park," Adam says. "After Central. You can't beat Central."

"I heard on the news that they are talking about turning the piers into a park, with grass and everything," Ben says.

"No way," Adam says. "That will never happen."

A group of college students approaches the fountain. One guy is pounding on a hand drum and the others are chanting. *Safe sex is hot sex! Safe sex is hot sex!* They make their way along the paved path and circle the fountain, handing out condoms to people as they go. A girl with waist-length braids and a flowing skirt with fringe at the bottom holds out a handful of condoms to Ben.

"No thanks," Ben says politely.

"They're free!" she insists. "Safe sex is hot sex!"

Adam takes the condoms. He turns them over in his hands, like mysterious relics. "It's hard to believe that something so small can . . ." His voice trails off. He sets the condoms down.

Ben turns his eyes to his feet in the water. He hates his toes. He tries to squish his feet together to cover them up.

"Can I ask you a question?" he says.

"What?" Adam says.

"Do you ever get scared? Of HIV, I mean."

"Don't you?"

"Yeah, I guess it's a dumb question." Ben tries to cover his toes again. "Sometimes I don't know if I'm afraid of catching it, or if I'm just hoping I can put it off for as long as possible. Do you know what I mean? Like, even with all the precautions and every-thing it just seems like, I don't know. It seems like it's everywhere. There's no escape. You know?"

"No escape," Adam says. His voice is flat. His body slouches.

"Are you scared to get tested?" Ben asks.

"Scared?"

"I mean, because of—because of what happened?"

"Because of Callum?"

"I don't know. I can just imagine that maybe it's easy to make a mistake, you know? To get caught up in the moment and lose control and do something wrong."

"Do something wrong? What's that supposed to mean?" Adam sits up taller.

"That's not what I meant," Ben says. "I just meant—"

"Are you saying that people with HIV did something to deserve it?"

"No! I didn't mean that! I just—" He's choking on his words now. He's said the stupidest thing imaginable. Idiot. Stupid idiot. He opens his mouth to apologize but he's afraid he'll screw that up, too. His mind races. How can he take it back? "That came out wrong."

"You don't know what the hell you're talking about."

"I'm sorry," Ben says. "I really didn't mean to—"

Adam stands up. "I need to go," he says.

"Wait," Ben says, but it's as if he's become invisible. Adam doesn't even look at him as he splashes out of the water and walks away. He crosses the park in his bare feet, his shoes dangling from his fingers. Ben wonders if he'll ever see him again. He doubts whether he even deserves to.

ADAM

"Over here!"

Jack is calling Adam's name from the far end of the crowded lunch counter. It's one thirty in the afternoon at Eisenberg's Sandwich, and as usual, the tiny diner is filled with customers munching on egg salad sandwiches and finishing the crosswords in the copies of the *New York Post* left behind by the breakfast crowd. Adam gets a nod from the balding man behind the register, who's chewing on a matchstick while ringing up a woman whose blue rinse stayed in a little too long. Adam slips through the patrons to an aluminum and Formica table where Jack and Victor are already sipping cups of coffee.

"He's alive!" Victor jumps up to give Adam a hug.

"I'm sorry I disappeared the other day. I needed some air."

"You would have loved Caryn's rendition of 'She's Like the Wind' after you left."

"How does a BLT on white bread sound?" Victor asks.

"I'm not hungry."

"Well, you've got your work cut out then, because I ordered yours deluxe."

"Corned beef hash for me," Jack says with a grin. "Poached eggs on top. I love all-day breakfast."

After the waiter brings a Coke for Adam and more coffee for Jack and Victor, Adam fidgets with the salt shaker.

"So, there's an elephant in here," Jack says.

Adam nods.

"I know this is a shock," Jack says. "We're shocked, too. But my test result is the biggest reminder ever that we need to grab life by the neck and wring every last drop out of it, you know? I'm sorry that we freaked you out. We probably should have told you in a different way."

"That's okay, it's just, I don't get it. How did it, I mean, how did you—"

"You're asking how he got it," Victor says.

"I just thought that if you're monogamous, you know. That's what they always teach us."

"Life is complicated," Jack says.

"Yeah," Adam says. He tries to take a sip of water but his hand is shaking.

"Careful there," Victor says. "You're like Charlotte Vale in that first scene of *Now, Voyager*."

"I'm just so worried about you," Adam says, turning to Jack. "Have you been sick or anything?"

"No," he says. "I'm healthy as can be."

"Are you taking anything? AZT? Vitamins? How are your T cells? What about prophylaxis for pneumonia?" Adam catches a sob in his throat. "I can't lose you, Jack. I can't lose you, too."

Jack gets up and stands behind Adam, surrounding him with his arms. "Shh. You beautiful boy. You sweet man. Do you know how much we love you? How much I love you? You're not getting rid of me, you know."

"But you're leaving."

"Yes," Jack says. "But we'll be back. And I want you to come along on a trip with us one of these days. Maybe we could all go bungee jumping in New Zealand together. Or surfing in Costa Rica. Something crazy and fun."

But what about when you're gone forever? Adam thinks. *What if Victor is next?*

"Please don't give up," he whispers, almost too quietly to be heard.

"Never." Jack smiles softly when he says it. Victor smiles, too, but Adam can see that these aren't smiles of satisfaction, or anticipation, or joy. They are steely smiles, meant to comfort Adam. But steel, no matter how solid, is cold to the touch. He doesn't smile back.

"I'll be there," Adam says. "I'll be there for everything. No matter what. I won't let you down."

"I know you won't, kiddo," Jack says. "Family."

"I have an idea," Victor says. "Let's change the subject. Who was that cute boy we met at Pride? The one with the black baseball cap."

"You mean Ben?"

"That's it, Ben. He seems like a nice guy."

"I barely know him," Adam says. "I don't think I'll see him again. He made me mad."

"How so?"

"He asked me if I'd been safe with Callum."

"What's wrong with that?"

"It's none of his business."

"True, but isn't that the kind of thing friends ask each other? I asked you the same thing once."

"It was the way he did it," Adam says. "He asked if I'd lost control, or made a mistake, or did something wrong. It felt like he was saying that you only get HIV if you do something wrong. Like it's your fault. He was basically asking if I'm stupid. Or if Callum is stupid. Callum isn't stupid."

"Wasn't," Victor says. "Callum *wasn't* stupid."

"Victor," Jack says.

"What? Callum isn't here anymore. We have to live in reality, right?"

"He's right," Adam says. "I have to get used to this."

"Well, I don't know the kid," Jack says. "But I could tell at Pride that he really cares about you. He almost didn't let you go with us."

"Really?"

"Yeah. He made sure that we knew you."

"Oh," Adam says, freshly ashamed of the mess he made of himself that day.

"Maybe he got tripped up on the words he used when you guys talked about this," Jack says. "But the truth is, we're all trying to figure out how to talk about this stuff, aren't we? We all need to give one other a break every now and then. I'm sure you've said things that came out wrong, haven't you?"

"I guess so."

"Me too. Millions of times. And I got news for you: It never ends. Every time I turn around, I find out that there's another word we're not supposed to use anymore, or a new word that we *are* supposed to use. Usually for very good reasons, but keeping up isn't easy. Like, I'm trying to get used to the way people use *queer* lately. Every time I hear it, I flinch, because that's the name I got called when I was a kid. But they're using it in a new way now, and I'm trying to get on board."

"I can't even picture you as a kid," Adam says.

"Thanks a lot," Jack says. "I'll have to show you a picture

sometime. I know it was the Stone Age, but we had cameras back then, believe it or not."

Adam sighs, and then mumbles very quietly, "Callum didn't have anyone with him."

"He had you," Victor says.

"That wasn't enough," Adam says. He bites the inside of his cheek.

"I know how you feel," Victor says, and Adam believes him.

"You won't be alone, Jack. I promise. Not ever."

"I know," he whispers. He smiles at Adam. It's a soft smile, dipped in sadness. "I know."

"Speaking of not being alone," Victor says, handing Adam a piece of paper. "Phone numbers. After you left the apartment the other day, we all started talking about you. Everyone agreed to keep an eye on you while we're traveling. Don't worry, they aren't spies. Just good people, and they know how much you mean to us. You can call any of them, anytime, if you need someone to talk to or even if you just want to hang out."

"I don't know about this," Jack says. "Some of these people could lead him to sin."

"He should be so lucky," Victor says, grinning.

Adam tries to laugh, but it comes out more like a cough.

Victor pats him on the back. "You all right?"

"Yeah," Adam says. "Is it selfish that I don't want you to go?"

"I promise that you'll always know where we are," Jack says.

"Yes," Victor says, opening his fanny pack. "And if you get too lonely without us, I made you a set of keys to our place. You can go over and sit there and rummage through all of our stuff. Just, you know, keep it clean, all right?"

"Really?"

"Really. And if you don't want to go over, that's fine, too. There aren't any plants to water. I hate houseplants. All they do is attract bugs."

"Wow," Adam says. "Thank you for this. I promise I won't rummage."

"Oh, and please make sure there's booze left in the liquor cabinet. If I don't fix Jack a martini within five minutes of his return home from traveling, I have to hear about it for a week."

"We love you, kiddo. Remember that, okay? Family."

Adam feels the warmth of Jack's hand covering his. Victor reaches over, too.

Don't go, Adam wants to say, but he doesn't. Soon the sandwiches appear. Jack asks for extra mayo, and the three men eat. Jack and Victor tell Adam all about their plans for their trip to Italy. Victor even brought his copy of *Fodor's Italy* to point out all the towns they plan to visit and all the attractions they plan to see.

When Adam is back at home, he unzips Callum's backpack and overturns it onto his bed. Here are his Walkman and his cassettes. Adam counts six tapes—Bach, Beethoven, Chopin, Debussy, Mozart, and more Bach. Here is his notebook, filled with musical markings and ideas. A half-empty jar of aspirin, which Callum must have used to keep his fever down. Is that why he carried this extra undershirt, too? Here's a small jar of Tiger Balm, for the aches in his joints. Oh, Callum. How many days were you sick and didn't say so? How many ways did you suffer?

Here are Callum's shoes, the beautiful brogues, spotless and perfect. Adam tries them on, but they're too big. He'll keep them anyway. He'll keep them under the bed.

Adam lies down. He exhales and feels the sorrow slither around him again, returning to him now that he's alone, pressing against his chest, forcing out the oxygen, rendering him smaller and smaller into himself, crushing him until everything is flattened, and silent, and numb. He pulls the covers over himself. He stays here in this darkness for a very long time.

And then, Adam takes a leap of faith. He takes another breath.

Six

SEPTEMBER/OCTOBER 1990

No choice your voice can take me there.
—Madonna, "Like a Prayer"

ADAM

How can it possibly be September? Adam is due to check in at the NYU dorms tomorrow by ten thirty, but he's only just started to put clothes into his duffel bag. His mother hands him a package of socks. "Take these," she says.

"I don't have room."

"That bag is gigantic."

"I already have eight pairs of socks."

"And now you have twelve."

"Mom."

"Don't *Mom* me. If you get run over by a Mister Softee truck and it knocks your sneakers off, and the picture in the newspaper is you on a gurney with dirty socks on your feet, it's all I'll hear about from my friends for the rest of the week."

"A whole week?"

"Yes, and honestly, I'll already have too much on my mind, given that the ice cream truck will probably have to take at least a day or two off, depriving the rest of us of ice cream. And I'll have to sit there staring at your dirty socks in the newspaper without even an ice cream sandwich to ease my pain."

He takes the socks. "Your imagination is disturbing."

She puts her hand on the closet doorknob. "Dare I?"

"Knock yourself out," Adam says, knowing she'll be pleasantly surprised. He's cleared most of the stuff from his closet over the past week or two, filling boxes with old toys and books and sweaters and jackets and carrying them over to Jack and Victor's apartment. They're busy riding the Trans Canada railway this month, putting Adam in charge of their annual "Ain't Nothing Going On but the Rent" sidewalk sale in their absence. Next month, Adam will put up the signs, set out the tables, blast Gwen Guthrie on the portable boombox, and collect the money for God's Love We Deliver.

"Wow," she says, looking over the neatly organized jackets, sweaters, and shoes. "This closet has a floor? I never knew. You know, now that you're moving out, maybe I could rent this as a bedroom. What say I put a notice in the *Voice* and see what happens? I bet we could get a couple hundred bucks a month. The tenant would have to sleep standing up, but hey, this is New York, right?"

Just then, Pop shouts from the kitchen. "Frankie! We need to scram."

Mom takes Adam's shoulders and kisses him on the forehead. "We're meeting Jasmine and Stan for lunch at Baby Buddha. Do you want me to bring anything back?"

"Nope."

"He wants noodles, Frankie!" Pop shouts. "Extra hot sauce. I know my boy."

Adam and his mother roll their eyes in unison. "I'll bring them just to make him happy."

Adam follows her into the kitchen.

"I love this song," she says, diving for the clock radio to turn it up. "Have you heard of this girl? Mariah Carey? She's so good."

"Let's go, Frankie!" Pop says. "I'm starving."

"Love takes time, ya big lug!" She kisses Adam on the cheek. "Bye, hon."

"Bye." Adam grabs the phone and heads back into his room. He wants to see how Lily's packing is going.

She sounds incredulous when she answers. "I haven't even finished packing my hair stuff. I hate this. Can't we go to the Angelika and see *Paris Is Burning* again instead? I've only seen it twice."

"Not until you finish packing."

"You're so lucky. You can just run back to the apartment if you forget something. I can't do that from up in Siberia. Or Greenland. The North Pole. Wherever the hell I'm going."

"Lily. Hunter College is on Sixty-Eighth Street."

"Exactly. Canada. Call Bob and Doug McKenzie and tell them I'm on my way, eh?"

"Think of all the uptown fabulousness you'll encounter."

"That's a good point. Maybe I should get a membership to the Vertical Club. I hear Mick Jagger works out there."

"You could finally meet the rock star boyfriend of your dreams, right there by the StairMaster."

"I'd just end up stalking him. Speaking of which, what ever happened with that cute boy Ben? Is he still stalking you?"

"He's not a stalker."

"But is he cute?"

"I guess. But Lily, you know I'm not—"

"Oh my god."

"What?"

"You just said he was cute. You have a pulse. I'm calling *Page Six*."

"Zip it. You know I'm not thinking about anyone that way. I probably never will."

She sighs. "I know. I just keep hope alive."

"Thanks."

"What about being friends, though?"

"That's what I have you for," Adam says.

"Best, I'm going to level with you. As your elder."

"You're like a month older than I am."

"Like I said. Your elder. So you have to listen."

"Fine."

"I am the best friend you will ever have. And you are the best friend that I will ever have. This is indisputable, the eleventh commandment. It won't ever change. Right?"

"Right."

"But Best, you need some gays in your life."

"Gays? You make us sound like pets."

"Seriously, I can only do so much. I can only explain why *Xanadu* is the superior Olivia Newton-John vehicle to *Grease* so many times. I can only explain the vital significance of Diana Ross's *Swept Away* period so many times. I can only explain the difference between Kim Wilde and Samantha Fox so many—"

"Wait, what's the difference between Kim Wilde and Samantha Fox again? I forgot."

"I hate you."

"No you don't."

"Fine. But the point stands. I need backup."

"But—"

"Oh, by the way, semi related. You have plans on Monday night."

"I have plans on Monday?"

"Yes. Every Monday from now on. We're going to ACT UP. They meet on Mondays."

"Lily, you know the meetings are in the Village, right? You'll have to take two subway trains."

338

"Don't remind me, but also, I don't care. I've selected my courses to accommodate sleeping in on Tuesdays, because we're going out to Nell's on Mondays after the meetings."

"I'm scared to go to an ACT UP meeting. I'm afraid I'll have a complete breakdown and embarrass myself."

"You might. But I will hold your hand. We're going."

Adam knows there's no diverting Lily once she gets an idea in mind. "All right. Starting when?"

"Monday, dumbass. Are you not listening? Start picking out something cute to wear."

"Does a cute outfit even matter at an ACT UP meeting?"

"Does a cute outfit ever *not* matter?"

"I have to double-check my calend—"

"You're going. There will be no further discussion."

"Aye aye," he says, knowing she's right to insist, knowing that he wants to go.

"Brains, looks, money," she says.

"Brains, looks, money. I love you, Lily."

"I know."

She hangs up. He stares at the phone for a while. Why does he feel so alone? Lily loves him. His parents love him. Jack and Victor aren't around, but he knows they love him. He knows he has an entire page of phone numbers of people he can call—Caryn, Dennis, Robert, Diane, Carlos and Alexey, Lalita, Joe-Joe. There are so many people there for him, but still.

He steels himself, picks up the handset, and dials a number he's kept on his desk for weeks now. The phone rings only once before a friendly voice answers. "Gay Men's Health Crisis AIDS hotline. How may I help?"

BEN

The Meatpacking District is aptly named. The area, just one neighborhood up from the West Village, is mostly warehouses, food distributors, and, as its name promises, meat packers.

The streets are nearly empty of traffic except for the big delivery trucks that thump along, delivering meat. Every now and then you'll see one with its back door open, exposing giant sides of raw beef, pink and ribboned through with sinew and fat. Animal blood pools between the cobblestones, and you're just as likely to step on a discarded chicken neck as you are a discarded piece of gum or a smashed cigarette butt. A few small shops wedge themselves into the tight corners here, under the abandoned elevated train tracks.

"This neighborhood is going to be the next SoHo," Rebecca says. "It's gonna be nothing but chic boutiques and tiny little restaurants. You watch. You heard it here first."

They round the corner onto Gansevoort Street and step into Florent, a tiny, twenty-four-hour diner-style restaurant that Ben has read about. It's famous for attracting artists, musicians, actors, models, club promoters, activists, drag queens, local shift workers, and assorted creative misfits from all over downtown. Rebecca points him toward two seats at the counter, where a server wearing heavy black eyeliner and a backward cycling cap brings glasses of ice water. He smiles. Ben can see his nipple rings through his tank top.

Ben reads the menu board on the wall.

SALADE NIÇOISE
COLD SOUPE VICHYSSOISE
CROQUE MONSIEUR OU MADAME

CARGO PANTS WILL MAKE YOU FAMOUS
75% HUMIDITY—SWEAT STORM WARNING
$144 ROUND TRIP TO TOLEDO (OHIO)
620—480—320—515

"I love the menu board," Rebecca says. "It's different every time I come in. I guess they just put stuff up there to make you think, or laugh, or whatever."

"What are those numbers at the bottom? Six twenty, four eighty, three twenty, five fifteen?"

"Those are the owner's T cell counts. Five fifteen isn't so bad. Seems like he's doing okay."

"Why does he put them up there?" Ben whispers. "Doesn't it freak people out?"

"Maybe, but it's a statement, you know? Just a few years ago, people were getting kicked out of restaurants if they even looked like they were gay, because people were so scared that they'd be contagious, too. Those numbers are like a sneaky middle finger to all that. I love it."

She orders a plate of French fries and an omelet. Ben asks for a bowl of soup.

"So, talk to me," she says. "What's wrong? You spent the whole shoot today moping."

"Sorry," Ben says, shaking his head.

"Is it Gil? Is he being a jerk again?"

"No, Gil is fine."

The server slides a plate of French fries in front of them. Rebecca immediately grabs a handful. Ben takes one, tastes it, then showers the plate with salt.

Rebecca leans closer. "Is it a boy?"

Yes. It is a boy. It is Adam. Ben can't shake him, not even with his nights out, not even with his growing collection of telephone numbers. The idea of Adam just sits there in his mind, permeating his thoughts and keeping him awake, because Ben feels like he's seen inside Adam, over and over again. He's seen his pain, his fear, his insecurities. Every time they've met, no matter how strange, Ben's come away wanting to know more.

He looks toward the back of the restaurant, where a beautiful young man with a shaved head and long arms sits alone reading a magazine. He looks like a dancer, Ben thinks, or some kind of athlete. Two other young men approach him. One grabs a chair from a neighboring table, and the other sits in his lap. They laugh and light cigarettes.

"Kind of," Ben says, finally answering her question.

"Well, that certainly clears it up," she says.

"Sorry."

"It's a well-known fact that boys are confusing," she says. "Including you."

"It's just, I think I screwed it up. I said something stupid and I can't take it back."

"Oh, babe," she says, reaching over to run a thumb across his scar. "Can I let you in on a secret? You're eighteen. You're supposed to screw things up. It's part of the deal, you know? Also, if you don't start eating some of these fries, I will devour them all."

Eighteen. Is that all? Ben feels so much older. He feels like he's lived a lifetime, just this year. Everything's become more complicated, including himself. It's like he missed his chance to be simple. Even Rebecca thinks he's confusing now. He orders a cup of coffee.

"Just so you know," Rebecca says, staring at nothing. "The confusion doesn't go away. But that doesn't have to be a bad thing. You just have to figure out how to take that confusion, and turn it into something beautiful."

"I wish I knew how to do that."

She reaches into her handbag and pulls out a big manila envelope. "I printed out some of the photographs we've done together. My agent wants to meet you, but you need to put together a portfolio of your work first. These will get you started."

"Really? Your agent? Like to help me get styling jobs?"

"Yes. I know you're not getting enough work with me. If you're going to make a go at this, you need to be booked six days a week for a few years. Eventually people will start to know you, and they'll see what you're capable of, and you can start charging enough to set a better schedule. But right now, you need to be out there in the mix paying your dues, and not only with me."

"But I like working for you."

"Oh, you'll still work for me, don't worry." She lights a cigarette. "Open the envelope."

Ben does. Inside is a stack of eight-by-ten photographs. The first two are from their very first shoot together, the beautiful, colorful parkas sweeping across the images, shiny and alive.

"*Elle* was so happy with these," Rebecca says. "Thanks to you."

The next two are from the denim shoot on the roof downtown, the shoot where he first met Justin. In the images, the models stand like windswept statuary in front of the downtown skyline.

"Look there." Rebecca points to a reflection in one of the towers. Ben squints. It's the Statue of Liberty. "Bet you didn't think I could get her in the shot, did you?" Ben smiles.

The next photo is the two models in backless dresses and piles of necklaces, posing with big holiday smiles. The Louis Vuitton bag is barely visible.

"I can't believe how stressed out we were about that damn bag," she says. "And of course, *Vogue* chooses a picture where you can't even see it."

"These look great," Ben says.

"There's one more in there," she says. "A portrait of an artist."

"An artist?"

She nods. He pulls out the last photograph. It's printed in black and white, a young man in profile, concentrating intensely on something just out of frame. The dappled light makes the planes of his face look both soft and sharp at the same time. Both distant and near. Confident, like he knows things. Curious, like he doesn't. He is beautiful.

Ben draws a breath. "It's—"

"You," she says.

ADAM

Adam got to the walk-in clinic early today, but he still has to wait. Dozens of people were already here when he showed up, lined up like customers at Sonia's Village Video before a snowstorm. He was tempted to leave, of course, like he's done every other time. But today he's going to follow through. He's feeling brave, after his most recent session with his therapist at NYU.

When they call Adam's number, he follows the clinician into a small room at the end of the hallway. She's about Adam's mother's age, give or take, and her braids are finished with beads that click as she walks. She closes the door behind him and points to a chair next to a small table. She picks up a clipboard.

"Name?" she asks. She clicks her ballpoint pen, and Adam is reminded of Dr. Nieves.

"Adam."

"Are you sure? Most people who come here are named John or Jane."

"John," Adam says. "Okay."

"John Johnson, right?" She begins writing on her form.

"That's me."

"Age?"

"Eighteen."

"Have you received safer sex counseling within the last year?"

"You mean at school?"

"Yes or no will do, Mr. Johnson." She's not being unkind, just efficient.

"Yes," Adam says. She checks a box with her pen.

"Have you had unprotected sex within the last six months?"

"No," Adam says, but quickly changes his answer. "I don't think so."

She raises an eyebrow.

"I don't know," he says.

She checks another box. "Any intravenous drug use?"

"No."

"Any partners with HIV or AIDS?"

"No," Adam says. "I mean, not anymore. He—"

"I understand," she interrupts, without looking up from her clipboard. "Have you eaten today?"

"No."

She opens a drawer in a file cabinet underneath the table and retrieves a Nature Valley granola bar. "Here," she says. "It's better if you have something in your stomach."

"Thank you."

After a few more questions, she says, "We will draw six vials of blood today. Afterward, you and your sample will both be assigned a number. Your blood will be tested two ways to help guard against any errors. Do you understand?"

"Two ways?"

"Yes. The ELISA test and the Western blot. Each has a small potential for a false result, but when we do both tests, we can be nearly one hundred percent certain of accuracy."

"Nearly?"

"Nearly. Do you understand?"

"Yes."

"Now, the tests take about ten days, but we say fourteen just in case. After fourteen days, you will call the clinic, provide us with your assigned number, and we will make an appointment for you to come in to receive your results. Do you understand?"

"You can't just tell me over the phone?"

"No. Do you understand?"

"Fourteen days," Adam responds. It sounds like a short time, but also an eternity. "I understand."

She checks another box.

"All right. Rest your arm on this surface, please. Palm side up." She pulls two rubber gloves from a box on a shelf above her, then ties a length of rubber tubing around his bicep and taps the soft skin on the inside of his elbow. Callum's part. *I gave it to him.* She rubs the spot with an antiseptic pad.

Adam watches as the needle approaches his skin, then presses against it, straining it inward. A sudden prick, a pop, a shot of sharp pain. The clear plastic vial starts to fill in a rush of liquid. He's transfixed by the vibrancy of its color, almost electric red. It gives itself up so easily.

In less than a minute, she has six vials of blood. She slides the needle out and presses a cotton ball onto Adam's skin.

"Hold this please," she says. She applies a length of surgical tape to hold it in place. "Be sure to drink a little extra water today, all right? And eat that granola bar."

She hands him a pamphlet, "How to Survive the Wait." Then she hands him a slip of paper on which she's written his assigned number.

"Don't lose this number. If you do, we won't be able to provide you with your results. Do you understand?"

He doesn't answer. He watches her slip the vials of his blood into a plastic box, little containers of himself he'll never see again. He wonders about the journey they'll take. How far will they go? What will happen when they get there? Do they even belong to him anymore?

"John? Do you understand?"

"I'm sorry. Yes. I understand. You said fourteen days?"

"That's right. I know it's not easy."

"No," he agrees.

"Take care, Adam," she says, finally smiling.

"Thank you," he says. "Thank you very much."

He exits back out into the street, holding his hand over the inside of his arm, over Callum's part, to protect it.

BEN

Ben was asleep a minute ago, but then the phone rang and now he's trying to find the ON button without his glasses. The October issue of *Vogue Paris*, the one with Isabella Rossellini on the cover, slides off his stomach and onto the floor, landing with a *thud*.

There it is.

"Hello?"

"Hello? Is Ben there?"

Ben knows it's Adam from the first aspiration of the *h* in *hello*. It's been seven weeks, a lifetime, since the last time he saw him. They had their feet in the Washington Square fountain then, and Ben said something stupid. So much has happened since then, and also, nothing has happened at all.

"Adam," he says, sinking back into the couch. "Hi."

"Hey," Adam says. "I wanted to see if you wanted to do something. Go for a walk or something. I don't know."

Ben sits up. "Like right now?"

"I know it's late."

"That's okay. I mean, I'm up. What do you feel like doing?"

Adam is quiet for an agonizing minute. Ben pictures him staring at his shoes, or pushing his hair out of his eyes, or regretting calling in the first place. Maybe Ben should offer an idea. But what? Think, Ben. Think.

"I just thought it would be good to see you," Adam says. "You know?"

It's so strange, Ben thinks, how a person can be a mile away or a thousand miles away, but the voice on the phone still seems so close, like a whisper in your ear.

"Ben?"

Suddenly, Ben knows exactly what they should do. "What time is it?" he asks.

"Eleven. Just after."

"Meet me in thirty minutes."

"Where?"

"You know where," Ben says. He hangs up before Adam can respond. He pulls on his shoes and zips up his sweatshirt. In the mirror by the door, his hair looks just fine. He leaves his baseball cap behind. He doesn't need it tonight.

ADAM

Adam does know where to go, but he takes a roundabout route to get there. Instead of heading straight there, which would take only five minutes, he hikes first up to Horatio Street. He walks the length of it, from Hudson Street to the river, inhaling the cool air deeply as he goes. This is still Callum's street, he thinks. This is still Callum's air.

In the months and years to come, Adam will find himself here on days when he's happy, on days when he's unhappy, on days when his mind is nothing but a tangle of confusion and worry and guilt and sorrow and regret. In the summertime he'll be glad for the shade from the linden trees, and in the wintertime he'll wonder whether they'll ever bloom again. He'll sit on a stoop sometimes, but sometimes he'll just walk. He'll never tell anyone where he's going when he comes here. The only one who needs to know already knows.

At the West Side Highway, he jaywalks across in two bursts, first waiting for a break in the uptown traffic, then the downtown traffic. The pier is not busy tonight. Just a guy with stringy hair leaning over his mountain bike talking to a girl with a buzz cut, and a group of teenagers walking slowly downtown, silently voguing as they go.

Adam climbs carefully over the chain with the KEEP OFF sign and out onto the Jane Street pier. He walks slowly, careful to avoid the potholes and cracks. He wonders how he'll film this scene, how he'll create the soft glow of the city lights reflected in the river. He wonders if it's even possible.

At the end of the pier, with his feet at the very edge, Adam turns to face the city. He listens carefully for its chorus, its music. He closes his eyes and raises his arms as if to conduct.

Music everywhere.

A gust comes from nowhere, testing his balance. He steps to one side, then the other, catching his foot on a loose plank. He swings his arms in circles to regain his balance. He doesn't fall in.

Sit, he tells himself. He'll be here soon.

ADAM AND BEN

"I want to know more about you," he says.

"Like what?" he says.

"I don't know," he says. "A lot of things."

"I'll tell you anything."

"Anything?"

"Anything."

He considers. "Okay. Tell me when you knew for sure."

He answers, and then he asks a question in return. For an hour, two hours, three hours into the night they sit with their sneakers dangling over the river, trading questions for answers and back again. *Tell me how you made it through. Tell me what you hide. Tell me where you want to go.* They surprise themselves with the things they know about themselves, and with the things they don't. They talk to each other, and listen to each other. They laugh a little bit. They lose track of time.

"Do you ever wonder why?" he asks.

"Why what?"

"Why everything, I guess."

"Yeah," he says, grasping the edge of the pier. "All the time."

"Me too."

The breeze off the river is warmer than you'd expect this time of year, he thinks. He's happy for that. He knows the colder air is coming, and then it will be winter. Before long, it will have been a year since everything changed.

In a moment he will exhale, and he will feel his friend's hand graze his own. It will be a faint touch, just a breath. But it will send a pulse of electricity through him, and it will fill him with courage and clarity. He will close his eyes to feel it. He will wish the feeling could last.

And he will tell himself: Maybe it can last. Maybe it will last. Maybe.

Author's Note

There was this guy who came into the record shop all the time. You know the one. Spotless Filas, complicated hair, always bouncing to the background music. He'd spend hours in my section, the twelve-inch singles, and if he wanted to hear a track I'd play it for him—Shannon, Colonel Abrams, Dead or Alive, Madonna. It was 1986, the year I turned eighteen. He was older than me. My crush on him was monumental.

Once he waited for me after work. To talk, to flirt. To kiss, I hoped, but he just wanted to hold hands. Okay, I said. Let's hold hands. It felt like something. But he stopped coming around after that.

Some weeks later I asked a common friend if she'd seen him and she said you didn't hear? I said no. She touched my arm. I'm sorry, she said. Don't make me worry about you, too.

I kept a lot of secrets in those days. I didn't open up because I knew what people would say: *Be careful.* Those words didn't mean *look both ways* or even *use a condom*. They meant *don't be gay. You can't do this to me. Please change. Don't you watch the news?*

Five years later I was keeping fewer secrets. I found a cheap apartment on Avenue C and fell into a tricky, restless kind of love with a boy over on Eldridge Street. You should have seen his smile. He'd keep me out all night dancing then take me over to the river all day. We'd stay until it was dark again, listening to Ten City and imagining fugitive futures. We'll go so many places, I said. We'll do so many things. He didn't believe me. He was right.

They say that memories fade with time but I don't believe that's true. You carry them with you like stones in your pocket. Sometimes when it's quiet you take them out to roll between your fingers. Then you put them back in your pocket, safe again. You don't leave them behind.

AIDS is an exceptionally insidious condition that doesn't follow a script or timeline. The HIV virus depletes its host's immune system to clear pathways for terrible infections: Toxoplasmosis, encephalitis, histoplasmosis, cytomegalovirus infection, tuberculosis, pneumocystis pneumonia—the list goes on. Things happen fast, or slow. Every patient's experience is different, often radically so.

Without the kinds of sophisticated treatments developed in the late 1990s, a person with AIDS might face a relentless procession of troubles. Common bacteria or viruses that healthy systems block away every day would attack with devastating effectiveness. You might recover from an infection just in time for another one to burst through. You might get sick, then get better, then get sick again in a different way, over and over. Treatment side effects could be brutal. Even with the best care, predictability was off the table. So much depended on timing, and privilege, and luck. But even with luck, the outcome was almost always the same.

In 2001, the Centers for Disease Control reported that of all

AIDS cases identified from 1981 to 1987, over 95 percent were fatal. For the period 1988 to 1992, it was just under 90 percent.

When You Call My Name takes place in 1990, a cusp year with one foot in the eighties and the other foot searching for solid ground. Everything was in flux: Pop culture, politics, technology, the future. What would the nineties be? Who would we be in them? Would we even be here at all?

It's no hyperbole to say that many of us weren't so sure we would be. There was an inevitability to the way the virus picked through us—a friend, a crush, a rival, a trick, a true love—while the rest of the world wore red ribbons and waited it out, or worse. I remember once seeing someone on television say that the best thing to do would be to send all the gays to an island to die off. A convenient way to deal with an inconvenient group of people. My boyfriend wondered if we'd at least get to pick the island. A beautiful one please, temperate, not too many mosquitoes, maybe a pleasant beachside bar. No need for a lifeguard budget. Dark humor was a strategy. Oh, I miss him.

It is 2021 as I write this, and HIV/AIDS is still very much with us. There is no cure, no vaccine. Tens of millions of people worldwide live with the virus today. Hundreds of thousands die every year.

Still, hope lives. After decades of extraordinary science and activism, we have drugs now to help minimize the presence of the virus in the body, and to help prevent its transfer from person to person. These drugs have saved countless lives. But they remain violently out of reach for millions who need them. Inequity has always been at the center of the story of HIV/AIDS. Inequity, ignorance, stigma, bigotry, and greed.

And yet, also sitting at the center of the story: Collaboration, creativity, intellect, persistence, pride. And love. Always love.

When You Call My Name is fiction. It represents only the tiniest sliver of the continuing experience of HIV/AIDS. None of its events happened in real life, not exactly. None of its characters existed in real life, not exactly. St. Hugh's Hospital, Dome Magazines, Sonia's Village Video—none of these places existed in real life, not exactly. But you exist in real life, and I exist in real life, and that means hope exists in real life. Find it and hold it tightly, because hope will grow in your grasp.

The HIV epidemic is not over, not by a long shot. There are still so many stories to be told and heard. We must tell them and hear them. There is still so much to learn. We must learn it. There is still so much work to do. We must do it. We can't let go.

Please don't let go.

Acknowledgments

Thank you

To editor and collaborator **Mark Podesta,** who gave this book a life, who transformed it with unselfish brilliance, and to whom this book belongs. To agent **Dan Mandel,** whose generosity is a super-power. To **Christian Trimmer,** who believed. To **Hayley Jozwiak, Trisha Previte, Alexei Esikoff, Jie Yang, Chantal Gersch, Kristin Dulaney, Jordan Winch, Kaitlin Loss,** and the rest of the team at Henry Holt Books for Young Readers and Macmillan Childrens Publishing Group.

Thank you

To **Susan Ottaviano,** who protects me. To **Jorge Ramón,** my beloved lifelong brother. To **Tim McCoy** and **Brian Ruhl,** who took me in and built a family with me. To **Bryan Roof,** who keeps me tumbling forward, always forward. To **Buzz Kelly,** who keeps me up too late to talk about beauty and hope. To **Paul Zakris,** who proves that laughter is indispensable. To **Jay Inkpen** and **Steven Kolb,** who swaddle me in warmth no matter how far away. To **Marc Leyer** and **Christopher Barillas,** who help me see deeper into still waters. To my Body & Soul dance partner **Alex White.** To **Doc Willoughby,** who provides constant ballast. To my dear **Lisa Kennedy,** who moves me toward patience and fortitude. To **Geoffrey Shaw** and **Alec Baum,** who hold the future.

Thank you

To **John Shea,** who knows why. To **Dr. Michael Liguori, MD,** who saved my little life. To **Ryan Kull,** who converted me to optimism. To **Karen Ramspacher,** who showed me compassion I did not deserve and will never forget. To **Scott Sanders,** who sees better things. To **Tom, Peter, B.J., Todd,** and the rest of the rogues from those first years. To **Danny Goldstein, Andrea Boone, Chris Israel, John Torres, Cody Lyon, Gant Johnson, Mac Folkes, John Bowe, Sarah Pettit, Michael Goff, Roger Black, Trine Dyrlev, Mark Tusk, Tamar Brazis, Chris Echaurre, Spencer Cox, Brett Mirsky, Rachel Clarke, Alan Zaretsky, Luiz DeBarros, Antonio Branco, Grace Young, Andy Lerner, David Cicilline, Elle Simone, Brian Franklin,** and **Sally Holmes.**

Thank you

To **ACT-UP.** To **Gay Men's Health Crisis.** To **Community Health Project/Callen-Lorde Community Health Center,** especially **Health Outreach to Teens.** To the **Hetrick-Martin Institute.** To **@theaidsmemorial** on Instagram.

Thank you

To **248 E. 2nd, 237 Eldridge, 35 Bedford,** and **90 Bank.** To **Casa Magazines.** To **Field Six** at Jones Beach. To **Sound Factory.** To **The Bar.** To **the Boy Bar Beauties.** To **Shelter.** To **Body and Soul.**

Thank you

To **Patrick Kelly, Scott Ross, Ian Charleson, Jermaine Stewart, Keith Haring, Rudolf Nureyev, Rock Hudson, Freddie Mercury, Tseng Kwong Chi, Derek Jarman, Arthur Ashe, Paul Monette, Tina Chow, Max Robinson, Anthony Perkins, Dorian Corey, Dack Rambo, Alison Gertz, Liberace, Tony**

Richardson, Alvin Ailey, Halston, Pedro Zamora, Gia Carangi, Brad Davis, Eazy-E, Sylvester, Michael Callen, Dan Hartman, Marlon Riggs, Way Bandy, Robert Mapplethorpe, Hervé Guibert, Herb Ritts, Vito Russo, Willi Smith, Randy Shilts, Ilka Tanya Payán, Emile Ardolino, Michael Bennett, Denholm Elliott, Ricky Wilson, Antonio Lopez, Patrick O'Connell, Joe MacDonald, Robert Moore, Leonard Frey, Arnold Lobel, Willi Ninja, Robert La Tourneaux, Fabrice Simon, Harold Rollins, Bill Connors, Colin Higgins, Juan E. Ramos, and the millions of others who continue to inspire. They had so much more to say.

Thank you most of all

To **Steven Cuba,** you thrilling, sexy, funny, creative, confounding, stubborn, beautiful, unforgettable heartbreaker. I miss you so much. At night, when the world is quiet, I can still hear you call my name.